Totally Bound Publishing books by Isla Dennes

Single Books
Sex, Spoons and Salsa

For Heaven's Sake
Heavenly Pleasures

I0691661

For Heaven's Sake

HEAVENLY PLEASURES

ISLA DENNES

Heavenly Pleasures
ISBN # 978-1-83943-841-7
©Copyright Isla Dennes 2018
Cover Art by Posh Gosh ©Copyright January 2018
Interior text design by Claire Siemaszkiewicz
Totally Bound Publishing

HEAVENLY PLEASURES

Dedication

To my wonderful children,
Liam, Erin, Alanna and Kaitlin.
They are my greatest life achievement
and my biggest fans.
Thank you for being amazing xxx

Chapter One

"What the hell is wrong with you?" Scarlett asked, taking in my pale face and trembling hands.

"Some bloke just walked in here and asked me to have sex with him!"

Uggh! And he'd been all greasy black hair, gold fillings and overgrown 'tache, like an aging porn star. I stifled the urge to throw up.

Shaking her head in disgust, Scarlett rolled her eyes. "Hate to break it to you, precious, but you *are* working in a brothel, you know."

"But—"

"But nothing. What the hell did you expect him to ask for, a burger and fries?"

"I kept telling him I was only the receptionist, but he didn't seem to care. He told me he'd pay extra if he had to." I fought to calm my racing heart and queasy stomach.

Scarlett's eyes narrowed. She didn't look happy. It occurred to me that maybe I should have kept my mouth shut.

"What do you mean *extra*? How *much* extra?"

"Um…" I swallowed hard. "Three hundred dollars."

The temperature in the room plummeted as a blast of ice-cold fury filled the air.

"*What!*" she screeched. "*And you turned him down?*"

"But—"

"Jesus Christ!" she hissed and bolted over to the waiting room. "Shit, where the hell is he now?"

My glance flickered toward the door. Scarlett's followed. For the briefest of moments, I thought she was going to drag him back in and make him apologize for being an insensitive bastard.

Instead her eyes widened in shock. "*What!* You let him walk out of here? You selfish fucking cow. You mightn't have wanted him, but what about the rest of us girls? Three hundred bucks and you just let him walk out of here? Jesus! Prue is going to go off her nut when she hears about this."

Prue was the Madame and owner of Heavenly Pleasures. An outwardly serene woman with immaculate hair, but nonetheless seriously scary with a sinister reputation, not unlike Cruella DeVille on a bad day, and therefore someone I did not want to cross.

"Oh, please don't say anything," I begged, on the verge of tears. "Look, I promise if he comes back in, I'll call you out straight away—before JoJo. Just don't mention it to Prue. I was just a bit taken aback, that's all, and didn't know what to do."

This part was true. Haggling for sex wasn't something we'd covered in secretarial college. Maybe it was the look of pure terror on my face or possibly Scarlett was in a rare compassionate mood, but after a moment's hesitation she stopped scowling, her expression softening in what could well have been pity.

"Okay. I won't say anything—this time," came with reluctance. "But of course I'll expect some more bookings, *if* you get my meaning."

Yes—her meaning was loud and clear. She was blackmailing me, but I was in no position to protest. I nodded.

Her mood lightened. "Hey, cheer up, will you? So what if some ugly punter wanted a poke? Jeez, you're not the first one to have the hard word put on them by some tosser, believe me. Guys come in here, think they're God's gift to women and although they know you're not a worker, it gives them a sick thrill to think they can convince you to drop to your knees for a blow job—even if it is for three hundred dollars." She threw me a disgusted look and shook her head in disbelief. "I reckon in their pathetic little minds they're convinced they've seduced you with their hot looks and charm. Losers, that's what they are. Anyway, I suppose it's probably just as well you didn't take him up on it."

"Really?" I brightened, seeing it as a sign I was forgiven.

"Yeah, the girls would have flattened you if you had."

Oh, God. I felt ill. What on earth had happened to my perfect life?

Two months ago, I had never met or even *spoken* to a prostitute. Two months ago, I'd had no idea brothels even existed outside the red light district of King's Cross. Two months ago, I'd thought French, Spanish and Greek were southern Europeans rather than hooker code for certain sexual practices. And two months ago, I'd been happily looking forward to marrying my fiancé, Brad, an up-and-coming lawyer who planned to be the youngest junior partner in the law firm where he worked.

Yes, two months ago my life had all been mapped out before me.

But that was before a day out in the city to catch up with an old friend triggered a series of events that would ultimately bring about my downfall. Yep, it was at that point I can honestly say my life had bit the big one, nose-diving to newly discovered depths of desperation and despair. I was completely screwed and I didn't have anyone to blame but myself...

Chapter Two

"Oh, go on. Buy it, you deserve it. And besides, it looks totally divine with your coloring."

My heart was racing, threatening to burst from my chest as a rush of pre-purchase adrenaline hit me. Oh, God, it was beautiful. And Sophie was right, it did go perfectly with my new honey, copper and blonde highlights. Rich Bitch Blonde, the stylist had called it. Well, a girl could dream.

I took a deep breath and tried to drag my eyes and my heart away from the burned-orange silk pashmina draped seductively over my arm. Just holding it against my skin infused me with a greater confidence. I felt all of a sudden glamorous, attractive, successful — special, in other words.

No, I told myself firmly, taking a deep breath. *Have some control. And anyway, where would I possibly wear it?*

But the feel of it, cool and decadent against my flushed skin, was breaking down my defenses, together with my better judgment. Already I was picturing myself wearing it with the caramel-colored slacks I'd just been admiring down the road. Thankfully they had run out of my size so I was saved from having to make excuses to Sophie for my non-purchasing.

I tingled all over.

It was better than sex.

God help me, I wanted that pashmina more than life itself. It had to be the single most exquisite item of clothing I had ever laid eyes on. Unfortunately, along with its luxurious silken texture and delicate hand-stitched embroidery came an even more luxurious price tag—a whopping three hundred and ninety dollars!

Ouch!

"Come on, Brooke. What's stopping you? Buy it," urged Sophie, clutching what must have been at least a dozen designer carrier bags.

Sophie didn't appear too concerned about my dilemma. Why would she? She was out-shopping me ten to one. According to Sophie, *I* was the one letting the side down.

Big deep breaths, I kept telling myself. *Breathe...in...and...out...*

"I don't know, Soph. It *is* a bit pricy, don't you think?" I said, biting my lip.

Sophie looked up at me in surprise. "God, no! Not for a designer label like that, it isn't. Just think of how stunning you'll look in it. And, besides, what are you worried about money for? You must be rolling in it."

I opened my mouth to protest, but Sophie cut me off.

"God, don't I wish I had a successful business like yours. PR—now that's something I should have gotten into."

She wasn't the only one. Right then I desperately wished *I'd* gotten into it, as well. I also wished I hadn't hinted I had a successful career in PR in a stupid, vain attempt to impress her when we'd bumped into each other a few weeks back.

Why, why, why?

Even now the memory of that one thoughtless act was enough to make me cringe. Once the horrible lie was out there, I was gone. How could I possibly back-pedal or play it down now? It was without doubt the most foolish thing to ever have passed my lips.

PR. I knew *nothing* about PR. Zip. Nada. I might as well have told her I was a bloody rocket scientist. In other words, I was in deep shit.

Unfortunately, for the time being, I had little choice but to brazen it out and pray I could figure a way out, and soon, before she cottoned on to the truth and I was outed as a lying loser.

Hence the shopping trip into the city to catch up on old times — and far, far away from my real life — and equally hence my awful dilemma over the hideously expensive pashmina currently sending my shopping hormones into a tailspin. But, then again, as far as Sophie knew, I *was* supposed to be a wealthy businesswoman to whom money was no object, *not* a part-time receptionist at a local doctor's surgery, scraping by on a pathetic fourteen-dollars-an-hour pay. And if that wasn't bad enough, I also had a fiancé who would positively freak out if he discovered I was walking around the haute couture floor of the downtown department store, seriously considering spending almost four hundred dollars on a pashmina when we were supposed to be saving up for our wedding and, beyond that, a house.

"It must be wonderful to have such a glamorous career," she continued, eyeing an obscenely expensive Collette Dinnigan dress, oblivious to the agony of indecision raging in my head. "My Dominick would never hear of me going out to work. He *insists* I spend my days pampering myself and my nights pampering him, of course," she whispered, dissolving into little-girl giggles.

I smothered a sudden rush of irritation. Yes, Sophie was the one rolling in old money thanks to an advantageous marriage and I was happy for her, really. I just felt so inadequate next to her.

"Come on, Brooke. What else are you going to wear to that fabulous wedding you're organizing—whose is it again?"

Panic stations.

"Oh, I don't think you would have heard of her. Her father is high up in some investment bank somewhere."

"Yeah, but if he's *that* rich, the wedding is bound to end up in the weekend society pages. Just think, if they ask you to pose with them, this little investment will have been worth every penny." Sophie paused briefly before grabbing my arm. "You know what? I just had the most brilliant idea."

Oh, no—

"How about you get Dominick and me onto the guest list? After all, I imagine you'll be organizing the seating, so surely it wouldn't be any bother to slip us in somewhere inconspicuous, would it? I know at my wedding—did I tell you it was held in a seventeenth-century chapel on the family estate—"

Only about seventeen times!

"Well, apart from my parents and a few close friends, you know, *London* friends…" She cast me an apologetic look. Needless to say I hadn't gotten an invitation. "I barely knew anyone, so no one will suspect we aren't strictly friends of the family—yet!" She winked. "It would be perfect. Dominick and I would surely make it into the society pages *and* make a few valuable social contacts as well. What do you say?"

What I *really* wanted to say to Sophie's suggestion could easily have gotten me thrown out of the haute couture floor of David Jones. Or out of any shop, really. God, didn't I wish I could pull a successful PR career — or a rich, aristocratic husband for that matter — out of my arse.

Alas, I was no magician.

Although I certainly had the arse for it.

I groaned inwardly. I needed a diversion and I needed it now.

"Um, look, I can't promise anything, Sophie. The list is set in concrete, I'm afraid. You know, for security reasons and all that." Sophie's expression darkened. "*But* if there are any last-minute cancelations, I'll see what I can do," I added quickly, desperate to restore her good humor.

The situation was fast getting out of control. The pressure of Sophie's scrutiny was beginning to make me sweat and I was starting to panic.

"Jesus, Brooke. I don't see why the huge decision. It's only four hundred dollars, for God's sake!" she huffed.

Standing in her shoes, I suppose I could see her point. My mind was racing and, in my current state, common sense wasn't terribly forward in my thoughts. Then a sudden thought struck. Of course, why hadn't I thought if it before? *Buy the pashmina and, once Sophie's out of the picture, I simply return it. Perfect!* Problem solved and maybe, just maybe by the time I saw Sophie again, I'd have worked a way out of this stupid fictitious PR-lady mess.

"Well, I suppose you're right. It *is* only one little pashmina." And with that I draped the much-desired wrap over my arm and made my way over toward the sales counter. This was it. It appeared the much-coveted pashmina was mine, if only for a brief spell until I could sneak back in and get a refund, hopefully restoring some equilibrium to my finances.

By the time I reached the haughty saleswoman standing guard alongside the Dolce & Gabbana and Chanel displays, my earlier bravado was retreating at breakneck speed. I was sweating buckets and, perhaps even more alarming, how on earth was I going to pay for this?

Until that moment, the snooty sales assistant had been eyeing me with a distinctly distasteful glare, her finger poised above the panic button under the counter, *potential shoplifter alert* written all over her face. But as I laid the pashmina with the utmost care on the tiny glass top, her nostrils flared slightly, no doubt catching the whiff of an impending sale—not to mention the accompanying commission—and her haughty look of disdain transformed itself into a patronizing smile.

"Madam certainly possesses a refined taste in accessories," she purred. "*And* I must say this particular piece is one of the standouts of the spring collection."

What. A. Poser.

Appearing beside me, Sophie interrupted our exchange in her recently acquired posh Kensington accent. "Oh, you know the designer, then?" she asked.

"Um, only by reputation," came the saleswoman's hesitant reply.

Sophie made a point of searching out the woman's name tag. "Oh, that's nice. *Sabinne-with-an-extra-N* — how original!" she sneered.

Sabinne's faux-smile evaporated in an instant, along with any remaining semblance of civility. All redirected my way. Of course.

"Does madam realize the price of this pashmina is three hundred and ninety dollars—Australian dollars, that is?" she announced in a voice sharp enough to slice through rope. Behind me, it seemed every woman within a twenty-foot radius held their breath in anticipation of what was quickly degenerating into a world-series bitch-off with me the hapless stooge stuck in the middle.

My composure was rapidly crumbling before Sophie's shrill voice rose above the ambient music playing in the background.

"Oh. My. God. Did you hear that! We had no idea," she cried out, gaining the attention of the entire floor. "What a *bargain*, Brooke. I can't believe it! They're practically giving it away. Darling, now you really will have to buy those divine Gucci shoes we spotted earlier—you know, the black ones with the diamante-encrusted heels."

The look on Sabinne's face said it all. She knew when it was time to admit defeat and backed down in a second, hastily wrapping the pashmina before almost bundling it into a black and white plastic bag. Sophie, meanwhile, moved off to amuse herself by rummaging through a pile of artistically folded designer sweaters as though she was racing the clock at a Boxing Day sale, while I swallowed my disappointment. It seemed I was not destined to receive a designer tote bag that day.

"Cash or credit?" Sabinne snapped, by now not bothering to disguise the irritation that she directed toward me.

"Cr-credit," I stammered, pulling my wallet from my fake Louis Vuitton handbag.

Bloody hell, what was I going to do? I had four credit cards. My Virgin card was about as pristine as an Amsterdam hooker. My Amex was A-Maxed out and my Visa card was a passport to nothing. So that only left my last remaining retail lifeline, my Diners Club card. Sadly even that was in imminent danger of suffering an aneurism with all the abuse it had copped recently. God, this was going to be close.

I relinquished my Diners Club card to Sabinne's expectant fingers.

As if caught up in a bad dream, I monitored its snail's-pace progress toward the EFTPOS machine with a feeling of impending doom. *Please don't die on me*, I prayed as she swiped it hard through the electronic terminal. Already I could visualize the beefy security men springing out from behind the Versace display to *escort* the broke punter from the top floor down through the bargain basement and back onto the street where Sabinne clearly thought I belonged — and where in truth I *did* belong.

It was as though Sabinne could smell my fear, for she sadistically punched in the details of the sale at an even slower snail's pace, dragging out my agony until I was almost ready to crack and dissolve in a blubbering heap on the floor, confessing the true state of my finances. My voice of reason screamed at me to simply say I'd changed my mind. Yes, a moment of embarrassment in front of a sales person I would no doubt ever lay eyes on again sounded like the smartest thing to do under the circumstances, but before I had the chance to swallow my pride, the machine swallowed my money and sent an approving *beep* signaling the transaction had gone through.

Sabinne then thrust the plastic bag toward me and immediately turned her back and stormed off to the other side of the counter.

"Christ, wasn't that sales girl a complete cow?" sniffed Sophie fifteen minutes later as we made our way out through the large glass doors and back onto Market Street. "Honestly, Brooke, you should have really let her have it. Scene or no scene, it would have been worth it just to see that little hag put back into her place. Thought she was so high and mighty. Pretentious little fashion diva, yeah, right. My mother's bloody Spaniel has more class than her."

"Soph, I'm sure she didn't mean it personally. She probably just had a bad day, that's all," I said, desperate to forget the entire episode.

However, Sophie was on a roll by this stage. "Anyway, let's take a look at that lovely pashmina." Standing by the intersection, waiting for the crossing lights to turn green, I experienced a pang of doom as Sophie reached out and grabbed the bag off my arm. *Please be gentle with it*, I prayed, mentally stealing myself for the humble pie I was going to be choking on later when I snuck back into the store to return the precious item.

Sophie whipped it out of the bag like a magician pulling a rabbit out of a hat and my stomach lurched dangerously. "No point wasting a minute enjoying this little beauty," she uttered, almost to herself. And to my utter horror, she proceeded to rip the price label off before draping the pashmina around my shoulders. "Wow, it looks better on than it did in the store," she gushed.

As if in slow motion, I watched her carelessly drop the tag into the waste bin at the intersection just at the moment the crossing lights turned green. I found myself swept across the road in with the tide of tired shoppers heading over to the other side toward the underground rail.

My strangled yelp of horror was drowned out by the passing buses and, in what was in reality probably no longer than fifteen seconds, my plans to rescue myself from the precipice of financial doom had been shot to shit.

"Sophie! Why did you do that?" I shrieked as we reached the other side.

"Do what?" she replied.

"Take the bloody price tag off, of course," I stammered trying to keep my cool.

Sophie laughed, yes, actually laughed! I thought I was going to be sick. "Well, silly, you can hardly go around wearing it with the tag on, can you?"

"And what if I need to return it?" I replied, anger boiling up inside as my face started to redden.

"Yeah, right, it's not like it can be the wrong size."

Well, there was no arguing with logic like that.

Still, it didn't help that I was hovering only inches away from an economic black hole. Clinging on to solvency by a mere thread. In this case, a silken burned-orange thread.

Alas, similar to an addict's desperate desire for instant gratification, the moment I'd finished signing the credit slip, my cravings for the above-mentioned pashmina had begun to wane. All of a sudden, it wasn't quite so mouth-wateringly delectable draped around my shoulders as it had been on the androgynous mannequin moments before. I felt sick. What had I done?

It seemed only moments ago I'd been basking in the grip of an exhilarating pre-purchase adrenaline rush. I should have known it wouldn't last and now I plunged headlong into an all-too-familiar post-purchase depression. To make matters worse, as a result of Sophie's flagrant disregard for the precious nature of my current situation, and that of the pashmina, my plans of sneaking back in and returning it, and in doing so restoring some much-needed equilibrium to my finances, were now down the toilet.

I took a deep breath, trying to dampen down the panic rising inside. No, I wasn't about to start crying over it now. It was a done deal and, besides, there would be plenty of time for tearful regrets once the credit card statement arrived next month.

"Okay, where to now?" queried Sophie, looking up and down Elizabeth Street for a taxi.

Clearly, she still had money to burn and plastic to swipe — unlike me.

"Oh, I don't know," I responded without enthusiasm, desperately trying to come up with a viable excuse to cut loose and go home. The last few hours trailing behind Sophie and her shopping frenzy had not only now cost me a fortune but also highlighted the raging gulf that existed between Sophie's lifestyle and my own humble existence.

"Look, I'm sorry, Soph, but I really think it's time I called it a day. Brad will be home by six and if I don't leave soon, he'll be wondering where I am."

Sophie waved away my concerns. "Oh, don't worry about him. I'm sure he can manage without you for an hour or two. Make up an excuse. Tell him you were entertaining a potential new client or something. Pretend I'm an A-list celebrity. Then you can surprise him with this lovely treasure we found today." She ran her fingers over the pashmina.

That was exactly what I feared and I stifled a groan.

"No, seriously, I also have an early morning breakfast meeting tomorrow," I lied. "And I still need to go over a mountain of paperwork to prepare."

Sophie seemed to consider this for a moment before sighing. "In that case I suppose you should make a move. After all I wouldn't want to be the cause of you falling asleep in your granola tomorrow morning in front of some VIP, would I."

I silently admonished myself for stooping to the PR lie again, but I was desperate to leave while I still had the money for train fare home.

Air-kisses and promises to meet again soon and I watched Sophie vanish in a taxi. Thank God that was over. She was on her way to spend an obscene amount of dosh and I was on my way home to face the consequences of my day of excess.

Chapter Three

As usual the train terminal was total anarchy. Only my fear of negotiating the kamikaze inner-city traffic maze had made me decide to leave my car at home, a decision I was now regretting. Luck was on my side for once and, a few minutes later, my train inched its way out of Central Station and I leaned back against the cold vinyl seat and breathed a sigh of relief. *What a day.* I was exhausted, my feet were killing me and, if that wasn't bad enough, an enormous headache was coming on. Great, all I needed now was some alcohol-soaked weirdo to plonk their butt down next to me and attempt to discuss the meaning of life for the duration of the two-hour, all-stops-to-Newcastle train trip and my day would be complete.

It was some kind of divine penance, I was convinced. My punishment for breaking Brad's cardinal rule and, in the process, breaking my bank balance, for at this particular point in time, I honestly couldn't see myself ever paying off those wretched credit cards behind his back. Hell, lately even keeping up the minimum payments without him finding out was becoming harder and harder to manage.

Brad, in what he saw as a magnanimous gesture, paid off all my cards just after we announced our engagement. At the time he pointed out that he didn't want the taint of my past debts and bad habits casting a shadow over our future life together. We, or should I say *I*, was starting fresh. A clean slate, as it were. Of course, there was a proviso to his generosity and Brad's only condition was I destroy my precious credit cards once and for all. I, having lived under the shadow of debt for the better part of my adult life, was completely bowled over by his generosity and agreed heartily.

I swear to God I meant it at the time.

Then, just as I was experiencing a lean week money-wise, I spotted these wonderful new-season cut-off jeans. I hate to say it, but the lure of plastic was too much for a poor retail junkie like me to withstand and after much agonizing, I eventually dug out a much-neglected credit card from where it had lain hidden and almost forgotten in the depths of my wallet. It would just be this one time, I told myself. I would pay it off as soon as I was paid — promise! But then, a couple of days later, a pair of gorgeous tan suede ankle boots caught my eye at a never-to-be-repeated bargain price of seventy-five dollars. What was I expected to do? If I'd waited another month until I had the cash, they would have been long gone and I would have been looking at one hundred and fifty dollars at least to buy the very same pair of shoes. The way I saw it, I was saving *him* money, buying them at the time.

Alas, as a result of that one little indiscretion, my credit card abstinence was broken. I honestly didn't know how it happened. Yes, I was ashamed. Mortified, in fact, but following that initial fall, it was a slow slippery road back to credit card dependency for me.

Brad, of course, had no idea and I wasn't about to tell him, especially seeing as he'd once hinted if I didn't gain some control of my spending addiction, he was going to call off the engagement. Like he pointed out at the time, how was I expected to become a responsible wife and mother when I couldn't even master the basic concept of household budgeting?

He was right. I didn't even know why I had this overwhelming compulsion to spend. My cousin, Trudy, who I must point out is a hairdresser and therefore only one step away from being a psychologist, suggested my shopping addiction was a form of comfort seeking. It made sense at the time. While some people, according to Trudy, eat, or smoke or bite their nails when they're under stress or bored, I unfortunately head straight for the nearest factory outlet store.

What could I say?

At least I wasn't fat or coughing up chunks of blackened lung tissue.

No—I was just broke. Very, *very* broke and right then I wasn't sure what was worse.

By now my headache had upgraded itself from economy to first-class pain. Added to that, I was sitting on the wrong side of the carriage and the afternoon sun was streaming in through the window, tormenting me with sharp splinters of glare. It was too late to move to another seat now. Every available spot on the passenger-friendly side of the train was by this stage occupied by train-smart commuters rustling their way through the newspaper or cracking open a can of beer in preparation for their afternoon wind-down.

I noticed the only seat left in the entire carriage was the aisle seat next to mine. Needless to say, I fully intended to guard it with my life and set to work rearranging my bag on it to discourage anyone from sitting there. With my migraine currently boring a hole right through my right eye, I knew I couldn't cope with any more interference and rested my head against the window, hoping to ride out the tempest raging in my head.

Moments later, a heavily accented female voice filtered down through the pain. "Excuse me, lady, is this seat taken?"

Damn it!

What choice did I have but to cram my bags down at my feet to make room for this woman, who by the look of her was a nurse? Oh well, at least it wasn't a verbally incontinent, pissed old man leering down my top. The ID pinned to her blouse together with the general weariness surrounding her told me she had just come off a shift and no doubt was only interested in getting home and putting her tired feet up. Thank God. It seemed I was saved from having to contribute anything more meaningful than a polite nod and I closed my eyes and tried to ignore the pain raging inside my skull.

What a horrendous end to what had generally been a stressful day.

Since I'd unexpectedly run into Sophie, an old school friend, a couple of weeks back, she had taken to calling me regularly for a girlie chat. At first, I'd been flattered beyond belief, but as I was soon to learn it turned out nearly all her old friends had either moved away from the area or were knee deep in babies and unable to manage a single sentence that didn't revolved around breastfeeding, colic or the bowel patterns of their darling infants. So, by the process of elimination, it seemed I had climbed up in her social estimations. Admittedly the PR lie helped.

Now, in light of my 'lie', I was glad I had only given her my mobile number. The last thing I wanted was for Brad to answer the phone when I was working an evening shift and spill the beans about my lowly position at the surgery.

It wasn't as though I wasn't thrilled to hear from her after all those years, because I was, honestly. All throughout high school, we'd hung out together until Sophie had left to live in England with her parents and from there, she'd gone on to get a job as a clerk at some insurance company. It was apparently then Sophie had met her blue-blood husband, through a friend of a friend — naturally. For, as Sophie had pointed out, guys picked up at bars and nightclubs were fine for a romp but definitely not keepers. And from the first time she'd laid eyes on Dominick — and his accompanying pedigree, I suspect — she knew he was without doubt a keeper.

Not that my own romance with Brad wasn't a match made in heaven. It was. Only rather than meeting over a fancy candlelit dinner party in Notting Hill, we met when he was rushed into the surgery where I was working by his team-mates one night following a particularly brutal clash with another rugby player in a local Union competition.

Three stitches later, I was smitten.

Looking back now, I'm not sure what it was exactly about him that caused my heart to melt. Maybe it was his wide muscular shoulders, or his cheeky little-boy grin, or his dirt-smeared face and grazed knees, or the way he winced as the doctor sutured his head.

Brad occasionally jokes it was the painkillers talking that night, but as he left the surgery, urged on by his mates, he asked me out for a drink the following weekend.

Right from the very beginning, he was everything I had ever dreamed of in a man. Good-looking, smart, ambitious and, as my mother pointed out, a proper gentleman. My parents of course just loved him and he in turn did an admirable job of tolerating them. Their relief I had finally found a boyfriend who they considered worthy of their precious only daughter was evident in the way they welcomed him into the family with open arms. Mum in particular was clearly delighted he was a lawyer and more than once hinted that she hoped his maturity and level-headedness would rub off on me. Eight months after that first date, I moved in with Brad and, a year later, much to my parents' delight, we announced our engagement. At the time, we agreed to postpone the wedding until we had saved enough for a deposit on a house.

It was all part of his five-year plan, he patiently explained to me whenever I voiced any disapproval at being rationed nonstop. Five years to own the house of our dreams. Five years to start or continue a family — accidents do happen, he kept telling me, despite me constantly assuring him I was in no hurry to get sprogged up. And five years for him to become senior partner at the law firm where he's worked ever since graduating from university with a prestigious law degree. Big plans for the future, he has.

Big plans or not, I am caught up in a budget hell. Sure, to begin with, I was all on board. Enthusiastic, even, about planning for our future financial stability. But really, three years later and three years of retail abstinence was too much for anyone to expect. Trudy keeps reminding me that I too go to work and contribute to the finances and I shouldn't feel like I'm always going without. But it was my future, too, I remind her, and a future without Brad was too much to bear.

Hence my solemn promise to curb my spending.

And hence why I will be in deep shit if he ever finds out about today's shopping blow-out.

As the train jerked out from another station, I opened my eyes, fighting off a wave of nausea and praying I was nearly home and my nightmare trip almost at an end. It was then I noticed we were barely out of the city and I groaned, as much from pain as from disappointment.

Can today possibly get any worse?

"I like your hair," trilled the nurse sitting beside me in what I guessed to be a heavy Eastern European accent.

What an odd thing to say. I gave a weak smile and turned away from her to look out of the window, strangely unsettled by her incongruous comment. Then if that wasn't disturbing enough, a few minutes later, she began touching and stroking my hair. I flinched in horror, desperately trying to melt into the wall of the carriage and out of her reach. Then it struck me.

Oh, holy hell, a loony in disguise.

Very clever, dressing up as a nurse like that. Probably a mental patient escaped the asylum after clubbing her nurse to death and stealing her clothes.

Why. Why me?

I swear to God I must have a stamp on my forehead inviting loonies far and wide to come and sit next to me on trains, or any form of public transport, for that matter. I was a nutter magnet. A beacon to which all weirdos gravitated like moths at a floodlight. But still, for all my horror, I found it next to impossible to simply tell them to bugger off and leave me the hell alone.

"My name is Maria. Vot is your name?" she asked loudly, her thick accent seeping into every grimy crevice in the now very quiet carriage.

Someone tittered a couple of seats ahead of me and I cringed inwardly.

"Brooke," I whispered out of the corner of my mouth.

I should have made up a name! What if she *was* a psycho? What if she tracked me down, moved into the house next door, stole my fiancé and murdered me in my sleep? What if she cut off all my hair and saved it as some kind of sick trophy? I didn't want to die bald.

"Brooke," she repeated even more loudly, her voice permeating throughout the carriage like a toxic cloud. "Vot a pretty name. I knew a patient called Brooke once. I am the nurse, you know. Vell, training to be the nurse..."

Okay, so she isn't an escaped psychiatric patient – just weird.

I attempted to juggle my level of attentiveness as not to appear completely rude but then again not to seem too keen, either. Yes, no direct eye contact and no communication of more than one syllable. Not that Maria picked up on the leave-me-alone vibes all but screaming from every pore in my body. No, she carried on relentlessly.

"Dis poor, poor Brooke, she has terrible cancer of dee...dee..."

Maria was by now looking down meaningfully to her lap.

"How do you say – dee ut-er-us. You know, dee womb," she shouted, this time, gripping her lower abdomen just in case I was in any doubt as to where my ovaries were located.

"Terrible it vos. Just a young pretty girl like you and nothing to do but to cut out her womb. No babies vor

30

her. Ever. It vos such a shame. She cried and cried. Do you have little babies?" she inquired.

As her voice rang out over the seats, the carriage fell into a deathly silence. Not even a lone rustle of newspaper. No doubt they all thought my mad neighbor was infinitely more entertaining than the latest political scandal unfolding in our nation's capital. I was just dying!

I shook my head and kept my mouth firmly closed. Yes, it might have been rude, but I sure as hell wasn't about to encourage her.

"Oh, never mind. Maybe one day, then ven you find nice husband, you have little babies of your own, ya?"

At that came a muffled giggle from the lady diagonally opposite. *Bitch!*

Oh, God, will this nightmare never end?

Thankfully, my prayers were answered a couple of minutes later when my mobile phone went off in my bag. Yippee, a valid excuse to ditch psycho nurse. Fishing my phone out of the bottom of my bag, I forced a polite apologetic smile at Maria before rudely turning my back on her.

"Hello."

"Brooke, where are you?" demanded Brad.

"I'm on the train. I should be home in another hour. Why?"

"Why? I thought you would be home by now, that's why. You know I have training tonight."

"I hadn't forgotten," I sighed. With the pain in my head slowly crushing my will to live, I was beyond taking offense at his attitude. "If you're hungry, there's leftover fried rice in the fridge, or if you can wait until after training, I will cook you dinner when I get home. Look, I can't talk now. I have a terrible headache and we're just about to come up to the tunnel. I'll see you later..."

"But I can't find my footy shorts..." he whined, just as the train raced into the tunnel, thankfully cutting short his whine as my phone lost reception.

Great. Just what I needed, another evening navigating around one of his bad moods. I threw the phone angrily back into the bottom of my bag, where with any luck I wouldn't hear it if he chose to ring back and nag some more.

Brad sounded a little annoyed. Still, by now I knew better than to take it personally and reminded myself once again that he had a very important job and was under immense pressure at work. Every day he carried the weight of other people's problems on his shoulders, so it wasn't unusual that he occasionally needed to vent. Not that he'd voiced any objection as such, but I suspected he was a little uneasy about my trip to the city. Just the thought of letting me loose in the retail capital of Australia was enough to cause him to break out in hives.

I only hoped he never discovered the truth.

The low rumbling of my nausea was by now gaining momentum, keeping pace with my headache. Of course, I could have asked Maria if she had an aspirin on her, but I didn't relish the thought of the entire train carriage being privy to my entire medical history so I slowly reached down to gather my bags. I'd finally had enough. I was out of there.

"You leaving?" Maria sighed as I stood up, her face falling.

"Um, my stop is coming up soon," I lied tripping over her legs in my eagerness to put some distance between us.

I desperately needed to get some air. Beads of cold sweat were gathering on my top lip and a hollow whooshing sound booming in my ears. I didn't feel well at all. Brad's phone call had been the last straw, and I knew I was about to be ill.

For the first time that day, luck was on my side. Thank God I had chosen a carriage with a toilet, saving me the humiliation of either chucking out of the door—very dangerous and messy—or vomiting in a plastic bag—hopefully after I retrieved my pashmina from its depths—in full view of a carriage full of commuters.

I squeezed myself into the tiny cubicle with barely a second to spare. The moment I slammed the door shut behind me, bile hit the back of my throat and I heaved. God, I felt wretched. So wretched not even the disgusting state of the standard issue CityRail stainless steel toilet bowl was enough to deter me from making use of its evacuative facilities.

By the time the train pulled into my station some forty minutes later, I was feeling human once more. A little cold water splashed over my pale face and wrists and no one would have suspected I had spent over twenty minutes crouched over a metal toilet bowl heaving my guts up while fully expecting my head to split open like an over-ripe melon. On the plus side, at least I had escaped from psycho-nurse and her hair fetishes. My day of a thousand trials was almost over and I was looking forward to getting home, pulling on my pajamas and curling up in bed.

Brad could get his own bloody dinner.

I alighted from the train and shuffled along the platform toward the station exit and the waiting buses, relieved to know I'd be home in less than fifteen minutes. I was counting on Brad being safely out of the house at footy training, leaving me free to surreptitiously stash away my meager purchases before I found myself having to justify my spending. I shouldn't complain, though. After all, Brad was doing this for us and many years from now when I looked around at our fabulous home and family, I would be thankful for his restraint.

Mind you, one person's idea of restraint is another's definition of meanness and Trudy considered Brad the stingiest man on earth. As I tried to explain to her, he was only looking out for my best interests. Yes, he was everything I had ever wanted in a man and I looked to my future role as Mrs. Brad Cooper, wife to up-and-coming lawyer Brad Cooper with a sense of pride and excitement.

The only downside to his chosen career, of course, was after dealing with crooks — not to mention other lawyers — day in and day out, he'd developed a bullshit barometer and could sniff out a lie a mile off.

I, on the other hand, was a terrible liar, which went a long way to explaining my recent stress-induced migraine.

It was then I saw him. Large as life in his faded jeans and Australian rugby jersey, peering through the crowds of approaching commuters.

Shit! Shit. Shit.

Why was Brad waiting for me at the exit gate? A dozen different scenarios rugby-tackled my tender brain at once. Sophie had found out my home number and phoned to see if Brad had liked my four-hundred-dollar pashmina. Or maybe the credit card company had called, demanding to know why I was so grossly overdrawn on my credit account.

For a brief moment, I prayed that it was a death in the family.

No, that was a dreadful thought.

A serious illness would do just as well. A few seconds later he saw me and my heart sank. He didn't look happy. It transpired that for once I was not the cause of his bad mood. Not today, anyway. Apparently footy practice had been canceled at the last minute, explaining why he had decided to come out and pick me up from the station instead. Still, Brad was not a happy camper. There were only a few weeks left before the start of the new footy season and he was determined that this year they would finish in the top half of the local competition ladder. So with that in mind he didn't consider Danno's twisted knee, Jacko's wife's childbirth *or* the coach's kitchen catching fire sufficient grounds to cancel training for the night. Union was a serious sport, he continually told me, a thinking man's sport, and as such was to be taken seriously.

By the time we got home, Brad's huffy mood had burned itself out and his attention turned to me.

"So," he said, his forty-watt smile as always lighting up my heart. "Tell me about your day. Did you have a nice time with your friend?"

I had to think quickly. If ever there was a loaded question spoken, this was it.

In the end I decided to play it safe.

"Yes, I suppose I did. It was great seeing her again after all these years, but I can honestly say being pushed about by thousands of people in the city is not my idea of fun."

Brad looked at me in surprise bordering on disbelief. "I thought you loved going into the city?"

"I do," I said quickly. "At least, I used to. But I don't know. Maybe I'm getting old, but it wasn't as much fun as I remembered. Also there was this weird woman on the train touching my hair..."

"I see it didn't stop you from shopping, though." Brad's smile slid off his face at the sight of the carrier bags I had just placed on the dining table.

"Oh, those. God, don't worry about them." I laughed. "Sophie and I had a trawl through a couple of clearance sales in the city and you'll never guess what we found and for virtually nothing."

"Really. *Nothing*, you say."

"Well, almost nothing."

Brad smiled indulgently. "Okay what did you get?"

I decided to out the pashmina while all was going well. Better to get this over and done with while the going was good. After all, it wasn't something I could hide for long. As I held it up for his approval, he looked genuinely confused.

"What the hell is it?"

"It's called a pashmina, silly. You wear it like a wrap, over little tops or strappy dresses. They're really in fashion at the moment."

"Seriously? It reminds me of my granny's kitchen curtains when I was a kid. Back in fashion, you say? Wow!"

Thankfully his attention was soon drawn to the footy game about to begin on the telly. I was home free, off the hook, and could finally relax, safe in the knowledge I had dodged a bullet. My heart was thumping with relief while lurking in the back of my mind was the nagging thought that one day my 'luck' was going to run out. Then I would no doubt need a flak jacket to wear under my pashmina, for those bullets would be coming in thick and fast.

* * * *

I woke the next morning feeling as though I had been given a get-out-of-jail-free card. I still couldn't believe I had gotten away with it last night. But, still, it had been a close one. As a measure of my relief, I'd even gifted him with a quick shag when he'd come to bed that night after the rugby finished. Considering it was somewhat out of character for me to be the initiator, Brad had been understandably taken aback by my sudden interest.

It wasn't as though I was *never* enthusiastic in the sack. I could do a fairly convincing rendition of Meg Ryan's café orgasm when the occasion warranted it, but sex wasn't high on my list of must-haves — as opposed to the silk pashmina. I would have liked to have slept with it instead of Brad. But rather than it being a cause of conflict between the two of us, I suspect this was one aspect of our relationship where we were in complete accord. Brad made no secret of the fact he considered sexually aggressive women, citing precisely which female celebrities he found unfeminine, unbecoming and a bit of a turn-off. I did itch to point out at the time that I didn't see he had much chance of being hunted down and screwed to death by either of them any time in the near future.

By the time I woke up the following morning, it was after nine and Brad had already left for work. The house was so quiet I could hear the birds outside my bedroom window and the distant barking of dogs somewhere in the next street. As I stretched my sleep-taut muscles and rolled over, I noticed a cup of coffee sitting on the bedside table atop a saucer and smiled. How sweet of him. Almost worth the twenty minutes' sleep I sacrificed last night indulging him. It was stone-cold of course, but it was the thought that counted.

I had the morning off and briefly considered what to do with it—something cheap, of course. A walk in the park? A stroll around an art gallery? A walk along the beach? Some place where I wouldn't be tempted to spend money. After yesterday's close call, I realized I desperately needed to conform my thinking to include non-retail-related pastimes.

I determined from this moment on to pull in the reins and avoid anything that might plunge me further into debt. Yesterday I'd stuffed up big time, and the entire incident with the pashmina had been a warning shot across the bow. *Yes, sacrifices have to be made and unfortunately some of us are expected to sacrifice a little more than others*, I thought, citing Brad's new golf clubs as a prime example.

Seeing I wasn't rostered on at the surgery until four o'clock, I had a good seven hours to fill. Wednesday night was Dr. Fairweather's late night in the surgery. In the four months since having started at the surgery, I'd come to enjoy working with Dr. Fairweather. He was a real sweetie, only a couple of years from retirement and therefore winding down for a new life on the golf course. As a result, he never yelled at me for getting out the wrong file or booking in an entire family of hypochondriacs in one appointment space. I think he saw me as a kind of pseudo-granddaughter and indulged me accordingly.

Pity I couldn't say the same for that cranky bitch Dr. Chisholm.

Now *she* was a right dragon. Always on my back for something *and* she made no secret of thinking me a complete airhead. Just because *she* managed to fluke her way through medical school—I have absolutely no proof of this but the thought gets me through the day—

it didn't give her the right to treat everyone as though they were mindless imbeciles.

Chapter Four

Happily flicking through that month's *Marie Claire*, I heard the phone ringing in the next room — Mum calling to see how yesterday had gone.

Since my parents had moved up the coast almost a year ago, my relationship with my mother had improved out of sight. Indeed, I've come to appreciate she might not have been put on this earth merely to spawn me and, following that, devoting the rest of her life to making mine hell. In fact, in the last couple of months, I had begun to look forward to her frequent phone calls, much to my amazement.

"Hel-loo," I sang into the phone as I pulled a chair over, ready to make myself comfortable.

"Good morning," came a formal masculine voice. "May I speak to Miss Brooke Jillian Delaney, please?"

Well, one thing was for sure. It wasn't my mum.

"This is Brooke Delaney speaking," I replied, experiencing the pang of nervousness that usually accompanied hearing someone refer to me by my full name and title.

"Good morning. My name is Geoff and I am calling from Optimum Communications. I have to inform you this call may be monitored for training purposes and if, for any reasons you have any objections, please say now and I will connect you to my superior."

Great. Another long-winded call from yet another phone company wanting to improve my telephone service. If I hadn't been brought up to be pathologically polite I might have shouted down the phone that they could improve their bloody phone service by *not* wasting my time every few days calling me with stupid time and money saving options that never seemed to live up to their promise of actually saving me money *or* time. Funny that.

"No, go ahead, I don't mind," I responded, resigned to yet another ten minutes of listening to this boring bloke on the phone bleat on about long-distance carriers and free-time communication. But, hell, it was keeping him in a job, I suppose.

"I am ringing in regard to your mobile phone account."

"Oh, thanks, but I'm happy with my current plan," I gabbled, in the hope of cutting him off before he settled into his lengthy well-rehearsed spiel.

"No, ma'am, I am calling from the finance department in relation to this month's account."

"If it's about last month's bill, I can assure you it has been paid in full," I replied, growing a little indignant at the suggestion I was attempting to dip out of paying my phone bill. My mobile bill was one of the few bills I *did* pay on time. "Monday, I think it was. I paid it over the phone and have a receipt number to prove it."

"Yes, that is correct. It is this current month's account we have a concern with, Miss Delaney."

"Um and what exactly is the problem?"

"Well, Miss Delaney..." I wished he would stop calling me *Miss Delaney*. The official tone in his voice was making me feel uneasy. "Have you in the past couple of days made any prolonged telephone calls, or perhaps any overseas calls?"

I racked my brain. Sure, I had been on the phone to Sophie once or twice, but so what?

"No, I don't think so. Nothing out of the ordinary, anyway."

"And, Miss Delaney, has your phone been in your possession for the past few days?"

"Yes, of course it has."

"Well, Miss Delaney..."

Oh, God, there he went again. An ominous feeling crept over me.

"Is there any reason you can think of to explain your current account balance of, um...let me see...four thousand, two hundred and ninety-two dollars?"

"What?" I spluttered, smothering the urge to laugh out loud.

"Is there anything—"

"No! The amount! *How* much did you say?"

Obviously I hadn't heard right. There must be something wrong with the line. How ironic.

"Four thousand. Two hundred. And. Ninety-two dollars," he overenunciated, to make himself perfectly clear.

A cold wave of dread rolled over me like a London fog. "You *are* joking, aren't you?" I whispered hoarsely, the breath squeezed from my body. Then it dawned on me. *Of course.* Jesus, I was so gullible. "This is one of those radio show 'gotcha' calls, isn't it?"

Trudy! Of course, it was just what she would do. She was the only one who knew how freaked out I was about my money situation. I was going to kill her for this. But still I loved listening to those prank calls on the radio. Poor bastards fell for it every time and made a right fool of themselves.

"No, Miss Delaney. I can assure you this is not a hoax call."

"Sure it is." I laughed, not wanting to sound like a totally humorless idiot on the radio. "That's you, isn't it? Paddy—from the Morning Crew? I'd recognize your voice anywhere!"

There was a brief silence on the other end of the phone before *Geoff's*—or Paddy's—voice came back on line, this time sounding a little more forceful.

"Miss Delaney," he began. "We have it recorded on our system that at five-thirteen yesterday afternoon you received a call on your mobile service from this number." He recited a string of digits. "Is that correct?"

"Um, yes," I replied, slightly thrown.

It had been Brad calling me on the train to whinge about his bloody footy shorts, of all things. I was hardly going to forget that, was I? But so what? Then a thought suddenly struck me. If Paddy knew about that, maybe it was Brad behind the gotcha call and not Trudy, as I'd first thought. Still, it wasn't like Brad to have a sense of humor...unless of course he was trying to teach me a lesson. *Bastard!*

"Then," he continued, "at five-twenty-seven another call was placed *from* your mobile service *to* an overseas number."

"But I don't even know anyone overseas, at least not someone I would call on my mobile." *Jesus, Paddy really put some effort into this one.*

"Miss Delaney, whether you know someone in Brazil or not, we have it confirmed on our records that a call *was* placed from your mobile service to a number in Fortaleza for a duration of more than five hours."

"But—"

"*And* as a result of that call, an amount of four thousand, two hundred and ninety-two dollars is owed *by* you to the Optimum Communication Network," he finished curtly. In the background came the faint murmur of concerned voices and the first stirrings of dread wound themselves around my chest.

It was then my eyes were slowly drawn to my handbag, sitting innocuously in the corner of the dining room, exactly where I'd thrown it as I walked in the door the night before.

Oh, shit!

An hour later, I called the phone company back.

I knew by this point in time it was *not* Paddy from the Morning Crew targeting me for a hoax call.

It was, just like he had said in the first place, Geoff from the mobile phone company and I was in deep shit.

And how did I know this? Well, after dropping the phone down on the cradle in shock, I inched my way over to my handbag to retrieve my mobile from its depths. I was almost loath to touch it, knowing once I did, I couldn't go on pretending this was all a dreadful mistake or some wanker's idea of a joke.

The first thing that struck me was the phone lock wasn't on and my heart sank. *Damn.* I was always careful to lock the phone after every call. Then, not daring to so much as breathe, I scrolled through the menu until I got to Call Register and the last call option.

A wave of nausea rose up the back of my throat and settled in my gullet.

44

The number displayed was at least *sixteen fucking digits long*!

This wasn't a hoax. Geoff had been serious.

My panic dial was wound up to about warp nine by now so rational thought wasn't high on my agenda. I was having enough trouble just breathing. The only explanation I could come up with, other than the fact my life totally sucked, was after I'd thrown the phone back into my bag following Brad's call and dashed off to the toilets, I must have sat on it or leaned against it or something.

How could I have been so stupid? But then in my defense, I'd been feeling like shit at the time, *and* I had been dead tired, *and* hiding out from the weird nurse with the hair fetish.

Finding someone at Optimum Communications who was willing to talk to me was proving to be more difficult than I would have imagined under the circumstances. The trouble was, as soon as I mentioned who I was and why I was calling, I was immediately placed on hold, where I spent the next ten minutes suspended in a telecommunication no-man's-land listening, ironically enough, to some poor bastard being set up by a local radio station. Finally, when they figured I had been tortured enough, my call was tossed from one edgy customer service operator to another until I was eventually transferred back to Geoff. My circle of humiliation was complete.

Talk about stigmatized.

Let's just say I knew exactly how Typhoid Mary felt.

Geoff didn't sound particularly thrilled to be reunited with me on the phone, either. It was obvious by the weary tone of his voice he had drawn the short straw and was now doomed to deal with the hysterical phone fiend until such time as a suitable arrangement could be found. In other words, until I either coughed up the dough or they sent the sheriff around to the house to cart off the telly, fridge, washing machine, Brad's new golf clubs and almost anything else they considered to be of value.

What was I going to do?

Normally, when faced with a crisis of this magnitude, I would have turned to Mum and Dad for the money. They, of course, would have it. Only because they'd insist I come clean with Brad did I resist. Even in my current state I realized telling Brad was completely out of the question. The mere thought of how he would react was making me feel faint—we'd be finished if he ever found out. After all, a four-thousand-dollar phone call made my four-hundred-dollar pashmina seem like a mere trifle.

Paying it off on a credit card? That wasn't an option, either, seeing as I didn't have enough credit points left to buy a Happy Meal, never mind paying a phone bill the size of the Brazilian national debt. Lastly, there was Trudy, of course. God love her, she was always willing to help me out of a sticky situation, but I was fairly certain even she didn't have that much cash, despite owning her own hairdressing business.

So there I was, up a Brazilian creek without a paddle. My life was over.

* * * *

"What am I going to do, Trud?" I cried, fighting back tears.

Had I stayed in the house on my own with nothing but the looming specter of doom for company, I would have been ready to end it all by lunchtime, so in desperation I'd made my way down town to Trudy's salon, ironically called Dye Hard, praying all the time she would have some hope to offer me.

"What did the phone company say again?" she said in her usual business-like manner as she stood rinsing the suds from the hair of a client, who was stretched back uncomfortably into the basin in front of her.

"Only that I was legally responsible for any debts occurred while the phone was in my possession," I parroted word for word, which wasn't all that difficult considering the entire conversation was now engraved into my brain.

"Pass us that towel, will you. So you are saying that if your phone had been stolen, you wouldn't have had to pay?"

I nodded glumly, reaching across and lifting a towel from the top of the pile next to the basin. "Apparently, it would have been covered by my phone insurance."

"Well, what's the problem then? Tell them it was stolen. Simple! Phones are stolen every day. God, tell me someone who *hasn't* had their phone nicked at some time or another. I've lost four of them over the past two years and claimed them back on insurance. Everyone does it!" Trudy shrugged, vigorously rubbing the freshly washed scalp in front of her. "Okay, Mrs. Patterson. I'll just move you over here and get you a nice cup of tea. Becky won't be long."

After Trudy relocated Mrs. Patterson across the room to a station gleaming black and chrome and passed her a pile of magazines, I followed her out into the back room. Trudy filled the kettle and sat down on the small stool in the corner, eager to rest her tired feet for a few moments. I seriously didn't know how she managed to stay happy *and* polite to everyone all day when her feet and back must be killing her. Surrounded by hundreds of small boxes containing various color treatments, I eventually located the coffee, concealed behind a white plastic bucket of bleach, just as the kettle came to a boil.

"So tell me again, why don't you just report the phone as stolen?" she asked, reaching out for the steaming mug of coffee I set down beside her on the bench.

"It's not as simple as that, Trud. They have it on record that Brad rang just ten minutes before and for them to buy the story I would have had to report the phone missing to the police and the phone company *before* the charges came up on their records."

"So you'd thought of that already then?"

I nodded miserably. I'd thought of a great many things but nothing that was going to get me out of this mess. "Trudy, what am I going to do?" I pleaded, my voice trembling.

I was hovering dangerously close to losing it completely.

Trudy put her arms around me for a hug and I battled to keep my tears at bay.

As busy as she was running the small but hip salon with Becky, Trudy was always available for a shoulder to cry on. She was my cousin and, with us being the same age, she was the closest thing I had to a sister. Our mothers were sisters, twins in fact, and although Trudy had two younger brothers, growing up she'd tended to spend more time at my house than her own to get away from them. Seriously, Trudy was the dark to my blonde or at least she was this week, with her long black hair cascading like a shiny waterfall almost to her waist. Some people say we could be mistaken for sisters. But looks were where the similarities ended. She was certainly the genetically blessed one when it came to brains and maturity, unlike me.

"Look, why don't you stop torturing yourself and tell Brad? Everyone makes mistakes, even him, I'm sure. You're only human after all. You never know, he might even surprise you by being really supportive."

I cast Trudy an incredulous look. "Yeah, right!" I sniffed. "If he finds out, I'm telling you now, I will be out on my ear and the wedding will be off — for good."

"Oh, come on, Brooke! You don't honestly think that, do you? I know Brad and I haven't exactly hit it off — "

"You don't say," I mumbled.

Trudy rolled her eyes and smiled, refusing to rise to the bait. I pretty sure they'd rather hit each other than hit it off, but, since the engagement, for my sake, they had thankfully settled into an uneasy truce and agreed to disagree. Not willing to take any chances, though, I had since made it my quest in life to keep them at opposite sides of the universe from each other.

"Look, Brooke, it's no great secret I think he can be a king-size pain in the arse at times but I seriously doubt he'd break up with you over something like this. Sure, it's a lot of money and all, but shit, it isn't like you've been sleeping around behind his back or dealing drugs to primary school kids. Apart from going off at you for being a stupid cow, which of course you are, by the way, I'm sure he'll get over it."

"I don't know. Maybe you're right, but I am not about to take that chance. Things are stressful enough at the moment."

"Jeez, what is it this time? Not the wedding plans *again*?"

"What wedding plans? He's *still* balking over a date. I've been trying to pin him down to, say, February, but he's refusing to commit to an actual *date*. I don't think he has any idea how much there is to organize. Christ, anyone would think we were planning his bloody execution, not his wedding!"

Trudy laughed. "It can't be that bad, surely?"

"Have I told you what his latest excuse is?"

Trudy shook her head, trying to smother a smile.

"Apparently, now he's decided against getting a bank loan to pay for the wedding, so we're saving for that as well. Have you any idea how much weddings cost, Trudy? At the rate we're going, I'll be about ninety before I finally get to the altar. So, can't you see, if he finds out I've blown four grand on a stupid phone call to Brazil, it'll give him the perfect excuse to put it off forever."

I sank further into despair.

"Trudy, you have to promise me, whatever happens, you won't breathe a word about this to anyone — at all. You know how word spreads."

"Of course I promise. But don't you think it's going to be a bit obvious if debt collectors start suddenly banging on the door?"

I sighed, trying to shut out the image in my head. "I was hoping to get a few more shifts in the surgery."

"*Four thousand dollars' worth?*"

"I know. I know. But what else can I do? They gave me the option of payments over a twelve-month period and I couldn't see I had any choice but to take them up on it."

"Well that doesn't sound too bad, I suppose. What's that, about three hundred a month?"

I nodded. "Something like that. *But* the bad news is, if I default on any of the payments, or I'm late, I have to pay the remaining sum in one hit—within fourteen days."

"Jesus, Brooke, that's going to be tough."

"You don't have to tell me. I know!"

Slumping down on the nearby stool, I had never felt more depressed and alone in my life.

* * * *

By the time I got home from the salon, I had descended to a whole new level of misery. How could I have been so stupid? Four thousand dollars might not appear completely unattainable to some, but with my current credit rating, it might as well have been four million.

Suddenly my phone rang, startling me out of my dark fog. *Mum.* As much as I wanted to ignore her call, I'd failed to return it least two in the past couple of days and I knew I couldn't fob her off again.

"Hi, Mum," I sighed.

"Hello, Brooke. You sound a bit flat. Is something wrong?"

Tamping down the urge to cry, I took a deep breath in an attempt to swallow my misery. I wasn't ready to share my recent woes with my mother, knowing she would immediately berate me for being so stupid.

"No, of course not. Why would there be anything wrong?" I babbled, trying to keep my voice light.

"Oh, I don't know. You just sounded a bit funny when you answered the phone, that's all. You and Brad haven't had a tiff now, have you?"

"No, of course not," I spluttered. "What on earth gave you that idea?"

"No reason. It's just I know there are a lot of stresses on young couples these days."

Well, she was certainly spot-on with that one and right now I was one big steaming ball of stress, but lightening the load by sharing my money woes with my mother was out of the question. A lecture was the last thing I wanted to hear.

"And what's brought all this on, then?"

Mum sighed. Not a good sign. *Here we go again.* I was about to be handed a boarding pass for the Guiltsville Express. "Oh, I'm sorry, Brooke. Don't pay any attention to silly old me. I'm just feeling a bit down, that's all. It's just Joan. You remember Joan, don't you?"

"Yes. Of course."

Mum's old neighbor wasn't easy to forget. Believe me, I've tried.

"I was speaking to her on the phone yesterday and she was in a terrible state, poor thing. It appears her eldest daughter Clare just upped and left her husband. Just like that! Arrived on their doorstep out of the blue with their two small children in tow. It was a dreadful shock. Joan naturally thought they were blissfully happy together. And who wouldn't be with a huge house and two BMWs? Her son-in-law is a doctor, you know. Highly respected. I have to say, I was very surprised. Your father and I were at their wedding, you remember. Huge affair, it was. Two hundred guests and no less than *eight* bridesmaids. Cost an absolute fortune, I hear. Not that it mattered. Joan's son-in-law comes from a very wealthy family. And now the silly girl has walked away from it all. Joan doesn't know how she'll manage with two little ones in the house after all these years. She and David were planning a trip to Honolulu later on in the year, but I suppose in light of what's happened, that will all have to be postponed. Poor woman, just when she thought they could stop worrying about the family and start enjoying their retirement."

"*Mum*, listen to me. I'm fine. Brad and I are fine. I was a million miles away and the phone startled me is all."

Ever since we'd gotten engaged, Mum had lived in mortal fear that I might somehow let him slip away before I got that all-important wedding ring on my finger. I was beginning to get a complex.

"Well, I can't tell you how relieved I am to hear that, dear. You really are a lucky girl, you know. Brad is such a lovely young man and I don't have to tell you that we would be heartbroken if anything came between the two of you."

Already I was regretting answering the phone.

"Look, Mum, I've got to go. I start work soon, but I'll give you a call later in the week."

"Okay, darling. And don't forget to give our love to Brad."

"Will do," I replied through gritted teeth. "Bye."

I considered calling in sick for work — after all, how could I be expected to concentrate on work when I had a million things on my mind?

Alas when you work alongside doctors and they pay your wages, chucking a sickie isn't always as straightforward as ringing in and rattling off some crap about having a stomach bug or something equally vague. For, as I learned the hard way, not only do they want to know *all* your symptoms for a quick phone diagnosis, but if you go overboard or pick the wrong ones, like protruding lumps on your neck, for example, you can be in all sorts of strife.

But apart from the fact I hadn't the strength left in me to come up with an excuse that might sneak under their radar, I had to admit, with a debt the size of a small third-world nation hanging ominously over my head, I had no choice but to go. That bloody phone bill wasn't going to pay itself off, was it?

By six o'clock that evening, I suspect Dr. Fairweather might have been wishing I had called in sick after all. I had to admit that even by my lowly standards, I wasn't much help. I kept losing files and getting Dr. Fairweather's provider numbers wrong or putting Dr. Chisholm's number in instead. In the end even Dr. Fairweather's legendary patience was starting to crumble and, after I'd caused the computer to crash for the third consecutive time that evening, he called me into his office for a little "chat".

"Is there anything troubling you, Brooke?" he asked, after sitting me down next to his desk.

I shook my head. I knew if I began unburdening my heart, I would fall to pieces. As much as I would have loved to share the burden weighing down on me, I knew, if no other reason than to keep my sanity, I had to get a grip.

"Are you feeling unwell?"

Again I shook my head.

"Troubles at home?" he suggested gently.

"No. I am really sorry, Dr. Fairweather, I know it's no excuse, but I am just a bit out of sorts tonight."

I had a sudden brainwave. The wedding. Of course. Didn't all brides complain that planning their nuptials did their head in?

"It's the wedding, you see," I blurted out.

"Ah!" said Dr. Fairweather, understanding dawning on his tired face, "Of course. Very stressful they are.

And expensive. I remember my daughter's. It cost a fortune and that must have been more than twenty years ago now." He shook his head. "Boy, I'd hate to think how much you'd be up for these days."

"From what we originally estimated, the prices have almost doubled."

This was true in part.

He nodded in sympathy. "I can well believe it."

"Dr. Fairweather, I've been meaning to ask you if you might consider giving me a few extra shifts? I know I haven't been here as long as some of the other girls, but the extra money would really help with the wedding costs, and all."

By the look of silent apology in his eyes I knew straight away I wasn't going to get the extra work.

"If it was only up to me, Brooke, I would be happy to give you the extra shifts, but unfortunately Dr. Chisholm organizes the staff and rosters and I know she would consider it unfair on the other girls if you were given preferential treatment above those who have been here longer."

He didn't say but I could read between the lines that if it were up to Dr. Chisholm, I would be out on my arse in a moment. It was only because Dr. Fairweather had a soft spot for me that I had lasted here as long as I had.

"I understand, Dr. Fairweather, honestly. Thanks, anyway. I'll make sure I don't make any more mistakes—I promise."

Another door had slammed shut and I was no closer to figuring out a solution.

By the time the last patient left the surgery, it was after nine so, while Dr. Fairweather took care of some paperwork, I set about straightening magazines in the waiting room and fishing out toys from behind the pot plants.

It was then the phone rang and I groaned.

Great, just what I need. A late patient. Why did it always happen to me? Just as I was set to leave for the night, some frantic mother always rang up in a panic, convinced her kid had meningitis or rabies or worse and I was stuck here for another hour waiting around until Dr. Fairweather reassured them it was merely teething problems or a touch of colic.

Tonight, though, luck was on my side. It wasn't a patient. It was Trudy and she was practically jumping through the phone with excitement, insisting I come over immediately because she had some fantastic news for me.

After the day I had suffered, fantastic news was in desperately low supply, so I finished off my jobs in record time and was out of the door in less than ten minutes, pausing only long enough to call Brad and let him know I'd be late home as poor Trudy needed a shoulder to cry on.

Chapter Five

Trudy must have been watching out of the window for me to arrive, for the door to her flat was flung open before I even had chance to ring the buzzer.

"You are going to thank me forever." She beamed, dragging me in off the landing and into the flat she shared with Becky.

Their place was small, even by city standards, but open plan with a sizable deck and views looking out onto the bay, so they were happy to trade off a bit of room for the view.

"Hi," I called out to Becky stretched out on the lounger in front of the telly enjoying a glass of white wine.

"Oh, hi, Brooke. Trudy was telling me about the stuff-up with the phone. What a shit of a thing to happen, you poor thing."

Yes, poor me!

I turned to Trudy. "Okay, tell me what it is that I will be thanking you forever over? Oh, and by the way, if

Brad happens to mention anything about tonight, you have just broken up with Tony again and are inconsolable."

Trudy rolled her eyes. "Righto. But listen up. I think I may just have the answer to all your problems."

Following Trudy into the kitchen, I helped myself to a glass of wine from the open bottle on the bench.

"Jeez, let me guess. You've won the lottery?" I couldn't disguise the cynicism in my voice.

Trudy carried on cheerfully, unfazed by my churlishness. "Unfortunately, no, but the next best thing, though. I may have found you a job and it pays, like, thirty bucks an hour—in the hand. Can you believe it?"

"Yeah right." No, I didn't believe it at all. "And who exactly do I have to murder, then?" I asked, taking a large mouthful of wine.

"Get serious, will you? It's as a receptionist. Dead easy and the hours are flexible. You could work it in with your job at the surgery and Brad would never know. Honestly, it's perfect for you. You'll have that bloody phone bill paid off in next to no time and you might even be able to get rid of some of those credit cards while you're at it."

Nothing was this perfect. Not in the real world, anyway, and I was waiting for the 'but', the 'catch', the 'just one thing, though'. There had to be one.

"Um, and how exactly did you come to hear about this *job* then? Surely, if it's as good as you're making out, people would be lined up around the block, waiting for it. I don't have to tell you if that's the case, with my references, I'd have absolutely no chance of getting it."

"Don't be so negative, Brooke. Anyway, the best thing is, it hasn't been advertised yet. One of my clients was telling me about it this afternoon in the salon. Apparently, one of the other receptionists where she works just upped and left and now they desperately need someone to fill her place, starting almost immediately."

"Jesus, Trud, why didn't you ring me straight away? I've been almost beside myself with worry all afternoon."

"Sorry, hon, but I didn't want to get your hopes up until I knew more about it. This client of mine, she just works there, you see. She had to wait until she went in to work to talk to her boss before she could ring me back with the details. And it seems they haven't got anyone yet, so you're in with a chance. A huge one, actually."

"Are you serious?" I asked, desperation no doubt stamped all over my face.

Trudy smiled and, for the first time, I felt a glimmer of hope.

"Yes, of course I'm serious. I wouldn't joke about something like this. I told her how responsible you are..."

I couldn't help but gawk in disbelief. God, she was laying it on a bit.

"Don't look at me like that," Trudy chided. "I was building you up, wasn't I. Jesus, somebody has to, when you have the self-confidence of a gnat. And while I was at it, I also told her you were smart and reliable, not to mention very discreet and open-minded. By the time I'd finished, I had her all but convinced you would be perfect for the job."

Despite my pessimism, Trudy was right. It did sound like the answer to my prayers, which left me wondering why it was I was feeling decidedly uneasy about it.

"Well?" Trudy pressed. "What do you say? If you want it, I reckon the job is as good as yours. All you have to do is go around tomorrow morning and have a chat to the woman who runs the place."

Trudy pushed aside a couple of bright pink cushions to make room on the lounger next to Becky and I settled in beside her, feeling I might as well get comfy as I was likely to be here for some time.

"Hey, wait on a sec, Trud." My head was spinning and I couldn't help feeling she was keeping one vital piece of information from me. "What *exactly* did you mean when you said I was discreet and open-minded?"

"Well, you are, aren't you?"

"Well, yes, I suppose so. But what I meant was why is it so important?"

Trudy looked away, suddenly avoiding all eye contact.

This wasn't good. Something was up. I was sure of it.

"Trudy. Look at me! Where exactly is this wonderful, well-paying, flexible job no one knows about and isn't being advertised?"

Trudy looked back at me, grinning like a loon. "Heavenly Pleasures!"

"Heavenly *what*?"

"Heavenly Pleasures," Trudy repeated.

"Jesus, what kind of a name is that? Sounds like either a brothel or a chocolate shop."

"You were right the first time, actually," Trudy admitted, grinning at the stunned expression on my face.

"Oh, God. Tell me you're joking, Trud. Please tell me this is a joke."

Trudy continued grinning, looking oh so pleased with herself.

Me, well, I was still waiting for the punch line.

It was then it dawned on me she was actually serious.

Great. The light at the end of the tunnel instantly flickered and went out, much like the last ember of warmth on a cold night. Instantly my brief feeling of relief vanished.

My stomach lurched dangerously. Trudy my best friend, cousin and honorary sister, had set me up to work in a brothel of all places. My God, I didn't even know brothels existed outside of the red light district of King's Cross. What on earth was she thinking? Brad would have a stroke if he found out.

Despite her and Becky's assurances that these days the sex industry was a perfectly legal, legitimate business, I had serious reservations about the entire thing. A *brothel.* I tried the words out in my head. *I work in a brothel.* It would certainly raise a few eyebrows next time one of my relatives asked me what I am doing with myself these days.

I shook my head in disbelief. Christ, I couldn't believe I was actually considering it. What was wrong with me? I needed to get a grip.

"Have you gone completely mad? No way!" I yelled. "How could you even think I would agree to work in a place like that?"

"But why not?" she said, "Look, before you dismiss the idea, at least think about it for a minute, Brooke. It's perfect. Good money. Easy. What more could you want? And, besides, it isn't as though they're expecting *you* to have sex with strangers. All you do is answer the phone and make appointments and stuff like that, which, I might point out, is *exactly* what you're doing at the moment."

"Except you're forgetting one small thing here. Where I work now the employees tend to leave their clothes *on*," I sniped.

"Brooke," admonished Trudy. "I never pictured you as a prude."

"I'm not a prude," I denied. "I have nothing against people making a living any way they want. It's a service, after all, like hairdressing I suppose. Mind you it's a tad more personal than cutting hair. I'm sure these hookers—"

"I think they prefer to be called sex workers," offered Trudy, trying not to smile at my obvious naivety.

"Okay, I'm sure these *sex workers* are perfectly nice people going about their business. I'm not judging them, Trudy, honestly. Sure, offering my body to total strangers for money is not something *I* would ever do, but then I've never been put in that position, have I?"

"Until now."

"What do you mean?"

"Have you forgotten already? You still own the phone company over four grand, remember. At least this way you might have a chance to pay it back before Brad finds out about it."

Well, when she put it that way, there was no denying Trudy had a point…

* * * *

Lying awake in bed later on that night, listening to Brad softly snoring beside me, I had ample time to consider my options, none of which particularly filled me with joy.

First of all there was always the option of coming clean and telling Brad about the phone fiasco before someone else beat me to it. But even on the off-chance he forgave me, he'd never trust me again. For the rest of my life, I'd have to account to him for every penny and even then I suspected it would only reinforce both his and my parents' view that I was irresponsible and in need of a stabilizing influence in my life.

But then again, even that was preferable to being single again.

No, I couldn't bear the thought of going back to my pre-Brad days. If we split up my life would be over. I'd be reduced to moving back in with my parents, at least until I paid off my debts—which in my case could easily be for the next fifty years. Eventually, I'd turn into one of those sad, middle-aged spinsters, wearing tracksuit pants, hand-knitted cardigans, sporting a bad haircut and trailing behind their mother at the shops. People would stare and whisper, assuming I was not quite right in the head. Either that or a total loser.

No. Trudy was right. This was a lifeline. The answer to my prayers. If I didn't take up the offer, I might never get another opportunity like this again. So what if it wasn't exactly the type of job one usually wanted to appear in their résumé? It paid well and besides, it was only temporary. A couple of months at the most, just until I was once again debt-free.

Yep, I desperately needed money and Heavenly Pleasures could provide me with it.

My decision was made.

God help me, I'm going to work in a brothel.

* * * *

Pulling up at yet another set of traffic lights heading into town, I took a few deep breaths in a desperate attempt to quell the swarm of butterflies bouncing off the walls of my stomach.

A woman walked past my stationary car on the footpath beside me, smartly attired in a corporate-designed floral blouse and sleek navy-blue skirt.

I couldn't help staring. It didn't feel like that long ago I'd been at business college, full of ambition and determination while struggling to comprehend the complexities of a computer keyboard — what kind of freak can type sixty words a minute, anyway?

Back then, I, too, looked forward with bright-eyed eagerness to a fabulous and glamorous career flying up the corporate ladder. My future plans naturally included rising swiftly to the ranks of personal assistant to some hotshot executive in the city. Gazing out of my fortieth-floor office window onto a sweeping view of Sydney Harbor and enjoying three-hour business lunches in trendy city restaurants and nights out on the town with my cool-as-sin co-workers.

I was going to show them how it was done.

Sure, I might have only graduated high school by the skin of my teeth, but I was determined to demonstrate that personality and determination could conquer the limitations placed unfairly on us teenagers and highlight the gross injustice of an educational system that expected us to sacrifice our adolescence to endless hours of mundane study.

Yeah, right.

I'd showed them all right — *not!*

And so where did that leave me now, six years on? Skulking into town, desperately hoping I might just have the required skills to secure some skanky job in a brothel...

I felt sick. This was worse than a visit to the dentist — or a pap smear, for that matter. Given the choice, I'd gladly sell one of my kidneys to raise the required four grand, rather than what I was about to do.

But, alas, it had to be done and I'd already put off leaving the house as long as I could, agonizing over what to wear. I was due to meet the *Madame* in ten minutes. Madame. I hated that word. It immediately conjured up an image of Dolly Parton in the *Best Little Whorehouse in Texas*. Did they still call themselves Madames — or even Mesdames, for all I knew — in this day and age? Probably not. After all, this *was* the new millennium, where everything was politically corrected to within an inch of its inoffensive life. Her official title was probably Sex Agent Coordinator or Fornication Facilitator — who knew? But, still, the last thing I wanted to do was insult my potential new boss by showcasing my complete ignorance on the ins and outs of the sex industry.

The address Trudy had written out for me last night was sitting on the seat next to me like an unwanted passenger. Its very presence taunted me, reminding me once again that had I taken two seconds to lock my bloody phone that fateful afternoon, I wouldn't be currently on my way to an interview at some sleazy brothel secreted away at the back of a dodgy old arcade at the far end of town. Trudy said it had been operating there for years. Apparently, it was common knowledge. Common knowledge to everyone but me, that was. Hell, I must go around with a bucket on my head if what Trudy had said was true.

Clearly, I had led a very sheltered life.

As I sat there, summoning up the courage to get out of the car, my only hope was that my parents never discovered the thousands of dollars they'd spent putting me through business college in the vain hope I might embark on a long and satisfying professional career was about to land me a job in a brothel.

A fresh wave of gut-churning nervousness hit me and I struggled with the growing urge to turn my car around and flee. Only the fact that, once again, Trudy had gone out of her way to help me out of a bind halted my panicked retreat. I couldn't bear the thought of letting her down after she had gone to all the trouble of finding me a way out of this, my recent financial disaster. I had no choice. It was either this or sit at home and wait for the debt collectors to knock on the door.

Alas, it was time to face the consequences of my actions — or lack of, as the case may be.

It being early in the day, there were relatively few people wandering around this end of town. Even so, I couldn't help feeling a million eyes were trained on me, watching me and waiting for me to walk into the brothel arcade. Oh, Jesus, what if they took me for a prostitute? I suppose it was for this very reason I had decided to wear the same clothes that I usually wore to the surgery — white shirt, a very demure gray skirt and matching jacket. Very boring and guaranteed not to attract any attention. In the back of my mind, I was kind of hoping they might consider my attire completely inappropriate for the position and offer the job to someone else. At least that way, I'd be off the hook with a clear conscience. Mind you, I'd also be no closer to paying off that bloody phone bill.

I was fast running out of options.

Of course, it was vital that Brad never know, for there was little doubt in my mind he'd consider what I was about to embark on as unforgivable, and he'd never understand that I was doing it for the sake of our future happiness.

Halting briefly outside the entrance to the arcade, I took one last glance around me before making my way into the tiled walkway.

Once inside the arcade, it was fairly clear why I had never bothered exploring the shops within. To say it wasn't very inviting was putting it mildly. Apart from a lonely, run-down launderette on the corner, the rest of the shop fronts were securely boarded up and from the multitude of posters and graffiti plastered over the concrete-rendered walls, I was in little doubt that they had been empty for some time—all but the shop right at the very end of the arcade that was, which, to my surprise, sported a small red light above its entrance.

This was it.

HEAVENLY PLEASURES
For your intimate pleasure
Please enter!

It was written across the heavily frosted glass door in a discreet but classy flowing script and, for the first time since Trudy had announced her grand plan to rescue me from financial ruin, I felt my spirits lift a fraction.

Maybe Heavenly Pleasures wasn't as tacky and tasteless as the image that had been festering away in my mind? Maybe it was one of those super-classy but covert operations that Arab sheiks, politicians and footballers frequented? Yes, granted, the red light was a dead giveaway, but then there were certain standards within any kind of industry. At least the telltale red light ensured against poor misguided chocolate lovers making a complete fool of themselves.

By now, it was a few minutes past ten. I knew I couldn't put this off forever.

I took a deep breath and straightened my skirt before pressing the buzzer set discreetly into the wall and standing back to wait.

A few moments later, the door opened and I was greeted by a petite woman aged somewhere in her late fifties with immaculately styled blonde hair and wearing cream slacks and a white halter-neck top. I couldn't help but stare. She didn't look like a prostitute, or what I envisioned a prostitute would look like, anyway. She was too old, for a start, and apart from a fundamental lack of makeup — a basic requirement for the job, I imagined — her clothing suggested that she could very well shop at the same stores frequented by my mother. They might easily have smiled to one another at some time over the top of a sales rack and stopped to exchange polite chitchat. In other words, she looked normal.

I was relieved but at the same time strangely disappointed.

"Um, hello. I'm Brooke Delaney," I announced. "I have an appointment for ten o'clock."

"Brooke? Oh, yes, of course, you're here for the job, aren't you?"

"Yes, the receptionist's position," I added quickly, ensuring that she knew straight away that I was not applying for any other positions—horizontal ones, especially.

Sensing my nervousness, she smiled. "Hello, I'm Prue, the owner. Come in." She had a deep raspy voice, a by-product, I guessed, of a long and loving association with the tobacco industry.

As I followed Prue into Heavenly Pleasures, any hopes I had been briefly cultivating of elegance and modern sophistication instantly plummeted. Whatever I had been hoping for, this was not it. The reception area, although clean, reminded me of a cheap run-down motel. The dark wood-paneled reception desk itself had clearly been retro the first time around, as had the faded orange carpet, which I suspected might have been originally red.

Seedy was the first word that came to mind.

Brothel came a close second.

Of course, when Trudy had said Heavenly Pleasures had been around for years, I'd never imaged that she meant *literally* years. Christ, the place must have been operating since the seventies, if the décor was anything to go by. I felt as though I was standing inside a time capsule. It could have been a museum. I'm sure people would pay good money to see original artifacts like these.

"As you can see, we like to make a favorable first impression on our clients, Brooke," Prue announced, looking around her, clearly mistaking the expression of astonishment on my face for admiration.

Taking in the purple bubbly light fittings and hideous orange-tinted glass-topped coffee table, on which sat disfigured tribal statues with grotesquely over-exaggerated erections and mammoth boobs—and some with both—man-boobs?—I could only stare in wonder. It was like the Brady Bunch revisited, possibly under the influence of drugs?

"Brooke, before we begin, have you any experience in the sex industry?"

"Um, no, I'm afraid not. I do have experience in general office duties, though. Answering phones, filing and that sort of thing. Oh, and I am proficient in Microsoft Office," I offered, all the time praying that I wouldn't be called upon to demonstrate my so-called computer *skills*.

A quick glance over toward the office failed to spot any computers or for that matter any hint that Prue and Heavenly Pleasures had embraced the twenty-first century at all and I couldn't help but feel relieved. Of course I could use a computer — I was a whiz at solitaire — it was when they added columns, spreadsheets and invoice files I tended to come unglued.

Prue looked a little concerned. "So am I to take it that you have *no* experience in the sex industry?"

"No. Sorry. I am willing to learn, though. I'm flexible and I have my own transport."

I don't know exactly at what point it occurred, but suddenly the thought of *not* getting this job as well as the accompanying humiliation of knowing that I was incapable of landing a job in a naff escort agency overrode any remaining reservations I might have previously had. I desperately needed this job and like they say, beggars can't be choosers.

"Well, I don't suppose your lack of experience poses too much of a problem," she eventually conceded after a brief pause. "We do provide training, after all. The most important thing in this industry is that you have good people skills." Prue gave me a meaningful look before continuing, "Do you have good people skills, Brooke?"

"Um, yes, I do."

Clearing my throat I launched into my well-rehearsed but rarely successful *please hire me* spiel. "My previous jobs have primarily been in doctors' surgeries, where good communication between both patients and staff is very important."

Prue seemed to consider this for a moment and I prayed that she wasn't about to request a reference. I was almost certain that Dr. Chisholm wouldn't be laying on the compliments for my so-called people skills — or *any* work-related skills.

Prue sighed. "Look, I have to be honest here, Brooke."

My heart sank. Going by past experiences, job interviews and honesty were a lethal mixture and usually resulted in nothing but tearful regrets and numerous trips to the Welfare Agency.

Honesty. Whoever came up with the concept that honesty was the best policy was cracked in the head. It sucked. Honesty would see me confessing to Brad the entire phone-call-to-Brazil cock-up. And honesty would have me telling Mum in no uncertain terms that we were not getting married in a bloody church. And honesty would make sure I enlightened Sophie about the fact that I wasn't in PR but simply a desperate loser hoping to gain employment in a sleazy brothel. And of course if I were to be completely honest with Prue, I would have to divulge to her that the very idea of pairing perfect strangers together in order for them to have sex and engage in God knew what carnal practices for money made me feel decidedly queasy.

Whoever this honesty freak was, I wanted to kick him in the nuts.

I felt my chances of getting this job and saving my relationship slipping away from me. Damn it. I knew I should have worn something tartier!

"Look, you seem like a very nice girl." Only a Madame could make 'nice' sound like an insult. "As you might imagine, most women outside the industry tend to find this kind of service a little confronting. It is an extremely personal one and discretion is vital, not only for the privacy of our clientele but also the girls who work here. For that reason I'll warn you now that anything you see or hear while you are on duty is to be kept strictly confidential. At Heavenly Pleasures, we value our customers and want them to feel at ease when they come here to be pampered. Do you think you are able to cope with the delicate nature of your duties?"

"Um, sure, I don't have a problem with it," I answered, with a damn sight more confidence than I was feeling.

Some might say that I was putting on a brave face.

"That's good, Brooke. And are you able to start on, say, Monday?"

"Yes," I responded enthusiastically.

The sooner I started, the sooner I'd be able to pay off my debt and forget my seedy sojourn into the adult sex industry.

"Well, that's good. Before we discuss rosters and the like, I think now might be a good time to show you through the place. The girls don't come in for another hour and even then most of them are booked out on calls."

"What, this early in the day?" I asked not quite able to mask my surprise. Don't ask me why, but I imagined that most of the action, for want of a better word, would take place after dark. In fact I found the very idea that men might hire a hooker before lunch quite sordid.

Prue smiled indulgently.

"Yes. We usually have a couple of girls available from about eleven in the morning. A few of our older clients like to have regular appointments earlier in the day so they can be assured of the girls of their choice, but generally it is later in the day that most of our customers come in or ring up for a call-out. Come on, I'll show you through to the lounge."

Walking ahead, Prue pushed aside a beaded curtain and beckoned me to enter.

"This is where our clients wait to meet the girls." Prue motioned toward two large plush sofas, upholstered in dull brown leather. It looked just like a normal lounge room complete with coffee tables, fake pot plants and a large wide-screen television in the corner — the first hint that Prue was indeed living in the twenty-first century. Very comfortable and normal, I noted with relief.

That was until I took a closer look at the magazines placed neatly on the coffee table. *New Idea* and *House & Garden* they were not! Of course it shouldn't have come as any surprise to learn that *Spank!* and *Bad Biker Bitches* were the reading matter of choice at Heavenly Pleasures but it was still a shock to find the reality of sex business out on show for all to see.

"It's your job to greet the clients at the door and bring them through here to the lounge. You're to make sure they're comfortable and relaxed while they wait for the girl of their choice to escort them through to one of our luxury suites out the back. Some of our clients can be quite nervous when they first arrive, especially if it's the first time they've used a service like ours, so the more relaxed you are, the better. Understand?"

I nodded.

Easier said than done, I thought, finding myself staring at a shaved pussy displayed proudly on the cover of *Bare Babes.* I kept this thought to myself, though, and wondered what Prue's policy was on receptionists stopping off for a swig or two of Dutch courage before commencing work.

"Oh, and another thing," continued Prue. "As part of your duties you need to make sure that there are a range of magazines available. I like to offer a variety to cater to every taste, so ensure there are also a few lesbian and bondage publications available for clients to flick through."

Lesbians. Bondage. Pornography. Oh, my!

Not unlike Dorothy in *The Wizard of Oz,* it occurred to me that I wasn't in Kansas anymore.

"But keep an eye on them, Brooke," she went on to warn. "You'd be surprised how many magazines go missing. They are quite expensive to replace so any that go missing on your shift will be docked from your pay. Do you understand?"

I found myself nodding manically despite not knowing quite how I was supposed to police Prue's porn policy.

"*And* under no circumstances are you to tolerate any of the clients masturbating in this room. Ever. It just isn't on. I can't stress this enough. We are not operating a peek show here. They either book one of the girls and pay for a service, or they leave the premises and wank over their own porn and in their own time. These are strictly for paying customers!"

Oh, God. I stood there frozen to the spot, trying to imagine myself walking in on a man mid-wank and telling him off like a naughty schoolboy before ordering him to leave the premises. *Fuck!* It was beginning to dawn on me just how much I was in way over my head. Not that Prue had picked up on my reservations, as she blithely carried on with her orientation.

"The porn mags are primarily to get our clients turned on before the girls come out to greet them. It saves time," explained Prue matter-of-factly, in the same tone as a home science teacher might explain to a class of fourteen-year-old girls how to make the perfect sponge.

"We also find that if the girls are, well, not quite to their taste, ensuring they are aroused to begin with safeguards us from the event that they might change their mind and leave before securing a booking. Which brings me to the next part of your duties," she said, picking up a remote off the table and pointing it toward the large TV in the corner. Before my unbelieving eyes came a graphic image of a busty naked girl bearing an uncanny resemblance to a well-known and big-titted Hollywood actress giving a huge black man a blow job while another equally naked woman appeared to be doing something quite inconceivable with the biggest dildo I had ever laid eyes on.

Oh. My. God.

"Now, Brooke," began Prue, oblivious to the fact that my eyes were almost popping out of my head. "Whenever there are clients on the premises, the DVD *must* be running at all times. Remember this, as it is important. Make sure you keep an eye on the TV so you know to change the movie as soon as it's finished. *Don't* do what our last receptionist did and simply put it on repeat. That is pure laziness and it will not be tolerated. There are a large variety of X-rated movies stored in a cabinet in reception. They are not to be left out when they are not in use or they *will get stolen*. Do you understand?"

"Yes. DVDs stay in reception. Change the discs as soon as they are finished and clients are not to wank on the premises without first paying for it."

It felt like the words were being spoken by someone else.

Prue smiled. "Exactly! Very good. Do you know what, I think we're going to get on just fine."

It was surreal. Here I was standing in front of a pile of porn magazines, watching three people have graphic sex on the TV while matter-of-factly discussing masturbation rules with a brothel owner called Prue. And it wasn't even ten-thirty in the morning.

"Great. Now we have that covered, I'll show you the rooms where the girls work."

Here goes. I strapped myself in for the ride to Kinksville.

God help me!

Chapter Six

Looking up from the Sunday night football on telly, Brad cast a disparaging eye over my almost empty wine glass and frowned. "Brooke, how many glasses of wine have you had?"

I tried to remember. Three? Four? More?

"Why?" I replied defensively.

It had been a challenging few days to say the least and an afternoon spent in the company of Brad's despotic mother hadn't helped matters, either. God, the woman was a cow. Totally ignored me the entire time we were there while cooing and fussing over her number-one son like he was the bloody Dalai Lama. Under the circumstances, I figured I was more than entitled to relax with a glass of wine as a reward for my suffering.

Oh, God, talking about suffering—every time I thought about beginning my new job tomorrow, I felt sick. Could I go through with it? Just the idea of revisiting Prue's Porn Cave turned my stomach. *Yuk.*

I gulped down the rest of my wine in one mouthful.

Oh, God, what on earth had I let myself in for? One thing was for sure — whatever I had been drinking tonight wasn't enough to quell the horrible churning inside my stomach.

"Brooke, are you *drunk*?" queried Brad sternly, staring at my now empty glass balanced on the arm of the sofa.

I didn't need to be psychic to figure out that he was far from impressed by my alcoholic consumption.

"Of course not," I responded primly, taking extra care over my pronunciation.

Damn. Rather than confirming my sobriety I sounded a lot like the Queen. Well the Queen after a few drinks, at least. Brad gave me a funny look.

Was I drunk?

No!

Well, at least, I didn't think so.

Not yet, anyway.

"Would you like me to get you a glass of wine?" I offered, eager to dispel any notions forming in his mind that I was indulging myself in a spot of solitary drinking. Brad's eyes narrowed, summing up my intentions before the words left my mouth. I wasn't about to be put off, though, and defiantly scooped up my empty glass and headed off to the kitchen. If he didn't want to join me for a drink, well, that was his problem, not mine.

As I walked past, he flashed me a disapproving look before dourly accepting my offer. "I suppose so. Just the one, though," he added pointedly, making it crystal clear that it was going to be my final glass for the evening as well.

Great, even the bloody wine's rationed now.

What next? Air?

I didn't exactly know why I was feeling so resentful. It certainly wasn't Brad's fault that I was drowning in debt. Hell, it wasn't like we were dirt-poor. Far from it. Brad earned a good wage and, if he made partner someday, it would hopefully double overnight. So what was the big deal if every now and then I felt the urge to treat myself to a pair of boots or a new jacket or a to-die-for designer pashmina? Weren't all us modern girls supposed to be shopaholics?

By the time I returned from the kitchen and handed Brad his glass of wine, the footy had finished. Thank God. Football, the most boring pastime on the face of the earth. Totally self-indulgent. Grown men chasing each other through the mud and piling on top of one another wearing skimpy shorts while groping each other's private parts.

And they consider it to be a manly display of skill and dexterity.

I think not!

I snatched up the remote to flick through the channels in search of something to distract me. Something on the plight of oppressed Middle Eastern women maybe, to remind me that despite my current feelings of resentment, I was indeed lucky to be living in a progressive Western society, where after decades of struggle, women were finally able to live their lives free of the burden of patriarchal tyranny.

"Brooke, you did remember to pick my suits up from the dry cleaners today, didn't you?"

Suits, what bloody suits?

Then I remembered.

Oh, shit, those suits.

"Oh sorry. I'll get them tomorrow," I cast back, sounding not at all remorseful.

"You said that yesterday," Brad continued, with a hint of annoyance.

Yep, I thought, two thousand years of feminist struggle and I might as well be dragging my weary arse down to the nearest creek and beating the shit out of his suits against a flat rock.

"Look, I *said* I'd get them tomorrow! *Okay?*" I said, gritting my teeth. "Jesus, if you were that desperate for them, why didn't you pick them up yourself?"

"Because I thought you were, that's why," he replied, shaking his head.

"Well, there's nothing I can do about it now, is there? Jesus, the way you're going on about it, anyone would think I'd forgotten your mother's birthday!" I muttered sarcastically.

Brad cast me an impatient look, which suddenly softened as he appeared to remember something. "Um, talking about my mother…"

I'd rather not. Actually, given the choice I'd rather stick pins in my eyes.

"Well, she rang me at work today to let me know she had come across the perfect venue for the reception."

That certainly got my attention.

"Whose reception?" I frowned.

"Well, ours of course. Who else's wedding would I be talking about?"

"Ohhh, so we are talking about *our* wedding then, as opposed to your *mother's* wedding!"

I knew I was being a prize bitch, but this was the first time in months that Brad had voluntarily brought up the subject of our wedding and what should have been a moment of exquisite triumph on my behalf was marred by the suspicion that the only reason he was bringing it up now was because his mother had made him. Oh, to have that kind of power. God, I hated that woman!

"Brooke, what on earth is wrong with you tonight? You've been nagging me for months about getting things moving with the wedding plans — "

"And *you've* been constantly dodging the subject or telling me that the time isn't right. But now that your *mother* has decided to poke her nose in, it's suddenly on the subject list again."

"Well, as you know, I still feel it's a little early to set an actual date. After all, didn't we agree to wait until my career was more established?"

"The way I remember, it was you who wanted a long engagement, not me."

"Well, in that case, what are you complaining about? Honestly, Brooke, even though we aren't ready to set a date just yet, I don't see that it could do any harm just to look into a couple of places."

I felt like screaming.

"Brad, I would love *us* to start planning the wedding. *Us. You and me.* Not your mother."

"Christ, you should listen to what you're saying, Brooke, and have a think about it. Here my mother is kindly offering to help you with the arrangements and suddenly you're acting like an ungrateful bitch."

"Ohhh, so I am a bitch now, am I? That's just charming."

Generally, even at the best of times, the mention of Brad's mother was pretty much guaranteed to send my blood pressure soaring, but tonight, combined with the few glasses of wine I had consumed and my mounting nerves over the new job, I knew things were about to get ugly — real ugly. I was ready for a showdown and who better to kick off the proceedings than my future mother-in-law from hell.

"No, of course you're not. Look, I'm sorry, Brooke. I didn't mean it the way it came out," he apologized, furiously back-pedaling as he took in the dangerous expression spreading like poison ivy across my face.

"Well, tell me, then, what exactly *did* you mean by it?" I asked angrily, not willing to let it go that easily. It wasn't often I got Brad on the back foot and I was enjoying the feeling of power it gave me. "Because it *sounded* to me like you were calling me an ungrateful bitch!" I glared at him.

Instantly contrite, Brad sighed. "Look, Mum has merely offered to help with the wedding, that's all."

"My mum did too, remember? Before you told her we wanted to organize it ourselves."

"I know I said that, but your mother is a busy woman, what with your father to look after and that big house of theirs. Ever since Dad died, though, Mum has been at a bit of a loose end. I was hoping that helping you with the arrangements might just give her back a little direction in life."

Yeah, and I suspected the direction she was heading for at full throttle was smack-bang in the middle of our lives. Something that Princess Di once said sprang to mind. *"There were three of us in this marriage."* It had a horribly prophetic ring to it. Over the past few months, it had begun to dawn on me that I wasn't only marrying Brad but his mother as well and I had to admit it was taking a bit of getting used to.

Brad, meanwhile, was giving me that pleading little-boy look he knew I couldn't resist and my anger began to melt as the wine finally reached my brain.

"Think of it from my point of view, Brooke. I can't very well tell her to stay out of it. She'd be crushed. It is the first good thing she's had to look forward to since Dad died."

Brad's father had been a lovely man, which had made the shock all the more dreadful when he'd succumbed to a heart attack last year. More than anyone else, I also knew how much Brad missed his father and since his death had felt responsible for his mother's wellbeing. In one way I could see his point, but it didn't help matters that she was milking the situation for all it was worth to the stage that she only had to say jump and he'd ask how high.

"Please, baby, for me," he pleaded. "I know Mum can be a little overbearing at times, but she really does mean well."

"A *little* overbearing?"

"Okay, you're right, I admit she is quite domineering, but it's only because she wants the best for us."

"She wants the best for you, not me," I responded bluntly, knowing full well that she thought of me only as an appendage to her son, an appendage that, if given half the chance, she'd happily cut off.

"No, you're wrong. I know you refuse to see it, but she really thinks the world of you, you know. And Dad, well, of course we all know Dad loved you like a daughter. If he were alive today, he'd have been so excited about the wedding and I'm sure he would have wanted you and Mum to become closer. You just have to give her a chance to know you like I do, that's all."

Before I knew what was happening, his sweet words began gnawing away at my conscience and before long I did feel like a bit of a bitch.

"At least just have a look at this place, Brooke. If you don't like it, that's fine, but it can't hurt to check it out, can it?" he suggested, sensing my weakening resolve to keep his interfering mother out of my life.

"All right. But, listen, I'm only doing it for you," I eventually yielded, my earlier ire tempered.

Brad beamed. "Thanks, Brooke."

I rolled my eyes.

"No, hon, I really appreciate it, honestly."

"Okay, where is it then?" I asked, ignoring the look of relief on his face.

"The function room at the bowling club. You know, the one near the lake."

"The *bowling* club?" I spluttered, desperately hoping I had misheard him.

"Yes, the bowling club," he countered, sounding a mite defensive. "Mum tells me they've recently done the place up and it's every bit as nice as those flash reception places — *and* half the cost, I might add."

Great. Bloody marvelous. My dream wedding. The wedding I'd been planning ever since I was a little girl and now, to complete the picture of romance and elegance, I was expected to celebrate my marriage in a bowling club. Already I could hear the sound of poker machines going off in the distance, cutting through the music as Brad and I took to the floor for our bridal waltz.

Bowling club?

Over my dead body!

Or Brad's mother's.

Or Brad's, for that matter…

* * * *

I woke the next morning feeling really out of sorts. It wasn't just the hint of a hangover that was bothering me. I felt as though I'd been played. Our conversation the night before was still making the rounds of my head and, as a result, I was having difficulty containing my growing irritation toward Brad's interfering mother. It wasn't as though she was offering to actually *pay* for the bloody wedding. No, that burden was squarely on our shoulders now, thanks to Brad declining my parents' generous offer to fund the entire event. Brad, at the time, stated that he wouldn't hear of them depriving themselves of their retirement funds.

Not that he would ever admit to it, but I was starting to suspect the real reason he'd turned down their offer was that he — together with his ego — didn't want to feel indebted to my parents for anything. At the time, he'd reasoned with me that if we wanted to go all out with the plans for my promised fairy-tale wedding, we wouldn't feel guilty for lumbering the cost onto my parents.

Going all out.

What a joke!

Going all out at a bloody bowling club was like having a romantic dinner at McDonald's.

Of course, not even this latest drama could distract me from the knowledge that today was the day I began my new career in the sex industry. I felt ill with nerves and had practically worn a path to and from the bathroom ever since waking at the crack of dawn.

I was due to begin my new job at eleven o'clock, which left me barely two hours to pull myself together. I had to say that, after having talked to Prue last week, I was relieved to discover that I wouldn't be expected to wear a negligee or plastic hotpants. Blouse and skirt or trousers had been Prue's suggestion, but she didn't seem too worried about any particular choice. I think she guessed, quite correctly, that I would choose something as far from provocative as possible, preferring to come across all matronly rather than run the risk of being mistaken for one of the girls.

Speaking of that, there was another thing sending my stomach into knots. *The girls.* The workers. The prostitutes. I couldn't stop thinking about them and what they'd be like. Apart from Prue, the only hookers I had previously seen were on sleazy American cop shows and even then they were usually drug addicts with big hair, thick makeup and a fetish for neon Lycra and fake fur.

Did that sound disapproving? Oh, God, I hoped not. *What if they decide I'm a prude and take an instant dislike to me?* Or, worse still, what if we got on really well and they expected me to join them for after-work drinks? Everyone would assume I was one of them!

Shit, there I went again. This was awful.

I sounded just like my mother.

Glancing down at my watch, I groaned. Nine o'clock already. Another hour or so and I would have to get ready to go.

I began to do a mental inventory of my wardrobe. As luck would have it, thanks to my ill-begotten shopping addiction, it was simply bulging at the seams with perfectly suitable office-type apparel. I kept buying it in the vain hope I might one day land a real job in a real office, but suspected it would take me until I retired to recoup the cost.

Boring, boring, boring.

On the plus side, at least there was little danger of me walking in there looking like a tart. Even if I'd wanted to, there was no way Brad would ever have let me be seen outside the house — or inside for that matter — in anything too revealing. But that was one of the other things I liked about him. He was a gentleman through and through and in this day and age that was a quality almost impossible to find in a man.

I had to admit there *were* the odd times that I, or rather my ego, reflected back fondly on the good old days — my pre-Brad miniskirt-wearing days — when I'd been silly and immature. I recalled the odd occasions when I'd found myself on the receiving end of a leer or two at the local nightclub, or a lone wolf whistle pealing out from the odd building site. I can also remember my girlfriends bemoaning how insulting it was to be objectified and lusted after by every prat equipped with a penis. But, then, in those days we were caught up in the grip of equality fever and harbored a desire to be respected for our minds rather than our bodies.

Unfortunately, harsh reality has since caught up with my youthful ideals and soundly beaten them into submission.

Had I known then how much worse it was to feel invisible, know the shame of walking past a silent-as-the-grave building site where not even the most sex-deprived laborer would waste a look away from his *Penthouse* for a quick leer, I would have savored those long-ago pervy looks and considered them flattering.

Not that I could ever reveal this to Brad. He'd be horrified.

After a few drinks, some of my friends occasionally talk about sharing their sexual fantasies with their boyfriends. Not me. It would be beyond embarrassing. And, besides, Brad would think I was ready to be committed if I asked him to don a tool belt and hard-

hat and swagger into the bedroom in nothing but a pair
of torn cut-off Levi's. I tried to will from my mind the
image of Brad, sweaty and dirty, his muscles glistening
in the sun, pounding away at a truss.

I took a deep breath.

What on earth is wrong with me?

One glimpse at a porn movie and I was turning to
mush!

Suddenly, not three feet away, the phone sprang to
life, scaring the daylights out of me. Instantly, I was
transported back to that cataclysmic phone call last
week and my heart skipped a beat. Phones, the bringer
of bad news, the malevolence courier of misfortune and
ruin. God, I hated the little fuckers.

"Hello," I answered cautiously.

"Brooke, is that you?"

My hand flew to my chest. It was Mum and I almost
combusted with an odd mixture of relief that it wasn't
my own personal phone ghoul Geoff and acute shame
that she'd caught me fantasizing about Brad in a hard-
hat.

"Mum, what a surprise," I squeaked.

"Brooke, is everything all right? You sound a bit
funny."

Thankfully, the sound of my mother's voice proved
to be the proverbial bucket of cold water, effectively
putting an end to my construction-site fantasies.

"Oh course I'm all right. What's up?"

"Well, the reason I'm calling is I'm thinking of coming
down later on this morning. I haven't seen you for ages
and thought it might be nice to catch up for a late
lunch."

"Sorry, Mum, but I have to work."

"Oh!" She sounded a bit put out. "I thought you had mostly evening shifts this week?"

"Well, I do," I stammered. "But one of the girls is off sick today and they've asked me to come in and cover her shift."

"Oh, what a shame, and I was so looking forward to seeing you, too. Oh, well, I suppose work is work after all and the extra money is sure to come in handy, what with the wedding to think about."

"Yeah, I suppose so," I replied glumly.

Knowing that Mum had been trying to pin us down on a date for the big day for months I should have been more prepared for what was coming.

"Soooo…any closer to coming up with a date, then?" she asked casually.

Not that I was fooled by her nonchalance. Not for a minute. She was simply dying to know the date so she could begin planning dressmakers, hair and beautician appointments to coincide perfectly with the big day. Mum wasn't one to leave anything to chance. She'd rather arrive at the wedding minus Dad than risk being caught out sporting a single gray hair or chipped nail on the big day. To the outside world, she might be only the mother of the bride, but make no mistake, this was her defining moment of glory. Trudy and I had been joking about it for months.

"Well, now you mention it, we were thinking about sometime early next year. February maybe?" I said, desperate to change the subject.

It wasn't strictly a lie. I had been trying to get Brad to agree to a February wedding for ages, but he kept skirting around it. Honestly, getting him to commit to a date at all was like trying to nail jelly to a wall.

I could feel her excitement bubbling up through the lines.

"Oh, in that case have you spoken to Father Brockway yet? He is a very busy man and if you are looking at February, I don't think you ought to leave it too long."

Oh, God, I should have known this was coming. Mum just assumed we would be married in a church — her old church actually. But after having suffered through one too many church ceremonies over the years, I was determined not to torture my friends with a three-hour sermon from senile old Father Brockway. The trouble was that I hadn't found quite the right moment to tell her.

I groaned inwardly.

Just as I was contemplating ripping the plug from the wall, I was rescued by my mobile phone going off.

"Mum, sorry, but I've got to go. My mobile is ringing. But I'll try and talk to Brad about it tonight," I promised, if only to get her off my back.

"Okay, sweetie. Just don't leave it too long. It would be dreadful if Father Brockway was booked up already."

"Yes, Mum."

Dreadful, my arse. It would be a divine act of mercy.

Reaching for my mobile, I deliberately shut out any further thoughts of Mum and Father Brockway.

"Hello."

"Brooke, darling, how are you?"

"Sophie! What a surprise."

"I haven't caught you in a meeting or anything, have I?"

My stomach did a little flip-flop. I hadn't spoken to Sophie since that day in the city. Instantly, I tried to put my head into Important Business Woman mode.

"Um, no, that's fine. My nine o'clock just rang to say she'd be a little late so I am all yours."

"Terrific. I have to say you're a difficult woman to get hold of. I tried ringing you a couple of times, but I kept getting redirected to your message bank."

Not that Sophie had any idea, but in the wake of my monstrous phone cock-up I'd switched my phone off over the weekend.

"Oh, sorry about that. I had wall-to-wall appointments all day Friday and the weekend was just mad. It's been bedlam in here all morning so I haven't got around to checking my messages yet. But enough of my whining. How are you?"

"Wonderful. Found these to-die-for ballet flats in Prada after you left the other day. Honestly, you should have come. Their winter collection is simply divine, I tell you. And what about you? Sounds as though work has you totally snowed under."

If only she knew!

"Yes, well, it's mostly boring routine stuff, but it keeps me out of trouble."

God, I was beginning to sweat. This ridiculous charade had gone on way too long, but unfortunately I was still at a loss as to how to extradite myself with my dignity intact. The only thing that kept me from blurting out the whole ugly truth was the thought that Sophie would be heading back to England in a few short months and I would finally be off the hook. But could I hang in there for that long? That was the six-million-dollar question.

"You might say it's boring, but what I wouldn't give to be in your shoes," Sophie said wistfully.

I stifled the urge to laugh out loud. *My shoes.* Who in their right mind would want to be in my shoes right now? *I* didn't even want to be in them.

"No, honestly, it isn't that exciting at all."

"Yeah, right. I don't believe you. Anyway I'll be quick. I'm just on my way out to see Ricardo."

"Ricardo?"

Sophie laughed. "Oh, don't worry, hon, I'm not having it off with the pool boy. Ricardo's my stylist, gorgeous, but not *that* way inclined, *if* you get my meaning. Anyway, I was wondering if you've managed to organize that wedding invite yet?"

What wedding?

Then it all came rushing back. *That* wedding. The wedding Sophie was expecting an invite for. The wedding that didn't exist. The wedding I was desperately hoping that she'd forgotten about. How could I have possibly thought I was going to get away with it?

Shit!

"Um..."

"I hate to be a pain, Brooke, but it's just I don't think we'll be able to make it after all."

Instant relief gushed through me. *There is a God after all!*

"Really? What a shame."

"It happens we're heading back to London next month. It's sooner than I thought, but Nick's really eager to get back and I must admit I can't wait to rejoin the rest of the civilized world again. No offense, but I mean, once you've lived in London, Sydney does seem a little provincial. But we really will have to get together before I leave. Maybe the four of us could get together for dinner. I'm sure Brad and Nick would get along well."

A cold tendril of dread crept up my spine. This wasn't good. In fact, this was catastrophically bad. It was one thing to bluff my way through my lies on my own, but I would never get away with it with Brad present. I desperately needed to buy some time.

"That sounds really nice, but do you mind if I get back to you on that?" I rustled the phone book in front of me. "I can't seem to find my planner to check my dates."

"That's all right. Either way, we will get together before I leave and maybe do lunch."

"I'll give you a ring."

Chapter Seven

"Hi, I'm Leanne. I'm one of the receptionists here. You must be Brooke."

I nodded.

"Nervous?"

Again I nodded, mute with first-day jitters.

"Don't be. It's dead easy. Don't worry, though. I know how you feel. When I first started here, I was shit-scared."

"Really?"

"God, yes. I remember on *my* first day I almost chickened out at the last minute. Honestly, I came *this* close to pissing off before I reached the door. I'm glad I didn't, though."

Warm relief streamed through my veins, thawing the icy grip of nerves currently strangling my innards. Thank God I wasn't the only coward.

"Um, how long have you worked here?" I asked in an attempt to mask my nervousness with small talk.

"Oh, a bit over a year, I suppose. But, really, it's great. The money is good, Prue's not a bad boss, all things considered, and the hours are flexible which suits me fine seeing as I'm studying at the moment."

"Really. What are you studying?"

Wow, so the Julia Roberts thing wasn't that off-target after all—except of course Leanne was the polar opposite to Julia Roberts in the looks department.

"Business management." She laughed as my eyes widened with surprise, "I know it's hard to imagine looking at me, but when you're single and on the wrong side of thirty, it's time to give up on the Prince Charming fantasy and take matters into your own hands. And, hey, you never know, I might open up an escort agency of my own one day. I tell you, there's great money in it if you can stomach the stigma attached to this kind of industry."

I decided straight away that I was going to enjoy working alongside Leanne. It wasn't only her bubbly disposition and cheerful smile that chased away my anxieties, but the general air of confidence that surrounded her. In her presence I felt safe. Although I tried not to sum people up by their outward appearance, *bright* was the first word to come to mind when attempting to describe her style. Indeed, she looked like she'd collided with a paint truck. On top of that was her wild hair. Long, curly and almost black, I reckon it was only a stiff wind away from turning into dreadlocks. I don't think Leanne had ever heard of subtle. She was larger than life and in comparison I felt spectacularly boring and now regretted dressing like a Sunday school teacher.

"Seeing as my classes are mainly evenings this semester, you'll probably be on with me most of the time."

My immense relief must have shown on my face and Leanne laughed loudly. "Cheer up, petal. You'll survive. I promise. Roslyn, the other receptionist, does most of the evening and weekend work as she has a couple of kids and it works out better with her babysitting. You'll probably meet her next week sometime and also Prue is in a couple of nights a week, too."

All of a sudden, the door behind me was flung open and an angry dark-haired woman wrapped up in a black duffle coat stomped through the door, clattering her fancy cowboy boots noisily over the tiled entrance.

"What's got you in such a fucking good mood, moonbeam?" she snapped at Leanne, plainly irritated by the sight of the cheerful hippy receptionist. To my surprise, Leanne didn't appear in the least upset by being verbally set on by this walnut-faced woman.

"Scarlett." Leanne smiled, ignoring her surly attitude. "Come and meet Brooke. She's the new receptionist."

Scarlett gave me a once-over. Clearly unimpressed with what she saw, she swung her bag over her shoulder and stormed off through the lounge and out the back without so much as a word of greeting.

"Don't mind her," Leanne whispered as Scarlett disappeared. "She's always a right cow in the mornings. You wait, once she has had a couple of bookings, she'll thaw a bit."

Oh, God, I certainly hoped so.

"Scarlett, what an unusual name," I commented, wondering how such a nice name ended up with its mismatched owner.

Leanne's eyes widened in amusement and she laughed. "It's not her *real* name. None of the girls use their real names in here. You don't have to, either. It's up to you. Me, well, I don't give a stuff if the blokes that come through that door know who I am. I'm not the one fucking them, after all!"

I blinked in surprise at Leanne's casual attitude.

"Um, well, if it's all right I think I'll stick with my own name as well. Christ, I have enough trouble remembering people's names as it is without inventing another one for myself."

"That's the way! But you *will* have to get used to the girls' names here. They're all written down on the roster behind the desk. I've also written out a brief description of each of them as well, just until you get used to the way things run around here."

"What, so I'll recognize them when they walk in?"

Leanne's booming laughter once again filled the room. "God, no! You'd have a hard job spotting them from these profiles, believe me. No, they're for the clients. When a man comes in the door or rings up for a booking, you need to describe the girls available to them. Think of it like a menu. You're the waiter and you're describing the soup of the day. You know, make them sound like they're getting Lara Croft when in reality they're about to get up close and personal with Nanny McPhee." She grinned. "Get the picture now?"

I nodded like a dashboard poodle.

"Let's just say quite a bit of creative license comes into play," she added, winking.

The whiteboard hanging discreetly out of sight of the door was marked out in various grids with the girls' names written in different colors.

"Oh yeah, that's another thing. If they're out on a call, we write them up in red. Blue if they're in-house and with a client and green if they're free. That way we can keep track of who's where and, more importantly, for how long. It's Prue's way of keeping tabs on them, ensuring they don't stay on at, for example, a half-hour booking, and pocket the extra money. Believe me, more girls get sacked for that offense than turning up for a shift shit-faced on drugs."

I swallowed hard. Was it too late to change my mind?

"Either Scarlett, Olivia or Angel are usually available for in-house and, if you know what's good for you, you'll try to share out any clients evenly between them or they tend to get a little ratty. Believe me, we don't want that, or it's likely to get real ugly."

At my puzzled expression, Leanne leaned in and whispered, "Poor things are getting on a bit and since Prue brought in some new younger blood, they've been feeling a bit threatened." Leanne shook her head. "There really is nothing sadder than an old tart."

Across on the board, I noticed two names, JoJo and Sienna, whose time spaces were almost entirely blocked out in either red or blue, a stark contrast to the pastoral green that stretched out endlessly from Scarlett's, Olivia's and Angel's.

"I gather that JoJo and Sienna are quite popular, then?"

"Yeah, you could say that. Most of the blokes who come in would love to book them. The ones that can afford them, at least. You see, they won't take any bookings less than an hour and even then Prue insists the punters fork out extra for their services. Mind you, she gets away with it. They are real stunners. JoJo's a uni student, only been here a couple of months.

Nineteen with long blonde hair and looks like a model. And Sienna is twenty, olive skin, dark hair and legs up to here." Leanne held her hand to her neck. "Gorgeous! They bring in more business between the two of them than the others put together, which is probably why Prue lets them get away with murder. Spoils them rotten, she does, which, as you might imagine, doesn't go down too well with the other girls. You probably won't see too much of them because they're usually out on calls. I only hope they have the good sense to put some money away before they end up like poor Scarlett here."

I knew it was rude, but I couldn't help asking, "How old *is* Scarlett then?" I figured she must be somewhere around mid-fifty by the look of her, which started me wondering what passed for retirement age in the prostitution game.

"Jesus, um, I don't know exactly. About forty, I'd imagine. Mind you, she could be a couple of years younger than that. It's hard to tell with some of them."

Seeing the shocked look on my face, Leanne continued, "Before Prue brought her up to the coast, she had a hard life, that one. Worked Darlinghurst for years, apparently, some of it out on the streets, too. Back in those days the police weren't quite so…let me just say *people-friendly*. She doesn't talk about it much, but I reckon she did have it really tough. Living like that it would have to harden you, I reckon."

Suddenly I saw another person behind the small, wizened, angry woman who'd stormed through the door in a cloud of animosity and Poison. The perfume, that was. What Leanne said certainly made sense of Scarlett's caustic nature and I found I couldn't hold it against her. There but for the grace of God…

"Now, did Prue go through the front of house rules with you?"

"If you mean her porn and anti-wanking policies, yes, she covered them quite thoroughly the other day."

Leanne smiled. "Well, I have to say you're handling it very well. I've known a few girls who've taken off, never to be heard of again after one of Prue's interviews. If you managed that all right, the rest of it should be a breeze."

If only that were true, but so far it hadn't been as bad as I'd feared.

"Before I go through the booking procedures with you, did Prue explain about the deal with the condom book?"

"The *what?*"

Leanne rolled her eyes. "Figures. She's totally paranoid about the girls robbing her blind and that goes for the condoms as well, I'm afraid. God knows why, but she insists on keeping them locked away in the same cupboard as the porn—just here behind us. The way it works is, after we get the client settled in the lounge area, it's up to us to nick out the back and make sure whatever suite the girls have chosen has a towel and two condoms laid out on the pillow. Most places apparently have a box of them in the room, but as you will find out, this is not like most places. Anyway, every condom has to be accounted for in this book here." She pulled out a black folder from beneath the desk.

I was baffled. After all, it wasn't like they were in short supply out in the real world. Hell, you couldn't walk into a public toilet without being confronted by them around every corner. This being a brothel, I'd imagined the place would be knee-deep in them. Surely I'd misunderstood.

"Sorry, but I don't think I'm quite following you."

Leanne opened the folder and explained. "If you look here, you'll see that every condom supplied is recorded next to the individual girl's name. I've found it's best to do it straight away or you tend to lose track. Prue then comes in at the end of the week, does a tally and takes the amount owing off their wages depending on how many they've used."

"You mean they have to *pay* for them?"

"That's right."

"You're joking!"

"I'm afraid not. And just between you and me, it's a bloody disgrace. Sadly, I've known girls who, rather than pay the extra, have opted to risk it when money's tight."

"What do you mean, *risk it*?"

"Risk it! Service a client without a condom. Use only one condom instead of two. Spit rather than swallow! Get the picture?"

Unfortunately I did, in glorious Technicolor, and it didn't conjure up a particularly pleasant image.

"But surely these days that's a bit dangerous?"

"A *bit*? It's *very* dangerous! And not only that, but if Prue ever found out they were doing it, she'd have them out the door in a flash. And in case you were wondering, yes, she does check the book regularly, so it's best to keep things straight, for your own sake."

Blinking back my surprise, I looked upon the big black book with a growing sense of distaste. It seemed, if there was a buck to be made, some people would stoop to anything to make it.

Just then the phone rang.

Clearly my orientation was over. It was showtime.

By the end of my shift, I was beginning to relax a little bit. Having to sit there listening to the grunts and moans coming from the video in the lounge next to us was going to take a bit of getting used to, though, despite Leanne's assurances that I would in no time. She claimed it was like living next to a railway and that eventually I won't even notice the sounds of urgent theatrical orgasms and the constant cries of "Ooh, baby," "Ooh, you're sooo big," or "Ooh, give it to me *real* hard."

All in all, for my first day, it hadn't been too bad. I wasn't called upon to evict any masturbating timewasters — thank God! No one stole any of Prue's precious porn mags, ensuring my pay packet remained intact, and Leanne decided to take it easy on me and did all the meeting and greeting, allowing me to ease myself slowly into my new role. Only Scarlett and Olivia, a rather chubby Philippino in her early thirties, were in-house and apart from one or two snide comments, they were generally civil to each other, which, according to Leanne, was bordering on miraculous.

Then there were the clients themselves. Much to my relief, the few men that Leanne greeted at the door didn't appear to be socially inept perverts. Quite the opposite. They were quite boring and normal. Today, they were mostly regulars and chatted freely with Leanne before disappearing out the back with a minimum of fuss. They might well have been coming in off the street asking for a ham sandwich and a Danish pastry. I didn't even have to straighten up the porn mags — the only job I felt even remotely qualified to carry out.

Thanks to Leanne's excellent tutoring, I now knew that ten minutes with a girl set the lucky punter back forty bucks and an hour would cost them one hundred and fifty. Any kinky or unusual requests—my imagination was doing flip-flops by this stage but Leanne refused to elaborate—were extra and at the discretion of the girls. Call-outs cost an extra fifty plus the taxi fare and I was to always request Ken, Steve or Barry when booking a taxi as they looked out for the girls and minded the money when the girls were on the job.

And from Scarlett, whose favorite non-sex-related pastime was evidently shock the new innocent receptionist, I learned more about multiculturalism than I ever thought possible. *French, Greek, Spanish.* And I have to point out that she was definitely *not* talking about salad dressings there...

"I tell you, I do it all—and more." Scarlett grinned, enjoying the look of discomfort spreading across my rapidly blushing face. "Most of these young prissy workers draw the line at Greek. Frigid cows."

All in all, it was a huge eye-opener. Leanne was clearly appalled at my lack of knowledge of the street terminology for various services provided by the girls and vowed to get me clued up before I did something stupid like get a client's request confused with the dinner order. But *Greek*—well, I got a lesson in cultural diversity that I wasn't likely to forget in a hurry.

But despite all this, it seemed I had passed my baptism of fire without so much as a hint of sunburn to show for it. Leanne informed me that I'd been lucky to strike such a quiet day to start, although she was quick to point out that it generally got a whole lot busier after dark. Apparently Friday and Saturday nights were bedlam, with dozens of horny blokes spilling out from the clubs and pubs looking for some action after striking out with the local girls. Thank goodness I wasn't rostered on for a weekend shift just yet.

Finally five o'clock rolled around and, to my surprise, I had survived my first day in a brothel. *Yay!*

Chapter Eight

"Guess what?" Brad sang out as he walked in the door after work.

"What?"

"Robert Fletcher has invited us to a dinner party at his house on the fourteenth!"

By the beaming smile that lit up his face, he was clearly thrilled at the prospect. This, I might add, was somewhat out of character. Brad absolutely detested his boss and generally referred to him only as *that pompous dickhead*. Not that Robert Fletcher would have any inkling of Brad's animosity, seeing that, at least to his face, Brad waxed lyrical over his courtroom skills and personal charisma. This had to be important.

"Of course, I told him we'd love to. You haven't got anything planned, have you?" he asked.

"Um, the fourteenth, you say? No, I'm pretty sure that's fine."

Fine — it was perfect, actually. I rejoiced that I was off the hook for Sophie's dinner invitation without having to resort to yet more lying. Not that I had been intending to tell Brad about it anyway, on the off-chance that he insisted we go. After all, stranger things have happened. "It's nice of them to invite us."

"*Nice!* Are you kidding? This is better than *nice*, Brooke," he cried with all the delight of a twelve-year-old boy announcing he'd made the football team. "It's been common knowledge around the office for months that Robert is talking about retiring at the end of the year—thank God! Now, everyone's just waiting for him to make the official announcement. Before he goes, though, he and the other partners will have to make their minds up about who they're going to offer junior partnership to. And, just quietly, I think I'm in with a big chance there, unless they bring in someone from outside to fill the spot, but that's fairly remote. So, at this stage, I reckon it's between Simon Parsons and me."

Faced as I was with his obvious excitement, anguish twisted in my chest. Brad's desire to gain a partnership wasn't exactly news to me and he'd be completely devastated if he were overlooked in favor of someone else, especially this Simon Parsons.

There was no love lost between the two of them. According to Brad, Simon was the office flirt and all-round party boy, complete with flash car and broken hearts strewn all over the place. Simon's exploits both in the courtroom and in his private life were anything but demure or respectable. But, despite his colorful private life, he was beginning to garner a certain reputation as a legal trailblazer, much to Brad's chagrin. Therefore, it was little wonder he was Brad's stiffest competition in the race for partnership.

"That's wonderful news, but remember, just because we've been asked out to dinner, it doesn't necessarily mean they're going to offer you the partnership."

"Well, it's a damn sight better than being snubbed, isn't it?"

"Why, what do you mean?"

"Simon Parsons wasn't invited." Brad beamed. "You should have seen his face when I happened to drop it into the conversation. He looked like he'd been kicked in the guts. Hah! Serves him right. From what I gather, it's going to be just the other partners and their wives and us. I'm thinking they're keen to see how we fit in as a couple. After all, it's a big decision they'll be making for the future of the firm, so of course it makes sense that they'll want to make sure I'm the right kind of man for that type of responsibility. No, I'm telling you, this is great news. This is so big—what do you say we go out to dinner to celebrate?"

"We don't know for sure if we *are* celebrating," I suggested gently, but Brad wasn't listening.

Who was I to pollute his euphoric mood by playing devil's advocate? A night out at a fancy restaurant was still a night out and I was determined to make the most of it.

* * * *

Two hours and a bottle and a half of Cab Sav later, Brad pushed aside his half-eaten tiramisu and, in a halo of seriousness, dropped his bombshell.

"Brooke, I really think we need to talk."

His words floated across the table toward me and something inside me froze. I knew I should have expected something. He had been acting a little weird of late, sort of detached and even more difficult than usual. I put it down to the stress he was under at work, which was partly why I was willing to overlook his occasional churlishness and lack of affection. But, despite his burst of excitement earlier, he had grown steadily more and more morose over dinner. Now I knew what was wrong. Oh, God, he was having second thoughts about getting married. After all, apart from that ridiculous bowling club idea of his mother's, he's been sidestepping the issue for months.

Oh, shit, this was it. He was about to end it with me!

Brad's face was rigidly somber and for a moment I thought I was going to be ill. *This can't be happening to me. That's what this bloody dinner was really about. He didn't want to celebrate his invitation to some stupid dinner party – he wanted to avoid an almighty scene so he opted for the coward's way out – a public dumping!*

He frowned. "Did you hear what I just said?"

How could I *not* have heard him? Great, not only did he expect me to take this calmly but also wanted my undivided attention as he callously ripped my heart out.

"Yes," I responded flatly, fighting off a rush of tears.

The way he was tugging at his collar, anyone would have thought he was about to be hanged with it and, for a moment, I wondered if he was having second thoughts about bringing this up in such a public place. After all, he couldn't be *absolutely* certain that I would take it in my stride. I might very well throw myself at his feet and beg him to take me back *or* hurl my glass of wine furiously in his face and stomp out, yelling across the crowded restaurant that I'd faked all my orgasms.

Not a likely scenario, I'll admit.

Clearing his throat nervously, Brad fixed his intense gaze on me. I braced myself for heartbreak. "Brooke, I've been meaning to talk to you about this for a while now, but I know I can't keep putting it off." The other diners seemed to retreat, melting back into the walls as my world closed in about me. "I know this seems out of the blue, but I really think it's time we set a firm date for the wedding."

Off in the distance, a pot clattered onto the floor.

"What?"

That was a strange way to dump someone.

Brad looked a little perplexed. "I thought you'd be pleased?"

Suddenly the full meaning behind his words hit me and I was engulfed in a blinding sense of relief. What on earth was wrong with me tonight? And to think, here I was imagining he was about to call off our engagement.

Stupid me. Stupid, stupid me.

My face glowed with love for this man, my man, sitting across from me and a warm rush of pleasure coursed through my veins, lighting up my heart from within. To think he loved me enough to want to spend the rest of his life with me! How could I have ever doubted him? He was my knight in shining armor, my Romeo, my Brad!

"Pleased? I'm thrilled!"

The evening suddenly took on a sparkling magical ambience and I shivered with pure delight, gazing across the candlelight at my soon-to-be husband. This was exactly what I had been waiting to hear for months and what better place to discuss our future together than over a romantic candlelit dinner and a bottle of wine?

But why the change of attitude? Not that I was complaining, or anything. Far from it. But, every time I tried to pin Brad to a particular date, he came up with a dozen reasons as to why it wasn't suitable.

"In fact, I think that's a wonderful idea," I gushed. "I've also been thinking about it for the past few months and, well, what do you say to the eighteenth of February?"

After obsessing about the date twenty-four-seven for God knew how long, I wasn't about to let this moment slip through my fingers. I'd even looked up an astrology site on the internet in between patients at the surgery and been advised – for a fee – of the best celestial date for our forthcoming nuptials. I wasn't leaving anything to chance. If I'd had a piece of paper handy, I would have been drawing up seating plans and writing out our wedding vows right there in the restaurant. After all, a girl can't be too organized, can she?

Brad sat there, silently twirling his glass for a moment with an indulgent smile playing on his lips. "Well, I'm not saying that February wouldn't be nice, but, um, I was kind of thinking about bringing it forward a little."

Hello, this is unexpected, but, hey – "Okay, that's fine. How about the beginning of February, then, say, the fifth? That way everyone will be over Christmas," I suggested enthusiastically. This was getting better and better. For one brief heart-stopping moment, I'd feared that Brad was about to set the date back further, like ten years back.

"Um, well, you know what, I was actually thinking about the beginning of October – this year."

Immediately, I began choking on a mouthful of coffee-flavored dessert.

"*This year?*" I spluttered.

Brad nodded, smiling at me lovingly, his beautiful blue eyes glowing seductively in the soft candlelight.

"Why not? We've been putting this off for ages and it's about time we made some firm decisions concerning our future."

We? What was he talking about, *we?* I had wanted to set a date from the moment Brad first proposed. It had been him who was keen to wait until the time was right. Now, out of the blue, it seemed October was perfect?

"It doesn't give us long to organize everything," I said with a smile, careful not to discourage him.

Christ, even February was pushing it! According to the pile of bridal magazines I'd been accumulating steadily over the past few months, it took a minimum of twelve months to organize a wedding properly. October was only five months away. Bloody hell, Mum was going to have a fit.

"Nonsense. Of course we can do it, Brooke. What is there to organize anyway? Church. Reception. Dress. Simple. I've known people who have managed it in a few weeks, not months."

Yeah, right. The ones who settled for a dodgy celebrant in a park and a rented hall for the reception, no doubt. Apart from that, I didn't want everyone thinking I was pregnant! Our union was going to be a glorious symbol of our undying love, not a symbol of our lackadaisical attitude to contraception. I was keen to tie the knot as well, but not at the expense of my fairy-tale dream wedding.

Sensing my hesitation, Brad leaned across the table and gently took my hand in his. "I know you want a wedding with all the extras and I promise you I'll see to it that you're not disappointed. We could even fly out to Fiji for our honeymoon, if you like."

"*Fiji! Really?*"

Brad smiled. "Really. Anything for you. So, what do you say to the first of October? It's the long weekend, so the relatives living interstate will be able to fly down for the big day."

"October the first sounds perfect." I beamed and Brad topped up my glass of wine.

Mrs. Brooke Cooper. Wife of Mr. Brad Cooper. It had a delicious ring to it.

Chapter Nine

"Oh, my God, this is huge!" Trudy threw off her tinting apron and rushed up to me for a hug. "I can't believe it. Just think, by Christmas, you'll be an old married woman."

"Well, married anyway. Enough of the old." I laughed, punching her playfully in the arm.

After a moment's hesitation, her smile slipped a little. "And how do you feel about it? Are you sure you're ready to throw away your freedom and settle down with one man for the rest of your life?"

Ever since the engagement announcement, Trudy had been dropping hints that I was throwing away the best years of my life for matrimonial monotony, and I threw her a *look*. "Don't be like that. You know how much I love Brad, so why can't you be happy that I'm happy?"

"Believe me, I *am* happy for you. I just worry about you sometimes. That's all."

"Why?" I frowned.

"I know you're old enough to make your own decisions, but are you absolutely certain Brad is the one for you?"

"Trudy..."

"Okay, okay. I'm sorry. I just want you to be happy and I'm not a hundred percent sure Brad appreciates you for the wonderful unique person you are. Look, just remember you can always count on me to be there for you. If things don't turn out the way you imagined or you start to have second thoughts, you don't have to go through with it."

I laughed at the absurdity of Trudy's words. Hell, this was what I'd wanted since the first time I'd laid eyes on Brad. "Christ, can you image what my mother would say if I called it all off? Shit, she'd have a stroke I reckon."

"Talking about your mother, what did she say when you told her? She must have been over the moon."

I rolled my eyes. "That's putting it mildly. The way she went on, I reckon she was starting to think that Brad had no intention of ever agreeing to a date. Can you imagine? I'd be disinherited if I managed to lose him. As it was, I swear to God she practically collapsed with relief. And as soon as she stopped crying, she started panicking about Christ knows what, from the reception to the church..."

"You haven't told her yet, have you?" Trudy accused.

I winced. "No."

"Brooke, you are such a coward. You can't put it off forever, you know. Don't you think your mum is going to figure out that something is up when she arrives at the church on the big day and you're not there?"

"I know. I know. I'll tell her the next time I speak to her, I promise. But it's going to kill her. I just know it.

Then, you know what she's like. She'll put on that big martyr act of hers and I'll feel like the worst daughter in the world — again."

"You've got to be strong about this and stick to your guns. You let people push you around too much. You're so worried about letting other people down you forget about yourself sometimes. If it helps, why don't you try keeping the image of senile old Father Brockway dribbling all over your wedding vows fresh in your mind?"

I shuddered. "Oh, Jesus, that's horrible, Trud."

"But true. I reckon they have to exhume him every Sunday to take the service."

"Yuk, that's gross! Anyway, there will be definitely *no* dribbling at my fairy-tale wedding and *no* Father Brockway, for that matter!"

"Thatagirl! And, remember, if you're determined to get shackled to Brad for the rest of your life, at least make sure it's on your terms. Okay?"

"Okay."

"Jesus, I can't believe I nearly forgot! How did you go yesterday at the House of Ill Repute? You did go, didn't you?"

"Of course I did!" I responded, a bit hurt. Did everyone think I was a spineless wimp? Or only those who knew me best? "Did you think I'd pike out or something?"

"To be honest, the thought had crossed my mind," she confessed, slightly shamefaced.

"Trudy!"

"Well, you have to admit you were pretty freaked out about the whole brothel thing the other night. I thought maybe once you'd slept on the idea, you might decide to take your chances and tell Brad about the phone bill, after all."

"I think, under the circumstances, I had every right to be a little freaked out. After all, it isn't a proposition I get confronted with every day, now."

"Well, that's true."

"And, anyway, for your information, I didn't wimp out. Brad has no idea about the phone bill *or* my new job. Both him and Mum think I've got extra shifts at the surgery, so don't you dare breathe a word about it—not even as a joke. I know what you're like, Trudy Baxter. You have a sick sense of humor. And as far as the job goes, I got on very well, thank you. It was really interesting—not at all what I thought it would be like."

Trudy's eyes lit up with interest. "Well, come on, then, spill the beans. How was it? Did the hookers all loll about in skimpy underwear, painting their nails?"

Like most women, I suppose, Trudy was convinced that all the girls looked like Las Vegas showgirls and had fantastic bodies—a result of a diet rich in drugs, naturally—and for the first time in my life, I didn't feel like the naïve one. Now *I* had one up on my worldly cousin.

"No, they didn't. They sat around the kitchen in jeans, watching the soaps on TV and reading trashy celebrity magazines. *And*, Trudy, I think they prefer to be called sex workers."

Clearly surprised by my recently acquired wisdom, Trudy widened her eyes and I couldn't help smiling.

"Leanne, the other receptionist I was working with, was lovely, a real sweetie. She's a student, would you believe, studying business management. You'd like her. She's really cool. And as for the owner, Prue, they don't see too much of her, thank God. Apparently she's an ex-working girl herself who runs another brothel in Hornsby with her girlfriend and only comes up every few days to check up on the girls."

"What, she's a lesbian?" Trudy shrieked.

"Well, apparently she has a gal-pal so, yes, I suppose so."

"But..." This latest snippet of information clearly had Trudy poleaxed. "If she's a lesbian, how could she stand to, you know, screw blokes for a living? Jeez, it would be like a vegetarian working in an abattoir."

"Don't ask me! But I suppose after doing what they do all day, it would put anyone off doing it after hours as well—and for free? Who knows? Anyway, Leanne reckons about a third of the girls on the game are lesbians or at least bi."

"No!" Trudy gasped.

"Well, that's what I've been told anyway."

"Jesus Christ! And the girls, come on, Brooke, what were they like? Pretty—"

"Old!"

"Old?"

"Well, yes. Granted it was a really slow day, so I only met two of them, but they had to be pushing forty."

"*Get out of here!*" screamed Trudy, causing the lone customer currently straining to hear us from under the dryer to jump and bang her head. "God, you'd think if a guy wanted to screw some old flapper, they'd just wait until the nightclub in town ended and pick one up then. Shit, how hard could it be?"

"Don't be so judgmental, Trud," I admonished. "They aren't all eighteen with looks like models, after all. What do you think happens to them when they reach thirty or forty? What, they suddenly decide to get married, have babies and join the local tennis club?

Where do you think they go when they get older and lose their looks? Honestly, Trudy, some of these girls have had really horrendous lives — worse than you or I could ever imagine. I don't think they have too many options available after being on the game for that long." I thought of Scarlett. "What are they going to put on a résumé, 'Proficient in French, Greek and bondage'?"

"Okay. Okay. Enough. I get it. Christ, Brooke," said Trudy throwing her hands up in surrender. "One bloody shift in a brothel and now you're ready to die for their cause. Who would have thought it? So when are you on next?"

"I start at eleven," I said, glancing down at my watch. "So I'd better get a move on because I also have a shift at the surgery tonight."

"It's all go for you, isn't it!"

"Ha ha."

"But, seriously, when are we going to get a chance to catch up? We haven't had a girlie night in for ages and we do have a wedding to organize, remember."

"Um, how about later on in the week, say Friday night? I've got the day and night off and Brad will be at footy training."

"Great. Come around to my place. Say about six-thirty?"

"Terrific. See you then."

* * * *

"Well, congratulations. When's the big day?"

"October the first," I replied, feeling a little hesitant.

Typical of me. Been working there five minutes and already I was revealing my life story to anyone willing to listen. It wasn't my intention to go blurting out to

Leanne that I was getting married, but she was so friendly and easy to talk to and, besides, I was too excited to get a grip on my runaway mouth. As soon as my news was out, though, I began to experience certain reservations.

"Leanne, I hope you don't mind me asking you this..."

Leanne's eye widened in surprise. "Oh, my God, don't say another word," she cried, leaping up from behind the desk before throwing her arms around me, practically smothering me in her matronly bosom. "I know we haven't known each other long, but of course I'd *love* to be your bridesmaid."

What? Bridesmaid? Leanne? Shit, what had I said? I reeled back in shock, frantically trying to think of something to say that would get me out of this hideous situation.

In response to the frozen look of shock on my face, Leanne gave me a sheepish grin before dissolving into a fit of giggles. "Oh, God, sorry hon, that was rotten of me, I know, but I just couldn't resist. The look on your face was priceless." She chuckled. Then, adopting a more remorseful tone, she added, "Don't you worry. You'll get used to me. What was it you were going to say?"

Regaining my composure, I took a deep breath. "What I was *going* to say was would you mind not mentioning anything about my wedding to the others yet? I don't want them to think that I'm, oh, I don't know..."

"What? Happy, with a normal life and in a normal functioning relationship?"

"Well, sort of, yes," I replied awkwardly.

What I really meant was that I didn't want the girls to think that I was rubbing it in or parading my happiness around in front of them.

Leanne smiled at me kindly. "Don't worry, petal, your secret's safe with me. Actually, it is probably best to keep it to yourself anyway, at least for now. It's not like your average office situation in here where everyone comes in on a Monday morning and talks about their weekend and their wild nights out on the town. These girls tend to keep their outside lives to themselves. I still don't even know where they all live, what they do other than this and I see them every other day."

"So I take it they only socialize with each other, then?"

Leanne shook her head. "No, not even that. Once they leave here after a shift, I suspect most of them would cross to the other side of the road rather than acknowledge each other out there in the real world. I know it seems weird, but once you've been here for a while, you'll understand better."

In response to my puzzled expression, Leanne continued, "Look, no one ever wakes up one morning and thinks, 'Hey I might give this prostitution game a go — sounds like a great lark!' Sadly, it's something they usually fall into when things get really tough. They all have their scars, some physical and some emotional, and it makes them see everyday things differently from, say, you and me."

"Like marriage and that."

"Yeah, like marriage and that."

"I suppose I can see where you're coming from. I can't imagine working here and having a husband or boyfriend works out too well."

Leanne shrugged. "It can. But it's rare. Some of the girls I know have had relationships outside."

"Really?"

"Yeah. Look, I'm not saying they're something out of a romance novel or anything, but sure. Why not! But listen, keep this to yourself, though. Prue doesn't particularly approve."

"You're kidding. Why? And besides what business is it of hers what the girls do when they're not working?"

I was shocked. What kind of a place was Prue running here, where you weren't even allowed a boyfriend? Noticing my mounting ire, Leanne came to Prue's defense, to my surprise.

"Well, you see, that's the trouble. It doesn't always stay out of the brothel. A couple of months ago one of the girls came in for a shift and the night before her fella had beaten her up. Worked her over real good and, by the time she showed up here, the poor girl was black and blue and not in any fit state to work. Despite Prue's offer to put her up for a few days, the poor thing refused to call the cops. She left not long after and took off back to Sydney, I think."

"But surely that's hardly her fault now. Why should she be the one to suffer because of her abusive boyfriend?"

Leanne shook her head. "That's the problem, though. The vast majority of them have no family or financial support and think they have no choice but to go back to the situations that quite often put them here in the first place. It's not just what goes down away from the place, though. Just before I started here, apparently a fellow came in here in a jealous rage and threatened to torch the place. He'd been going out with one of the girls for a few months but couldn't cope with the thought of her with other men. Happens a lot. A couple of the girls ran out the back and called for help, but by the time it came, he'd smashed the place up and scared the daylights out of everyone.

"Prue may sound tough, but she's been in the business long enough to know the pitfalls. In the end, she's only trying to protect not only the girls, but, I suppose, her business, as well. Sure, she knows she can't control what they do on their own time, but she prefers them to keep their private life well away from the place, and that goes for drugs and booze, too. If any of them turn up high, you'd better keep an eye on them or be prepared to call Prue and let her know. If she finds out you've been turning a blind eye, your neck will also be on the chopping block."

I didn't know what to say. How could I possibly start to understand what kind of lives these girls had lived? Compared to them I felt like Pollyanna.

Fifteen minutes later, the door buzzer sounded. Engrossed in a magazine article about a woman who'd stabbed her abusive husband to death, I resolutely ignored it until Leanne nudged me none too gently.

"Hey, what was that for?" I cried out, rubbing my arm.

"Go on," she urged. "This one's yours."

"What!" I shrieked in alarm. "I don't think I'm ready to greet anyone yet."

"Sure you are. You watched me all day yesterday. Come on, the poor bloke's waiting out there. Move it."

Leanne's expression told me she was not going to be swayed by the look of distress that arced across *my* face.

"Go. What are you waiting for?" she urged.

In all fairness to Leanne, I realized without her bullying I would never have volunteered. After all, this was my job and I had put it off for long enough. So with that in mind, I figured in this instance it was better to take the plunge and just get it over and done with.

I rose from behind the desk and made my way over to the door. My mind felt as though it wasn't quite connected to the rest of my body and, by the time I reached the door, I was numb with nerves. Perhaps sensing my growing hesitation, Leanne called out from the desk, "Pretend you're inviting them into your house. Be friendly. You'll be fine."

Okay, I thought. *Friendly. I can do that.*

As instructed, I quickly checked the fellow out through the security viewer before opening the door to my first official customer.

Leanne had given me strict instructions yesterday that under no circumstances were we to admit any more than two customers at any one time — mainly for security reasons, she'd explained. Not that she had ever experienced any trouble on one of *her* shifts, but still Prue was adamant that they always take precautions, especially late at night when occasionally blokes turned up at the door drunk and proceeded to take great offense when they discovered that, yes, they were in fact expected to pay for a root.

This fellow wasn't a drunk, nor did he look potentially abusive. He looked quite nice. Very nice in fact. To say I was surprised was to put it mildly. Mid-thirties, perhaps a bit younger, he had sandy-colored hair, an open friendly face and was wearing nice jeans and a neatly ironed blue shirt. By the leather satchel he was carrying, it was my guess he'd come straight from work. Granted, it was a little out of the ordinary to be nicking out from work for a fuck, but, all things considered, it might have been a whole lot worse. He looked up at the camera and smiled. Instantly, some of my nerves slid away.

This was it. I opened the door.

"Hello. Welcome to Heavenly Pleasures. Please come in," I announced, calmly smiling back at him.

Leanne gave me a brief nod of encouragement. This was going well. I could do this.

"How can we assist you?" I asked, after closing the door again behind him.

"I was hoping to see one of the girls for half an hour," he requested, confidence in his tone.

I almost swooned with relief. By his relaxed attitude, he clearly wasn't a first-timer as I had dreaded.

"Of course," I responded with enthusiasm, all the time praying he wouldn't see through my thin veneer of faked confidence and realize I was practically a work-experience kid. In fact, I know fifteen-year-olds who would probably have loved this kind of gig. A great laugh, they'd no doubt think. Me, I was only hoping I could get through this without making a complete idiot of myself.

I cleared my throat. *Time.* "Currently, we have four lovely girls available waiting to meet you. First, we have Angel, a lovely lady, twenty-seven, with long blonde hair and generously endowed. Very kind with a cheerful personality. Second, Cherie, five foot five, a voluptuous size twelve with soft honey-colored hair and a flair for making a man smile. And we also have Scarlett. Long, wavy dark hair, petite, in her early thirties and eager to see to your every need. And Vivian, a mature but stunning brunette. Five foot two and a tiny one hundred and five pounds, she has ample experience in every aspect of erotic pleasure."

Well, in reality we only had Angel and Scarlett in-house, but Leanne had instructed me to use a little imagination to make it sound as though we had an entire harem of girls out the back rather than the two watching the morning chat shows and drinking endless cups of tea. Mystery, Leanne had stated at the time, was the secret. We wanted to create mystery. After all we were in the fantasy business as well as the sex-for-money business.

He thought about it for a few minutes before deciding on Angel. I wasn't surprised. Leanne said most blokes went for the big tits and blonde hair.

"Fantastic choice. I am sure you will be pleased with her services," I crooned, gaining some confidence at last. "Now, if I can just get your payment details, I will take you through to our client lounge where Angel will be with you shortly."

As I handed Leanne his credit card to process, she winked at me. I had passed my first test.

With the payment out of the way, I pulled aside the beaded curtain and invited him into the lounge, ignoring the grunts coming from the video.

"Please sit down and relax and Angel will be with you in just a moment."

"Thanks…?"

"Brooke. My name is Brooke." I smiled.

"Well, thanks, Brooke. First day?"

I colored. *Was it that obvious?* "Second, actually."

"You did very well." He smiled back.

"Thank you," I replied, just about swooning with relief. If all the blokes who frequented Heavenly Pleasures were as nice as this fellow, I figured I just might survive the experience.

Once back out at the desk, I took a deep breath before collapsing into the chair.

"Well done," whispered Leanne, "I told you it was easy. But don't get too comfortable there. You have to go out and get Angel and for God's sake make sure she has some makeup on and her hair brushed."

I froze. Scarlett was also waiting out the back. This was bad. Again this morning she had arrived in a complete fouler of a mood and quite frankly I was terrified of her, even more so now seeing as I hadn't managed to get her a booking. Then, on top of that, the two of them had been hurling black looks at one another and I feared it wouldn't take much to provoke a full-blown war between the two of them. And the root of all this animosity? Apparently it was a result of Angel, who from what I was told practically hijacked one of Scarlett's favorite customers last week by brazenly flashing her fanny at him as she walked through the lounge room on some flimsy excuse.

Considering the fellow in question hadn't yet paid for a service and therefore was not entitled to any sneak previews, Angel's flirty foray into the client lounge was practically a sacking offense. Under the circumstances, though, Leanne decided to take pity on her and didn't report her to Prue as Scarlett, it seems, had just about flayed the poor girl alive, reducing the normally placid Angel to a quivering mess by the time she was through with her. Leanne therefore considered a bollocking from Scarlett to be punishment enough.

Scarlett and Angel were sitting out the back in the kitchenette, both sullenly reading magazines and smoking furiously in between shooting evil looks at one other. The hostility in the room was almost as thick as the cigarette fog and I experienced a twinge of fear as they looked up at me expectantly. I sent up a prayer and hoped I'd make it out of there alive.

"Angel. A half-hour booking in the lounge room for you. And Leanne told me to ask you to put some makeup on and fix your hair," I announced, figuring it was best to adopt the short-but-sweet method in this instance.

Ignoring Scarlett's venomous glare, I smiled at Angel reassuringly. "Don't worry, he seems really nice."

Angel rolled her eyes and stubbed out her cigarette in disgust at my little pep talk before standing up and dumping her cup in the sink behind her.

Once out of there, I let out a sigh of relief and prayed that Angel would do something with herself or I seriously feared the bloke in the lounge would take one look at her and demand his money back on the grounds of false advertising. Mind you, I hadn't been lying when I said she had big boobs, I just omitted that the rest of her was a little on the large side as well. On the plus side, she did have a pretty face and blonde hair, even if it was a result of a bottle.

While she disappeared to get ready, I made my way into the suite Angel had chosen and put out a couple of towels and a condom on the bedside table next to an economy-sized pump-action bottle of lube. Leanne had said whoever finished up the night before normally checked the lube was filled, but it was always wise to double-check. Also it was our job to ensure the girls had removed any used condoms, towels or anything else that may have been left behind from a previous session as it was definitely *not* our place to clean up after them.

Looking around the room, I gave thanks to whoever had been in last night. Thank God they'd done their job, because I didn't know how I would react to being confronted with the sight of a used condom or, for that matter, a renegade dildo peeping out from under the bed.

To my relief, some thirty minutes later Paul – I sneaked a look at the credit card slip – emerged from out the back via the lounge room and thanked us politely before making his way out of the door again. He seemed happy. Well, he had just had sex, so I suppose it was mission accomplished, from our point of view. I was relieved, to say the least. I had just effectively seen to my first customer and I had survived the experience. I was now a full-fledged brothel receptionist!

I felt immensely proud of myself.

After my successful initiation, Leanne put me on door duty for the remainder of my shift while she took care of the call-outs. They were a little more involved than simple meet and greets as they involved booking taxis, checking with the respective motels that the customer was indeed booked in – thus safeguarding us from sending out a girl to a vacant motel room as occasionally happened if the fellow in question got cold feet or his credit card limit was breached and he took off to avoid having to deal with a furious hooker. Sorry – sex worker.

After Paul, things got a little easier and, by the end of the shift, I had not only managed to get Scarlett two bookings, but also conquered my fear of the porn DVDs. Leanne had been right and by the time I left for the day, the relentless moans and groans didn't seem quite so distressing.

When I got home from the surgery that evening, I was exhausted. Brad was watching telly and smiled as I let myself in through the door.

"Hi, hon. I've left you some Chinese takeaway in the fridge." He glanced up from some big budget blow-'em-up type movie playing. "Hope you don't mind, but I got chicken and almonds for a change?"

I frowned. Brad knew I wasn't fond of chicken and almonds. But tonight I was so hungry, I was prepared to eat anything.

Throwing down my bag, I stumbled into the kitchen and placed the plastic takeout container in the microwave before heading to the bedroom, kicking off my shoes along the way. Seeing as I hadn't had time to come home before starting at the surgery, I felt like I had been in the same clothes forever and wanted nothing but my comfortable PJs and an hour of mindless television before going to bed.

Sitting across from Brad watching telly, I had barely finished eating when my eyes started drooping with exhaustion. Counting both shifts, I had worked almost ten hours straight and, unaccustomed as I was to long working days, I was completely knackered.

The surgery had been packed with patients when I'd arrived and it had taken most of the night to work through them, by which time I was getting used to the hostile glares and muffled condemnation directed my way about receptionists who had no idea of the concept behind appointment times. It wasn't my fault that Dr. Chisholm insisted on stopping for a coffee break after every second patient. But regardless of that, I was still on the front line of their displeasure while Dr. Chisholm was greeted with grateful smiles when she eventually got around to seeing her patients.

Despite all this, it hadn't been such a bad night, I supposed. For once, I hadn't screwed anything up and thus had avoided Dr. Chisholm's wrath, which made a nice change from the usual lecture I received at the end of each shift that went along the lines of, 'get your act together or get another job'.

The longer I thought about it, the more I came to realize that I preferred working with prostitutes than the viperous Dr. Chisholm. Sure, the girls at Heavenly Pleasures were a bit of a handful sometimes, but at least they didn't look at me like I was scum. If it weren't for the fact that it was the perfect front for my clandestine job, I would tell Dr. Chisholm where to shove her nasty temperament together with the shitty work hours and pay.

"You look tired," Brad commented, making his way over to rub my aching neck.

As he massaged the tension away, I groaned. "I am. It's been a really long day."

"I'll say. Your mum was telling me they called you in for a morning shift as well today. That's a bit rough, isn't it?"

My heart froze.

"When were you talking to Mum?"

"Oh, she rang about an hour ago. She said you'd been called into work this morning."

"Well, not until one, really. I went down to the salon to see Trudy first," I explained carefully, not wanting to rouse his suspicions as to why I'd gone from scraping by on the odd four-hour shift to working doubles.

"Well, at least it sounds like you're finally settling in there. You never know, with any luck these extra shifts might lead to full-time work."

Yeah, right, not likely. Besides, the thought of having to walk into the surgery and face Dr. Chisholm each and every day was enough to send me screaming to the unemployment agency—hell, I'd rather *work* at the unemployment agency for that matter.

"You never know," I replied vaguely, reminding myself that it was the perfect alibi for my shifts at the brothel, after all.

"Your mum sounded really excited about the wedding. Kept going on about some Father Brockway and how happy he'll be to marry us. Sounds to me like she has her heart set on us having a big church wedding."

I groaned. Mother from hell had woken from the grave! Break out the pitchforks and sharpened stakes!

Brad sounded a little puzzled. "Do we know a Father Brockway?"

"I do, you don't." I rolled my eyes. "She has it in her head that we're getting married by Father Brockway at St Cecilia's. You know, the Anglican church in town." Brad opened his mouth to speak. "But don't you worry. There's no way I'm letting my mother bully us into having a church wedding."

"I was just about to say that a traditional church wedding might be quite nice, and it means so much to your mother, maybe we should think about it at least."

"No!" I cried. "Absolutely not! There's no way I am going to stand in some stuffy church and listen to some decrepit minister go on about how a woman's place is in the home and cap it off with a three-hour lecture on the evils of premarital sex and divorce. Little wonder brides faint at the altar. Bloody hell, it's the only way they can get out of being bored to death."

Brad laughed. "Surely he's not that bad? And besides, wouldn't you like to walk down the aisle like a princess?"

"No. Sorry, Brad, but my mother is not going to force this one on us. There will be no church and definitely no Father Brockway! This is *our* wedding day we're talking about and not hers. Just because she got married in some musty old church wearing what was *the* most hideously vile wedding dress known to either man or beast doesn't mean she's going to inflict the same torment on me."

Brad held his hands up in a gesture of surrender. "Okay. I get it. I won't argue. No church. Fine. Have you given any thought to where you do want the wedding, then?"

"I don't know. I really do love the idea of a nice garden wedding, surrounded by flowers. I hear the Japanese gardens at the Arts Center are beautiful. Or maybe the beachfront somewhere. The only trouble is that we're really at the mercy of the weather. If it were to pour with rain on our big day, I think I'd have a breakdown. What about you? Any ideas — apart from a church, that is?" I added firmly just in case the idea was beginning to grow on him.

"No. It's your big day and it's your decision. I'll marry you anywhere."

My heart melted at his sweet words.

"Well, if it's all right with you, I was planning to go around to Trudy's while you're at training on Friday night. Thought I'd take a pile of bridal mags with me. Surely among them I'll see something that's prefect for us."

"I'm sure you will." Brad shifted awkwardly clearing his throat. "Um, while we are on the subject, I've been meaning to talk to you about the reception?"

Something in his expression warned me I wasn't going to like what he was about to say.

"What about it?" I replied cautiously.

"I hope you don't mind but Mum was on the phone to me *again* today," he began, shooting me a pained look meant to convey the impression that he was under immense pressure so was to be forgiven for what he was about to say. "And, well, I kind of told her that you would at least have a look at the bowling club with her — tomorrow, maybe?"

I opened my mouth to protest, but Brad got in first. "I know what you said the other night, and I agree one hundred percent with you. It's our decision. But, Brooke, all I'm asking is that you just have a look at the place. Please. For me. There's no pressure, honestly, but it would mean a lot to me if you and my mother could just try to get on a bit. Just make her feel included, that's all."

I had to admit he had a point. After all, I wouldn't like it if Brad hated my parents. All I had to do was look around this place and leave. How long could it take — five minutes, tops? Brad would be happy, his mother would finally be off my back and following that he could deliver the news to her that we had decided *not* to go with the bowling club idea. *Everyone's happy. Simple.*

"Okay, I'll have a look," I eventually conceded. "But just remember I'm only doing it for you, *not* your mother, okay?"

"Oh, you're an angel. Thanks, hon. By the way, Mum said she'd be around to pick you up at about ten tomorrow morning. Okay?"

Chapter Ten

"Just follow me and I'll take you through a list of the special services our club has to offer."

I felt as though I was listening to a recorded message. Every aspect of the stylish young events coordinator was impressively shiny and flawless, from her tailored burgundy suit to her matching burgundy tights and shoes. She could have passed for an airline hostess or a museum guide. Clearly, she'd been hired for her presentation skills — or, failing that, by an elderly all-male board of directors. But no matter how much she tried to tart up the place, the sad fact remained it was still a bowling club and currently the local hangout for, I suspected, every pensioner in a ten-kilometer radius. I was totally off the idea already. Pity the same couldn't be said for Brad's mum. With brisk efficiency, she fired off question after question as if she was reading them off a list as we were led on a grand tour of the club's facilities.

As I followed sullenly behind, I couldn't help feeling I was being manipulated. One thing was for sure, Brad owed me big-time for this. If this didn't gain me some brownie points, I didn't know what would. *It has to be love*, I told myself.

But after viewing the club's entertainment facilities, I was even more determined to hold firm to my original resolve to sever any link between my upcoming nuptials and any recreational facilities for the over-sixties. If I didn't stick to my guns on this one, I shuddered to think of where it might lead.

"Brooke, can't you picture the bridal table set up against the glass doors? What a lovely outlook," whispered Brad's mother, Rose, or Mrs. Cooper as she liked me to call her.

"What, the bowling greens?" I queried, churlishly refusing to give in to her fantasy.

Just in front of me someone yelled out *Bingo* at the top of his lungs, almost frightening the life out of me.

"Yes. Don't you think with the floodlighting and the beautiful gardens it would be a perfect backdrop?"

No. I didn't. It might have only been eleven o'clock in the morning, but the only view I wanted to enjoy was from the bar.

As we followed Sonia, our guide, back to the foyer, Brad's mother looked superbly pleased with herself. "I am sure once Bradley sees the place he will agree with me that it is the perfect venue to hold the reception," she announced, purposely avoiding all eye contact. "You'll be pleased to know I have already inquired about the availability and, as luck would have it, the function room is available for the first of October."

Turning back to Sonia, she continued waffling on, oblivious to the fury building on my face. "Thank you very much for your time this morning. I am confident we will speak to you tomorrow or possibly the day after with a confirmation for the first, just as soon as I have checked with my son on the matter."

I stood there mute with rage. Was I dreaming or had she had practically booked the reception?

It wasn't until we walked out into the club car park I felt able to speak without losing it altogether. "Rose," I called out, deliberately using her Christian name, knowing how much it annoyed her. Her shoulders tensed and I smothered a satisfied smile.

"Yes?" she replied coolly.

Start as you wish to continue, I said to myself.

"It's like this, *Rose.* Brad and I really appreciate your help, *Rose,* but we still have a number of other places to look at before we make our decision, *Rose,*" I informed her through gritted teeth.

"Nonsense."

Nonsense? Did she just say *nonsense*? The horrible —

"Trust me, *I* know my son and I am positive he will just love the idea," she continued brazenly, dismissing me with a wave of her hand. "Why waste *our* precious time and energy trudging around countless function centers when the perfect venue is right here in front of you?"

With the effort it took not to strangle her, I could already feel an ulcer eating away the lining of my stomach. By the time we reached the car, battle lines had been drawn. There was no doubt about it. This wasn't a question of our wedding, anymore. This was war!

I smiled woodenly, staring her down. "It's no problem at all, I assure you. Anyway, Brad was more than happy to leave the decision-making up to me. So, as much as I appreciate your kind offer to help, I would really like to look at some more venues before *I* make the final decision."

If that didn't scream out 'fuck off, you overbearing cow' I didn't know what would.

For a moment, I thought she was going to argue, but then, to my surprise, she smiled sweetly and said, "Of course, Brooke. I wouldn't dream of interfering."

Yes, Brad owes me big-time for this.

Chapter Eleven

"Where the fuck is my damn taxi?" yelled Sienna, throwing me an accusing look. "You did remember to book it, didn't you?"

"Yes, I rang ages ago," I spluttered defensively. "It should have been here ten minutes ago."

"Well, can you ring them again and see what the hell is going on?" Out the back a car horn tooted. "That's them now," she grumbled, grabbing her bag and racing out through the kitchen to the taxi waiting in the back street.

It was my first evening night shift and already it was proving to be chaotic. Between the nonstop ringing of phones and answering the front door, I had barely had time to think. Leanne effortlessly juggled phone calls, credit card payments and clients while I did my best to ensure the girls were ready and organized for what was proving to be a really busy night.

It was barely nine o'clock and already Sienna and JoJo were beginning to show the strain. Taxis not showing up on time were only part of the problems we'd had to deal with. There were also the usual drunk timewasters and another bloke who, after making a booking for a nearby motel, got cold feet and did a runner before Scarlett got there, putting her in a fouler of a mood.

"How long before my next booking?" yelled the new girl Candy from out the back.

"You've got a half-hour in five minutes," replied Leanne, marking her down on the whiteboard.

"Shit! I'm fucking starving out here. Can't someone nick out and get me a burger or something first?"

As another call came in, even Leanne was beginning to look a tad flustered. "Christ, she's a pain in the neck," she muttered, picking up the phone before quickly covering the receiver with her hand. "Brooke, sorry to do this to you, but have you a minute to run out and get Candy in there something to eat before she starts eating the damn furniture?"

Although I didn't have so much as a minute to scratch my arse, I jumped at the opportunity to escape from the madness, even if it was only for a few minutes. At least I could take a breath and try to clear my head a bit. Behind me, I heard the unmistakable sounds of an argument brewing so grabbed some money from the cash tin under the desk and made a run for it.

By the time I got back five minutes later, calm had been restored and Candy's next booking was waiting happily in the lounge, his eyes glued to some big-breasted black Amazonian woman wielding a whip at a likewise voluptuous but clearly terrified redhead. I looked away.

"Here, Brooke, give me Candy's burger and I'll dash through with it. You'd think she hadn't eaten for a week the way she's carrying on out there. And can you go and tell her next booking that she won't be long?"

My gaze flickered toward the lounge and I took a breath. If he had his hand down his bloody pants, I swear I was going to scream. The one thing I'd discovered since starting there was that there was nothing remotely sexy about a bunch of horny blokes gagging for a root at any cost. Honestly, it was enough to put you off sex for good and I wondered how the girls did it day in and day out.

As I collapsed into my chair, safely back behind the desk once more, Leanne gave me a worried glance. "Um, I think that's your mobile going off."

Above the grunts and groans emanating from the lounge, I too recognized the sound of my phone. Damn it, I'd meant to turn the bloody thing off before I started my shift. I pulled out my phone and looked at the caller display. *Fuck.* My heart practically stopped dead in my chest.

"What's wrong, petal?" asked Leanne, clearly alarmed at my pallor.

I shot her a panicked look. "It's Brad!"

Instantly, she summed up the situation.

"Here, quick, run out the back and into the alley. It's a bit quieter out there."

I didn't need to be told twice and bolted for the relative haven of the laneway that ran behind the arcade. Slamming the door shut behind me, I lifted the phone to my ear.

"Brad, hi. What's wrong?" I panted, trying to calm my racing heart.

Through the closed door behind me came a muffled burst of angry hooker — Scarlett, I think.

"Nothing's wrong, I was just wondering what time you were coming home, that's all. Bloody hell, what on earth is going on there? Sounds like someone's getting murdered or something."

I forced a laugh. "Oh, it's just a woman getting an injection. Yellow fever, I think. A nasty one, apparently. Poor girl. It doesn't help that Dr. Chisholm's a sadist, either," I whispered. "As you can hear it's bedlam around here. Dr. Fairweather is off sick and there are people everywhere. At the rate things are going around here, I don't think I'll be finished for ages yet and I promised Trudy I'd pop over and see her afterward."

"Oh, okay then. Well, in that case you won't mind if I nick off to the club and have a drink with Danno?"

I let out a sigh of relief. "No, of course not. Stay as long as you like. God, the way things are, it's going to take half the night to clear the place. I probably won't be home until closer to midnight, anyway."

"All right. I'll see you later on."

"No problems."

I turned the phone off, closed my eyes and slumped back against the door. My heart was practically bursting from my chest and my legs were shaking. *Shit, that was a close one.* I felt sick to think of what would have happened if one of the girls had got to my phone first.

At least if he was down at the club, he wouldn't notice that I was working a damn sight later than I usually did at the surgery. I knew I couldn't keep using Trudy's tragic love life as an excuse for coming in at all hours. No, I needed to mix them up a little. Maybe I could pretend the surgery was extending its hours until midnight?

Taking a few deep breaths, I pulled myself together and made my way inside.

Back at the reception desk, Leanne was furiously tapping a pen on the side of the phone. She looked more than a little annoyed.

"Ten dollars!" she yelled into the phone. "That's not even enough to get you a hand shake and a boot up the arse, sonny, so I suggest you go back to your bloody X-Box before I ring your parents and let them know what you've been up to. Oh, *really*? I hate to break this to you, but we have caller display and I *do* know your number."

Slamming down the phone, Leanne looked across at me and winked, trying not to smile. "Well, that got rid of the little bastards! Bloody kids. Damn nuisance they are, especially when we're flat out like tonight. Jeez, these ones couldn't have been any older than thirteen. Still, I reckon they'll be sweating it for the next hour or two."

Noting my grim expression, Leanne frowned. "Everything all right now?"

"Yes, thank God, but it was a close one."

Leanne smiled. "Let me guess, your other half hasn't got a clue about your job here."

I shook my head. "God, no! He'd go mental if he found out. He thinks I'm working late at the doctors' surgery."

Leanne raised her eyebrows. "Really, it's not as though you're working on the other side or anything."

"Doesn't matter. Believe me, he'd freak."

"Well, in that case, you'd better be careful then. Have you got someone to cover for you?"

"Yes, my cousin. She was the one who got me the job in the first place."

Trudy was the perfect alibi, considering Brad generally avoided her, knowing what she really thought of him. It was weird, really, because at first they'd seemed to get on all right but a month or two before we moved in together, something happened, some kind of argument and since then they'd barely spoken to each other. Neither of them would let on what it was all about. At the time, I got the impression it was some comment Brad had made concerning a friend of Trudy's.

"Brooke, I hope you don't mind me saying this, but I think maybe you should tell your fellow about this. From experience, I know that while he might be a bit shocked at first, he'll get over it eventually. But, on the other hand, if he finds out you've been lying to him, it can only end in tears."

Of course she was right, but it didn't change matters. Had this been any other situation, I would have been the first to agree, but as things stood between Brad and me at the moment, telling him was out of the question. The only consolation was this job was only temporary. As soon as I got that damn phone bill under control, I was out of here. So, as long as I was careful, Brad would be none the wiser. I'd be out of debt and off the hook and we'd live happily ever after.

"Thanks for the advice, but I think I'll take my chances there. He works in a law firm and any hint of a scandal would reflect badly on him."

Leanne was continuing to frown.

"I'll be careful, I promise. No one will know. And, besides, I can pretty well guarantee that no one I know would ever visit a place like this."

"I wouldn't be too sure of that. You'd be surprised. We get all types come in to see the girls. Married, single, uni students, old men living in nursing homes... And as far as professions go, you're looking at everything from factory workers to judges."

I'm sure Leanne was right, but still I wasn't worried. So long as I kept a low profile and didn't do anything stupid, like leaving my mobile switched on, I felt confident that I could pull it off.

By the time I left Heavenly Pleasures, it was just after midnight. Leanne was staying on until two, but seeing as things had finally settled down, she told me to go home and get some sleep. Thank God for that. I was completely knackered and couldn't for the life of me imagine how the girls managed it night after night.

Climbing into bed some twenty minutes later, I found Brad curled up against my pillow snoring softly and I smiled.

No matter what Leanne and Trudy said, it was worth the risk.

Chapter Twelve

"You know your mum came into the salon today?" Trudy said guardedly, pouring me a glass of wine.

I moved over, making room for her on the lounge.

"Really? She didn't mention anything about it to me. I only spoke to her an hour or two ago."

Not that Mum visiting Trudy at the salon was all that unusual. Although my parents now lived up the coast, Trudy had always cut mum's hair. Granted, she did it for free so Mum was happy to make the ninety-minute drive down, but still I wondered what the big deal was.

Trudy looked a little uncomfortable. "*So*, she came in to give me something."

Intrigued, I looked at Trudy questioningly. "To give you something? Like what? Your birthday was months ago!"

"Like this," she said, handing me a small blue book with faint silver writing across the cover. At first glance, it looked like one of those romance novels Mum was so fond of.

A little perplexed, I took a sip of my wine. "What is it?"

"Just look at it, will you."

I did and almost choked on my wine. It was a wedding etiquette book.

"Oh, I don't believe it!" I gasped.

For a brief moment, I was torn between amusement and rage before eventually settling for the latter. In the space of less than two seconds, I was furious, first of all at my mother for insinuating that Trudy was incapable of being my bridesmaid without her guidance and then at myself for putting up with her interfering all these years. Would I never be allowed to grow up? And poor Trudy. I almost combusted from shame. Christ, the audacity of my mother never ceased to amaze and dismay me.

"Oh, Trudy, I'm so sorry."

And I was. Jesus, between Brad's mother with her damn bowling club and my mother with her etiquette, I was almost ready to consider eloping. What bothered me most was the horrible suspicion that this was only the beginning of my woes. Lurking in the back of my mind was the very real fear that the two of them might decide to join forces and, believe me, my life wouldn't be worth living if that were to happen. One mother was bad enough, but the two of them together on my back — well, it didn't bear thinking about.

With this in mind, I'd have to do something, and soon.

Alas, this was a problem I was all too familiar with and I knew it was going to be tough. Had I been blessed with other siblings, at least I would have had someone to commiserate with, someone to help shoulder the burden of shame when at times — like now — my parents did something truly indefensible. Well, my mother at least. My poor father, God love him, had discovered years ago that my mum was a force to be reckoned with and any attempt to control her was a wasted endeavor.

"Tell me, did she say anything at the time, or just slip it to you like she slipped that booklet on becoming a woman into my school bag when I was twelve?" I asked, gritting my teeth. It was one thing for mum to try to control my life, but I objected when she started on my friends.

Trudy fell about the place, laughing. "Oh, wow, I'd almost forgotten about that. Now *that* was hilarious."

"No, it wasn't," I cried. "How can you of all people possibly say that? It was horrific and I still haven't forgiven her for it either."

Not even the passage of time could erase the memory of what had to be easily the single most embarrassing moment of my life thus far. And this is coming from someone who could make embarrassing themselves into an Olympic event.

Suddenly I was right smack-bang back in the middle of second period history. Alas, I remembered it like it was only yesterday. I opened my bag to retrieve my pencil case and, in a moment that will stay with me until the grave, that wretched book fell out on the floor, only to be seized upon by Dean Edwards, the class jerk, who then proceeded to read out loud the hideously embarrassing contents, including references to menstrual cycles, hygiene hints and sanitary napkins. It took poor ruby-faced Mr. Caruthers almost twenty minutes to regain control over the class again, but unfortunately the damage was already done. I was labeled the Personal Hygiene Chick. Or PHC for short.

The stigma from that one incident stayed with me for months and every time Dean walked past me, he asked me if I was a woman yet. Never mind a woman – had I been a bloke, I would have gladly smashed his leering face in.

"Well, she said that I might find it helpful, seeing as I'm chief bridesmaid – just to save me from making any embarrassing faux pas."

"The bloody cheek of her," I cried, my outrage building. "Ever since we decided on a date..."

"A week ago!" grinned Trudy.

I groaned, throwing my head into my hands. "Oh, God, has it only been a week? I don't want to think about what she'll be like by October. Between her and Brad's bloody mother, I swear I'm going mental. Would you believe she's already started on about the church, to Brad?"

Trudy's eyes twinkled as she tried to smother a smile. "That can't be good, surely?"

"Well, thank God he isn't too worried either about us not having a church wedding. He said he was happy to leave it up to me."

"Great. Well, what's the problem, then?"

"It might be just my imagination, mind, but I get the impression that she isn't going to let up on the whole church thing. Mum is trying to get to him and I don't want to think what'll happen if she manages to get him on her side."

"I wouldn't worry about that too much. Somehow, I can't see Brad caving in to your mother's demands."

"I know, but I can't believe she would go behind my back and try to get Brad on her side. It is so manipulative – even by her standards. And don't let me get started on Brad's bloody mother."

By the time I'd finished filling Trudy in on the entire bowling club fiasco, she was as angry as me about it all.

"It's your wedding and, considering you guys are paying for it, just tell them both to butt out, for God's sake. Anyway, they can't *make* you do anything. You're not a little girl anymore and I think you should start by telling them that, starting with your mother."

"That's easy for you to say. You're not the one who has to face up to her." I miserably, pictured the all too familiar tight, wounded expression of disapproval that always sent torrents of guilt pouring into my conscience. I could almost hear my mother's voice ringing in my ears. *Ten years we prayed to God to bless us with a baby. Ten years of disappointment we suffered until the day you were born. It was the happiest day of my life. Seeing you happily married will be the icing on the cake.*

I'd heard it all before and it just killed me. Talk about pressure.

"Hey, but enough of this. How about you get those bridal mags out and I'll grab some chips and the rest of the wine. Becky will be home soon and I'm sure between the three of us we can come up with something that will be guaranteed to turn both Brad's mum and your mum's hair gray. Maybe a druid priestess or an Elvis impersonator to perform the ceremony?" she suggested, a mischievous glint in her eye.

By the time Brad pulled up out the front to collect me, some four hours later, I was twisted drunk. The only excuse I could come up with for my sudden alcoholic splurge was my mounting anxiety over my mother and the wedding in general— together with my secret new job that had to remain that way. It had been a stressful week, after all. But regardless of my motives, by then there were magazines scattered all over Trudy's lounge room floor and at least four empty wine bottles together with the crumbs that had survived our savage chip attack.

Sadly, despite our high spirits, we were still no closer to coming up with a possible location for the wedding. It had been a good night, mind you, with Trudy and Becky being far more interested in hearing my exciting tales of brothel life and middle-aged hookers than veils, bridesmaid's dresses and wedding rings.

Trudy, especially, was riveted. The whole 'secret sex' business had her completely intrigued. "How many guys, guys we know, say, do you reckon have visited a prostitute at some time in their life?" she pondered after a couple of glasses of vino.

It wasn't something I had ever considered. Until the last few days, I would have said hardly any. Sure, some guys might go for a while without a girlfriend, but I had overheard more than my fair share of masturbation jokes in the club bar after Brad's football games to know that guys didn't blink an eye at taking care of business themselves. Besides, most of the fellows I knew would see it as a gross insult to their ego to have to pay for sex, like admitting they were total losers when it came to the seduction game and therefore were down to paying some chick to root them. Humiliation at its worst.

But then I thought of Paul. Nice-looking Paul who didn't seem at all embarrassed to request thirty minutes of sex with the slightly less than alluring Angel. He hadn't been ugly or old or, to my eye, lacking in any social graces. In fact, I had to admit, he seemed really nice. Someone I'd find attractive myself if I wasn't engaged to Brad. Surely he was capable of finding a woman to have a relationship with?

It was about at this point of the evening — post-schoolgirl giggling but just prior to the onset of syllable slurring — that Trudy came up with another one of her legendary pearls of wisdom — or so it seemed at the time, anyway, after a bottle and a half of cheap Chablis. This latest gem pertained to her theory that to a male psyche, visiting a prostitute for sex was considered akin to one of us girls sneaking out to the local Indian takeaway for a chicken marsala, cucumber raita and cheese naan bread when a perfectly functional frying pan and spice rack languished unused and neglected at home. Sure, it was shameless and slovenly, but it filled a need despite the inherent risk of contracting food poisoning or VD.

At this point I vaguely recalled suggesting that she should give up the hairdressing trade and join a Confucian monastery where she could contemplate the meaning of life and write great works of philosophy. Or, failing that, greeting cards and calendars.

Like I said, I was fairly legless at the time.

Guttered, actually.

* * * *

I woke the next morning feeling like shit. *What on earth had I been drinking last night?* I stared into the backs of my eyeballs, trying to ignore the lightning bolts of pain ricocheting off my screaming retinas. Overnight, my mouth had transformed itself into a cat litter tray and I tried unsuccessfully to work up some saliva to lubricate my swollen dry tongue. *Yuk!* As for the state of my head, I didn't feel up to compiling a damage report just yet, but suffice to say I was drowning in the morning-after horrors.

Of course, it was all Trudy's fault. Every time we got together, she seemed to lead me astray, usually with the result that I'd spend the remainder of the night with my head in the toilet bowl trying to blot out Brad's accompanying lecture condemning what he considered to be my adolescent behavior. Maybe he was right. I was getting too old for this kind of torment. Unfortunately, my rampant hangover was the least of my problems that morning and, although I was convinced my head was about to detonate, I knew it was time to take some kind of stand with my mother.

Three painkillers and a gallon of brain-cell-reviving water later, I felt sufficiently hydrated to face the unenviable task of confronting my mother. I picked up the phone. I put the phone back down before picking it up again. Why was I such a coward? My hands were shaking as I punched in her number. I prayed it was simply nerves rather than the onset of DTs.

"Mum, we need to talk," I announced bravely after getting all the usual pleasantries out of the way. This had to be done and the sooner the better. And, besides, considering the state I was currently in, I was fairly certain that not even Mum's legendary martyr*ish* sulks could possibly make me feel any worse than I did already.

"About what, dear?"

I took a deep breath. Here goes. "It's about my wedding..."

On the other end of the line I heard a very un-Mum-like squeal and I recoiled painfully as her shrill voice threatened to splice my head clean in two.

"Oh, Brooke," she cried out in delight, "I was wondering when you were going to ask me about it."

"Sorry," I stumbled, slightly confused, battling a sudden attack of nausea.

"Oh, darling! I've been keeping it a surprise, but I suppose now is as good a time as any to tell you."

A feeling of cold dread rolled over me. My mother and surprises never boded well. "Tell me what?"

Maybe she and Dad were migrating to Finland or setting out on a walking holiday around Australia and this was the last time I'd hear from her for months? Was it possible? No, I couldn't be that lucky.

"Oh, this is so exciting," she cried.

I heard the rush of the ocean in my ears and seriously feared I was about to throw up. "Mum, what?" I gasped, willing myself not to spew.

"Oh, Brooke, darling, I've been waiting twenty-six years to tell you…"

Oh, please let it be that I'm adopted!

"That it would make me the happiest mother alive to watch you walk down the aisle on your wedding day in the very same wedding dress I married your father in!'

No, it had to be a joke, a nightmare, the DTs. Please, God!

Mum, of course, being genetically immune to subtlety, took my silence entirely the wrong way.

"I know how you feel, sweetie," she sniffed. "Believe me, I got a little choked up myself when I lifted the dress out of its box a couple of months ago to get it dry cleaned. You won't believe how well it came up. And I must say it is every bit as beautiful now as it was the day I married your father."

The room started spinning. *This cannot be happening to me.* I was supposed to be making it clear to her I was not going to be bullied in respect of my own wedding, and now this?

"Isn't it wonderful? Think about it, Brooke, it's like a family heirloom. Well, at least it will be after you wear it for your big day, and who knows? If you have a daughter of your own one day, you can pass it down to her to wear on her big day as well!"

In my opinion, that was as good a reason as any not to have children at all. How could I possibly inflict this mad woman on to some poor innocent baby? Child cruelty, that was what it would amount to.

"I can't wait to see you in it. I'm sure you'll be absolutely beautiful. Oh, darling, I can't tell you how happy I am right now. It's like a dream come true," she continued, oblivious to my horrified silence.

So it is true. One person's dream is another's nightmare.

Or perhaps it was just me?

Just say no, a voice inside my head screamed out. And, now, quickly, before it's too late. I opened my mouth, but nothing came out.

"Mind you, I was quite a few pounds lighter than you when I got married," she continued with her customary tact, though clearly delighting in the fact she was still a dress size smaller than me.

"But, then, girls these days all seem to be a little, well, *stouter* than they were in my day. I read somewhere recently it's to do with the hormones they inject into chickens. Fancy that."

Oh, great, now I'm obese as well.

"But you are not to worry about that, dear. I've lined up your Aunty Pat to do the alterations and she thinks if she adds a panel or two of lace she should manage to fit you into it."

"Not Aunty Pat!" I squeaked in alarm. *No, please, have mercy.*

"Yes, of course, dear. You don't think I would let just *anyone* work on your wedding dress, do you?"

I was revisited by a nightmarish memory of standing on Aunty Pat's dining room table, rigid with fear. Every year I suffered her ill-placed pins in silent agony while she fitted my school uniforms, dancing costumes and, even worse, when I was asked to be flower girl for some distant cousin on my father's side. By the time I followed the blushing bride down the aisle, I swear to God I looked like a cross between the Scarecrow *and* Dorothy from the *Wizard of Oz*. A one-girl traveling freak show!

Oh, God, it was official now. I was in wedding hell.

"Mum, I...I..."

"I know, darling. There's no need to thank me really. Just seeing you in that dress will be all the thanks I need. But I really do think you should come up for a fitting in the next few weeks. We wouldn't want to leave it all to the last minute now, would we? And besides, Aunty Pat's getting on a bit and her eyes aren't as sharp as they used to be."

I bet her pins are, though. She's probably sharpening them as we speak.

Oh, fuck, could this nightmare possibly get any worse?

"I'd love to stop and chat, but you've caught me on the hop, I'm afraid. I've joined this wonderful poetry group and we have a meeting at the leisure center in, oh dear, twenty minutes. But before I go, dear, I've got more exciting news. I can't believe I almost forgot. It must be the excitement of the dress and all, but, anyway, I know just how busy you and Brad are so I've spoken to Father Brockway for you and you'll be relieved to know that he is free for the first of October. Isn't that just wonderful news? Anyway, have to go darling. Ta-ta."

And with that the line went dead.

Oh, God. Oh, holy Jesus. What the fuck just happened?

It felt as though I'd been mown down by a herd of wild buffalo and left bleeding and battered, wondering where the fuck they'd come from.

One five-minute phone call to my mother and my entire wedding if not my life was in ruins. From my dreams of a classic hand-beaded damask and pearl wedding gown, it now appeared that I would be wearing a frothy, frilly, flouncy nightmare-from-the-eighties fashion faux pas, complete with big satin bows and padded shoulders, *and* being married by Father Drool himself.

I wanted to die.

Chapter Thirteen

After listening patiently to my latest tale of woe, Trudy put a comforting arm around me, her face set in a grim line. "Well, honey, the way I see it, you haven't any other option."

"What do you mean?"

"Well, you're simply going to have to pay a hit man to take her out, I'm afraid."

I looked at her aghast.

Trudy shrugged, not at all perturbed by the expression of horror on my face. "Honestly, no one would blame you and I can't imagine there's a court in the country that would convict you under the circumstances."

"Please, this is serious, Trudy!" Although the idea *was* rapidly beginning to grow on me. *Sick, eh?*

"Sorry, hon." She shrugged, trying to suppress a smile.

"I can't believe she wants me to wear that horrible... Oh, God, I can't even bear to think about it. Brad will take off in fright if he claps eyes on me wearing that car crash of a dress."

The salon was packed, not the best time to walk in and land this on her, but what could I say? I was desperate and, not for the first time, it dawned on me that I didn't really have anyone else to turn to.

Leanne, with her eclectic fashion sense, might be offended or, worse still, mystified by my abhorrence of floral nylon and lace and Sophie would simply think I was ready for the nut house or, horror of horrors, realize my 'glamorous' life was indeed a sham. Most of my other friends from school had gradually drifted away in the past couple of years since I'd started going out with Brad—apart from Trudy, who refused to be intimidated by anyone, least of all Brad with his golf membership and wine appreciation pretenses.

God love her, she really was my last life line. This was awful. I had turned into Nigella-no friends. I was a loser, and God, a loser with a psycho mother possessing a nauseating fashion sense and a morbid desire to inflict it on her only child.

"Brooke, I *am* serious. It so happens that I've had the misfortune to see your parents' wedding photo and, believe me, it should have been a hanging offense to wear that dress the first time around, not to mention your father's brown velvet suit! Jesus, just what kind of drugs were they on at the time?"

"Ha ha." It was the drugs my mum was *currently* on that were of more concern to me.

"Seriously, you are really going to have to tell her. The church was bad enough, but this, Christ, this is ten times worse."

"I know. But she'll be shattered. Trudy, you weren't there. You didn't hear her going on and on about it.

Honestly, anyone would think she was bestowing the secret of the universe on me."

"Instead of the world's most revolting wedding dress, you mean?"

"What am I going to do?"

"Tell her. You'll have to and soon. The longer you put it off, the harder it'll be, you know."

A few minutes later, Trudy saw her client to the door and came out the back where I was sitting staring glumly into a cup of coffee.

"I feel like calling the entire thing off, I do. Not even the prospect of being Mrs. Brooke Cooper is worth this kind of torment."

Trudy put her arm around me. Despite my misery, it occurred to me that I was forever dumping my problems on her and I felt terrible.

"I'm so sorry, Trudy. I hate whinging to you all the time and you must be so sick of me coming in here when you're busy and bringing the mood down?"

She dismissed my concerns with a wave of her hand. "How about you make yourself useful then, and gather up some towels and put them in the washer."

Looking around at the chaos that surrounded me, I felt a wave of guilt. "I know you're flat out. I shouldn't be here bothering you with this," I muttered, scooping up an armful of towels.

Trudy winked before smiling back. "Hey, don't worry, for most of the clients, this is *the* only excitement they get. And believe me, lately your life is more drama-filled than *Neighbours*."

I smiled weakly. Yes, my life was turning into a soap opera. It was nothing to be proud of, though.

"I have an idea."

Oh, please, make it a good one, I prayed. Not that the hit man concept wouldn't have solved quite a few of my problems, but it might have proved a little difficult to explain to Dad why Mum had to die because of a wedding dress.

"Granted, it's not brilliant, but under the circumstances it's worth a try."

"What is it?" I asked, fully aware of the desperation leaking from my voice.

"What if I ask my mum to have a little chat to your mum, you know, sister to sister. It couldn't hurt."

"Do you think she'd do it?"

She was my only chance and I prayed that Trudy's mum, my Aunty Tina, would come to my rescue.

Trudy laughed. "Are you kidding? Did you ever see the bridesmaid dress your mother made *her* wear?"

I nodded. She'd looked as though she was wearing a bedspread with tassels.

"Well, I suspect Mum has waited for thirty-two years to get some revenge. Trust me when I tell you she doesn't want to be revisited by the sight of that hideous dress any more than you do."

Chapter Fourteen

"Scarlett, you can't sit out here. Prue will be popping in sometime this afternoon and she'll sack you if she catches you."

"Fuck off, moonbeam. I'll bloody well sit here if I want to, so bugger off!" came Scarlett's venomous reply.

Across the client lounge, the sounds of elicit shagging that had until recently been emanating throughout the brothel from *Barbara's Backdoor Boudoir* was now replaced by Oprah's nasally voice welcoming some over-inflated Hollywood starlet onto her show, eager to waffle on about her ten-year battle with drugs and depression and her amazing recovery to conquer the world stage again in her Oscar-nominated new film. Bloody show-off!

Leanne walked back into reception, shaking her head in despair. "What are we going to do with her?"

We? My stomach churned with growing apprehension. I didn't like the implication that Leanne considered Scarlett's defection from the kitchen to the client lounge a shared responsibility. The thought of confronting Scarlett in her current mood quite frankly scared the shit out of me.

"I don't know," I whispered back, casting a worried glance in the direction of the lounge. Right then the only buffer between us and Scarlett's psychotic rage was a flimsy beaded curtain and I didn't fancy my chances of walking out of there unscathed if push came to shove and I was called upon to evict her.

Half an hour earlier, the tension that had been steadily brewing all afternoon between the girls out the back erupted into a full-on, hair-pulling free-for-all catfight. The violence that followed had been terrifying. Chairs were scattered, coffee upended and more than a few strands of hair unrooted. Had it not been for Leanne's intervention separating the two warring factions, it might have ended up as a bloodbath out there in the kitchen.

And all this over a dress!

In all fairness, it wasn't just any old dress, but a stunning black designer dress Prue had sent up from Sydney last night especially for JoJo.

The main trouble was that the other girls had had no idea that Prue had secured a booking for JoJo to spend the night at some flash Sydney hotel with an A-list American actor currently in the country to promote his new film. Through a contact of hers in Sydney, Prue had pulled off the coup of the century when she had been asked to supply him with her best girl — or JoJo, as it happened. Probably not surprisingly, he was also the same actor currently caught up in a messy divorce from his equally famous wife on the grounds of his well-documented serial adultery, a lot of it with hookers.

All would have remained peaceful in Prue's house of carnal pleasure had JoJo chosen to follow Prue's advice on the matter and not advertised her stroke of luck to the other girls. JoJo, being JoJo, had decided to disregard this and flounced her way into the kitchen wearing the aforementioned designer dress, effectively starting World War Three.

It was only then that the screaming and shouting that infiltrated through to the reception area alerted Leanne and me to the trouble brewing out the back.

I'll say this for Leanne, if she ever decided to change professions she really ought to consider a career as a bouncer. I was very impressed. Not only did she succeed in physically separating the warring hookers, but thanks to her quick thinking, the dress escaped unscathed, as did JoJo. I would hate to think what would have happened had Leanne not gone through to sort them out when she did. One thing was for sure, someone's head would have been on a pike if JoJo had turned up to her once-in-a-lifetime booking sporting a black eye.

"When *is* Prue coming in?" I whispered, glancing toward the beaded curtain anxiously.

Leanne shrugged. "Dunno. But, knowing Prue, she could be here at any moment."

This wasn't good. Prue expected us to keep the front end of the business running smoothly. It was part of the job description. What the girls did in the privacy of the rooms out the back with their clients was their business and any problems were sorted out by Prue personally, but the money and reception were our domain and therefore, under the current circumstances, it seemed so was Scarlett. If Prue arrived to find her camped out in the client lounge, she'd go ballistic and blame us for not sorting it out.

"Maybe we could ask JoJo to apologize?" I suggested carefully for want of a better solution.

Leanne gave me an incredulous look and laughed darkly. "Yeah, righto! How about you go back there and suggest it to her then?"

Granted, it was a stupid idea, but it was the only one I could come up with under the circumstances. Thinking under pressure was not my forte.

As if we didn't have enough to worry about, the buzzer sounded, alerting us to a waiting customer. Leanne and I both froze, torn between relief that it wasn't Prue, who would have let herself in with the key, and concern that we were still no closer to figuring out how to get Scarlett out of the way.

Alarmed, Leanne scrambled to her feet, her shirt of a million tassels sending pens and booking sheets flying in all directions. "Right, Brooke, this is what we are going to do," she began, casting urgent glances from the lounge area to the door and back again as if measuring the distance for a possible escape route. For who, I don't know. Us maybe? "You answer the door and stall them for as long as possible."

"How?"

"I don't know. Just think of something and I'll see what I can do with Gandhi in there," she said, motioning to the pair of crossed ankles, presently the only part of Scarlett visible from the desk, perched defiantly atop the porn mags.

Smoothing out imaginary creases from her voluminous shirt, Leanne looked across at the lounge with an expression of fierce determination pasted on her face. "Wish me luck," she whispered grimly and, with head held high, she quickly disappeared through the beaded curtain into enemy territory and I sent up a prayer for her safe return.

Once at the door, I checked the security screen and to my relief found it was Paul on the other side. It had been a couple of weeks since I'd stumbled through that first introduction and I experienced a pang of pride that he'd returned. I must have done something right—or at least Angel had.

Just like his previous visit, he was wearing jeans and a neatly ironed shirt, this one white, opened loosely at the collar and like last time he was carrying a smart leather satchel. Very respectable and thankfully no sign of chest hair or chunky gold jewelry, I noted with relief, unlike the last fellow in here who'd sported more gold plate than a Wimbledon champion.

As I opened the door, his face brightened into a smile of recognition. "Hello again," he said cheerfully. "It's Brooke, isn't it?"

I smiled back and nodded, strangely flattered to find that he had remembered my name. "Yes, it is. You have a good memory. Please come in."

"Thank you. By the way, my name is Paul."

His smile lingered and I found myself looking away, pretending to wipe away an imaginary mark on my arm.

"So you survived your baptism of fire then," he continued. "I didn't expect you to stick it out."

I gawped. "You didn't? Jesus, was I that bad?"

Paul laughed. "No, not at all. I was just surprised to see someone as sweet as you in a place like this."

"Um, what?"

"Well, you look like you would be more at home working in a nice city office with views of the bay."

"Well, a girl can dream, but instead, here I am surrounded by porn mags and X-rated movies. Lucky me!" I replied.

"*Or* lucky me," Paul capped.

The drama in the next room was forgotten. My face began to heat and a pleasant warmth seeped throughout my body.

A brief moment of silence started my heart racing as Paul continued to look steadily into my eyes.

Oh, God, this was awkward. And also rapidly getting out of hand. What the hell was wrong with me? I knew I had to take back some control over my rampant hormones, assuring myself it was stress sending me stupid. Stress, and nothing else.

Taking a deep breath, I straightened and looked Paul right in the eye. "Anyway, Paul, how may we help you today?" My best professional voice should pull the focus back to the business at hand.

He smothered a grin. "Well, I'd like a half-hour booking again, if possible."

"Certainly. No problems," I announced confidently, belying the mini-panic whirring in my chest.

Sneaking an anxious glance over toward the lounge, I could hear Leanne's and Scarlett's muted voices occasionally rising above the whoops and yahs coming from Oprah's audience and prayed for a miracle. *Stall him. That's what Leanne said. But how?*

"Um...any girl in particular?" I asked, trying to distract him from the increasingly voluble exchange happening in the adjoining room.

It was by now no secret that Scarlett was resisting any attempts by Leanne to pacify her, but to his credit Paul tactfully ignored the commotion and smiled sympathetically.

"Well, is Angel available by any chance?" he inquired.

He might well have been asking after the health of my grandmother and the irony of the situation was not lost on either of us.

"I'm afraid not," I began apologetically before Scarlett's angry voice cut in over the top of me.

"I don't give a fucking toss, moonbeam. Tell that whoring bitch that if I see her skinny arse again, I'll fucking smash her, I will!"

I bit my lip and winced. Scarlett's vitriol was potent enough to peel the paint from the walls. The situation was hopeless. There was no point pretending anymore. "I'm so sorry, Paul. We're having a little bit of a problem with one of the girls at the moment. But you've probably gathered that by now."

By the expression on his face, I could have sworn that Paul was finding the drama currently unfolding in the adjacent room quite amusing.

"Bit of a handful, is she?" he asked, suppressing a grin.

"You could say that."

Another burst of anger spewed from the lounge room and I cringed.

To my complete amazement, Paul laughed. "Hey, what the hell. I feel like a challenge today. How about I take her off your hands for half an hour?"

I stared at him for a moment completely gobsmacked. Was he mad or did he have a death wish? Oh, God, maybe he was one of those men who liked to be abused during sex? I felt decidedly queasy at the notion of Paul engaging in such perversities.

"It's just somehow I don't think she is very good company at the moment." I cleared my throat.

"Wouldn't you rather I introduce you to another girl? We have three other lovely ladies available right now. I can bring them out and introduce you to them if you like?"

Paul rubbed his chin. "No, I think she'll be fine — that is, if she's available?"

Under normal circumstances that was a sure bet, but I still couldn't shake the impression that Paul was about to bite off more than he could chew and I weighed up the chances of him being carted out of Scarlett's room in a body bag.

Taking in the worried look rapidly spreading across my face, he laughed again, leaning in to whisper, "Hey, don't worry about me. I'll look on it as a challenge. But just to be on the safe side, I might forgo the blow job today."

Oh, God help me! I was on the verge of a meltdown and my face flamed bright magenta.

"Wouldn't want to leave with less than I arrived with, would I?" He winked.

Please let me wake up now!

But, alas, this was no dream and from a distance I heard my voice politely asking Paul to wait one moment while I checked with Scarlett that she was indeed available for a booking.

A few minutes later and if Paul was surprised by Scarlett's transformation from screaming harridan to slinky sex kitten, he hid it remarkably well.

Thank Christ we were off the hook. Thanks to Paul's noble sacrifice in taming the shrew, tranquility had effectively been restored to the establishment by the time Prue arrived to ferry JoJo to her assignment half an hour later.

Chapter Fifteen

"Brooke, where is Mrs. Clarkson's file?" Dr. Chisholm barked from somewhere out in the treatment room.

"It's on your desk, Dr. Chisholm," came my somewhat puzzled reply.

Or that was where I had left it barely five minutes ago when I'd escorted Mrs. Clarkson through to see her.

It had been scarcely an hour since I'd begun my evening shift, but already Dr. Chisholm had found about a dozen things to bitch about. Honestly, how was I supposed to know that we were running low on five milliliter syringes or gauze dressings? My last shift had been three days ago. And as for the ripped magazines languishing in the waiting room, anyone would think I'd maliciously torn the pages from them myself the way she'd carried on about them only ten minutes before. I knew by that stage that it was going to be one of those shifts that seem to go on forever. Her despotic mood was even more enhanced by the fact that it was

Dr. Fairweather's night off and, in his absence, bitch-face was making the most of every opportunity to make my life hell.

This week was going from bad to downright nightmarish and I was completely exhausted. And if I didn't have enough to worry about with my mother and the whole wedding dress impasse, the previous night Brad and I had had an almighty fight about, you guessed it, the fucking bowling club. I was still fuming. I can't believe I didn't see it coming. Yes, adding to my latest woes, it seems the whole hideous concept of the bowling club was starting to grow on him. After all that crap about including his mother in the wedding and the ultimate decision being mine, he was trying to convince me to come around to the idea. To say that I was resisting was putting it mildly. Of course, being slightly premenstrual and stressed to the max, I immediately began screaming that he was turning into a big squishy mummy-loving wimp, which I'll admit didn't help to resolve matters between us and, not surprisingly, from there things went from bad to worse. It was all his damn mother's fault, the interfering old hag.

Brad's mother, *Mrs. Cooper*, was putting the pressure on him big-time and, despite being able to reduce hardened criminals to tears in the dock, he was completely spineless when it came to sticking up to a woman whose hobbies include quilt making and collecting Toby jugs. Not that I was one to talk. All day I'd been in a lather every time the phone rang, expecting to hear my mother's hurt voice ever since Trudy rang through with the good news that her mum had agreed to rescue me from the dreaded wedding dress nightmare. Two days it had been and still no word from my mother. I don't know what was worse, the thought of her hysterics or her continuing silence. I felt as though I was sitting on a time bomb and it was only a matter of time before it exploded, blowing me smack-bang into the family counseling session from hell.

Behind me, Dr. Chisholm's thick rubber soles squelched noisily across the polished linoleum floor and I groaned. In full view of everyone in the waiting room, she came to a squeaking halt beside me and I could all but feel anger bristling out from her bleak gray woolen skirt and black polo neck jumper. My shoulders tensed as I prepared myself for another serve of her vile temper.

It was then I saw it. Mrs. Clarkson's file, that was — *in her hand*. What on earth was her problem?

"Do you mean *this* file?" She waved a dog-eared manila folder about in the air not three inches from my face. Across from me, those left in the waiting room had since forgone their magazine-flicking charade and were now looking on at the unfolding scene with morbid interest.

"Um, yes?"

Her expression was poisonous, her aura toxic and I experienced a stab of trepidation deep in my belly. Speared by her steely gaze, I understood how the Christians felt just prior to the Romans releasing the lions into the Coliseum. What was going on? I didn't have to wait long to find out.

"Look closer, Brooke," she growled, thrusting the file in question into my face. It took a moment for my eyes to focus but when they did, my stomach clenched in dread.

Mrs. J. Clayton, it read.

Oh no! Not again.

"Oh, yes," responded Dr. Chisholm, correctly decoding the look of horror on my face. "Mrs. Clayton! *Not* Mrs. Clarkson. When are you going to learn how to read, Brooke?"

It was my guess that not only every patient in the waiting room heard about my latest balls-up, but every person in a four-block radius of the surgery. My face flushed hotly with embarrassment as I fought to hold back a rush of tears. How could I have got it wrong? Sure, the names were similar, but I always took extra care to check these days. Dr. Chisholm wasn't interested in my mumbled apologies, though, cutting me off mid-grovel with an impatient wave of her hand.

"Forget it. I've heard enough of your excuses for one night, Brooke. Stay behind after your shift finishes, will you? I want to have a word with you."

Granted it was a monumental cock-up, *and* all my fault, but any reasonable person would have seen the funny side of what had been an honest mistake. Not Dr. Chisholm. No! As I was soon to discover not long after the last patient walked out of the door, the proverbial shit was about to hit the fan over what, in reality, was simply a harmless little mix-up. Sure, Mrs. Clarkson, the elderly wife of one of the local councilors, had been horrified when told she was suffering from gonorrhea by Dr. Chisholm herself, having read the wrong lab results from the wrong folder. Thankfully, it only took a cup of tea and a mild sedative to calm her and reassure her it was a mistake and her listlessness and dryness *down there* were nothing more insidious than a hormone imbalance.

No harm done.

Well, I didn't think so, anyway.

A happy result, if you ask me.

"I think it best if you collect your things now and hand back your name badge," Dr. Chisholm demanded.

It wasn't a request. It was an order and in those few words I felt the end of my career as a medical receptionist rapidly approaching.

Yes, I'd been sacked!

* * * *

"Hey, what are you worrying about? You hated that bloody job," Trudy reminded me on the phone the next morning. "You said it was only one rung up the ladder from cleaning toilets for a living, except you were expected to clean the toilets as well."

I shrugged. She had a point there.

"Anyway, I remember ages ago you told me that that soon as you found something else, you were going to tell the bitch where to stick her lousy job."

"But—"

"But nothing. It's probably the best thing that could have happened under the circumstances."

"Under the circumstances?" I repeated, stunned by her lack of concern. "Trudy, I have just been sacked—again! So explain to me how this is a good thing, will you? Because I just don't get it myself."

"Isn't it obvious? Now you'll be free to work extra shifts at Heavenly Pleasures! The pay's higher and you said yourself it's much better than being bossed about by that bitch Dr. Chisholm."

I began feeling the first hint of anger at her lack of empathy. Bloody hell, if I'd wanted a sermon, I would have rung my mother. Or maybe not. "You're forgetting one vital thing here. If Brad finds out I've been sacked from the surgery, it's going to be the kiss of death for my *other* job as well, isn't it now? Remember — Brazilian phone call from hell? Drowning in debt? What am I going to use to cover for all the extra hours I've been working?"

Through the phone, I could almost see Trudy's eyes rolling back in exasperation. "*Don't tell him.* Honestly, Brooke, it's only until you get the phone bill paid off, anyway, so surely it won't kill him not to know? And it's perfect. He was already used to you working all different hours so that covers you now for possible evening work. Besides, do you really think he's going to notice?"

"Probably not," I conceded glumly.

"There you go. So far, most of your shifts at the brothel have been day shifts, anyway."

"Apart from that one the other week." Even now I cringed thinking of how close I'd come to being found out.

"Well, now you don't have to show up at the surgery, you might even be able to pick up a few more evening shifts as well. But, hey, if you're that worried about Brad finding out, you can always tell him they're having a crackdown on personal calls at the surgery, so if he needs to get through to you, to SMS your mobile."

"I suppose you're right. Besides, apart from the other night, I can't remember the last time he rang me at work. He's so wound up with this whole partnership thing at the moment he doesn't even know I'm around most of the time. The only time I get any attention from him at all is when he wants sex — and even that's not all that often these days."

Trudy cleared her throat. "God, you two sound like an old married couple already. Hey what's happened to all that kinky premarital sex you're supposed to be enjoying? You know, bondage, swinging from the chandeliers and that sort of thing?"

"Ha ha. As if," I responded. "Brad's strictly a 'meat and potatoes' kind of guy in that department. *If* you get my meaning."

I felt Trudy's shock like a sharp slap to the head through the phone and I instantly regretted bringing the subject up. Sure, it was one thing lying in bed late at night wondering if I was ever destined to experience a real-life orgasm, or maybe I had and missed it, if that was at all possible, but another confessing to my best friend and cousin that my sex life was crap. *Humiliating is what it is.* Still, I'd read somewhere that the stress of planning a wedding can have that effect on a couple. I hoped so, as I was banking on a wedding night revelation in the boudoir.

"Jesus, Brooke, what on earth is going on with you two? You're not even married yet. If it's like that now, what's it going to be like between you both in ten years' time?"

I sighed. A few years back I would have been thinking along the same lines as Trudy. Too many lonely nights at home spent watching soppy chick-flicks had nurtured an impossible ideal of nonstop passion and multiple orgasms in both Trudy and me.

Alas, over the past couple of years, my eyes had been opened to reality and I'd come to realize that life in the real world is not like a Hollywood movie. Clothes-ripping passion might sound all well and good in theory, but when I thought of all those buttons to sew back on in the morning, not to mention foraging for knickers under the lounger and on top of light fittings — well, it seems like hard work to me.

I supposed I could see what Trudy was getting at, though. Not so long ago I, too, might have been concerned about our recent less than sparkling sex life as well, but these days I was so consumed trying to come to terms with being a responsible adult and soon-to-be wife I had little time to grieve over the lack of fireworks in the boudoir.

"Hard as it might be for you to understand, Trudy, sex isn't the most important thing in a mature long-term relationship," I replied primly, trying to throw her off with a serve of rational maturity. Not something that I resorted to often, believe me.

"Oh, bullshit, Brooke! This is me you're talking to, not your mother! Sounds to me like you need to spice things up a bit. If you want my opinion, I reckon you should get some advice from some of the girls at work. I'm sure they'd let you in on a trick or two. After all, it is their area of expertise."

I was fairly sure she was joking.

At least I *hoped* so.

It was Saturday morning and Brad was at training again in preparation for the start of the footy season only a week away. So, with the morning to myself, I arranged to meet Trudy at the mall for a spot of shopping. Just the thought of browsing through the shops sent a delicious thrill racing through me. Weeks of retail abstinence had only sharpened my appetite to blow the dusk off my credit card and shop till I dropped.

This time it was legit, though. Indeed, as an added bonus, Brad had given me the green-light, so there was no need to inflict any more damage on my credit rating. This was coming out of our joint account with his blessings. *Someone ring the Vatican and report a miracle!*

And what brought on this rare act of generosity? None other than the all-important dinner party with Brad's boss. It was next weekend and he'd suggested I splash out on something special. Something guaranteed to impress.

I didn't need to be told twice. No prodding was required. I was going shopping!

A couple of hours later my earlier euphoria had mutated into abject misery. What on earth had happened to all the lovely clothes that usually leapt out at me every time I walked past a clothing store? They couldn't have all disappeared in the last few weeks, surely? Normally, everywhere I looked a dress or skirt or top shimmied seductively out from where they'd lain waiting for me and simply begged me to take them home. But today they had all gone into hiding. Sulking, no doubt. A few short weeks and I'd been cast out of the loop. I was on the outside, staring in. I had lost my retail kudos. Oh, the shame of it!

"Come on, Brooke. Surely you've seen *something* you like?"

Trudy had trodden patiently behind me through countless boutiques, listening with a sympathetic ear while I cried over the lack of anything in the least fashionable to wear, but now I'd rejected yet another dress, the cracks were beginning to appear in even her normally unyielding tolerance.

"Okay, tell me what was wrong with that last one?" she huffed.

"What was *wrong* with it? Are you blind?" I cried, throwing off the offending item that looked divine on the hanger and totally hideous on my lumpy likewise hideous body. "What kind of woman has the kind of figure that would look good in *that*?" I asked, thinking back to the way my bum had burst from the lovely mint-green fifties-style cocktail dress like a mini explosion. I'd require at least a year's worth of Pilates to pull it off. That or emergency liposuction.

"It didn't look that bad—honestly!" said Trudy, glancing down at her watch for the umpteenth time. "Look, why don't we grab something to eat? I'm starving. And anyway we'll be able to concentrate better once we've had some lunch."

"Food! How can you even think of food, Trudy? Didn't you see how fat I looked in that designer dress back at Myers? Christ, I looked like I was five months' pregnant. I swear to God, if I eat so much as a bloody dim sum I'm going to have to move on to the super-size ladies department."

"Now you're just being stupid, Brooke. And if that designer dress was a size twelve, well then I'm Miranda Kerr's identical twin sister. It's a conspiracy, I tell you. They must be in league with Jenny Craig and think sticking a size twelve tag on a size eight dress is going to result in you fleeing to the nearest diet center to be robbed of everything but your unwanted pounds."

I looked at Trudy with near desperation in my eyes. "But what am I going to do? It means a lot to Brad that everything is perfect for this dinner party and I have to find something special." I glanced down at my watch and paled. "Oh, no, the shops close in three hours!"

"Stop panicking for a start. Anyway, we've got tons of time yet."

"No we don't," I cried, battling a surge of near hysteria.

"Brooke, for God's sake!" yelled Trudy, finally losing patience. "Get a grip, will you? Jesus, you've tried on at least three dresses that would be perfect. What the hell is wrong with you today? It's only a bloody dinner party, after all!"

I took a deep breath and tried to calm down. Trudy was right, of course. When all was said and done, it *was* only a dinner party, but, still, it was a dinner party that meant a great deal to Brad and I wanted to get everything right. I wanted him to be proud of me. Of late I couldn't help feeling I was letting him down. What with having lied to him about practically everything from my credit card spending to the phone fiasco and my secret brothel job, I desperately wanted to make it up to him. I wanted to be the woman he wanted me to be. I wanted to prove that I was worthy of his love.

Poor Trudy looked about to faint with hunger and I felt awful. She was doing this out of love. A day spent trailing after me through countless boutique shops wasn't exactly her thing. Flea markets and second-hand shops were more her style. She loved uncovering a bargain, whereas to me stepping into a frock that some stranger had worn and sweated in was enough to send shivers down my spine. *Yuk.* Still, I have known Trudy to turn up some really amazing stuff as a result of her infatuation for anything old and cheap. She insists vintage clothing is the best-kept fashion secret of the last few years and while she's yet to convince me that Hollywood stars rummage through charity clothing bins, I admit she looks a million bucks all glammed up and ready to party.

"Okay, then, why don't we get something to eat and afterwards we'll go back and have another look in Myers. Maybe I missed something."

"Thank God for that! If I don't eat soon, I'm going to die!"

By the time we got back to Trudy's place, *I* was ready to die. I was practically suicidal! Nothing I'd seen all afternoon came close to being vaguely suitable for a heifer like me to be seen wearing in public. I was doomed. Or I would have been had it not been for Trudy's insisting that she had the perfect dress at home for me.

And, to my utter amazement, it was! Ivory crushed silk with tiny embroidered oyster-colored flowers fell like a silken waterfall to my calves, covering my flabby thighs and disguising all my imperfections. It was perfect. More than perfect, actually. It was a *miracle*.

"Oh, my God, I can't believe it!" I cried when Trudy pulled it from her wardrobe. "Where on earth did you find it?"

"Some lady had a second-hand clothing stall up at the artisan markets last year and I couldn't resist it. Gorgeous, isn't it?"

It was more than gorgeous. "It must have set you back a fortune!"

Trudy smiled. "Fifteen bucks!"

"No! Tell me you're joking!"

"I'm not. I've been telling you for years to give the markets and op shops a look. Honestly, I reckon I spend as much on clothes in a year as you spend in a month. No wonder you're always skint. And half that stuff you kill yourself over, you never end up wearing. Such a waste."

Trudy was right. "And are you sure you want to lend this to me?"

"Of course I am. I only wish I'd remembered it earlier. It might have saved my sanity. You know I love you to bits, but if you ever ask me to endure another afternoon like today again, I swear I'll kill you."

Jumping up from Trudy's bed, I hugged her. "You're a lifesaver, Trudy."

Chapter Sixteen

"Would you care to explain, Brooke?"

Brad stood waiting for me in the kitchen as I walked in the door, bloated with anger and clearly ready for a confrontation. Beside him on the table were a scattered mass of flyers, disassembled weekend newspapers and a few stained coffee mugs. The place was a pig sty—a pig sty that no doubt I would be expected to tidy!

I groaned inwardly, trying to summon the strength to deal with him.

"Well?" he said impatiently when I failed to respond.

"Well what?"

Oh, God, I was tired. Strangely the elation, the rush I had come to depend on as I accumulated numerous bags bulging with everything from jumpers to socks and lip gloss, remained frustratingly elusive and in its place was a sense of emptiness. For the first time I could remember, the stress of a day's shopping had taken its toll on me. All I wanted was a bath and a glass of wine to help me relax, *not* another one of his inquisitions.

His face was flushed with anger. "At least tell me how many times you have lied to me then?" he bellowed.

Something in his expression roused me from my apathy and I saw through his steely control to the raging anger simmering just below the surface. My heart practically stopped dead. The first thing that came to mind was of course Heavenly Pleasures. *Oh no.* My lungs seemed to fold up in my chest and I struggled to breathe.

I felt caught in the headlights of the truth lorry.

How could he have possibly found out? For the past few weeks, I had gone to extraordinary lengths to cover my tracks, even turning my mobile off and parking behind the arcade, making use of the private entrance to avoid any awkward chance encounters that might get reported back to Brad or my parents.

"How many times, Brooke?" he demanded, his eyes narrowing dangerously. "Or are you totally incapable of telling the truth?"

Tunnel vision obscured the item in Brad's hand and I struggled to think of something to say, something to make everything right again, something to convince him that working at Heavenly Pleasures wasn't as sordid and ugly as it sounded. Yes, I was facing an uphill battle, but what choice did I have? It was either that or stand blithely by while my relationship crumbled around me.

I jumped as Brad's hand suddenly came crashing down on the table. "At *least* tell me what was so bloody important to you that you had to go behind my back and rack up more debts on your blasted credit card?"

What?

Hope sprang from my heart in spurts of dizzy relief when I noticed the familiar blue credit card statement pinned under his palm on the table. *My credit card!* He'd stumbled across my credit card statement. *There is a God, after all!*

Ignoring my startled expression, he continued yelling. "I trusted you to get rid of those bloody cards, Brooke, and you deliberately defied me. Is it just this one or are there others I should be aware of?"

Well, if I was going to be hung for one lie, I figured I might as well make it worth the effort.

"That's the only one. I cut the others up, I promise."

The lies flowed effortlessly from my lips without any threat to my conscience. I should have been ashamed of myself, but strangely I felt nothing more than irritation that not surprisingly was directed toward Brad. *Why should I have to lie, anyway?* I was sick of walking on eggshells around him whenever the subject of money was brought up. Lately, it was like being summoned to the headmaster's office for some minor offense.

Suddenly, an image of Paul sprang to mind. Paul, with his easy-going acceptance and friendly nature. Paul the peacemaker, whose timely appearance yesterday afternoon had averted an even bigger drama, had Prue chosen to arrive a few minutes earlier.

Why couldn't Brad take a chill pill and give me a break for once? Of late it seemed he was constantly on my back for something or other and justified it with smooth talk of wanting our life together to be perfect. A tiny thought fought to gain prominence in my head. Was Brad's prefect plan worth the effort? Was I going to be able to sustain the image he'd built of me? It all seemed too hard. I wasn't perfect and the effort it required to meet Brad's lofty ideals was starting to wear me down. Again I thought of Paul. Why, I have no idea, but with his image, I felt the twist of anger toward Brad grow into full-blown resentment.

"So what if I did keep one lousy credit card?" I yelled back. "I am not a fucking teenager anymore and, quite frankly, you're not my bloody father. Did I ask you to pay them off in the first place? *No!* And I'm sure as hell not asking you to pay them off now, am I?"

Brad could only stare back at me, stunned, his anger frozen solid on his reddening face. This was clearly not the reaction he'd anticipated from me and he had no response to hand for my unexpected burst of self-righteousness.

"*And,*" I continued, my anger gaining momentum, "while we're on the subject of crossing the line, just what the hell were you doing opening my mail in the first place?"

For a moment there, I thought I had him on the grounds of personal privacy and civil liberties. After all, no one lived with a lawyer for as long as I had and not pick up some impressive tit-bits of legal terminology. It didn't last long and his countenance once again resumed its original haughty expression.

"Well, now you mention it, I *thought* it was a response from the bank to the loan inquiry I made the other week," he responded smugly.

I felt as though someone had deflated me like a beach ball. All my bravado gushed from my body.

"What loan inquiry?" I asked weakly.

"I wanted it to be a surprise," he snapped, skewering me with his anger. "I thought that once we had a clear idea of the amount we could borrow, we'd finally be able to start looking around for a place of our own. Of course, at the time, I *thought* our financial situation was stable enough to commit to a mortgage. Until *this* came up, that is," he stated, waving the credit statement in front of him as if it was exhibit A and he was a Queen's Counsel.

I was exhausted, mentally as well as physically. All my heartfelt promises to Brad and solemn pledges that I would curb my immature urge to spend money came back to me in a flash of shame. I remembered then how nice it had been to be finally freed of debt, to feel looked after and taken care of. All I could see was the hurt in Brad's face and that I'd let him down — again!

"I'm so sorry, Brad. Really, I am."

And with those words, the stress and tiredness of the past couple of weeks caught up with me and I burst into tears. Instantly, Brad's previous anger fled and he moved in to comfort me, holding me close and murmuring gentle words of reproach into my hair.

I hated myself for caving in, but right then I felt helpless to defend myself in the face of his brutal logic and knew that even if I did stick to my guns, I would only end up feeling guilty for the tension that has sprung up between us again.

Within an hour, my little uprising was effectively suppressed. Brad's lecture was at last concluded and I was left suitably chastised. But I couldn't help asking myself why, in that moment of anger, my thoughts had gone of their own volition to Paul, and perhaps even more baffling was why he had ignited such a rage in me toward Brad. At least Brad didn't sleep with hookers. He was clever and responsible and, most of all, he loved me. Sure he might be a mite overbearing and uptight at times, but his heart was in the right place — wasn't it?

Later that night, as we cuddled up together in bed, I couldn't help thinking about the conversation Trudy and I had shared on the phone earlier in the day, the one concerning my less than sizzling sex life. It was difficult to admit, but, yes, she did have a point. It did seem as though it was a little too early in our relationship for the sparkle to fade—like twenty years too early.

We weren't even newlyweds yet but I felt as though we'd already settled into middle-age! I know I said before that sex wasn't that high on my priority list, but still sometimes I wondered just what it was that I seemed to be missing out on.

Brad's warm body pressed against mine and I wondered just what it was that the likes of Scarlett and Angel did that kept Paul coming back week after week. Granted, they were professionals and I was a mere amateur, but still I wondered if there was some beginners' guide to eroticism out there, *apart* from that godawful relic the *Karma Sutra*. Love manual? Yeah, right. Trudy had bought a copy a few years back for a joke—apparently—and I swear I'd have to be a contortionist with a vagina in my bloody navel to master some of those positions. They appeared to be anything but pleasant and I half-expected to find a health warning attached together with a contact number for the nearest chiropractor.

But, in all seriousness, I doubted the girls at work would see it as a definitive book on sex. Anyway, by her own admission Scarlett was up for anything and, lending credibility to her claim, the girls often referred with a sense of awe to the arsenal of vibrators, handcuffs, floggers, butt plugs and other instruments of torture—or pleasure, depending on one's preference—that she carted around in her large carry-all bag. Whether these were for her clients or herself I had no idea and quite frankly I didn't want to know. But I was getting ahead of myself here. *One small step at a time.*

I couldn't say I had ever been one to *really* initiate sex. Until now, this had suited me just fine. In some ways, I kind of liked the feeling of being desired, yearned for, pursued like the heroines in those racy bodice-ripping novels who lay back in a swoon and allowed themselves to be ravished by the dark, mysterious Count Raven.

In hindsight, though, my passive approach toward sex could have stemmed from laziness or perhaps inexperience on my behalf. Not that I'd exactly been a virgin when I'd met Brad. I mean, I was, like, twenty-two by then. A grown woman. Jesus, even my mother had been married by the time she was twenty-two. But I suppose my experience was limited to two *very* short-term relationships. Micro-relationships, in fact. One of them lasted only a solitary weekend. Well, if I'm totally honest, six and a half hours, stretching from Saturday night to early Sunday morning until the numerous Tia Marias wore off. Even then, the only sex we had was in the back seat of his car. Not particularly conducive to wild uninhibited lovemaking, especially when taken into account that he drove a Ford Laser. Christ, it was a miracle I hadn't had to resort to the Jaws of Life to extract myself after the deed was done.

Maybe Trudy was right, after all. Maybe it *was* time to spice things up between us, or at least try to.

Reaching out to Brad in the dark, I ran my hand across his hard, smooth chest noticing as I did his heart beating strongly beneath my fingertips. Very Harlequin romance, I know, but in the dead of the night, I experienced an almost magical connection to this man who in a matter of months was going to become my lawfully wedded husband and it stirred something within me.

Stiffening under my palms, his nipples began to respond to my caresses, sending a shiver of excitement throughout my body, encouraging me to explore further. I knew by his erratic breaths that he was wide awake, despite the stillness of his body. Emboldened by this, I continued to gently stroke the contours of his torso before gradually moving lower down his body.

Suddenly I was desperate to elicit some kind of passion in him, something that would stir an erotic response within him. Various scenes from the porn flicks at work flashed through my head and I found myself picturing us intertwined together in a haze of lust, sucking and licking and moaning, exploring every coveted inch of each other's flesh without any sense of inhibition and oblivious to everything else but our own carnal pleasure.

Very gently I brushed my hand over his pajama-clad groin, delighted to feel his hardening flesh straining against the fabric. Brad's breathing was coming in little short gasps and at that moment I knew for perhaps the first time what it was to feel that particularly heady mix of power and desire.

Now, usually at this point in time, Brad would roll me over, swiftly taking his pleasure while I wriggled around a bit and faked some semblance of enthusiasm. But not tonight. Tonight I was determined to experience something for myself and, for that to happen, I knew I'd have to send him a message that I was up for a little more adventure.

Quickly, I discarded my nightie and rolled on top of him as a wicked thought worked its way into mind.

"Brad," I murmured gently into his ear.

"Mmm," he responded drowsily.

"Let me blindfold you," I whispered above the sound of my heart pounding.

Brad sucked his breath in and licked his lips. "Why?" He was surprised, shocked even, but still I felt him hardening against my thigh.

Quickly I located a scarf and returned to him. By now Brad was clearly aroused by my spontaneous display of fervor and a wave of power rose within me. Suddenly I pictured another use for the scarf and smiled to myself.

Yes, what was needed here was an infusion of passion into our lives. Something to shake the apathy from our bland sex and right then I knew exactly what was required.

Brad, drowsy and languid with arousal, didn't seem to take in the fact that I'd wrapped the scarf around his wrists until such time as they were secured snugly to the narrow metal frame of our bed.

"What the—" He struggled, tugging against his bonds.

I smothered his utterances of surprise with my lips. "Shhh."

As I stopped to ponder what to do with my newly discovered dominance, a rush of adrenaline coursed through my veins, fueling my imagination with all sorts of wicked thoughts. The feeling was electric and I had to stop myself from climbing atop him and sinking down onto his erection. But no, not tonight. This opportunity was too good to pass up, knowing full well it was only Brad's surprise that had given me the edge, not to mention the bravado to go this far.

Sliding slowly down his body, I covered his chest and stomach with tender little bites, smiling to myself as he squirmed beneath me until I reached the bulge in his pajamas. I hesitated, wondering if I could go through with what I had in mind. Up until now, I had firmly resisted the very idea of oral sex. Yes, I know in this day and age my squeamishness in that department sounds pathetically Victorian, but, to be honest, the thought of doing *that* was anything but a turn-on. Strangely, tonight, the sight and feel of Brad's helplessness had somehow provoked a so far unprecedented desire to see for myself what all the fuss was about.

Moments later and with nothing but a sore jaw and a nasty taste in my mouth, I was still no closer to enlightenment on that score. My curiosity, though, had now been replaced by an unfamiliar bubble of need deep inside me that was just screaming out for release. I'd done my bit. Now it was time to surrender myself to his ardor. Finally, I was ready to lose myself to him, to shake off my inhibitions and let my passions flow.

Shaking with pent-up desire, I reached up and untied him.

"Jeez," he muttered, almost to himself, "what on earth brought that on?"

He lay there inert for what seemed like ages, panting and drenched in sweat. It was difficult to tell if his words were laced with awe or irritation.

Suddenly I felt cheated, for by this time it was becoming clear to me that Brad, now having had his jollies, wasn't in the least bit interested in delivering any reciprocating attention my way. Ever the eternal optimist, though, I continued to rub myself up against his unresponsive body, hoping that he might just take a hint. Slowly it dawned on me that even my less than subtle body language wasn't going to be enough to inspire any such action.

Clearly, this wasn't working. Christ, did I have to spell it out to him? I was burning up inside and so rare was the sensation I was certainly not going to let it pass without some further exploration. I wanted more.

"Brad," I whispered, my voice strangely hoarse.

"What?" he drowsily replied.

"Did you like that?"

"Mmm."

Now it wasn't that I was after a score out of ten or anything, but I must admit by this stage I was becoming a little peeved by his lack of appreciation.

"Brad."

"What?"

"You know, I think I'd really like you to do *that* to me as well? I am so horny right now."

Beside me, he tensed. The atmosphere in the room suddenly shifted.

"Do what exactly?" he asked sharply.

"What I did to you just then," I said shyly. "Don't you want to return the favor by going down on me?"

"Come off it!"

Just like that, the heat inside me froze.

"What do you mean?" I stammered uneasily.

"Jesus, Brooke!" he admonished. "What on earth is wrong with you tonight? First of all there was that kinky bondage thing—God knows where *that* all came from, and now you're acting like some kind of bitch in heat. I can't imagine what on earth's gotten into you lately. If I didn't know better I'd say you were on something. Really, it's disgusting." He exhaled impatiently. "Look, I have to be up early for golf tomorrow so, if you don't mind, I'd like to get some sleep. Good night!"

And with those final words ringing in my head, he rolled over away from me and promptly fell asleep.

I felt as though I'd been slapped. Shame washed over me in a rush of pain. Oh, God, what on earth had I done wrong? Yes, sure, I might be a little naïve, but I wasn't completely unaware that most blokes loved to be on the receiving end of a blow job. He certainly hadn't objected at the time, hadn't stopped me going down on him, but here he was now making out I was some kind of whore, that I'd almost *raped* him!

After that, I lay awake for what seemed like hours. Every time I thought of what had happened, I experienced afresh the smart of humiliation that his callous words had caused me. The sting of Brad's reaction had extinguished the desire that only moments before raged away inside me and I felt something inside wither and die.

I should have been expecting it, I know, but still when the call *did* come, I felt totally ill-prepared to deal with it.

I put it down to bad timing, of course. I was still reeling from the shock of Brad's rejection when the phone rang just after ten. Immediately, I thought of Brad and sort of hoped it was him ringing to apologize. In the space of three rings I had envisioned a tearful apology, flowers and the promise of a fancy meal out together with an evening of erotic makeup sex to compensate for his churlishness.

No such luck. It was my Dad.

I knew I was in trouble the moment I recognized his voice, uncharacteristically stern on the other end of the phone.

"Brooke, I'd like to have a word with you, if that's all right?"

Oh dear. My father rarely rang me. Well, if I'm going to be honest, he never rang, preferring to leave the parent bonding to my mother to handle. Thus, I knew I was in trouble. Typically Dad-like, he got straight to the point.

"Brooke, I want you to ring your mother immediately and apologize for whatever it is that you've said to upset her."

Just as I had feared, Mum had wound the martyr dial up to maximum and apart from hinting to my father that I had caused her heart to break, she was now stoically refusing to enlighten him on the root cause of our mother-daughter rift. Suddenly I was filled with a sense of injustice.

"Sorry if Mum's upset, but, quite frankly, I don't think I have anything to apologize for."

I'll say this for her, over the years she had honed her manipulation skills to a fine art and from what Dad told me, she had spent the better part of the last three days sobbing into some old dress of hers that had been shoved away in the wardrobe for years.

Yes, I did feel a bit guilty for hurting her feelings but not enough to cave in to her underhand emotional blackmail.

"Dad, listen, the only thing I can think of is a tiny misunderstanding we had last week over one of the wedding arrangements. Nothing for you to worry about. It's perfectly normal for emotions to run wild when you're planning a wedding. Besides, it might just be her hormone replacement therapy causing her mood swings, not me, but still I'll give her a call later on and talk to her, if you think it might help."

"Would you?"

Poor man sounded enormously relieved and I couldn't help feeling sorry for him. Living with my mother all those years would have been enough to crush the will to live from anyone and since they'd retired, I could only imagine that his oppression was verging on complete.

When I was young, Dad was always the one I went to for a kind word, lollies, money or permission to go to parties I knew Mum didn't approve of. When I think about it, I was always Daddy's little girl. I think in some ways he tried to compensate for the pressure Mum used to heap on me to be the perfect student or sports player or musician or dancer—none of which I ever excelled at despite the private lessons and tutors she paid out enormous amounts of money for. In the end, I suspect it was Dad who made her see sense when she insisted that I go on to university when really I'd barely coped with high school.

As I put the phone down, I realized it was cowardly of me to blame the situation between us on her hormones, but at least it bought me some time while not appearing to fall for her evil plan to get Dad involved. Jesus, she was pulling out the big guns this time and I wondered how she managed to wield that kind of power over him. Perhaps one day, when we were on speaking terms again, she might let me in on her secret.

One thing was for sure, the wedding dress issue was far from resolved.

Chapter Seventeen

"Hey, what's wrong, petal?"

Before I had the chance to open my mouth to voice some crap about feeling a bit off-color, Scarlett emerged from the back room, catching the tail-end of Leanne's concern.

"Yeah, what's up your arse today? Christ, the look on your face would frighten off fucking winter, it would."

Thanks. If I didn't feel bad enough, ten minutes with Scarlett and I'd be ready to slit my wrists.

Leanne swiveled around in her chair to face me. "Come on, something's obviously bothering you, so it might help to talk about it."

It was a really slow day and most of the other girls had gone out shopping or decided to go home for a few hours' rest before coming back in tonight. That just left Scarlett, Leanne and me to hold down the fort, which probably accounted for the fact that Scarlett, who normally wouldn't lower herself to seeking out our lowly company, had decided to bin her magazines and

wander out the front, gracing us with a rare social visit.
I really wasn't feeling up to a post-mortem on my
family problems, though.

"It's nothing really." I shrugged, hoping for a
customer to get them off my case.

Leanne and Scarlett were clearly not convinced.

"Come on, Brooke. You can tell us. Is it man
problems?"

Their combined scrutiny eventually got the better of
me and I nodded miserably.

"Is your fella knockin' you about?" Scarlett asked, her
tone eager, suddenly filled with a renewed interest in
my private affairs.

"No!" I gasped, horrified at the very suggestion.

"Doing drugs?"

"Of course not!"

"Fucking other women?"

"No, Scarlett!" I cried.

"Fucking other men?" she suggested, smiling
wickedly.

I didn't even dignify that with an answer.

"For God's sake, Scarlett, leave her alone, will you?"
yelled Leanne, rescuing me from her unwanted
interrogation.

"Jesus, I was just trying to help," she snapped,
flinging a filthy look Leanne's way. "I know what some
of those bastards are like. Total scum, they are. They
fuck anything that moves and they come in here and
complain that no one understands them. I understand
them. Wankers, the lot of them."

Right then I was tempted to believe her. Brad and I
had barely spoken for the better part of two days and,
together with my mother, he was giving me the silent
treatment. Despite our tense silences, he remained

unrepentant, unwilling to make peace and, if anything, seemed to be taking it as some kind of affront to his masculinity that I'd dared to take the initiative. He was convinced that I was somehow possessed by some kinky sex demon while I remained hurt, resentful and more than a little confused. Neither of us were about to back down so now it was an issue of who would buckle first. I knew it would be me and that pissed me off even more.

"Well, what's the problem, then? Come out with it," demanded Scarlett who was by now clearly becoming bored with the conversation and ready to walk if I didn't come up with something suitably juicy to entertain her with.

"I don't know. It seems everyone at home is on my back at the moment. It's like I'm losing control over my life. Brad is turning into someone I barely know anymore, and on top of that my mother has completely lost her mind and is doing everything in her power to ruin my life. Honestly, it all seems too hard!"

Scarlett rolled her eyes. "Jeez, things *are* grim, aren't they just." Which promptly earned her a filthy look from Leanne for being unsympathetic.

I could see her point, though. Who was I to complain about anything? Compared to her life, mine was perfect.

"Scarlett, if you can't be helpful, at least keep your opinions to yourself," announced Leanne primly, sounding a lot like my mother, which I found strangely comforting.

"Don't worry. I think I'll leave you two to moan amongst yourselves. If anyone needs me, I'll be out the back right, *thanking God* for my *wonderful* life!" And with that parting comment she swung her legs around and slid off the front desk, disappearing out the back together with her sarcasm.

Leanne turned to face me with an expression of concern. "What's happened, then? A couple of weeks ago you were over the moon about the wedding and now here you are having second thoughts by the sounds of it."

"Not second thoughts exactly. I suppose stress is making me a bit psycho. We've hardly started planning the wedding and already I'm wondering what I've let myself in for. My mother has this thing about me wearing her wedding dress and she's determined to take over the wedding plans together with Brad's mother and now Brad and I aren't talking…"

"So you have had a fight? About the wedding?"

"No, well, not just about the wedding."

"What, then? I'm sure it can't be that bad."

I shrugged, not wanting to elaborate. God, it was embarrassing enough just thinking about what'd happened the other night without having to actually *talk* about it. But be that as it may, since that particular night a raging gulf had opened up in our relationship. Now I didn't know how to bridge it without betraying a part of myself by committing to what I suspected would end up as a passion-starved life. The funny thing was Brad was behaving as though he was relieved he'd at last managed to put me in my place and now it was up to me to finally come to my senses and admit that I was wrong and he was right.

Balls, he was.

If the likes of Meg Ryan could have an orgasm — albeit a faked one — why couldn't I? But I could hardly say that to Leanne and especially in my current whereabouts.

"Can I ask you something personal?"

Leanne pushed her chair back and made herself comfortable. "Of course you can, petal. Ask away."

"Umm...this is a little bit strange I know, but how important do you think sex is in a relationship?"

"You mean in a husband and wife relationship?"

"Of course, what else would I be talking about?"

"Just checking. Being blunt here, but has this got anything to do with you and Brad?"

I hung my head in shame and nodded.

"Are we talking about no sex life at all here, or is it just things have slowed down a bit in the bedroom?

"Ground to a screaming halt as of the other night, more like."

"Don't worry too much. It can't always be hot and wild. Sometimes it's nice to take it easy." Leanne smiled kindly. "You wouldn't want to burn out before the wedding, would you?"

I took a deep breath. Why was it so hard? "That's the problem. It's never *been* hot and wild."

"Not even at first?"

I shook my head.

"But surely the passion's still there?"

I looked up at her, tears threatening to spill. "I don't really know for sure if there ever was passion as you call it between us in the first place."

Leanne looked concerned.

"Don't get me wrong now. Brad and I are madly in love with each other..."

"But he just doesn't do it for you, is that it?" Leanne intervened.

In a nutshell.

"What am I going to do? I love him and really want to marry him."

"Have you considered trying something different? You know, something to fire things up in the bedroom? Most fellows get a kick out of sexy lingerie, furry handcuffs, that sort of thing."

Somehow after my last effort I didn't think furry handcuffs were a good idea.

"Hey, I know," quipped Scarlett, walking back out from the kitchen where it appeared she had been listening to every word. "Get yourself some of those crotchless latex hotpants and matching bra and pretend he's your bitch. Guys really get off on that fantasy. You could try spanking his bare arse or, better still, I've got this huge black dil—"

"Enough, Scarlett!" cried Leanne. "Fuck, this is serious."

"I'm only trying to help," she sulked. "What's the harm in it anyway? You never know, Brooke's fellow might just get off with a bit of S&M. No harm in giving it a go at least."

"Thanks, Scarlett," I said. "I appreciate the advice, but I'm fairly certain that he wouldn't go for it."

Scarlett frowned. "He's not gay, is he?"

"Oh course not!" I spluttered. "My God, why would you say that?"

"Well, you know, it happens." Scarlett shrugged. "Blokes can't handle the idea they might be batting for the other side and instead of coming out of the closet, they try and convince themselves they're as macho as the next bloke by getting married or the like. Leanne, you remember that fellow—what was his name? Carl, I think? He used to come in every week for a booking."

Leanne looked confused. "Um, not the short one with the blond buzz cut?"

"Yeah, that's the one. Well, after about the first three minutes, his old-fella used to up and die on him. Didn't matter what I did – nothing happened. It took him about six weeks for him to admit that he wanted it up the arse."

Leanne gave Scarlett a warning look.

"What I'm getting at here is that it seems the poor bastard didn't even think he might be gay until then. He was gutted. Kept coming in for weeks after that just to cry on my shoulder and see if I could turn him back on to women. Sad fucker!"

"And what *exactly* has this got to do with my relationship?" I queried, becoming more than a little annoyed.

"I'm just saying…"

"Well, don't bother. Brad is certainly not gay, for heaven's sake, and I'm sure it's just the stress he's under at work."

"Okay, then, it's your life," snorted Scarlett, throwing her head back and stomping off to the kitchen.

Leanne leaned in toward me, making sure Scarlett really was out of earshot. "Don't listen to her. I am sure you and Brad will sort things out, but still, if you want someone to talk to about it, remember I'm here."

I smiled but thankfully was saved a response when the buzzer sounded.

"I'll get it," I offered in a desperate bid to put the subject, together with myself, out of range.

Opening the door, I smiled. It was Paul, thank goodness, possibly the nicest customer I'd come across so far working at Heavenly Pleasures. His presence was usually guaranteed to lift my spirits, but today it was an effort. I felt drained. I was in no mood to rattle on with the usual spiel pretending we had a dozen girls out the back just waiting to pamper him and see to his every erotic desire and instead told him the truth. The truth being that Scarlett was the only one available as the others wouldn't be back until five o'clock. It was either her or no girl at all.

"That's fine. Scarlett will do. Half an hour again?"

Strangely, Scarlett was delighted to find that she had scored another booking with Paul. In fact, so much so, I was even gifted with a rare smile taking the place of her usual scowl, as she went off muttering something about it being the easiest half-hour booking she'd ever had.

Back out in reception with Leanne twenty minutes later, I couldn't help thinking about Paul and, despite knowing that it was against Prue's rules and totally none of my business, I couldn't resist bringing the subject up. "I was just thinking, why do you imagine a fellow like Paul comes in here rather than having a real relationship? He seems so, well, *nice*."

Leanne gave me a funny look and opened her mouth as if to say something before thinking better of it. "Who knows?" she said indifferently. "Some of them are just lonely, I suppose, some too busy or too lazy to go and meet a partner and others, probably like Paul in there, like the whole no-pressure side to it. They come in, pay their money, have sex or whatever and leave. I suppose it's a whole lot simpler than having to deal with commitment and risk the emotion and financial cost when it doesn't work out."

"That sounds so cynical."

Leanne shrugged. "That's life. It isn't all chocolates and roses. But then again, maybe working in here has made me a little jaded. A lot of the fellows we see in here are divorced, but even more are married. After a while, it kind of warps your idea of relationships."

I couldn't help but be shocked by Leanne's attitude and it must have shown on my face.

"Oh, sorry, petal. Don't you go listening to me now, I'm sure your fellow is a one in a million catch. Why else would you be with him?"

Good question.

Lost in my thoughts a few minutes later, I didn't hear Paul approach and jumped at the sight of him only a few inches away leaning on the reception desk. "Sorry, did I startle you? You seemed to be a million miles away."

"Oh, I was just thinking, that's all," I mumbled inanely, embarrassed at being caught off-guard — especially as I'd been thinking about him and, worse still, what he'd been doing with Scarlett for the past thirty minutes. Christ, I was becoming obsessed with other people's sex lives. My face must have been ready to self-ignite.

Leanne had nicked out for coffee and for the first time I felt a twinge of shyness muscling its way into my gloomy mood.

"You look like you have the weight of the world on your shoulders. You know, it sometimes helps to talk about it."

Ha ha. Good one. Talk about my relationship problems with a man who sleeps with prostitutes? No, I don't think so.

"No, I'm fine, really," I replied, trying to muster a smile.

"Okay. But just remember, sometimes things aren't quite as they appear on the surface, you know."

And with that Paul smiled kindly and exited, leaving me wondering what on earth he was going on about.

Chapter Eighteen

"You can't be thinking of wearing *that*, surely?" complained Brad, referring to my four hundred dollar pashmina as though it was a dead cat or baby panda fur stole draped around my shoulders. "For heaven's sake, Brooke, didn't you buy it from *a second-hand clothing shop*?"

What could I say? That was the official version of events as far as Brad was concerned and for the sake of future harmony, that was the version I was strictly adhering to. And besides, I was sick of wearing it around the house. I wanted to give it a proper debut and what better place than a fancy dinner party?

"Okay, let me put it this way. Someone threw it out as a rag and now you want to wear it out to dinner with my boss?" he continued, ignoring my hurt expression.

Ignoring his jibe, I did a little twirl. "But you've got to admit, it does look wonderful with my new dress, doesn't it?" I pouted, hoping to shame him into one small compliment.

And it did look wonderful even if he couldn't come to grips with my so-called bargain. It was all I could do not to blurt out that the dress he had immediately approved of was from some second-hand stall at the local community markets and cost Trudy less than twenty dollars. Ironically, I found myself telling Brad that the dress cost two hundred dollars, two hundred dollars which he fully accepted without a hint of reproach. Like someone once said, truth is stranger than fiction.

"Well, yes, I suppose it does," he grudgingly conceded after a few seconds' deliberation. "But that isn't the point here, is it? I don't think I like the thought of you rummaging around in op shops like that."

I was itching to remind him that he hadn't seemed to have had a problem with it a few weeks back when he thought I was saving him money! However, now was not the right time to bring it up. We were due at Brad's boss's in exactly thirty-five minutes and I still had my makeup to touch up.

"Look, no one's going to know where it came from unless you tell them, so relax, will you? I'm sure they're not going to refuse you the partnership because your fiancée likes bargain hunting."

"Yeah, I suppose so, but just to be on the safe side, watch what you say, hon. Robert is straitlaced to the point of Puritanism and seems to disapprove of practically everything that doesn't involve praying or making money." He paused, tugging at his tie. "I know you're not going to say anything stupid, but, please, just for tonight do me a favor and keep the conversation neutral — for me?" He smiled beseechingly.

As much as I wanted to take offense at being told how to act around his precious work colleagues, I couldn't.

Brad had been trying to play down his nervousness all afternoon, but I knew he was desperate to make a good impression on Robert Fletcher and the other partners. For this reason only was I prepared to ignore his insinuation that I was incapable of conducting myself in polite company.

"Just for tonight I promise to behave like the adoring fiancée, okay?" I gave an encouraging smile. "Anyway, I'm sure everything will be fine, so stop worrying. In fact, I reckon they'll be begging you to take the partnership by the time dinner's over."

Brad laughed, and it came out tightly. "I hope you are right."

* * * *

Despite the wall-to-wall smiles and polite conversation, I sensed a definite undercurrent of tension presiding throughout the Fletchers' sumptuous dining room. What started off all so friendly and amicable had gradually shifted toward carefully chosen words meant to mask other less noble sentiments. To her credit, Robert's wife, Muriel, being a consummate expert at this level of socializing, eased any tensions as they arose by either offering more food or more wine to her guests. But I still got the impression tonight was going to end up being more of a hostile boardroom meeting than a chance to come together in more relaxed surroundings.

And the root cause of the tension? *Simon.*

His appearance at the Fletchers' not long after our own arrival was the last thing Brad had been expecting and the moment Muriel had escorted Simon through to greet everyone, all Brad's earlier confidence seemed to desert him, along with his genial attitude. It was then I knew that Brad was thrown into confusion by the appearance of his arch rival and even more so when Muriel placed him next to me at dinner, while keeping Brad at her side down the other end.

But, to my growing surprise, I soon discovered that rather than the lecherous self-obsessed bore Brad had made him out to be, Simon was actually wonderful company and the perfect dinner companion. He was funny, polite and the only one not wearing a suit, which earned him some brownie points for being an individual – in a slightly rock-star-ish kind of way and if I'm honest he looked a little like Robbie Williams with his cheeky grin and animated questioning eyebrows. Unlike the rest of us, he had arrived solo, not in the least awkward about being the only one at dinner without a partner and as a result, he lavished more attention on me instead, asking me about my job, among other things. I chose the safe route and filled him in on the dreary life of a medical receptionist, although by the cheeky warmth in his grin I got the impression he would have loved nothing better than to hear about my 'other' life as a covert brothel receptionist.

As the evening progressed, I found myself opening up to him about my childhood, our mutually annoying parents – he was an only child as well – and even my stupid PR lie to Sophie, which for some reason he found extremely funny. By the time Muriel brought out dessert it occurred to me that I hadn't felt this relaxed in ages. Brad and I used to talk for hours on end about nothing in particular, but recently with the stress of his work and my own worries, I couldn't remember the last time we'd laughed together like Simon and I were now.

To the others we must have looked like two silly teenagers, but tonight I didn't care. I was having a good time after all and Brad had instructed me to make a good impression on everyone and I felt myself lighting up in his company.

Across on the other side of the table, though, it was a very different story. I could almost feel Brad's disapproving gaze aimed like a laser at me, hot and penetrating, but for once I chose to ignore him. I defiantly drained the last drops of white wine from my glass and leveled an equally hard stare back at him. Just then, his little pep talk of earlier, along with his insinuations that I needed him to tell me how to behave, began to grate on my nerves. I wasn't a complete social retard, after all. At present, though, anyone would have thought I had defected to the enemy side by the sense of displeasure firing my way. It seemed I wasn't the only one to notice, either. Muriel, picking up on the vibes coming from Brad, tactfully turned her attention on him and attempted to lighten his mood by indulging him in a spot of flattery.

"Brad, Robert has told me how splendidly you handled that big embezzlement case last month."

"He sure did," boomed Robert, clearly enjoying himself on the crest of a few glasses of wine. "A real hairy one, that was. It could easily have gone either way, but Brad here uncovered a tiny but fundamental flaw in the prosecution's case and blew them right out of the water."

Brad gave a modest little shrug, but I knew that inside he was almost glowing as a result of Robert's voluble praise. "Well, it was obvious, really, when you looked at their initial deposition pertaining to the company status at the time. Anyone could have picked it up. All it took was a little diligence and dedication to the case," he said pointedly to Simon, throwing out a silent challenge.

Simon refused to take the bait and smiled back, raising his glass to Brad in a gesture clearly meant to convey just a bit more than simple congratulations. It was clear by the chill between them that the upcoming partnership wasn't the only issue. These two seriously hated one another.

In an instant, the ambience in the room shifted as Brad, belying his earlier modesty, began rattling on about company loyalty, swiftly moving on to the decline of today's morality in general and the need for communities to rise against those in society who threatened the moral fiber.

For some reason, I couldn't help but think of Scarlett and Angel. They didn't have the luxury of wallowing in such pompous ideals. Just getting through the day was a major challenge. Suddenly, I saw a particular hardness in Brad's eyes, a blind intolerance that I'd failed to notice before, and it sent shivers down my spine.

Beside me, Simon appeared unfazed, but still I got the impression that battle lines were being drawn. Things were about to get personal.

Placing his glass down on the crisp white tablecloth, Simon leveled a challenging look down the length of the table at Brad. "Come on, lighten up, mate!" He smiled, softening the edge to his voice. "Think about it, will you? If you get rid of *all* the crims out there, don't you think you'll be doing us all out of a job?" he continued, by now openly sliding me a sly wink. "Hey, don't get me wrong here. I'm as much for your Utopian dreams as you are, but there are certain practicalities to consider. For example, what are you suggesting we do with all these so-called undesirables? Throw them all in prison? Or maybe dump them on a deserted island somewhere? New Zealand, perhaps? And on what grounds?"

"Grounds?" sneered Brad. "On the grounds they are single-handedly corroding the principles that we" — he paused, gesturing to those around him — "the decent people of this society strive to uphold. Take those principles away and you may as well give in to an uneducated and lawless culture whose only future will revolve around crime, drugs and immoral behavior."

Despite his continuing civility, Simon's eyes hardened. "But honestly, Brad, what gives us the right to judge them just because they haven't had some of the benefits growing up that the likes of you and I have been lucky enough to enjoy?"

Brad's smile held neither warmth nor good humor and I inwardly tensed, sensing I was about to witness a side of him I would have preferred not to. Even worse, he appeared to be in his element as he glanced across at Robert and the other partners in an ill-concealed attempt to reel in support.

"Honestly, Simon, I know you mean well, but you're beginning to sound like one of those bleeding heart liberals on telly," he began smugly. "But the fact remains they continue to use the excuse of an unhappy childhood or coming from a broken home to ignore society's boundaries and sponge off the welfare system. If they got themselves a job and developed some kind of responsibility, they wouldn't have the time to steal cars, take drugs and hang about on street corners inviting trouble. No, I tell you, what's needed here is a tougher justice system and a stronger police presence on the streets. Only that way are we going to rid our community of those undesirables who are steadily eroding our family ideals."

Brad might have been my fiancé, but, right then, puffed up with self-righteousness, he was a complete stranger to me. Arrogant and judgmental were the only words I could come up with to describe him and, for the first time, I felt appalled at his callousness to those people like Scarlett and Angel who in their short lives had faced more heartache and tragedy than the likes of Brad or even I could ever fully comprehend.

When I thought about Leanne and Paul, even Trudy, I couldn't imagine any of them looking down their noses at anyone because of their background or social status. Sure, the girls at Prue's might never be considered society's debutantes, but at least they were trying to get on with life with what little they'd been given.

Claire and Denise, the wives of the other two partners, who up until now had spent the evening talking mainly of the agonies of bringing up teenagers and the cost of raising their tearaway offspring, nodded in silent agreement as he continued to hold court, shooting down Simon's proposition that instead of casting judgment, maybe society should look to the underlying causes for the answer. Simon's point was completely steamrollered by Brad, and Robert, his surprise comrade in arms, who, if anything was even more vehement about Brad's Nazi-style brand of social reform.

Thankfully, just when I thought I could listen to no more, Muriel came to the rescue once again, finally bringing Brad's lecture to a grinding halt by changing the subject to none other than our wedding plans.

"Oh, we're still looking at venues at the moment, but we really will have to decide soon if we're going to have any hope of booking for the October long weekend," I responded to Muriel's inquiry, grateful for the change of subject.

"Oh, you poor thing." Muriel threw a sympathetic look my way. "Sounds like you have your work cut out for you there."

I nodded, unsure whether she meant the wedding plans or my pompous fiancé.

"Things were a lot simpler when Robert and I got married, but then again, I suppose that was thirty-five years ago now. Weddings have changed since then. Now they're more like a Hollywood production than a simple exchanging of vows. When we were young, you simply went up to the minister after church and asked if they could perform the ceremony, and organize a few sandwiches for the guests afterward. There was none of this business of booking months in advance. If they were busy on the date you wanted, you either opted for a weekday or a morning wedding. We were married at St. Celia's right here in town, you know. In fact I believe the old minister who married us is still there."

"Father Brockway?" Brad blurted out across the table. Every one stopped talking and looked across at him in surprise. "It is Father Brockway, isn't it?" he asked innocently, as if realizing he was again center stage.

"Yes, my goodness. That's amazing. How did you know?" responded Muriel in surprise.

A cold chill rolled over me as Brad smiled triumphantly at both Robert and Muriel. "Brooke and I were hoping that Father Brockway might be free to perform our nuptials."

"What an amazing coincidence," one of the wives announced.

Ignoring my silent expression of horror, Brad straightened in his chair. "Well, I suppose it is, really. Up until recently, Brooke's mother was a regular worshiper there and knows Father Brockway very well."

Robert's booming laugh punctured the silence that had settled over the table, following it up with a congenial slap to Brad's back. "Well, well, did you hear that, Muriel? Fancy Brad and Brooke getting married in our old church."

Suddenly, I couldn't breathe. What on earth was Brad *doing*? I could barely believe what I was hearing. It was like being caught up in a bad dream, one of those where you sense that danger is near, but your throat closes up and you can't scream out for help.

"You and Muriel will come to the wedding, of course?" said Brad, in full suck-up mode. "All of you. Brooke and I would love nothing better than to have you all there on our special day."

"Of course, my boy," laughed Robert. "We wouldn't miss it for the world. After all it isn't every day that one of our young legal eagles decides to take the big plunge. So is it St. Celia's on the October long weekend?"

Brad's smile practically split his face in two. "Yes, that's right. All we're waiting for is confirmation from Father Brockway and it will be official."

The rest of the evening passed in a nightmarish blur. All I could focus on was Brad holding court down the other end of the table, waffling on about how we were looking forward to starting a family and buying a house once the wedding was over, all the time dropping sly references to the fact that a rise in both pay and career status was likewise high on the agenda. I barely said a word for fear I'd completely lose my cool and vent my fury at Brad in full view of his colleagues, making an utter fool of myself in the process.

Not that he noticed. Not that he gave anyone a chance to take the conversational spotlight away from him for that matter. Hell, I might have sprouted a pineapple out of the top of my head for all the attention he gave me now he had supplanted Simon as the office golden boy. But then he did have other things on his mind, didn't he? He was brown-nosing on a scale never before witnessed and, quite frankly, it turned my stomach. I had never felt such an impotent rage in all my life. If it hadn't been for Simon who made it his mission for the rest of the night to make me laugh and top up my glass with wine, I honestly think I might have stormed out of there or burst into tears.

I couldn't believe Brad, my Brad, the same man who I adored as my knight in shining armor, had done this to me. Showing off to his boss and acting like a pompous prat was one thing, but announcing that we were getting married by Father Brockway was an entirely different matter, seeing he knew how strongly I was against it. Now that he had invited practically the entire law firm, there was no way that I was going to be able to sway him to change it to a garden wedding, especially as Robert and Muriel had been married in the same church. In Brad's eyes, he was already part of their big happy family and saw this as the final step to secure the partnership.

How could I have been so blind to his blatant machinations? To think I'd been swayed by the candlelit dinner and his sudden change of heart concerning the wedding date. For the first time, it occurred to me that maybe the entire thing was just a plot to further worm his way into a partnership and the reality that he was prepared to use our wedding to springboard his career made me feel ill.

As we made our way home that evening, Brad was flushed with triumph. Positively gloating. In fact, had they harnessed his ego right there and then it might well have lit up a small town. For the remainder of the evening, he'd completely monopolized Robert as well as Tom and Will, the two senior partners, totally ignoring Simon, and by the time we'd left he'd been all but in their pockets. If Simon had been put out by Brad's atrocious behavior, he hadn't allowed it to show and, to his credit, remained polite and friendly.

We were almost halfway home before Brad even noticed I hadn't spoken a word to him since we'd gotten into the car.

"Well, tonight was a resounding success, don't you think, Brooke?" He beamed.

"A success? In what way, exactly?" I replied through gritted teeth, struggling to control my voice.

"In every way. For one thing, I certainly showed that prat Simon that I was to be reckoned with, for a start. Still don't know what the hell he was doing there in the first place. I guess he must have found out and pestered Robert for an invite. Bloody embarrassing if you ask me, him barging in like that, and on his own. Still, I noticed you tolerated him quite well."

"Excuse me?" I spluttered.

"Simon. Christ, talk about making a fool of himself. But, honestly, Brooke, you really shouldn't have encouraged him, you know," he chided, his dark mood clearly a thing of the past. "Blokes like that tend to get the wrong impression when you lead them on. But then again, I don't suppose you were in a position to do anything else, were you? Next time, I think I'll have a word with Robert and request that Simon not be allowed to ruin everyone's evening."

Next time? I wanted to scream out that if he thought I was going to subject myself to another evening like that, he was sorely mistaken.

"But, despite Simon's presence, I think I made a good impression on the partners," Brad continued to prattle on. "I know they couldn't say anything with him being there, but I'm certain I have that partnership in the bag. After all, Robert wouldn't have been so keen to come to our wedding if he was planning on overlooking me for the position, would he?"

I was ready to combust with rage.

Pulling up at a set of lights, Brad looked across at me. "Brooke, what's wrong with you? You've hardly said a word since we left. Aren't you pleased for me?"

That was it. The moment I finally exploded.

"Pleased? I am thrilled," I spat, "*especially* at your very public announcement that we're getting married at St. Celia's."

For the first time, Brad noticed the anger smoldering behind my words and at least had the decency to look slightly uncomfortable.

"Oh, that." He laughed nervously at my stony expression. "Honey, I didn't think you'd mind, all things considered. After all, I reckon it was the clincher with Robert."

"*Brad!*" I screamed out. "This isn't about your fucking partnership — this is about *our* wedding. How dare you use it as some kind of bargaining tool to boost your bloody career?"

The atmosphere in the car suddenly turned caustic as all the tension that had surrounded us for the past few days erupted between us.

"Well, might *I* remind *you*, Brooke, that my *career* is going to be supporting you and our future children, so I think it's time that you started respecting that," Brad said icily. "Besides, it doesn't matter where we get married. It's, what, an hour in our lives, if that. A few lines read out of a damn book. But my legal career will go on for the next thirty years or more. One hour, just one hour is all I'm asking of you. Yes, I understand that you weren't keen to get married in a church, but under the circumstances, you have to admit it is a small sacrifice to make."

I sat simmering with rage. The bloody hide of him. A small sacrifice, my arse. I had to ask myself at that point what else was I going to be expected to sacrifice.

Chapter Nineteen

"Jesus, Brooke, you're not thinking of letting him get away with it, are you?"

"I can't see that I have much of a choice right at the moment," I replied mournfully, knowing full well it was more than likely I would do just that.

Just as I had feared, ever since the wedding-dress issue blew up in my face, Brad and my mother had joined forces and were now putting the squeeze on me to conform. Brad looked upon my objections as selfish and counter-productive — his exact words — and as for my mother, aka The Traitor, she simply stated with her customary disapproving scowl that it wouldn't do me any harm to spend an hour or two in church for a change. Her lack of support being my punishment for rejecting her damn dress.

"Bullshit! Of course you have a choice. Everyone has choices," Trudy cried out, clearly appalled as much by my spinelessness as she was by Brad's deviousness. "Why do you always take the coward's way out? You give in to other people too easily. Stand up for yourself for once in your life and tell him he either drops this idea of a church wedding or you'll drop him. That should let him know you mean business."

This conversation wasn't going quite as I had hoped. What I'd had in mind was a sympathetic shoulder to moan on and possibly a shot of compassion, not a lecture and a proverbial kick up the backside. But then what did I expect? After all, it was no secret that I was a coward of the highest-ranking order.

"But what if he won't? What if he calls my bluff?"

"What do you mean? *He* was the one who asked *you* to marry him, remember. Seems to me that the ball's in your court now."

I had to admit Trudy's brand of logic had a certain appeal to it, but alas I wasn't prepared to risk my relationship just to score a point for sisterhood. "I've been thinking, maybe I *am* the one being unreasonable. After all, it's not as if I'm an atheist or anything, and besides, people get married in churches all the time. If it means so much to him, not to mention my mother, maybe I should learn to compromise a bit."

"Christ, listen to you. What on earth's happened to you lately? You never used to be such a victim—well not this much of a victim, anyway. Can't you see, Brad is walking all over you and you're just letting him?"

"No, I'm not. I'm just trying to behave like a mature adult for a change, rather than a spoiled child."

Trudy narrowed her eyes. "So that's how Brad thinks you're behaving, is it, like a spoiled child?"

Her expression darkened and I knew I'd said the wrong thing. Trudy was a borderline feminist. I say borderline because her feminist tendencies only surfaced when it suited her, like now when she was in the mood for a spot of man bashing, or, I should say, a spot of Brad bashing. All of a sudden, I wished I'd kept my big mouth shut or better still simply pretended I'd had a change of heart over the church issue. I was also beginning to have second thoughts about stopping off to see Trudy at the salon on my way to work, but I was going nuts keeping it all bottled up inside and, as far as Brad was concerned, the matter was closed. What I had in mind, though, was a sympathetic ear, not a lecture.

"I know you don't want to hear this, Brooke, but what Brad did was totally out of line. He's completely disregarded your feelings, not to mention going behind your back like that just to suck up to his boss. I would have been livid."

"I *was* livid. I couldn't believe it at the time —"

"*At the time?* What about now?"

"I don't know," I conceded, feeling suddenly exhausted.

Of late, I couldn't help feeling like everything in my life was on a collision course with disaster. First the phone debacle — of which thankfully I had earned enough to meet the first couple of payments — then my secret life as a brothel receptionist, and now on top of everything I had Brad and my mother ganging up on me and taking over the organizing of my wedding.

"Look, I hate to say this to you, Brooke, but Brad's a wanker."

"Jesus, Trud, don't hold back," I muttered, not bothering to disguise the sarcasm in my voice.

"Well, he is! Think about it for a minute, will you? If he gets away with this, what do you think it is going to be next? You'll never have a say in anything for the rest of your life. He'll get it in his head that just because he makes a buck or two he can go around making all the decisions and you'll be expected to go along with him without a word of complaint. Honestly, he's a total control freak."

"He's not!" I protested weakly, perhaps out of some sense of loyalty to Brad, but deep down my heart just wasn't in it.

Not that I was ready to admit it to Trudy, but of late I had been thinking the very same thing and, believe me, it wasn't something that sat easily on my mind. Generally, when these traitorous thoughts seeped into my head, I'd do my best to remind myself that I had no right to expect him to be perfect — I certainly wasn't and for that matter neither was Trudy.

However today, my *we are all merely human* approach to this latest problem wasn't working and I was finding it more and more difficult to defend him.

"Well, tell him, then. Tell him you are not being married by Father Brockway and he'll just have to live with it."

Sure, it sounded simple when *she* said it. *Stick to my guns. Be an adult. Put my foot down.* But, no, it wasn't that simple. Not for the likes of me, anyway. Once confronted with Brad's brand of logic, my own tends to roll over and die rather than stand and fight. It was hopeless. I had tried arguing with him in the past, but in the face of his dominant line of reasoning, I always found myself on the back foot, struggling to think of what I was fighting for in the first place. No, Trudy's idea of outright confrontation never got me anywhere. Not that I was willing to confess that point.

"I'll think about it, really. But now I have to get to work. I'll ring you later okay."

"Promise?"

"Promise."

* * * *

The moment I arrived at Heavenly Pleasures, I knew that something wasn't quite right. For one thing, the place was uncharacteristically quiet for this time of the afternoon with none of the usual squabbles leaking out from the back room above the salacious sounds of sex resonating from the waiting room porn. And, two, Angel who prided herself in being something of an ice queen was white as a ghost and being comforted by a grim-looking Leanne. Highly unusual. I felt as though I'd walked smack bang into the Twilight Zone.

"Brooke, thank God you're here!" cried Leanne, beckoning me over. "There has been a bit of a drama with one of the clients in the last few minutes. I've rung for an ambulance, but before they get here, I'm going to need your help."

After gently sitting Angel down behind the reception desk, Leanne came around and walked past me in the direction of the client lounge, beckoning me to follow.

"What's happened?" I asked, quickly falling in step beside her.

For one horrible moment I pictured Scarlett or Oliva bruised and battered at the hands of some deranged client and I felt a tight fist of fear in my chest. "Oh, God, it's not one of the girls, is it? Has something happened to one of them?"

Leanne shook her head gravely. "No, don't worry. The girls are fine. It's one of our regular clients. From what Angel said, he's been coming in for years. A nice bloke from all accounts and very generous with the girls, but from what I've learned in the last couple of minutes, it seems he has some unusual habits. Anyway the poor man's had some kind of a turn in the middle of a session."

Leanne stopped and turned around to face me, her face a mask of seriousness. "Angel's really shaken up. She's going to sit and wait for the ambos to arrive, so I'm going to need you to give me a hand with him."

"Sure," I responded automatically. After all, it isn't every day when you get called to help in times of need. Not that I was any Flo Nightingale, mind you, but I had seen my fair share of emergencies at the surgery.

"He's in the Red Suite and, from what Angel said, it sounds as though he might be in a bad way. Too much Viagra is my guess. These old codgers don't seem to know when enough is enough. It's for that reason Prue doesn't usually allow it in here, so I reckon he must have taken it before he came." Leanne glanced at her watch anxiously. "Come on, we'd better get him cleaned up before they arrive."

Cleaned up? Under the circumstances, it struck me as kind of odd. Surely if the poor man was having a heart attack or something, his appearance would be the least of his worries. What did Leanne have in mind? Combing his hair? Straightening his tie? Polishing his shoes?

Following Leanne into the aptly named Red Suite, it took me a few minutes to adjust my senses to the onslaught of what could only be described as...well...red! Red walls, red carpet and red furnishings, even down to the red light fittings and lamps. I felt like I had walked onto the set of a Stanley Kubrick film. Jesus, it was enough to give anyone a heart attack.

Then, if the room itself wasn't enough of a shock, to my abject horror I noticed a very naked man bound face-up and spread-eagled across the bed, his penis jutting up grotesquely, sheathed in what appeared to be a bright orange condom. Yes, definitely *Clockwork Orange*! Fucking hell! I couldn't take my eyes off it. It was huge! He must have been popping Viagra designed for elephants! Jesus, one thing was for sure — they weren't going to deflate *that* in a hurry.

My heart was pounding away and it wasn't only the red room causing it. Welcoming customers I could cope with. Being in charge of Prue's porn archives — just. Taking down their weird sexual requests I was slowly coming to terms with, but *this*, this was just too much and had my feet not been frozen to the floor with horror I would have turned tail and run.

"For fuck's sake, Brooke, don't just stand there gawping. Come over here and give me a hand," bellowed Leanne, looking even redder in the face than usual. "Fucking Angel could have at least untied the poor man," she muttered in disgust, tugging at a length of cord.

Act casual, I told myself, *and whatever you do, don't look at his dick!*

Don't. Look!

The poor fellow wasn't moving and hadn't made a single sound since we walked through the door. For a moment, I feared he was dead already. *What a horrible way to die! Not to mention the embarrassment factor. But then again I suppose if you're dead, it kind of negates the whole being-caught-dead-in-a-brothel issue.*

By now, Leanne was beginning to run out of patience at my inability to handle the situation. How did I know this? Because with the agility I didn't know she possessed, she stopped trying to untangle his limbs from Angel's expert bindings and reached out and grabbed my arm, dragging both me and my raging reluctance over toward the bed. "For God's sake, don't just stand there like a stunned mullet—help me with these, will you!" she snapped.

I was still reeling from the orange condom when, to my horror, I happened to glance upward to his protruding belly. I stifled an immediate urge to gag.

"Oh, my God, Leanne, what's that all over his stomach and legs? Tell me it's not contagious, please!" I gasped in shock, taking in the sight of what looked like some hideous orange blistering skin disease completely covering him right down to his knees.

"Get a grip, Brooke, it's only marmalade, for God's sake," she hissed. "Apparently he likes to be smeared with it before he can get his rocks off. Look, I know it seems strange, but, believe me, I've heard of worse. Quickly, go into the bathroom and wet some towels. If we don't clean it off him before the ambos arrive, it's going to be rather awkward explaining what he's doing moonlighting as a human citrus dessert!"

I knew then I'd never eat marmalade again, that is, if I could stomach the sight of food again, period.

As I raced across the room to gather some towels, I couldn't help stopping midway, in full rubberneck mode, to peek a look at the old codger with the ill-timed food fetish. Leanne was too busy trying to wipe the worst of the orange goo off on the sheet to notice me staring across at the bed. But by then it was too late. I had seen him and, worse still, he had finally regained consciousness and had seen me!

"Oh fucking Jesus!" he cried out, clutching his chest and frantically pulling against the ropes that held him.

I couldn't move.

"Brooke, what are you doing? Start wiping this stuff off, will you?" Leanne shrieked, clearly alarmed by his pallor and distress.

But I couldn't. I was frozen to the spot, for right there in front of me, in all his sticky orange naked erect glory, was Robert Fletcher, Brad's boss! *Fuuuuuuck!*

Leanne stood up and angrily snatched the towels from my unresponsive arms. Outside in the foyer I could hear what sounded like Angel speaking to the paramedics and Leanne looked up at me in alarm.

"Quick," she urged. "I'll clean this up, you grab that damn condom off him and get rid of it before they get in here, for God's sake."

This is not a time to be coy or squeamish, I told myself, taking a deep breath. "Oh, fuck it," I muttered as I leaned over Brad's prostrate boss and gingerly rolled the orange condom from his swollen pecker. To my relief, Robert looked to have passed out once more, but still I couldn't shake the suspicion that he was pretending to be unconscious to save us both added mortification. Me, well I'd never been so grossed out in my entire life and I had to repeatedly remind myself that this was a life-or-death situation just to make it through the ordeal without becoming hysterical or throwing up.

It *had* to be done, I suppose? I couldn't dare a look at him, fearing one flash of eye contact would see the one shred of composure I had left flee into the wild blue yonder. In fact, I doubted that I would ever be able to look him in the eye again, that is, presuming he survived this ordeal. If I were in his shoes, I'm fairly certain I'd be wishing I was dead right now.

How was he going to explain this to Muriel?

How was I going to explain this to Brad?

Five minutes later, Leanne and I were relieved of our responsibility. Robert left the premises on a stretcher in the care of the paramedics who, after attaching him to a heart monitor, assured us that he would most likely survive to screw another day once they got him to the hospital and on the right medication.

As much as I was relieved that Robert was going to pull through, my mind couldn't release the look on his face as he'd recognized me standing over his naked body. What was I going to do? Or, more to the point, what was Robert likely to do? Tell Brad or take his shameful secret — and mine for that matter — to the grave?

Thankfully, Leanne, knowing full well she was unlikely to get any more work out of me, decided to let me go home early on the grounds of emotional trauma. To say I was relieved was putting it mildly. I did not want to stick around for the aftermath. And the aftermath in this case was Prue, and boy was she pissed off! Not at us exactly, I hoped, but pissed off all the same. Because as soon as the paramedics had left, Leanne had phoned Prue and filled her in on the near disaster and as a result she was furious and, worse still, on her way up from Sydney to confront the girls and reinforce the importance of her No-Viagra policy.

This wasn't good. Up until now I'd only witnessed her carefully constructed tranquil side, but I had it on good authority from Scarlett that Prue on a verbal rampage was nothing short of terrifying. Adding weight to this, I could hear her gravelly voice from where I stood at the other side of the room, yelling through the phone at Leanne something to the effect that no elderly perverts were going to bite the dust in her brothel...

* * * *

"You'll *never* guess what happened to Robert today," Brad announced breathlessly, throwing his briefcase down on the lounger.

I had a fair idea, but in the interests of common decency, I decided to bite my tongue. Besides, I had spent the major part of the afternoon trying desperately to banish the horrible image of Mr. Fletcher, or, as he will forever be remembered, the Marmalade Man, from my mind.

I looked up from the magazine article I'd been reading on that latest Hollywood heartthrob's marriage woes to take in Brad hopping from one foot to another in the manner of a four-year-old needing a pee. An expression of morbid excitement was warring with one of faux concern on his face. Incidentally, morbid excitement was kicking butt.

"What?"

"The poor man was out playing golf this afternoon and had a heart attack way out on the fourteenth green. From all accounts, he could have died."

"Oh, that's awful. Not all on his own, I hope?" I responded, trying to mask the contempt in my voice. I should have known he would have made up some lame excuse. But the truth would have landed me in the shit as well.

"Yes, how did you know? Poor Muriel spoke to Tom about two hours ago now. Robert had just been taken to the cardiac ward from Emergency. Apparently, he'll be fine. It was just a minor attack, but just to be on the safe side, they're keeping him in for a few days for tests."

Despite Brad's concern for Robert, all I could think of was Muriel. Not for the first time today, I wondered if she had any idea what her husband, known by all as a pillar of the community, was up to in his spare time. That is, when he wasn't riding high, not only on his political lobbying to criminalize pornography, but also his moralistic campaign to eradicate all the undesirables from society — or at least all the ones he didn't want to fuck, anyway.

Yes, I know I should have left it at that. Maybe it was post-traumatic stress overriding the stop button on my mouth, but I couldn't help myself. I had to know what the little pervert had come up with by way of a cover story. "Um, what was he doing out playing golf on his own on a Monday?" I probed.

Brad hesitated for one brief but intriguing moment before responding, "Oh, well, um, he quite often takes off early to play a few rounds. Perks of being the boss, I suppose. He says it relaxes him."

Yeah, right. He was 'playing around', all right. Leanne said he'd been coming regularly for years — no pun intended. Little wonder the man was so bloody relaxed. Jesus, it was nothing short of a miracle that I'd managed to avoid him up to now, not that it was likely he'd be back. Leanne had been horrified when I'd told her who he was, and even more so when I'd added that I'd had dinner with him and his devoted wife of thirty-five years only days before.

Brad's expression was suddenly guarded and for the first time I wondered if he had any inkling of Robert's clandestine visits to Heavenly Pleasures. No, surely not! What kind of a man would admit to something like that? And even if he did, why would Brad cover up for him?

"But he's going to be all right, isn't he?" I asked, trying to dismiss the suspicion from my mind that Brad knew more than he was letting on.

"Yes, apparently he should be out of hospital by the end of the week. But still, it's kind of thrown everyone at the office. No one can believe it. He is one of the healthiest people I know. Never even takes a sick day!"

Why would he when he could bunk off to visit hookers on company time?

"But wait for this. Tom called a meeting before we left today to announce that Robert has decided to bring his retirement date forward to next month. He still has a couple of things to finalize but Tom doesn't seem to think it will postpone the decision." Brad could barely contain his excitement. "You know what this means, don't you? They have decided to bring the partnership announcement forward to the week after next."

Again the partnership. I was so sick of hearing about it.

"Oh, and, Brooke, while I think of it, we really should go to the hospital and visit Robert. You know, let him know we're thinking of him and wish him a speedy recovery."

I stared at him with an expression of sheer horror. Surely he didn't think he was being subtle. He had all the subtlety and tact of Cesare Borgia offering his enemy a friendly glass of wine.

"Not tonight, obviously," Brad hastened to add, misconstruing my rabid reluctance. "But possibly tomorrow or the next day, when he's feeling up for visitors. Of course, in the meantime it would be nice if you could give Muriel a call, you know, to offer her your support."

With my current knowledge of Robert's sticky, orange extra-curricular activities doing my head in, there was no way I'd be able to pull it off without experiencing a ghastly flashback to that horrible moment of recognition, a moment I feared would live on in my nightmares.

"Brad, I've only met her once. What am I expected to say? Anyway, I think the poor woman has enough on her hands at the moment without me bothering her."

I glared back irritably, hoping he'd take the hint that I was not about to be bullied into being a puppet in his Machiavellian games. Despite his outwardly virtuous motives, I wasn't fooled for a minute. I'd heard of ambulance chasers, of course — I was engaged to a lawyer, after all — but this went well beyond that. This was bordering on sick.

"Don't look at me like that. The man has been through a terrible ordeal..."

You don't know the half of it!

"...something no man should have to endure on his own..."

Especially smeared with marmalade and trussed up like a marinating pig.

"So I think it would be charitable of us to let him know that we are thinking of him, that's all."

Particularly with the partnership decision looming.

Yuck! How could I explain to Brad that the image of Robert splayed out in the Red Suite was not something I was likely to forget in a hurry — even though I was *desperate* to?

Chapter Twenty

Overnight, I had come to a decision, one I hoped would help to put my life back on track and, with it, I felt the weight of the past couple of months lift from my shoulders. I was going to hand in my notice at Heavenly Pleasures and look for another job. A job with prospects, prestige and power. Or failing that, a job where I wouldn't be called upon to peel orange condoms off elderly perverts covered in marmalade. Sure, it would mean coming clean — no pun intended — to Brad about losing the surgery position, but I was hoping that if he made partner, he might be able to swing a job for me in his office. I wasn't fussy. I'd file or make coffee. Hell, I'd clean the place, if that was required. Anything that didn't involve contact with bodily fluids or preserves of any kind was fine by me. After all, it was only for a couple more months until I got the damn telephone bill paid.

Why now? Well, I suppose, not surprisingly, the events of the past couple of days had seriously eroded my confidence and every time I recalled that horrible moment of mutual sticky orange recognition, I wanted to die. In a flash of mortification, I saw my current life flash before my eyes then, hot on its tail, my future plans colliding head-on into a proverbial truck and crumbling to dust.

What a disaster! Even now I was praying I'd wake up only to find it had all been a horrible dream, one I'd tell Brad about over breakfast and we'd both fall about laughing. Alas, this was no dream and I seriously doubt Brad would find anything at all amusing about his fiancée manhandling his boss's genitalia. On that score, thus far Robert had kept our little secret just that — secret. Not that I expected him to place a full-page ad in the local paper or anything, but still he knew and I knew and, what was worse, we both knew something about each other that we would have preferred not to.

Tossing and turning half the night, I came to the realization that I had taken enough chances and it was time to bring my life and my future plans back on to the straight and narrow.

I'd miss Leanne and the girls, even Scarlett, strangely enough. Admittedly, I was still terrified of her, but I knew she was for the most part harmless. If ever there was a case of someone's bark being worse than their bite, it was Scarlett's. But then again she hadn't bitten me — yet. All things considered, the girls had shown me a side to the world that, although confronting and, let's face it, a bit ugly at times, had certainly opened my eyes to the reality of some people's lives and made me realize how lucky I was to have been brought up in a secure and loving — if annoyingly protective — home.

Following a now familiar path toward the arcade, I tried to guide my thoughts away from Brad and his lecherous boss and focus on the task at hand. This, I must point out, was alien territory for me as generally speaking I was the one getting shown the door, not the one doing the resigning. Maybe this was the reason behind the sudden return of nerves, or maybe it was the thought that I was returning to the proverbial crime scene. I have to admit to my shame that I had been briefly tempted to take the coward's way out and phone in my resignation, but I knew I owed Leanne and the girls a face-to-face goodbye. They had accepted me, after all, with all my middle-class naivety, and this might well be the last time I ever saw any one of them as I was fairly certain that after yesterday's happenings I was never so much as walking down this end of town ever again.

Making use of the key Leanne had given me on my first shift, I quietly opened the door and let myself in, only to find the front end deserted. To my surprise, no one was in reception and, by the absence of moans and tacky background music drifting out from the waiting room porn, it was my guess there weren't any customers in-house at the moment, either. Still, that wasn't too unusual. After all it was barely two o'clock and in a few hours' time the place would be alive with phones ringing and girls snapping at one another out the back, not to mention Leanne yelling at them to keep it down or alternatively hurrying them on to waiting taxis.

The place looked as it always did, rebelling against its slightly worn retro feel, hoping to regain some fashion credibility. But, for some reason, the atmosphere had changed from one of carefully scrubbed sleaze to ominously subdued. I tensed as a fresh tide of nerves returned in a wave of dread.

Behind the reception desk, the door leading out to the girls' kitchenette and lounge was closed. That was weird. Since the fracas between Scarlett and JoJo the other week, Leanne had made a point of keeping it open so as to keep an ear out for any more potential riots. What on earth was going on? Surely it wasn't a staff meeting? Staff meetings didn't feature that strongly in Heavenly Pleasures, and along with girlie nights out and Bible study classes, they were generally seen as taboo.

Approaching the closed door, I could just make out muffled voices beyond, rising and falling in urgent but undecipherable tones. There was no point standing there. Had anyone opened the door right then, it would have appeared as though I was eavesdropping.

I knocked.

Suddenly the door was wrenched open and I was confronted by Angel, who, if anything, appeared more than a little irritated by the sight of me standing there.

"Oh, it's you," she grumbled.

Faced with Angel's hostility, I couldn't help feeling like an intruder. But then how could I not feel like an outsider? I didn't belong there and really I never had. I'd been thrown in by circumstances beyond my control and had there been any other alternative at the time, I probably would have taken it. I shouldn't complain, though. Everyone here had accepted me, made me feel as comfortable as I was ever going to feel working in a brothel and, in all honesty, had I been in their shoes, I would have been likewise suspicious of someone like me.

Still, I couldn't help but feel as though my normal upbringing had somehow barred me from their tight fraternity.

I could see their point, though. How could I be expected to understand where they had come from? I didn't have a drug habit. I'd never been beaten or abused as a child. I had two normal parents — I'm being kind here considering current happenings — and I had never been confronted with any of the problems the girls had faced.

I wanted to leave, to escape back to my seemingly perfect life and hang my head in shame that I ever thought I had any real problems to deal with. But that was how I tended to feel around the girls. The spoilt prissy one.

Angel's expression remained closed and I half-expected her to close the door in my face but she moved aside letting me through. "I suppose you'd better come in then," she muttered and I walked in.

The first thing I saw in the kitchen was JoJo and Olivia huddled protectively around Scarlett, who was being comforted by Leanne. A sob escaped Leanne's generous embrace and I realized the solemn atmosphere was Scarlett-induced.

I have to admit I was more than a little taken back by the disheveled Scarlett and whispered to Leanne, "What's wrong?"

Leanne's concern was obvious, despite her efforts to appear calm, which I suspected was more for the benefit of the girls, who, for the first time I could remember, had stopped their sniping and come together in support of Scarlett. "Poor Scarlett had a bit of a nasty incident last night with a client. She was called out to a booking at a private home and when she got there, he refused to pay up and attacked her."

My blood ran cold. Poor Scarlett, she couldn't have weighed any more than fifty kilos, at most. Against any fellow with even a moderate amount of strength, she'd have no chance of defending herself.

"Is she all right?" I whispered, looking anxiously at Scarlett's tiny crumpled and sobbing form, horrified that something like this could have happened in the first place. Sitting there beside Leanne, she looked like a child. A scared child and my heart went out to her. Of course, Prue was always on at the girls to be careful and call in any strange requests — especially if it was a call-out to a private residence — but I never honestly believed that something like this would happen. Maybe in the city, but somehow not up here on the coast. Then perhaps I was being naïve. Besides, Scarlett had more street-smarts than any one I knew. If anyone knew when a situation was out of control, I imagined that she would.

"She will be. Luckily she got away with only a few bruises. Unfortunately, the bastard who did this to her has pressed assault charges against her."

"What?" I shook my head. "Have I missed something? Didn't you just say that *he* attacked Scarlett?"

JoJo turned slowly around toward me, her face set in a grim mask. "Yeah, well, the fucking coward didn't know that Scarlett carries pepper spray with her, did he? By the time he had her down on the floor, she didn't have much choice but to give him a face full. Now the bastard is claiming that Scarlett tried to pinch his wallet and wants her done for assault and attempted robbery."

"But surely the police wouldn't have believed that. Did she show them the bruises?"

"He's claiming it was self-defense and in light of the pepper spray, and the fact she's already got a record, unfortunately the police are taking his side," Leanne explained.

"That's outrageous!" I cried.

Angel came over and placed a steaming-hot cup of tea in front of Scarlett, before looking across at me with venom in her eyes. "No, it's fucking typical of the cops around here, that's what it is!" she sneered. "Those bastards should open their fucking eyes to some of the bastards out there instead of harassing us all the time."

For the first time since my arrival, Scarlett raised her head from Leanne's shoulder. Her eyes were red and swollen from crying, her makeup smeared across her small features. "I don't give a shit about the fucking cops *or* what happens to me. It's Levi I'm worried about. I'll lose him, I just know I will. If they put me away again, I'll never see him again," she cried, desperation making her voice sound strained and very small.

"Who?" I mouthed at Leanne, totally confused.

Angel cut in. "Levi is Scarlett's little boy."

Scarlett let out a cry of despair. "Children's Services will be at the fucking door and on my case as soon as the court date comes up." Looking up at Leanne pleadingly, she said, "I can't deal with all that again. If they put me away again, I know I'll lose him and if that happens I may as well be dead. He's all I've got to live for!"

I couldn't help but stare, my jaw dropping like an idiot. I had no idea that Scarlett had a child, but then again I really didn't know anything about any of the girls here.

"He's only six, for God's sake—a baby," cried Scarlett, growing more and more frantic by the minute. "I can't stand to think of him in some damn foster place.

They're the pits. I know. I spent enough time in them as a kid. Ran away most of the time, mind you," she added grimly. "God, even living on the streets was better than the shit I put up with in those fucking places..." Putting her head in her hands she let out a sob. "What am I going to do? They can't take Levi away from me. I won't let those bastards do to him what they did to me as a kid."

I looked across at Leanne, but from the look of pity in her eyes she was feeling every bit as powerless as the rest of us.

Leanne put her arm around Scarlett once more. "We'll find a lawyer, a real good one, and see what they say. I am sure we will work something out."

Scarlett shook Leanne off and stood up, angrily grabbing her smokes from the table and lighting up. "I can't afford a fucking lawyer. I'm already two months behind on my bloody rent and they're threatening to cut the phone off on me. I'm skint and the fucking idiots they give you through the courts are next to useless. It's fucking hopeless. Anyway, even if I could somehow afford someone decent, there is no way they would agree to represent someone like me, or any of us girls. You know that as well as the next person. They think we're scum and deserve everything that comes to us."

Brad's callous remarks against these so-called blights on decent society came back to haunt me and, as much as it shamed me to admit it, I had to agree she was probably right. Looking around at the concern etched on the girls' faces, I had to do something.

It was then I noticed Leanne looking at me questioningly and my heart skipped a beat. Of course, she was the only one here who knew Brad was a lawyer. But how could I possibly tell her the truth? The truth in this case being that Brad would chuck a pink fit if I even suggested that he represent a prostitute. Just the thought of his reaction made me tense. But what could I do? Right then, I was ashamed to admit it to myself, never mind Leanne, but the sad fact was the love of my life was a bigoted snob who would most likely be the first one to suggest that Scarlett be thrown into prison and her son taken away to be raised by strangers.

Leanne continued to give me the hard stare. But what could I do? There was no point in giving Scarlett any false hope. The poor girl needed help.

An unbidden image of Robert in all his sticky orange glory sprang to mind and with it came an idea.

* * * *

Across the road from the private hospital, I sat silently counting the freckles on the back of my hand. To think the events of the past couple of days had reduced me to this. It was pathetic, really. I was turning into some nutter with a nervous compulsion, but it was all I could do to pull myself together and distract myself from what I was about to do. Official visiting hours were due to start in ten minutes and I was beginning to regret my rash show of heroics in offering to come to the rescue of a hooker in distress.

But poor Scarlett. To my shame, I have to admit that up until yesterday I had never thought of her as anything other than a hard-arsed, potty-mouthed hooker, but it was clear not only to me but to all the girls that she simply adored her little boy and treasured him more than anything else in the world. She'd tearfully produced a tattered photo from her bag, showing us a picture of her darling son. Even now I couldn't dispel the image of her sobbing, clutching a photo of her little boy. With his small elfin features so like his mother's and huge inquisitive eyes, he was simply adorable as he stood grinning at the camera with an ice-cream in his hand, his face pink with happiness.

Gazing lovingly down at his image, Scarlett's face had lit up, softening her normally brittle-hard expression. Clearly he was her only shining light in an otherwise harsh life and it was that image of her I kept fresh in my mind as a reminder of why it was that I was here in the first place. This was not about me, after all. It was about keeping a little boy and his mother together.

Across the road, a steady stream of ambulances were queued up outside the main entrance, unloading and ferrying patients into the Emergency ward. I kept waiting for teams of nurses to come hurtling out shouting orders like on those TV medical dramas. Sadly, my yearning for excitement was thwarted. It must have been a slow day for life-threatening emergencies, going by the sedate, almost bored pace of the paramedics as they chatted amongst themselves, maneuvering unmanageable gurneys to and from the ambulances.

There was no point putting it off, but the more I thought about what I was about to do, the more it occurred to me how risky and possibly even illegal it was. Blackmail was such an unsavory concept. Not that what I had in mind constituted blackmail exactly, more a firm request for a helping hand — reluctant as it may prove to be — as payment for my continuing silence about you-know-what. But what if he turned me down point-blank? Refused to see me in the first place or called security on me? Or, even worse, turned the tables on me and threatened to reveal all to Brad? Did I have the guts to follow through with this? Not for the first time since hearing of Scarlett's dilemma, it occurred to me that my attempt to help her could easily come back to bite me on the arse.

No. I had to think positively. This was about Scarlett and her little boy and someone had to step in and do something to keep them together. I would just have to put aside my misgivings and get on with it. Act like an adult. Show some gumption. Confront the man I had so recently peeled an orange condom from and try to pretend I hadn't seen him stark naked and smeared with orange marmalade in the middle of a bondage session.

No wonder I felt like throwing up.

Compared to many of the large public hospitals in the city, this one was fairly unimpressive from the outside. Single-story and surrounded by neat hedges and modest gardens, it was set back from the main road amongst private homes, including some recently converted into specialist consulting rooms, only distinguishable from the other cottages by the shiny brass plates displayed on the front doors. What it lacked in stature, it certainly made up for in sheer opulence once I walked through the sliding glass doors and into the oasis of elegance within. Seriously, this was no budget-starved state-funded hell-hole, but a luxurious, resort-style clinic for those whose wealth and status rescued them from lengthy waiting lists, dodgy doctors and overcrowded wards.

Looking around the foyer at the numerous prints by artists such as Pro Hart, Margaret Ollie and Russell

Drysdale—at least I *think* they were *prints*—it was abundantly clear that healthcare for the rich was as much about esthetic therapy as it was about medicine. After all, who wants to be sick in a hovel? But seriously, had it not been for the ambulances parked outside, the main reception area could have passed for a hotel. The only thing missing was the concierge and security cameras. Just to be on the safe side, though, I picked up a small but outrageously priced bunch of flowers from the kiosk on the way in to legitimize myself as a visitor as I asked for directions to Robert's room at reception.

For once luck was on my side—Robert was currently occupying a private room. Just knowing that we wouldn't have an audience lifted some of the pressure off me and some courage returned.

This was it.

I wasn't leaving until I got what I came for.

Tough words, I know.

Believe me, I was talking myself up here.

After passing what had to be about a million linen trolleys and nearly as many nurses' stations staffed with scary efficiency-crazed sisters, I came across his room and stopped a short distance from the door. Room 202. I found myself overrun by nerves. And why wouldn't I? All things considered, our last meeting hadn't exactly been a Hallmark moment.

What on earth was I going to say to him? Did I attempt to make light of the entire marmalade-brothel fiasco, or, just to be on the safe side, avoid mentioning the unmentionable altogether? Alternatively, did I come right out with what I came here to ask or at least make some feeble attempt at pretending I was there to wish him a speedy recovery? Of course, I could just turn around and flee like the coward I truly was.

As it happened, fate stepped in, in the form of Muriel, who at that moment walked out of her husband's room and straight toward me. Oh shit! I hadn't counted on that happening and knew it was going to put the clappers on my plans. What was I going to say? Oh, God, it was too late anyway. There was nowhere to hide. This was it. Showtime.

Muriel stopped a couple of meters away from me, somewhat startled, trying to place me in the unfamiliar surroundings before sudden recognition hit her and she smiled.

"Brooke. Hello. My goodness, what a lovely surprise to see you."

By her puzzled look, I was clearly the last person she had expected to see and instantly my face began to color. I cleared my throat. "Oh, um, I haven't come at a bad time, have I?" I asked, by now desperately hoping it was, getting me off the hook.

"No, of course not," she replied. "Robert is recovering wonderfully now. Thank goodness it was a relatively minor attack. So much so that the doctor assured us that he should be home tomorrow or the next day. Between us it is just as well, too. The poor man is bored silly and not taking well to being a patient, I'm afraid. In fact, just quietly, I think the nurses will be glad to see the back of him." Muriel smiled, but the lines of fatigue around her eyes belied her cheerful persona. She looked like she had barely slept and even now I could sense her anxiety.

"I'm sorry to arrive out of the blue like this. I know I should have rung first, but I was passing and just wanted to wish Robert well."

Muriel smiled, putting me at ease. "No need to apologize. It was nice of you to think of him.

Unfortunately, I was just on my way out. I've been here all afternoon waiting for the doctor to come and now I am supposed to be at the hairdresser's in twenty minutes." She glanced down at her watch. "But not to worry, they're usually running late anyway, so a couple of minutes isn't going to make much difference, is it? Come on in. I'm sure Robert will be glad of the company."

Little did she know!

I think the Grim Reaper would have been a more welcome sight.

Robert looked up from the book he was reading, surprise registering on his pale face at seeing Muriel back so soon and, as he took in the sight of me, his eyes clouded over with embarrassment laced with a liberal smattering of suspicion bordering on irritation.

"Look who I ran into outside!" Muriel announced cheerfully to her husband, ignoring his black look. "Brooke's come in to see how you are. Isn't she a darling?"

Not surprisingly under the circumstances, I found myself unable to make direct eye contact. At least he had clothes on this time. And no sign of sticky orange jelly! Still, there was no denying that this was probably the single most awkward moment of my entire life.

Saving me from making a complete idiot of myself, I remembered the flowers in my hand and thrust them toward Muriel. "Thought they might brighten the room a little," I blurted out lamely, feeling my face go up in flames.

"Oh, they're lovely dear," she said, holding them out to her stony-faced husband. "Aren't they lovely, Robert?"

Clearly flowers were not the ice-breaker I had envisioned and if he responded more than a curt nod, I missed it completely. Muriel didn't seem the least fazed, though, and smiled. "I'll just pop out and get a vase for these before I go. You sit down and I'll be back in a mo."

Moments later, I was left standing in awkward silence beside Robert's bed and wishing I was anywhere else but there. A sense of déjà vu assaulted me and I tried to block out the memory of the last time I'd stood next to him in similar surroundings. The only thing missing was the bondage, condoms and, of course, marmalade.

I cleared my throat nervously. Time for some small talk.

"Um, how are you feeling?"

"I'm fine," he snapped, staring out of the window.

"You gave everyone a terrible fright. They'll all be relieved to know you're recovering, I'm sure."

Robert turned his head, looking directly at me for the first time since I arrived, and I shrank from the anger radiating from his eyes. "What the hell do you want?" he barked, trying to keep his evident fury from those out in the corridor.

Despite his hostility, I wasn't fooled for a moment. Clearly he was as mortified by my presence now as he had been at the time of his untimely attack and I couldn't help but feel sorry for him.

"I didn't come in here to make you feel uncomfortable or to cause any problems, honestly."

"What exactly are you doing here, then?" he snapped, his eyes flaming in the manner of a lion cornered.

Muriel arrived at that moment, rescuing me from an immediate response. Thank God she hadn't heard our exchange.

"There we are, dear. I got the last one," she said cheerfully, placing the world's ugliest vase beside him on the bedside table. "I hate to run out like this, but I really do have to dash. It was lovely seeing you again, Brooke, and I'm sure we will catch up soon," she said before leaning over and giving her husband a light peck on the forehead. "And you stop being so grumpy with the nurses now," she chided, smiling at him affectionately. "Remember they're just doing their job and hopefully you'll be home tomorrow. Okay. Bye-bye, love."

Witnessing Muriel's almost maternal show of affection, I felt like an intruder and had to remind myself of what was at stake.

"Well? What do you want?" Robert demanded, the moment Muriel disappeared down the corridor.

I cleared my throat. This had to come out right. This wasn't a polite request, but having said that I was not about to plead with a man as blatantly hypocritical as to sleep with prostitutes whilst publicly condemning them as social lepers and a scourge of society. Still, not for the first time this afternoon, I wondered what I would do if he refused. "I need your help."

Robert raised his eyebrows, somewhat surprised. His skepticism practically filled the room. Clearly this wasn't what he had imagined.

"Not for me, exactly," I hastened to add. "It's actually one of the *girls* who needs your help," I announced.

Robert's face turned an alarming shade of red and I feared he was about to have another attack.

"You have a hide coming in here, you know. If you think I'm going to give them money to keep their mouths shut, you can think again," he growled, his voice low with menace.

I refused to succumb to his intimidation. Mind you, it's difficult to come across all authoritarian wearing a gown with one's butt hanging out.

"No, no one is after your money," I began firmly, trying to calm my racing heart. Mine was not the only heart needing calming, either. The monitor next to Robert had begun to go ballistic and I cast an anxious look over to the seismic activity displayed on the heart monitor. Great, all I needed was for a nurse to come in and I'd be ordered out quick smart. "Nothing like that."

"Then what the hell *is* it then?"

"It's Scarlett—at Heavenly Pleasures," I reminded him in lowered tones. "You know her quite well, from what I believe."

Robert stared back, his face devoid of any sign of recognition.

"The small woman with the dark hair…"

"Jesus, I know who you mean!" he snapped, glancing at the door nervously. "What about her?"

"Well, the situation is this. She had a nasty run-in with a client a couple of days back. Even though he attacked her, he's pressed charges and she's in trouble with the police for simply defending herself. Now the poor girl is beside herself with worry and desperately needs some expert legal help to get her off an assault charge."

A look of disgust passed over his face, prompting me to bring out the big guns of persuasion. "Look, the way I see it, those girls saved not only your life, but possibly your reputation as well, so I think it's the very least you can do for them."

I let the words hang in the air as Robert sat motionless for what seemed like ages. I wasn't put off by his stony expression. Having got that off my chest, I was feeling a lot better and not even his formidable presence intimidated me. Things were going better than I had envisioned. Well, at least he hadn't called security on me. So, as far as I was concerned, he could lie there all afternoon, but I was determined to stand my ground. I wasn't leaving until he agreed to help Scarlett.

"Okay."

Okay? I wasn't sure I had heard him right.

"Excuse me?"

"I said okay. I can't promise she'll get off, of course, that's for the judge to decide. But I *will* appoint someone to represent her *pro bono*," he responded gruffly.

This was too easy and I wondered what the catch was. "For free? She hasn't any money you know."

Robert shook his head and rolled his eyes, clearly exasperated. "What on earth do you think *pro bono* means? Tell her it won't cost her a cent. *But...*" He glared at me. "You can tell your *friends* I never want to hear a mention of *this* or, for that matter, any other recent *happenings* ever. Not even a hint or I swear to God I will see to it that the place is shut down. Do you understand?"

His threat, and I had no doubt he would follow through with it, was clear but I knew the girls well enough to know that his anxieties were groundless. After all, discretion was their business.

I smiled, my relief at pulling it off for Scarlett making me dizzy with happiness. "I understand perfectly! If you help out Scarlett with your best attorney, I'll give you my word that your, um, accident will be completely forgotten."

Telling Scarlett the good news later that afternoon had to rank as one of the most rewarding things I had ever done. In the time it took me to convince her that everything was going to be all right, I swear ten years of worry lifted from her tired, anxious face.

Chapter Twenty-One

For the next couple of days, not even Brad's persistent moodiness could shake my feeling of elation. Helping Scarlett had not only gifted me with a sense of confidence and purpose, but, safe in the knowledge that Robert was unlikely to be frequenting the establishment anytime in the distant future, I had decided to stay on at Heavenly Pleasures — at least for the time being. I was finally making inroads on the phone bill and, if all went well, in another couple of months I'd be phone-debt free!

Brad didn't arrive home that evening until later than usual, by which time I was happily camped out in front of the telly watching *Notting Hill* on DVD with a glass of wine in one hand and a box of chocolates, a gift from Leanne and the girls, balancing on my lap. I was in girlie heaven. Hugh Grant and Belgian confectionary were a combination no girl could refuse. In fact, I was just waiting for the day they make a movie involving Hugh Grant dipped *in* chocolate. Sort of *Charlie and the*

Chocolate Factory meets *Four Weddings and a Funeral*. Yum. *Four Éclairs and a Hunky English Stud*.

But the best part was I had them all to myself. Brad had left a message on the answering machine stating he had a late meeting and didn't know what time he'd be finished. Romantic? I think not! I didn't care. I had my evening planned to the nth degree. It was going to be *Notting Hill*, then following that *Chocolat* — I also fancied a bit of Johnny Depp — and, if I had the stamina, I was going to treat myself to a romantic serving of Colin Firth in *Bridget Jones: The Edge of Reason*, which had bonus Hugh Grant thrown in for good measure. Yes, an entertaining night of chick-flicks had been a long time in coming since Brad had outlawed them a few months before, inflicting a new regime of football, *CSI* and *Law and Order* in their place.

Sadly, as soon as my errant fiancé walked through the door an hour later, my plans for the evening were hurled unceremoniously out of the window. Snatching up the remote, he turned off the movie without so much as a word of apology. I could have screamed with frustration. Hugh was about to declare his undying love for Julia in front of a packed press conference. My favorite bit. I looked up and scowled at Brad. Talk about rude!

"Hey, do you mind? I was watching that!" I cried, incensed my romantic interlude with Hugh had been so rudely cut short.

Ignoring my growing fury, he threw down his briefcase and kicked off his shoes. "What the hell is that crap on for, anyway?"

"Excuse me?"

"Well, for Christ's sake, can't a man come in from work without being made to suffer that shit?"

My hackles rose. So it was going to be another one of those evenings. I took a deep breath and braced myself for yet another nasty altercation. "In case you haven't noticed, you're not suffering that shit, seeing as you just turned the bloody thing off."

"Well, someone has to save you from all that drivel. Christ, who wants to watch gay actors like that, carrying on like some soppy wimps, anyway? Set him up against the likes of Matt Damon and see who walks away from it."

Now walking in and rudely turning off *Notting Hill* was bad enough, but insulting Hugh Grant was pushing things too far. I saw red.

"*Excuse me*, but who are you to tell me what I can and can't watch?" I shouted, glad to give him back some of the filthy attitude I'd been putting up with from him for days now. "You weren't even here. I didn't know what time you were coming home, so you can leave your foul mood at the door, thank you, because, quite frankly, I am sick to death of it."

Brad looked slightly taken aback and I had to smother a smirk of satisfaction. I was getting better at this confrontation caper. "*So*, what the hell is wrong with you? And don't you dare blame the movie. You've been like this for days."

Brad heaved a very un-Brad-like sigh, shaking off his jacket and carelessly throwing it on top of his briefcase.

"I know I've been a bit out of sorts…"

He's been a complete prick.

"But, if you must know, it's bloody Tom at work," he complained, loosening his tie and pulling it free of his shirt collar. "He's dumped this crappy case on me for some reason—an assault charge. My guess is that no one else would touch it. Bloody hell, I'm up to my ears in work at the moment, but when I tried to refuse it he all but insisted I take it. He actually said if I wanted to be considered partnership material I'd be best to demonstrate to the others that I was a team player! Can you believe it! What the hell does he mean by that? Jesus, I of all people know what leadership and teamwork are all about. *I am the one who has been slaving my guts out for that company for almost five years.*"

"Well, didn't you tell him that?" I asked, more than a little annoyed that I'd been made to bear the brunt of his mood because someone else had pissed him off.

"Of course I did, for all the good it did me," he responded irritably. "Christ, I even suggested he pass it on to Simon the Boy Wonder to handle. I would have thought this would have been more up his alley, what with him being a bleeding-heart liberal an' all," he sneered.

Suddenly warning bells started to ring. No, ringing would have been somewhat pleasant. This was a case of ear-splitting, high-pitched, screaming sirens.

Assault charge?

Bleeding-heart liberals?

Brad in a fouler of a mood for the past couple of days?

Not Scarlett! How stupid was I? Of course it was. I was amazed it hadn't occurred to me before now, especially in light of the fact that Robert had been more than a little pissed off with my request in the first place. How better to get back at me than to assign Brad to Scarlett's case? Obviously, this was Robert's idea of payback. I felt sick. This was too close for comfort.

"Um, what's wrong with taking on an assault charge?" I asked nervously. "Didn't you represent some footballer a few months back, you know the one who knocked out a security guard outside the nightclub in town?"

I glanced over toward the signed football jersey Brad had scored when he'd gotten the guy off with nothing more than a warning.

"That was completely different," he replied sharply. "He was a first grade player and, had he been convicted, would have missed out on a place in the state line-up. Besides, it was clear he was provoked at the time."

"I thought the papers said he was blind drunk at the time?"

Brad sighed impatiently. "Anyway, the assault charge is not the issue here, Brooke. It's the bloody client they want me to represent I have the problem with."

It was Scarlett. It had to be, but as much as I wanted to drop the subject, something inside me started to churn and I couldn't let it go.

"What about the client?"

Running his hands through his hair, Brad shook his head. "Well, apart from the fact that she's a prostitute, it's bloody obvious she's guilty."

My heart plummeted. Great, not even her lawyer was on her side. What hope did she have? A spark of anger lit inside me.

"How can you possibly know she's guilty? Did she admit it?"

Brad looked across at me strangely. "Jesus, Brooke, don't be so naïve. Of course she didn't. But then people like *her* wouldn't recognize the truth if it leapt up and bit them on the arse. You don't know what these people are like. They're not like us, believe me. I see them in court all the time. Oh, sure, there's always an excuse. It's always someone *else's* fault. People like that have no concept of honesty or right and wrong. Believe me, I don't need to see the details to know that she's probably guilty as hell.

"The thing I don't understand is why on earth I've been lumbered with it. These cases are usually dealt with by Legal Aid — after all, you only get what you pay for. And apart from the fact that pushing this case on me is an insult to all the hard work I have put into raising the profile of the company, this isn't going to look good on my résumé."

I frowned, growing more and more anxious. "Have you told Tom this? Sounds like she'd be better off without you representing her, anyway."

"Of course I told Tom. Where do you think I've been all bloody night? I was in a meeting with him trying to convince him that this was more suited to someone else…well, Simon actually."

"And what did he say?"

"That's just the thing. He said that this had been earmarked for me especially, but not only that. For some reason it is going through as *pro bono*, for God's sake. Jeez, it's a bloody freebie. I'll be a laughingstock."

Clearly he was stuck with it — or should I say poor Scarlett was stuck with *him*. Bearing that in mind, I considered Scarlett's only hope lay in the chance that Brad saw this in a more positive light.

"It might not be as bad as you're thinking. After all, they must think highly of you if they think you can win the case and, in doing so, help her."

"*Help her?* For Christ's sake, Brooke, listen to yourself, will you? You're as bad as Simon. I'd be doing everyone a favor if I made sure she *was* put away."

I could only stare at him in disbelief. Poor Scarlett. If that was his attitude, she would be better off with Legal Aid. What on earth had I done?

"Jesus, Brad, what about some compassion? Surely she deserves that much?" I said, finally letting my disgust rise to the surface.

"Compassion? Get real. I saw her today. She's as hard as they come. Talk about a ball-breaker. My guess is she's a drug addict to boot. They all are, you know, and thieves as well. The victim is claiming she broke into his house, attacked him and attempted to steal his wallet. Where was *her* compassion when she practically blinded him with pepper spray?"

"That's just his story, surely?"

"Well, under the circumstances I'm inclined to believe him. After all, who am I expected to believe here, a successful businessman with his own car dealership, or a filthy whore? No, it's completely implausible that he would have lowered himself to hiring some prostitute in the first place and, as for attacking her as she's now claiming, well, it's just ridiculous. She must take me for a fool if she thinks I believe her lies."

A tide of apprehension rolled over me. The way he was talking, I couldn't help thinking that he would deliberately jeopardize his own case just to prove a point and suddenly I saw all my good intentions going up in flames.

"But if she is *your* client, don't you have a legal obligation to at least give her the benefit of the doubt? What if she *is* telling you the truth? Prostitutes do get attacked sometimes. I've read about it in the papers from time to time. Why couldn't she be telling the truth?"

Brad looked across at me, more than a little pissed off.

"Who the hell cares, anyway? As far as I'm concerned, one more off the street would be a blessing.

Reckon if we locked them all away, we'd solve more than a few problems."

All I could think of was Scarlett and her little boy and I was filled with nothing less than disgust for this man I used to think was noble and decent. *Hah, what a joke. He* was nothing but a joke of a man, a callous egotistical bastard.

"Hey, what's up? You've gone quiet," he said, finally noticing the frozen look of loathing on my face. "Sorry, hon, I knew I shouldn't have brought up the subject. It's hardly the type of thing you want to be thinking about. Christ, I don't want to be thinking about it either, and I'm the one who's *supposed* to be representing her!"

I swear if I had kept my mouth shut a moment longer, I would have burst a blood vessel. Suddenly all the rage I had been suppressing from as far back as the dinner party, if not earlier, bubbled up within me and something inside me cracked.

"Jesus, listen to yourself, Brad. I can't believe that you, of all people, *you* who goes around telling everyone how socially conscious and morally responsible you are, could be so callous, so *hypocritical.* You're a lawyer. You're supposed to represent people in trouble and now you think you have this God-given right to decide who's worthy of your so-called expertise and who isn't? What, so now it's only those people you approve of who deserve a fair go? What on earth has happened to you lately? You never used to be judgmental and high and mighty. You used to be nice, once."

"Jeez, Brooke, ease up, will you?" He laughed, seemingly amused by my outburst. "What is it to you, anyway? Why on earth do you care if some scummy whore gets thrown in jail where she no doubt belongs?"

It took all my strength not to slap the sanctimonious smile right off his face. "Why do I care?" I finally yelled, sucking in a lungful of air. "I *care* because this woman you so compassionately describe as a scummy whore happens to be a friend of mine, that's why."

As soon as the words were out of my mouth, I knew there was no going back. I had not only drawn a line in the sand but taken a hurling jump right over it into unknown territory. The air surrounding us seemed to freeze, trapping my words in suspended animation midway between us like an unexploded bomb.

"*Excuse me?*" Brad gasped, his face going from white to deep red and back to white in a matter of seconds.

This was the defining moment. I could either stand up for what I believed to be right and just, not only for myself but for those people like Scarlett who I had recently come to not only know but in a lot of ways respect, or I could regress back to the spineless wimp of old and claim I was confused, overworked or premenstrual or simply a little pissed and therefore talking shit.

"Are you telling me that you actually know this, this *woman*...what's her name again...? Carol Jane Potts, I think."

I took a deep breath, knowing full well what I was about to reveal. "If she works at Heavenly Pleasures in the arcade in town, then yes, I do know her—but as Scarlett."

There, it was out.

Brad appeared more than a little confused. "How?"

"Well, I wasn't intending on telling you this, knowing full-well what your reaction would be, but it seems you have left me with no choice. I work there—as a receptionist, mind you—but I've been working there for the past couple of months."

Brad looked as if he'd been kicked in the guts. "What on earth are you talking about? I don't understand. Have you gone mad, or is this a joke? What about the job at the medical center?"

"I got fired a few weeks ago."

As the truth of my words finally sank in, Brad was quiet for a few seconds before exploding. "*What!* A few *weeks* ago! So you've been lying to me all this time?"

"Oh, come on now, I think lying is a bit strong. More withholding, I'd say," I stated defiantly.

"Don't you bloody well get smart with me. How could you do this to me?" Slapping himself on the forehead, he turned on me. "Oh shit, now it all makes fucking sense. *You*. Oh my God, it was *you* who spoke to bloody Robert. I couldn't work out why he'd suddenly tell Tom to make me represent some tart on a crappy assault charge. Oh, God, I swear if this gets out my reputation will be in shreds. My career will be over."

"Is that all you think about? Your bloody career? What about us? What about Scarlett, or Carol? She has a little boy to think about. He's only six and he needs his mother. She needs your help, not your judgments. And, anyway, you can stop worrying about Robert. It won't get out. He's not going to say anything to anyone about it, I promise."

Brad was past listening to me, though. He was past a lot of things and reasoning was only one of them.

"Oh I can't believe this. I feel ill. I feel physically sick. Just to think that you've been coming home to me after being around those, those *people*," he spat in disgust. "Christ, what's next then? Planning on earning a bit more on the side, are you? Going to start taking in men off the streets...oh, God, I can't believe I've been *sleeping* with you!"

He was practically incandescent with rage and, with his fury filling the room, I couldn't help taking a step back from him, fearing he'd lash out at me.

"For crying out loud," I shouted, hot tears of rage building behind my eyes. "I'm just a bloody receptionist, for fuck's sake. Get a grip. It's a good job and, more than that, I actually *like* working there."

Brad stared back bug-eyed in disbelief. I was waiting for his eyeballs to shoot out of his head and bounce across the floor. "Are you telling me that you plan on staying there?" he gasped.

I shrugged. "Yes, I suppose I am!"

"No! No! No!" he yelled, shaking his head manically. "How can you possibly *imagine* that I would stand by while you blatantly drag *my* name and *my* reputation through the mud? How could you do this to me? You stupid, selfish fucking cow!"

"What exactly are you getting at?"

"What am I getting at? I can't believe you have to ask me that under the circumstances! What I am getting at is either you leave that disgusting job immediately and *never* breathe another word about it to me or anyone else for that matter—"

"Or?" I challenged.

"*Or*...or...or you can get out right now. If you want to run around with low-life scum like that, I don't want to have anything more to do with you. Jesus, you have jeopardized my career enough as it is."

As if I was watching on from a distance, a sense of calm trickled through my body. It was like someone had turned something off within me and, for the first time, I began to see my life with Brad with some kind of clarity.

"So that is it, then?"

Brad ran his hands through his hair. "Yes, if you want to remain here with me and become my wife, you are going to have to start behaving like one. *Not* some slut who thinks it acceptable to rub shoulders with the likes of *that* mob." Rolling his eyes toward the ceiling, he seemed to be talking to himself. "How could I have been so stupid? It all makes sense now. Your weird behavior. The secrecy. All those times your mobile was turned off..."

For the first time in months, if not years, I saw my future together with my dreams of a life of married bliss and realized it was just that, all some kind of a fantasy I had dreamed up in the hope that reality might just follow. The last few months I had been so consumed with planning the wedding I had deliberately pushed aside all the doubts plaguing me about our relationship. The fact he had alienated me from all my old friends bar Trudy should been a sign of things to come. His disapproval of my taste in music, clothes, hairstyles, not to mention his resentment of my love of shopping. I should have known.

Piece by piece, he'd chipped away at the essence of what made me *me*, until I feared there would be nothing left but his image of what a perfect wife should be, and that wasn't me. As much as I wanted to blame him for ruining everything, I had allowed him to bully me into being someone I wasn't, passing off his so-called concern and guidance as proof of his love. I realized now, though, that if he couldn't love me for what I was then he didn't love me that much at all.

It was as though I was slowly rising from the fog and seeing Brad clearly for the first time. Looking at him now, ranting on almost demented with anger, I finally realized the man standing before me wasn't my knight in shining armor but a mean-spirited, social-climbing control freak.

Inflated with rage, Brad loomed over me, staring me down like I was some criminal in the dock and I knew at that moment that I couldn't stomach the thought of waking up each morning wondering what fault he would find with me that day. I was tired. Tired of this and tired of him.

"You're absolutely right," I responded wearily.

Some of his anger melted on hearing my words and a sheen of superiority arose on his face. "Well, I'm glad to hear you finally admit it. Despite this mess you've landed me in, I really hoped you would come to your senses eventually. Mind you, I have to make it clear that I am still furious with you. What you did was unforgivable, but despite all that, I'm willing to give you *one* last chance to prove yourself to me. It's going to take me some time to trust you again, of course. You are going to have to earn my trust back."

"Brad, stop."

"What?"

"Listen, Brad, I don't want your bloody trust if it means having to suffer your bigoted, self-righteous opinions. I'm sick of them and I'm sick of you. If getting married to *you* means giving up everything that you don't like about me, I want nothing to do with it—and nothing more to do with you, either. You're selfish, a bully, you have no compassion and you lack any kind of conscience. And what's more," I took a deep breath, "you're totally crap in bed!"

Gobsmacked, Brad could do nothing but stare back.

"*And,*" I added, my voice rising to crescendo pitch, "you can stick your trust and you can stick your bloody career and while you're at it you can stick this damn engagement ring right up your arse! It's over. I'm leaving!"

Having got that off my chest, I wrenched the quarter carat diamond ring from my finger and hurled it at him with as much force as I could muster.

There, I thought. *I'm out of here.*

Chapter Twenty-Two

By the time I reached Trudy's flat, the adrenaline rush that had carried me through my earlier burst of whoop-arse had burned itself out, leaving nothing but utter emotional exhaustion in its wake. Still, knowing I had done the right thing did little to alleviate the feeling that my heart was about to break in two.

"I can't believe it's all over," I cried, accepting a box of tissues. "I thought he was the one. How could I have been so blind?"

"So it's all over then, like, for good?"

I nodded.

"So you're telling me that you're *not* going to go rushing back to him tomorrow and beg him to take you back or anything?"

I shook my head.

Trudy let out a sigh of relief and squeezed my hand. "Thank God for that."

"Why didn't you tell me what a total douche bag he was?" I sniffed, wiping the tears from my eyes.

This wasn't strictly fair of me as Trudy had been the only person to tell me. The only one who hadn't fallen for his smooth manipulative charm.

"Would you have believed me if I had?" she replied, drawing me into her arms.

I had to admit she had a point there, thinking about all the times I'd stuck up for Brad. What kind of a fool was I?

"I'm so sorry, but this was something you had to find out yourself. Anyway, I didn't think it was fair to make you feel as though you had to choose between us."

"But I would have never let him come between us," I cried out and for the first time I wondered what my life would be like without her.

I knew then what she said was true. Had I gone on to marry Brad, it would have become more and more difficult to balance my friendship with Trudy and at the same time keep the peace with Brad.

"I know, but, still, you're my best friend and I would never have forgiven myself if we'd fallen out over some lousy bloke."

I sniffed. "No need to worry about that now, is there? I don't think I'll be hearing back from him after what I said. Not that I'd want to."

Trudy chuckled. "Tell me again, did you really tell him he was a dud in bed?"

I nodded glumly. I felt a twinge of guilt. My mother had always told me not to mock the afflicted.

Trudy began to smile mischievously. I should have guessed what was coming.

"*Well*, come on, dish the dirt! Was he?" she asked, clearly delighting in the chance to heap some crap on him after keeping her mouth shut for months, if not years. After only a microsecond of hesitation, I sat down next to her on the sofa and made myself comfortable. It was time. Time, that is, to reward her for her ongoing patience with a titbit of delicious slander.

"Okay, let me put it this way, Trud. I reckon a vibrator has more finesse than Brad in the boudoir — and that's *without* the batteries!"

Trudy squealed and fell about laughing. Clearly this was just what she had been hoping for.

"Christ, that's just so sad," she choked, wheezing like an old lady before taking another breath and starting all over again. At this rate, I wondered if I'd need to find her some oxygen. I frowned. Surely my sex life wasn't *that* funny? Pathetic, maybe? I was beginning to feel like a total loser. But then I couldn't really blame her. Had it been the other way around, I would have been all ears.

I owed it to what remained of my dignity to shoot her a half-hearted look of annoyance before continuing, "No, what's even sadder is that I've spent the better part of the last three years waiting for him to find my bloody clitoris! A damn map might have helped, I suppose, but then he was never one to listen to instructions!"

Wiping a tear from her eye, Trudy finally stopped convulsing and smiled. "Oh, honey, welcome back. Thank God you didn't marry him. It would have killed me to stand there and pretend to like him. He was such a jerk."

I wasn't about to argue with her on that point.

"And just think," she continued, "the best thing is that not only you never have to sleep with him again, but you never have to lay eyes on that horrible mother of his, either."

Shit.

I blanched and looked across at Trudy, my face weighed down with dread. How could I have forgotten? If there was a hell on earth, I was about to fall in head first.

"*My* mother!" I gasped. "Oh, sweet Jesus. What am I going to tell her? She's never going to forgive me for this."

"Just tell her the truth about Brad and what he was really like. She'll understand."

I bit my lip. "I don't know if she will."

"Of course she will. She's your mother, for crying out loud."

I couldn't help but groan. "Don't remind me. She's also the woman who thinks the sun shines out of Brad's arse, remember? This is going to kill her. She looked on Brad as the one who was going to save me from myself. Finally, I was going to make her proud."

Trudy was looking at me strangely. "Can I say something without sounding like a complete cow?"

I shrugged. "Be my guest." At least she asked first. Most people I knew weren't that considerate.

"Do you think that maybe, just maybe, you were getting married to please your mother more than yourself?"

I went to speak, but Trudy beat me to it. "No, think about it, Brooke. Your parents loved him from the word go—especially your mum. For the first time I can ever remember, she wasn't on your case to get a better job—"

"Or get a job, period."

"Well, yeah. But more than that, for the first time that I remember, she was treating you like an adult. You guys were beginning to get along..."

"Until the wedding dress debacle, that is."

"Oh, well, at least you don't have to worry about that anymore, either."

"Am I really that pathetic?"

As ever, resourceful in a crisis, Trudy shot me a look of sympathy and stood up. "Do you know what I think?"

I shook my head, a picture of abject misery.

"I think we both need a drink, hon."

"Fucking Brad," I muttered.

* * * *

Locking the door behind me, my next move was to push the keys under the door and stand back for one last look at the place Brad and I had called home for the last couple of years. I didn't feel anything. Not regret, not anger, not even any great sadness. Trudy was a little worried at my lack of emotion, fearing I was in a state of denial. But if anything, a weight lifted from my shoulders as I contemplated a life free of all Brad's petty rules and regulations. Sure, I had wasted the better part of three years on him, but at least I had come to my senses. Better late than never. I'd had a lucky escape.

It was now the morning after the night before, or as it was now being referred to, the night of the Great Arse Kicking. Together with Trudy, who had insisted on taking the day off to help me, we waited around the corner out of sight until Brad left for work. Then, when the coast was clear, I let myself in and gathered up my belongings. Apart from my clothes, there wasn't really much to gather. I was happy to leave most of it behind with almost three years of shattered dreams. I was determined to get everything in one go as I had no intention of ever coming back.

Last night, I had surprised myself with how strong I'd been, but I wasn't willing to risk another ugly scene on the off-chance that I might regress back to the gibbering coward of old, or, worse still, apologize. Considering my parting comments, I wasn't holding any false hopes of our split being amicable. Really, I was amazed he hadn't shredded my clothes and scattered them across the front lawn like retail road kill, or smashed everything in the flat after I'd walked out last night. Like Trudy pointed out, though, he would rather swallow his bitterness than risk the neighbors learning of our less-than-perfect life. *Appearances. It's all about appearances. Yes, it's fine to be miserable as long as you put on a happy face.*

Partway through our second bottle of cheap plonk last night, Trudy had insisted I switch off my mobile phone, thus avoiding any nasty break-up messages or, alternatively, pleas for an eleventh-hour reconciliation from you-know-who. I could see her point. After completely annihilating Brad's character and calling him every name under the sun for the better part of two hours, she hadn't been about to take the chance that I'd experience a change of heart and call her a bitch for slagging off my boyfriend.

Yes, many a loyal friendship had in the past bitten the big one when a break-up went horribly wrong and the lovers in question reconciled. It's always the loyal girlfriends who suffered, she'd moaned. One minute you're enjoying a drunken post-break-up bitchfest with your broken-hearted man-hating friend and the next thing you see her and the bastard all loved up again down the street shooting vile looks your way. Ah, the hazards of modern friendships.

With this in mind, I shouldn't have been too surprised that morning to find I had twelve missed calls. Unfortunately, rather than nasty threats of physical violence from Brad, they were from my mother. *Crap!*

Within seconds of me turning it back on, my mobile came to life in my hand, its shrill tone and manic vibrating warning me that my mother was trying to get through. Trudy glanced across at me, her eyes full of sympathy. Yes, we all had mothers, but some were more of a handful than others. Mine was certainly high maintenance. Had she been a horse — sorry, Mum — she would have been one of those dancing Spanish ones, all elegant, agile and dignified, but as soon as some novice lets their guard down around them, they turn into flighty, touchy vicious Thelwell mares.

"You know you can't avoid her forever." Trudy frowned, biting her lip.

She was right, as always. This had to be done and, just like ripping off a sticky Band-Aid, it was best done swiftly. Sure, the pain was intense, but at least it was mercifully brief.

"Hi, Mum," I began cheerfully in an attempt to throw her off the scent.

"Don't you 'Hi, Mum' me, young lady," she snapped furiously. "What on earth is going on?"

Oh dear. My phone was practically crackling under the force of my mother's hostility. I half-expected it to start glowing in my hand. I groaned. It seemed the cat was out of the bag.

"Are you listening to me, young lady?"

"Yes, Mum."

"Well?"

"Well, what exactly?" I replied, standing my ground — or at least sitting very defiantly in my small hatchback surrounded by a mountain of clothes, including one burned-orange pashmina Trudy was currently eyeing.

Now, the Brooke of old, the wimpy, self-sacrificing one, would have blurted out everything, desperately hoping I might be forgiven for upsetting her, but I was a changed woman. This was the new stronger, independent version and I wasn't about to cave in under the weight of my mother's displeasure. I'll admit the eighty kilometers or so separating us helped.

"*Well*, it so happens I rang you earlier this morning to see if you wanted to meet me for lunch tomorrow and I was very surprised when Brad answered the phone. I thought he would have been at the office already…"

She paused, waiting for me to say something.

I didn't.

"Anyway, he sounded *very* put out," she continued, "to the point of being quite rude. And when I asked him if anything was wrong, he told me quite bluntly that you had walked out on him. Naturally, I assumed he was joking. Tell me he was joking…"

I took a deep fortifying breath. "No, Mum, he wasn't joking. I've left him."

"*What?*" my mother shrieked before making a little choking sound on the other end of the phone.

I braced myself for the wrath of Cyclone Jillian and all her destructive fury. I didn't have to wait long.

"Well, young lady, you can just forget about all that nonsense now. I don't know just what you think you are doing, but I am telling you this—you *are* getting married and, I might add, in less than five months…"

I almost expected her to finish with…whether you like it or not!

I felt like I was eleven all over again.

"No, I am not, Mum," I replied with a sigh of resignation. "In case Brad didn't tell you, I have called off the wedding."

"*Brooke Jillian Delaney…*"

I flinched at the much-dreaded triple-named address.

"I don't know what's been going on with you lately, young lady, but I want you to call Brad *immediately*, do you hear, and apologize. He's the best thing that's ever happened to you so don't you *dare* think you're going to ruin your life because of some ridiculous argument!"

"Is that what Brad said it was, a ridiculous argument?" I asked, my anger building. Trust him to drag my mother into this.

"If you must know, he was a bit cagey about it all — at first. But in light of what he eventually revealed, I must admit I am shocked and, more than that, I can quite understand why Brad wants nothing more to do with you."

"*What?*" I squeaked in outrage.

"Well, for a start, I too have noticed your behavior has been particularly off these last few weeks. Your carry-on over the wedding dress is one thing, but when Brad told me that not only had you been fired from the surgery but...and I can hardly believe this bit. Surely, he was exaggerating when he said you've been working...oh my God...in a...brothel..."

My mother's voice cracked as she began to cry and my temper exploded.

"*Mum!* I am *not* a bloody hooker, for crying out loud! I am a *receptionist!*"

By this point, Mum was past listening. "What am I going to tell your father?" she howled, all but deafening me. "What am I going to tell *Father Brockway?* Oh, my God, I'll never be able to show my face outside the door again."

I was going to kill Brad for this. I should have known he'd stoop to anything to get back at me.

"For God's sake, Mum, get a —"

"I'll be *ostracized,*" she wailed. "Laughed at, behind my back."

Granted, this wasn't going as well as I had hoped, but in a bizarre way it was a relief to have it all out in the open at last.

"Tell me, Brooke, what did I ever do to deserve this? Wasn't I a good mother? Didn't I give you everything? And this is the thanks I get."

"Mum, shut up for a minute and listen, will you?" I yelled down the phone to be heard above the sounds of wailing and gnashing of teeth — Mum's, that is.

Suddenly she went very, very quiet on the other end of the phone. I could practically hear her blood pressure building. Definitely not a good sign. Sadly the silence didn't last long. "I think I deserve a little respect, young lady."

"Yes, Mum, I understand, but I'm an adult now and I am capable of making my own decisions."

"You call this…this job…a wise adult decision? Your father and I spent thousands of dollars putting you through that secretarial college and now you tell me that *this* is the best you can come up with? You're working with *prostitutes*, for heaven's sake!"

"They're just people, like you and me. Nice people, in fact. And, besides, I don't intend to be there forever."

"Well, if that's the case, you can leave right now and, with any luck, Brad might decide to forgive you."

"No!"

"No?"

"No, Mum. I meant it when I said the wedding was off. I am not marrying him, not now, now ever!"

Trudy smiled across at me encouragingly, my pashmina now wrapped securely around her shoulders. It looked as if I was going to have a struggle on my hands to get it off her.

"But why?" pleaded Mum, once again on the verge of tears. "He's a lawyer, for goodness sake. Think of what you're giving up. You would never have had to worry about money or anything, ever again."

"But at a price. I would have to put up with his snobby attitudes and suffocating double standards. And on top of that, he's a complete control freak to boot. Look, I'm sorry, Mum, I know you're disappointed and I'm sorry things have turned out the way they have, but if nothing else, at least I know now that I wouldn't have been happy with him."

"But he's a *lawyer*..."

Chapter Twenty-Three

Leanne was the only one at Heavenly Pleasures who knew the real story behind my break-up with Brad. Admittedly, it was kind of hard to hide the sudden disappearance of the diamond — small as it may have been — and, within the hour, I had succumbed to her sympathetic glances toward my bare-naked digit and spilled the beans on my miserable excuse for an ex-fiancé. Apart from having a well-deserved moan, knowing what I now knew about Scarlett's new 'lawyer', I felt I had no other choice but to confide my belief that Brad would if anything be happy to see Scarlett thrown in jail and separated from her little boy. What a mess!

Understandably, Leanne was every bit as concerned as I was, but short of going back to Robert and asking him to appoint someone else to Scarlett's case, I didn't know what to do. Scarlett was so over-awed by her supposed good-fortune in landing the services of a real-live attorney that I couldn't bring myself to smash her new-found happiness with a massive dose of ugly reality. Besides, considering what she had recently been through, I didn't know how she would react to the truth.

In the end it was Paul of all people who came up with a possible solution. A couple of days later, walking back through to the reception area from what had of late become his standing weekly booking with Scarlett, he happened to hear Leanne and me discussing it. Careful not to mention any names, I filled him in on the dilemma facing my 'friend'.

"What's the big problem, then?" he asked, genuinely baffled by our apparent gloom. "Tell your *friend* to request another attorney. Simple. He's working for her after all, not the other way around."

"What, even if it is being done *pro bono*?" I queried.

"Of course. Generally, it's the company providing the service, not the individual lawyer. Tell your friend that if she isn't happy with the service she's receiving, she has every right to ask for another lawyer. There shouldn't be any problem with that."

"Well, actually there might be. The problem is she *thinks* she is practically home free and doesn't realize this fellow isn't exactly looking out for her best interests."

Paul frowned. "Sounds to me like she needs someone to step in for her."

Unfortunately, I knew he was right.

I looked up at Paul standing at the reception desk. I still hadn't figured him out. I'm not saying *that* was anything amazing, mind you. It took me almost three years to figure out what a wanker Brad truly was. But Paul was different. He didn't fit the profile of many of the other men who came through the door, most of whom carried a discernible air of ignominy about them, some of them downright cagey, booking in under obviously assumed names and paying cash not to leave any trace of their whereabouts by way of credit card receipts. Leanne was always wary of blokes like that, but mostly they were harmless. Married, of course, but harmless.

Paul didn't fit into any of those categories, though. He was divorced, he'd told me a few weeks ago, not in a steady relationship at the moment—amazing what some people will divulge to a brothel receptionist—and the way he referred to his business interests, I got the definite impression that he worked for himself.

Suddenly, one of the girls, Olivia I think, called out for Leanne, who excused herself and disappeared out the back, leaving me alone with Paul. After a few seconds of awkward silence I felt myself blushing under his intense gaze.

"I can tell you're really worried about your *friend*," he said, his face softening with concern.

I shrugged, frantically willing my color to return to its previously pasty hue. "There don't seem to be too many people queuing up to help her at the moment," I mumbled. "She's had it rough over the years and I'd hate to see her go down for something like this."

"This *friend* of yours is lucky, you know."

I gave him a look. I was fairly certain that luck and Scarlett weren't exactly on speaking terms.

"What I meant was, lucky to have a friend like you. Someone who cares about her."

I blushed even more, feeling like a complete fake. Until recently, I'd been scared shitless of Scarlett or Carol or whatever her name was, to the point of avoiding her at all costs. That didn't sound like the actions of a friend to me.

"It really isn't that big a deal, you know."

Paul leaned over the counter. His smiling face was less than a foot from mine. The rest of the room, including the urgent groaning coming from the DVD next door, instantly faded away. All of a sudden, I was painfully aware of everything about him, from the lovely shade of his blue with flecks of gray eyes to the subtle woody masculine scent of his aftershave.

"I think you're a very special person, Brooke," he remarked. "Not many people would have gone out of their way to help someone like Scarlett."

I blinked with surprise.

"Don't worry, she told me all about it just now," he added in response to my obvious surprise.

Wow. Scarlett must be a mistress of multitasking if she managed to have sex with Paul and relate her life history all in a half-hour session.

I didn't know what to say. Paul was looking at me as though he wanted to say so much more and I was overcome by a sense of confusion. Only a few days ago, I'd been preparing to marry Brad and now I couldn't even remember what color his eyes were.

Suddenly the floozy in the porn flick next door came to the crest of her Academy Award winning orgasm and stripped the room bare of any semblance of intimacy. Paul burst out laughing and I found myself joining in.

"God almighty, I think Meg Ryan has a lot to answer for, don't you?" he said looking across to the lounge, cringing.

"I don't know. I wouldn't mind some of what she's having."

As soon as the words were out of my mouth, I wanted to die. What the hell did I think I was doing, for Christ's sake? My already pink face went up in flames and I prayed for the floor to rise up and swallow me. Making matters ever worse, Paul looked across at me with an amused look on his face and chuckled. "Well, if I ever run into her, I'll ask her for the recipe. Mind you, if some woman started screaming like that on me, I'd think I'd make a bolt for the door."

Well, there really wasn't any appropriate way to respond to that so I wisely decided to keep my big mouth shut. Better late than never.

"For fuck's sake, you two, get a room!"

I spun around, horrified, to find Leanne watching us with a big smirk on her face. How long she'd been there I had no idea, but it was clear that she'd heard enough to set her imagination on fire.

Paul laughed and took a step back from the reception desk in a manner that suggested a guilty conscience. "I suppose I'll be off," he spluttered, clearly as embarrassed as I was. "Um, I'll see you next week, Leanne," and in a softer tone to me, "and you, too, I hope."

For the next ten minutes, all Leanne could do was grin stupidly. I desperately wanted to slap some sense into her. What on earth had come over her, saying something like that? And in a place like this? *Totally inappropriate.* I was so embarrassed I wanted to die. But then she didn't have the monopoly on run-away mouths, did she? Mine was doing a fine job of its own accord and every time I remembered what I'd said to Paul, I wanted to crawl into a hole and stay there until such time as I developed Alzheimer's and forgot all about it.

"Well?" she prompted when it was obvious I wasn't about to talk to her.

"Well what, exactly?" I responded irritably.

"*Well*," she said with meaning, "it seems to me like you have an admirer there."

I leveled a stony stare at here. "Don't be so stupid. He was just being friendly."

"Friendly you say? Any friendlier and I reckon you two would have started a bonfire right there in the middle of the room."

"Don't..." I warned.

"Don't what?" she teased, wide-eyed and innocent, by now thoroughly enjoying my discomfort.

"Just don't, that's all. I feel embarrassed enough as it is. I don't know what's wrong with me. Talk about make a fool of myself."

"Why? He's lovely. What I'd give for him to look at me like that."

I looked at Leanne as if she'd gone mad.

She burst out laughing.

* * * *

Later that afternoon, Scarlett came out the front and sat down next to me, bringing us both cups of coffee. I was on my own as Leanne had an evening class to attend, but it being mid-week I was hoping that it would be fairly quiet. Seeing Scarlett this side of the divide wasn't as rare as it had been a few weeks before. It was strange really, but ever since that fateful day in the kitchen her attitude had done a complete turnaround. Where she used to breeze past me with nothing more than a scowl by way of greeting, these days she stopped for a chat and sometimes a coffee, like now.

She'd revealed that she had spent two short stints in jail in Sydney for soliciting on the streets. That had been years before, when she'd had a serious drug habit to pay for, she confided in me. It was with some pride, though, that she proclaimed she'd been clean for almost seven years now. Mostly due to love of her little boy. Levi stayed with Scarlett's aunt Shirley when Scarlett was working but sadly Shirley had been recently diagnosed with cancer and, although she continued to look after Levi, it was too much to ask that she take over the sole care of him if the worse happened and Scarlett was locked up again.

"How's Levi?" I asked.

Scarlett smiled, setting down a mug for me on the desk. "He's wonderful, a real little trooper, that one. Did I tell you last week he lost a baby tooth? Didn't even cry. Put it under his pillow for the tooth fairy and told me that his friend reckoned he'd get two dollars for it. A little con artist in the making, I reckon."

"He sounds adorable, Scarlett."

"I suppose he is really, apart from when he's knee-deep in mud and refusing to get in the bath."

After a moment she put her cup down and turned to me. "They set the date. It's the beginning of next month." She had anxiety in her eyes, despite her attempt to put on a brave face. "I've got a time to see this lawyer fellow again tomorrow afternoon."

"Oh, that's good," I said trying to inject a positive note to my voice. My stomach felt filled with lead.

Scarlett bit her lip and asked quietly, "This bloke they gave me, do you know him?"

I nodded. *All too well, unfortunately.*

"He is all right, isn't he? I mean, do ya think he is a decent lawyer an' all?"

I swallowed a lump in my throat. "Why do you ask?"

Scarlett shrugged. "I don't know. He doesn't seem too interested in listening to anything I have to say, that's all. He even suggested that to be on the safe side I plead guilty to get a reduced sentence."

I stared back at her horrified. "He *what*?" I cried.

"I don't want to sound ungrateful or anything, because I can't tell you how much it means to me what you've done, but…"

"I hope you told him to go jump?"

She shrugged miserably. "And what good would that do? If he walks, I have no chance at all."

"But that's terrible. How could he even suggest such a thing? You were the one attacked, remember. I hate to think what might have happened if you hadn't had that pepper spray handy. Hell, it's that bastard who should be the one facing assault charges, not you."

She sighed. "Well, that's what it is like for us, isn't it? For people like me, I mean, not you. I should be glad I have a lawyer at all."

Bullshit, should she. She'd be better off with Father Brockway as her lawyer. I found myself shaking with anger and filled with a sense of injustice.

I couldn't shake the feeling that Brad was planning to sabotage his own case as some kind of payback at me for walking out on him.

"Listen to me, Scarlett. It doesn't have to be like that at all. You were the victim here and it's inexcusable that you should be punished like this. This so-called lawyer of yours sounds like total crap to me and I'm sorry I got you caught up with him."

Scarlett's eyes clouded over and my heart went out to her. Then suddenly something Paul said earlier came back to me and an idea came to me. "Look, I know another lawyer, someone who I promise isn't going to bully you into accepting a plea bargain. If it's all right with you, can I at least have a word to him about your situation and see what he has to say about it?"

Scarlett looked wary and after all she'd been through I couldn't say I blamed her.

"He is really nice, I promise," I coaxed.

Scarlett frowned, biting her lip as though trying to weigh up her odds.

"Please just let me speak to him. You have nothing to lose here."

"Okay," she relented after a moment's deliberation. "If you think it will help."

It certainly couldn't hurt.

Chapter Twenty-Four

"Brooke, what an unexpected surprise."

Scarlett and Olivia were currently occupied out the back with clients. Olivia was with one of her regulars and Scarlett had her hands full with a shit-scared first-timer to the brothel. So with both of them out of the way I figured this was as good a time as any to phone Simon. However, now faced with the reality part of my big plan, I couldn't help feeling a little nervous at the hint of confusion in his voice. And who could blame him? Clearly, I was the last person he expected to hear from.

"Er, if it's Brad you're after, I'm afraid you've just missed him. He left for court a few minutes ago."

Thank God for that! It would have been all I needed for some ditsy secretary to mindlessly patch me through to Brad's desk. For once the gods were smiling on me.

"Actually, Simon, it's you I wanted to speak to," I announced, trying to ignore a rush of nerves, knowing full well this could easily blow up in my face. After all, what I was about to propose was a big ask.

"Really? Lucky me," he teased and I could almost see him grinning on the other end of the line. "In that case, what can I do for you?"

"Um, actually, it's kind of a delicate situation. Have you got time to meet me for a coffee in town?"

"Well, I have to say, I'm more than a little intrigued. When did you want to catch up?"

"I don't suppose you have time this afternoon?" I responded.

An hour later, I spotted Simon waiting for me at one of the rear tables in a quiet café in the middle of town and sat down opposite him. He clearly had no clue what I was about to ask of him.

Taking a deep breath, I blurted out, "I know this might sound a little, well, odd, but I need some legal advice."

Simon frowned. "Um, don't you think you ought to be asking Brad about this?" he queried, clearly thrown.

"Well, seeing as one, it concerns him, and two, he isn't exactly speaking to me, I don't think he would be completely impartial."

"Oh, dear, do I sense dissention in the ranks?" he joked. "A lovers' tiff perhaps, or have you finally come to your senses and ditched the boring old fart?"

I winced. "Um, all of the above, I'm afraid."

"What?"

"I moved out and called off the wedding a few days ago," I blurted out.

There was an awkward silence before he found his voice, immediately launching into an avalanche of effusive apologies. "Oh, God, I am so sorry. Christ, talk about my big mouth. I honestly had no idea, Brooke."

This struck me as kind of odd, seeing as I imagined Brad had been happy to drag my name through the mud and at the same time playing up the aggrieved jilted fiancé angle for all it was worth.

"So are you telling me Brad hasn't mentioned anything, then—at all?"

I was torn. Should I be upset that he wasn't a complete gibbering mess or relieved I wasn't being portrayed as the callous heart-breaking harlot from hell?

"About you guys splitting up? No, not to me, anyway, but then I suppose it's fair to say that we're not exactly best buddies or anything."

Well, this was certainly interesting. I would have assumed that even if he had only mentioned it to the partners, the way office gossip circulated, everyone down to the tea-lady would have known by now.

Then it dawned on me. Of course. How could I possibly be so naïve? With the partnership decision looming, Brad would see it as vital that his image of a soon-to-be family man was maintained at all costs. A surge of renewed anger coursed through me.

"No. But now you mention it, he has been acting a little odd these last few days."

"How? In what way?"

Teetering on the edge of a breakdown kind of odd or racked with guilt for not appreciating me more over the years? As much as it shamed me to admit it, I was hoping he was crippled with remorse, going around the office unshaven and wearing the same crumpled suit he'd fallen into bed in the night before.

"Every time I see him, he's entrenched in a meeting with Tom or Will. By the way he's acting, anyone would think they're joined at the hip. I'd say he's in full suck-up mode with the partnership decision coming up next week."

Well, there goes that theory out of the window. I couldn't help feeling a little insulted.

"Oh, so you don't think it's because he has been trying to worm his way out of a case Tom assigned him last week?"

"What, you mean the Potts case?"

"You know about that?"

"Only what I heard during our last weekly briefing. Some working girl in town up on an assault charge, I think. Poor bugger. Strangely enough, this fellow she's alleged to have attacked has a history of violent offenses behind him. Big bloke, too, from what I hear. Ex-footballer who now owns some dodgy car yard out in the industrial estate. But now you mention it, Brad *was* really put out when Tom assigned that case to him. Furious, actually. I would have thought he'd be up for it, seeing it's clearly an open and shut case for the defendant. Can't imagine a single judge who would seriously believe the prosecution's story."

"Brad doesn't see it as such. Not only that, he's gone so far as to advise the woman to plead guilty."

"*He's what?*" Simon spluttered in sheer disbelief. "How exactly do you know all of this? Surely Brad hasn't been breaching client confidentiality?"

"This Carol...Potts..." It still seemed weird to call her that.

"The defendant?"

"Yes." I took a deep breath. "Well, actually, it happens that she's a friend of mine."

Simon leaned back in his chair and reached for his latte. "Really?" he replied, sounding more than a little intrigued.

There was no getting out of it so I figured it was best to come clean.

"Yes. I work with her at Heavenly Pleasures in town, and before you start getting any funny ideas, I'm a receptionist."

Simon burst out laughing. "Oh, my God, you *are* a dark horse. I can't imagine *that* went down too well with your loving fiancé?"

"Ex-fiancé actually. But no, he isn't all that happy, but then again I don't really care."

"Well, well, well. It appears the worm has finally turned. Not that I'm suggesting you are a worm in any sense of the word," he added hastily, all the time trying to keep the amusement from his voice.

"No, of course not! The thought never occurred to me," I responded dryly. "But getting back to Scarlett, or Carol or whatever you want to call her, I am really worried about her. She has a little boy. He's only six and if she loses this case and goes to jail, there's a good chance Child Welfare will put him in a foster home."

"And, let me guess, Brad is taking the moral high track."

"Exactly, but more than that, the way he's been going on about it, I wouldn't put it past him to deliberately throw the case to get back at me."

There was a brief silence before Simon finally spoke. "Brooke, ordinarily I would suggest that a lawyer throwing a case, as you put it, would be highly unlikely, but sadly I remember too well his stance that night at Robert Fletcher's."

"Can you see why I'm so concerned now?"

"Yes, unfortunately. But I'm not sure what I can do about it. Brad has her case and unless she requests another representative, my hands are tied."

"That's why I wanted to speak to you. If Scarlett…"

"Scarlett?"

"Oh sorry, Scarlett's her shop name... If she requests it, would you be prepared to take on her case instead?"

"Sure. If she wants me to, I'd be happy to help her out, but I have to point out here that this might not look too favorably as far as Brad is concerned. It might be seen as a bit of a slight to his reputation."

"What, being dumped by a hooker?"

"Precisely."

Bonus! "In that case, when do you think you could speak to Scarlett? Her court date has been set for the fourth of next month."

"It should be ASAP."

"What about tonight?" I suggested, terrified that he might change his mind if left to ponder on the matter. "She's working until late, but you could always come down to Heavenly Pleasures. I promise you won't be interrupted."

Simon burst out laughing. "It isn't exactly the usual office procedure, but, hey, I'm game. Tell Carol I'll drop round to see her about seven tonight."

* * * *

I glanced down at my watch and hurried my step. Simon was due at Heavenly Pleasures any minute and up until a few moments ago I had been stuck waiting in the queue from hell at the local Indian takeaway behind a woman who found it necessary to query the spiciness of every dish on the menu. *It's bloody curry — of course it's hot,* I wanted to scream.

Despite the girls' assurances that the food was to die for, I hoped it was worth it. Prue hated it when the girls ate curry on shift, following numerous complaints from the clients about the girls stinking of onions and coriander. Tonight, though, they'd declared a particular yearning for something spicy in celebration of the fact that Prue was not expected to put in an appearance. Apparently an American Navy frigate was currently docked in Sydney harbor with fifteen hundred horny sailors on board. Sydney would be rocking tonight.

So I, the lackey, had been dispatched to the other side of town to pick up three orders of chicken korma, a beef vindaloo for Scarlett, butter chicken — Leanne's favorite — together with a mountain of poppadums, cheese naan bread and an extra-large serving of rice. As I struggled back up the hill toward the arcade, I could already imagine the pungent smell of it wafting throughout the brothel and I suspected that rather than a genuine yearning for curry, it was nothing more than an intricate ploy to ensure the girls wouldn't be attracting too many customers tonight. After they finished with this lot, the arcade, not to mention the brothel, would reek like a Mumbai backstreet.

By the time I entered the arcade, my arms were burning from the heat radiating from the box I'd opted for over the usual plastic carrier bag. Not that I'm an environmentalist or anything, but in the past, plastic bags and sloppy fast food have proven to be a lethal combination, usually culminating in sauce dripping all down my leg. Boxes were definitely a better idea, even if they did scorch big red marks into my tender flesh.

I had my key with me but, weighed down with enough scalding hot Indian takeaway to feed a small impoverished village in outer Kanpor, I leaned up against the buzzer not to risk upsetting the spicy sauces all over my new white top. Trudy had insisted I resume my retail connection as part of my post-Brad therapy, and who was I to argue? There was nothing like transferring one obsession for another. At least I was in little danger of having my heart broken by a pair of mules.

As soon as the door opened, I sensed something was going on and prayed that Prue hadn't decided to spring a surprise visit on us after all. Considering my illicit cargo, I would be the first one fired. But rather than the usual angry outbursts I had grown accustomed to, the girls sounded like a bunch of thirteen-year-olds at a slumber party. *Strange. Very strange.* Then, out of the affray, I caught sight of Simon's glossy dark hair and it all began to make sense. I'll give him this much, armed with little more than a smile and a charcoal-gray suit, he appeared to be charming the pants right off the girls.

Perhaps that wasn't an appropriate turn of phrase, considering it generally didn't require any charm whatsoever to get them out of their knickers—a valid Visa or MasterCard generally did the trick, but he certainly had them falling over each other to get his attention.

Setting the now-forgotten curry down on the closest flat surface, a chair on this occasion, I rushed over, fearing poor Simon was about to be set upon by a gaggle of hookers.

"Simon," I cried out breathlessly above the giggles and some very inappropriate offers of a nature not entirely called for under the current circumstances. "I'm so sorry I wasn't here to let you in."

"Hey, no problems, the girls here have been very, um, accommodating while you were gone."

Oh, Jesus! This was dreadful. Poor Simon. It was nothing short of a miracle he hadn't made a mad dash to the door to escape. Anyone would have thought the girls had never seen a gorgeous-looking bloke before, albeit one who bore a striking resemblance to Robbie Williams!

"Scarlett," I called out loudly, attracting the attention of the girls. "This is Simon—the lawyer I was telling you about," I added, shooting them all a warning look.

"Yes, I know," she replied, licking her lips in a not very subtle gesture of approval.

"He's here to *talk* to you—not for anything else," I felt compelled to add.

Simon burst out laughing. "Well, maybe while I'm here..." He winked, drawing covetous looks from the girls who I feared were about to set upon one another for the privilege of providing some extra-special services on his person. "I might speak to Scarlett, is it?" Scarlett nodded, blushing like a convent-raised virgin. "And see how best to tackle her case."

The others, finally realizing they were not about to be shagged by the love-god Simon anytime soon, shot Scarlett a venomous glare and slunk off back into the kitchen, accompanied by Leanne who had rescued the by now rapidly congealing Indian takeaway.

"Sorry about that, Simon. I thought I was going to be back ages ago. Bloody queues."

"No worries. The girls were looking after me."

That was exactly what was worrying me.

"I must say Simon here is a huge improvement on the last stiff I spoke to about my case. Bloody pompous fucker he was."

I sensed rather than saw Simon's amusement over Scarlett's perceptiveness concerning Brad's character. I couldn't blame her. At least she was honest. I wish I had half her insight when it came to the opposite sex.

"We're certainly grateful for you coming in." Pulling aside the beaded curtain to the client lounge, I gestured to him to follow. "This is probably as quiet a place as you are likely to find at the moment, so come in."

I swooped the pile of porn off the coffee table to make room for his briefcase before tactfully backing out of the room, but not before catching Scarlett giving Simon the once-over. Poor bloke. He might look tough, but I couldn't help thinking I was throwing him to the wolves.

Chapter Twenty-Five

Picking up the TV remote, I pressed the Power button and watched the plastic-haired journo's face sputter once before blanking out. There was nothing decent on apart from the usual crap current affair programs interviewing sleazy politicians eager to get their big ugly faces on telly. My gaze drifted over to the pile of DVDs stacked precariously up against the wall, just waiting for one of us to stumble into them after one too many Chardonnays and cause a mini catastrophe. But tonight I couldn't stomach sitting through yet another serving of *Bridget Jones's Diary* and, believe me, that was something I *never* thought I'd live long enough to hear myself say. God, I was bored.

After ambling across to Trudy's bookcase in search of some much-needed mental inspiration, I glanced over her selection of reading material. Not particularly exciting unless anyone considered a dozen self-help books — that only help if a person actually *reads* them — a dog-eared copy of *Gone with the Wind* and a few odd novels by people I'd never heard of like Paulo Coelho and Gabriel Marquez Garcia to be good, juicy material. Not a Marion Keyes or Jackie Collins in sight.

It being Thursday, Trudy and Becky were working late at the salon and, despite being at a bit of a loose end, it was nice to have the place to myself for a change. Don't get me wrong now, I am not complaining. Trudy and Beck had done everything humanly possible to make me feel at home, but encamped as I was in their living room surrounded by the wreckage of my failed relationship, I couldn't help feeling I was living in a refugee camp for the socially dispossessed.

Now, two weeks on, I suspected their relief that I had finally come to my senses and ditched Brad had overridden all sense of practicality and I knew I'd have to start looking for a place of my own. And soon. Trudy's place was only small, tiny, in fact, and between her and Becky, they filled the flat's meager quota of habitable space, leaving me feeling a little like the fat kid who'd scoffed the last piece of birthday cake. Trudy, being the darling she is, insisted I stay with them for as long as I needed to get myself together.

Despite our cramped living arrangements, I was slowly being deprogrammed, thanks to Trudy and Becky, and, as a result, I no longer cried myself to sleep at night. But then what were friends for but to slag off bastard ex-fiancés and remind a girl there are plenty more men out there willing to worship the ground she walks on?

However, as much as the girls extolled the many advantages of being single, the truth was slowing beginning to dawn on me. Sure there might be decent blokes out there, blokes who brought you flowers, opened car doors for you, made an effort to get on with your friends and made you cry out in ecstasy in the bedroom. But the downside was I'd have to wait in line behind every other single girl on the planet desperately searching for that one perfect man to sweep them off their feet and whisk them away to the magical land of married bliss.

Then just as I thought my life was heading on a one-way trip down the toilet, Leanne emerged as my unlikely savior, kindly offering to let me move in with her. Apparently her spare room had lain vacant since her previous flatmate dropped out of his environmental science degree and started working on an oil rig somewhere in the Tasman Sea. It seemed the best available option, considering my only other viable alternative was moving back in with my parents.

God save all of us from that heinous fate.

My mother had all but begged me to come and live with her and Dad, but, knowing she would do anything to put a halt to my current working arrangements, I had my suspicions as to her real motives. They weren't suspicions at all. I knew for a fact that she looked upon my employment at Heavenly Pleasures as being the greatest insult I, her only offspring, could visit upon her. It even surpassed dumping a successful lawyer. This I was constantly reminded of as I endured her now daily calls pleading with me to retire from the sex industry or as she calls it 'that terrible place'. Mum never could bring herself to say the word sex. Oh, and I should beg Brad to forgive me.

Strangely enough, Dad wasn't fazed at all about his darling daughter working in a brothel and I might even go as far as to suggest that he was proud of me for showing some gumption and getting on with my life.

Talking about work—it had been almost a week now since Scarlett had emerged from the client lounge sporting a smile the size of Sydney. Simon, bless him, had restored her faith in humankind and lawyers and although he couldn't guarantee her acquittal, he did assure her that even in the unlikely event of a guilty verdict, he doubted she would receive anything more than a suspended sentence.

Now all I had to deal with was Brad's reaction—if any. After all, he couldn't know for sure that I had intervened and contacted Simon. Sure, he might have his suspicions, but I knew that Simon would keep mum and Scarlett assured me she would rather sleep with Quasimodo's older, uglier brother than speak to 'that arsehole' again. *Can't say I blame her.*

Much to my relief, I hadn't heard a peep out of him all week. By the next day he would have learned that Scarlett had shafted him in favor of Simon and I had spent the better part of the week waiting with some degree of trepidation for his reaction. I would have thought he'd be grateful to be let off the hook, but of course there was the issue of his ego, and as far as egos went Brad's was up there with Napoleon's for sheer arrogance. No, he would never take this kind of slight with a shrug.

Scarlett's hearing was scheduled for the following Wednesday morning at ten o'clock, and as much as she tried to make out that she wasn't in the least worried, we all knew she was quietly terrified. Quiet being the operative word. For the last week she hadn't screamed abuse at anyone, not even some weirdo who wanted her to get down on all fours and bark like a dog while he led her round the room on a leash.

The Scarlett of old would have sent him packing stark-naked out into the arcade as she flogged him to within an inch of his doggy-humping life. Instead she calmly told him if he wanted a pet, to go visit the pound, and walked out on him, instructing us never to book him with her again. No hysterics. No bloodshed. We were indeed worried. It was like all the fight had gone out of her and it affected the entire atmosphere of Heavenly Pleasures, bringing the vibe of the place down.

I wasn't the only one feeling disturbed by Scarlett's lethargy. Leanne confessed that she too had never seen her like this before and made a special effort to secure her more bookings to take her mind off her upcoming court date. And, to illuminate the gravity of Scarlett's situation, not only were Leanne and I accompanying her to court, but in a rare act of solidarity, the girls were also coming out to show their support. If nothing else it would certainly be interesting.

Trudy had rung a little earlier to let me know they wouldn't be home until late as they were run off their feet. After Trudy declined my offer to come down to the salon to help out, I decided to treat myself to a leisurely soak in the bath, seeing it as the perfect antidote for a terminal case of boredom-induced munchies.

I'd learned years before that to get the full benefit out of a bubble bath a little forward planning was the key. So, with that in mind, I locked the front door, raided Trudy's pile of CDs and put on some relaxing music, poured myself a glass of wine, dimmed the lights and, most importantly, took the bloody phone off the hook and put my mobile on silent, gifting to myself a much-needed reprieve from yet another one of my mother's nightly guilt trips. I was set. The mood was right, the wine and accompanying bottle placed carefully beside the tub that was filling with hot steamy water and, as an added bonus, I'd unearthed an old fashion magazine from under the pile of hair mags beside Trudy's bed. It was time for the spoiling to commence.

After lighting a lone scented candle and placing it on the vanity unit beside me, I very slowly eased myself into the scalding hot, mango-scented frothy water, all thanks to Trudy's fetish for fruity toiletries. It was luscious, like floating in a mango daiquiri. The heat instantly soothed my muscles and helped ease the tension I'd been carrying around all week.

Considering I was now single, homeless and officially the worst daughter in the entire world, I wasn't feeling too bad. Mum was continuing to make my life a misery and when I let myself dwell on it, I suppose I was horribly disillusioned with how my life had turned out, but all things considered, I was holding it together. I didn't require Brad's constant monitoring and guidance to get through the day, after all. Leanne, who I learned had been through her fair share of ugly breakups over the years, helped me sort out my banking details and advised me to get my mail redirected, and even went as far as advising me to change my mobile number if things between Brad and me got nasty. Better to be on the safe side.

Suddenly, from beyond the bathroom door, a horrible noise startled me and I jumped, sloshing suds over the side of the bath and onto Trudy's magazine. A second later, the front door buzzer went off again, rudely shattering the peaceful ambience that I, along with the aid of Trudy's pampering potions, had so briefly enjoyed.

Fuck it!

My first thought was to ignore whoever it was until they got the hint and pissed off whence they came. Alas, that idea was quickly laid to rest as I found myself unable to blot out the God-awful noise of a million shrieking bats that continued to assault my senses in a Morse code of angry bursts. *Fuck it!* So much for my bath.

Reaching out with sudsy hands to my watch balanced on the edge of the basin beside the candle, I saw it was barely eight o'clock and cursed whoever it was for their inconsiderate timing.

Again the buzzer rang out in an angry tirade, practically hurling obscenities throughout the place and hastening me out of the bath with its urgent demands. I vowed then to go out tomorrow and buy Trudy a doorbell that played *Greensleeves* or something of that nature.

Now my first thought as I reached out for a towel was that Trudy must have forgotten her key. But Becky had hers with her. Surely they couldn't both have lost them. No one could be that careless. Well, no one apart from me, that is. I had already locked myself out twice since moving in. Anyway, it couldn't be either one of them. They were currently neck-deep in customers and not due home for at least another hour and a half.

The noise continued to blast its way around the flat like a heat-seeking missile completely obliterating the soothing strains of Eva Cassidy coming from the stereo. Who the bloody hell was it? Apart from Mum and Leanne, no one knew I was staying here. I hadn't ordered pizza. Yet.

A male caller for Trudy? Not likely. Not since she'd given her latest fellow his marching orders a couple of weeks ago. Not that it was any great loss. His name was Blain — seriously — and he was a tosser of the highest caliber who introduced himself as an entrepreneur — go figure. So along with Becky and me, she was temporarily single at the moment, or, as she put it, tragically celibate.

I wrapped myself in a robe from the back of the door, ignoring the bubbles stubbornly clinging to my ankles, determined to get rid post-haste of whoever was rudely pressed up against the buzzer and rescue the shreds that remained of my evening of pampering.

"For Christ's sake, get off the fucking buzzer!" I screamed, my previous serenity by now nothing but a distant memory.

Considering the ongoing lack of buzzer control, it was clear they couldn't hear me over the din.

By the time I reached the door, I was boiling with anger. Not only had they ruined my bath, but instead of me feeling relaxed and peaceful, my hair was practically standing on end. I took a deep breath and prepared to deal with the buzzer fiend on the other side of the door. There had better be a fire in the place to warrant all the commotion. I couldn't smell anything burning over the scent of mango bath gel and I wondered for a moment if I hadn't overdone it a little. One thing was for sure, whoever it was had better have a decent excuse or they were going to cop a mouthful from me.

Unfortunately, it wasn't until I wrenched the door open ready to deliver the bollocking from hell that I saw there was one scenario I had failed to consider. And he was slumped against the buzzer wreathed in a halo of alcoholic fumes.

Chapter Twenty-Six

I stood there, staring dumbly, rooted to the spot with shock. It might have only been a week or two since I'd last seen him, but I couldn't help being stunned by the bitterness etched into his face. This of course wasn't helped by the fact that he was smelly, disheveled, swaying on his feet and clearly pissed off his face. Legless. Totally shit-faced. I had never seen him this drunk before and a slither of alarm shot through me. I pulled Trudy's bathrobe tighter around my rapidly chilling body.

Brad's face was frozen in a half-grimace, half-scowl, preserved no doubt by all the alcohol currently doing the rounds of his system, turning his once-clean liver into tomorrow's medical ad for abstinence. He was a mess. His tie was missing, along with the top couple of buttons of his shirt. By the dark patches down the front of his suit I could only imagine that the last couple of drinks had failed to find their mark and ended up flowing down his chest. I barely recognized him. Gone was his trademark smug composure and his carefully cultivated aura of control and superiority. In its place stood a man plainly rushing headfirst into a hangover of biblical proportions.

"Youuuu..." he slurred, vehemently staring at a point above my left eyebrow, clearly finding it too much of a struggle to focus both eyes on me and think at the same time. "*Bitch!*"

"Who told you I was here?" I spluttered, too taken back at his current appearance to take umbrage at the bitch comment.

Swaying unsteadily, Brad attempted to tap his nose in the manner of someone in the know, but in his messy state he missed his mark, almost taking his eye out. Unfazed, he continued his verbal purge. "Where else would you be?" he sneered. "No one wants to know you but that bloody cousin of yours. You're nothing but a whore like the rest of them. All you fucking women are the same."

Frozen to the spot, I wondered what on earth he was going on about. He was getting louder and louder and halfway in the door already, meaning I had little choice but to pull him inside before someone called the police and poor Trudy was called in front of the tenancy board to explain why drunken men were fronting up at her door and disturbing everyone in the building. In hindsight I'll admit it was a tad stupid, but considering the state of him, I didn't see him as a threat as such. It was nothing short of a miracle he was still able to stand.

"Bastarrrds! Fucking lousy bastards gave it to *him*."

I should have known this was coming. I had been waiting for a backlash over Scarlett's case ever since I'd walked out on him. I really didn't think he'd be *this* angry, though. Annoyed yes. Pissed off, most likely, but he was practically combusting with fury. Christ, he hadn't even wanted the case in the first place.

"You," he spat, "and that fucking whore have ruined my bloody career. I hope you're satisfied. I had it. It was mine before you ruined it. It's all your fucking fault."

"What on earth are you talking about? You didn't *want* it."

Brad was past listening. "They must have found out somehow."

"Found out what?" I yelled.

"You and your disgusting friends, that's what," he sneered. "Whole fucking lot of them should be thrown in jail. You too. Can't believe I was ever going to marry you. You're no better than the rest of those bitches out there. My mother was right. She always said you were a tart. I should have listened to her."

He stood swaying in the doorway to the lounge, bracing himself against the door frame. He was blocking my only escape route and I felt a spasm of panic deep inside. I had forgotten how big he was. He had a footballer's physique and, for the first time since I'd opened the door, it occurred to me I had done a stupid thing by allowing an angry drunk man into the flat. In his present state of mind, I didn't know what he was likely to do and while I'd never considered him capable of violence, I had never seen him in a state like this either.

Ordinarily Brad considered men who drank to excess to be somehow weak and despised them for allowing their vulnerability to show. He prided himself on the fact that he never allowed his control to slip — until now, that is.

I looked down at my watch, still clasped in my hand, and groaned. Trudy and Becky wouldn't be home for ages yet and although my phone was sitting on a shelf just inside the front door only ten feet away, Brad was between me and it and, even drunk as he was, I didn't fancy my chances of pushing past him. What was I going to do? I had to get him out of the flat and soon.

"Brad, go home, will you?" I ordered, trying to conjure up what I hoped was a commanding voice. He glared at me and I took a step back, knowing if worse came to worse I could always make a dash for the bathroom or Trudy's bedroom, both of which had a lock on the door. "Look, you're drunk. You can talk to me tomorrow if you want, when you've sobered up. But right now I want you to leave. Do you understand?"

"Drunk? I'm not drunk," he slurred, catching hold of the wall to steady himself. "I haven't even started to get drunk."

He didn't appear to be listening to me and my panic escalated. Every moment that passed, he seemed to grow bigger and more intimidating and in his current frame of mind I wasn't quite sure how to deal with him. One thing was for sure, though—antagonizing him wasn't going to make the situation any better, so I decided to change tack. All I had to do was get him out of the flat.

"Brad, what's wrong? This isn't like you at all," I said in an attempt to calm him down.

He laughed grimly, running his hand through his hair. He was sweating and flushed and I wondered exactly how much he'd had to drink. "Like *you'd* give a shit. You think I'm some kind of a fool, don't you? You have no idea what you've done to me. But you're the one who's the fool. Stupid fucking cow. You know what, I *never* loved you."

"You don't mean that," I stammered, watching him sway in front of me.

He smiled nastily. "I never *wanted* to marry you either, but Robert fuckwit Fletcher wanted a family man for the job, didn't he? Fuckwits, the lot of them," he raged.

Brad's face darkened and I took a step back, desperately praying that my legs would somehow get me to the safely of Trudy's bedroom and, more importantly, the security of a locked door without turning to jelly. Trudy was going to kill me for letting him in the flat in the first place. That is if Brad didn't beat her to it. He took another step forward and a shriek rose in my throat, before his eyes clouded over.

Suddenly he lunged toward me and I screamed.

* * * *

Trudy wouldn't stop giggling and it was beginning to grate on my already raw, bleeding nerves.

"For heaven's sake, stop laughing. This isn't funny, you know."

"Yes it is. Look at him." She pointed at the corpse-like figure at her feet. "It's bloody hysterical. Who would have guessed Boring Brad was such a pisshead?"

Brad hadn't so much as moved an inch since he'd hit the deck and passed out almost half an hour ago now, despite my urgent shakes and Trudy's well-placed kicks. Pissed or not he was going to be black and blue tomorrow. Maybe I should have dealt with him myself and not dragged Trudy into it? It was too late now, though. In a panic I'd rung Trudy at the salon and she'd rushed straight home, leaving Becky to finish off her last remaining customers.

I think she was expecting to find the place in a state of utter carnage, furniture upended, blood splattered up the walls, her DVDs snapped in half — that kind of thing. Instead, what she found was nothing more dramatic than me in tears and Brad's hulking form blocking her passage through to the kitchen as he lay snoring like a Mac truck in desperate need of a tune-up.

Attractive? Hardly.

Funny? Trudy thought so.

None too gently, she kicked him once more in the ribs with her bare foot. "Can't tell you how good that feels," she muttered, leaving me wondering if it was for my ears or Brad's.

"You know what? We have *got* to get a photo of this. He looks like roadkill. All he needs is the white chalk outline and the place could pass for a crime scene. Wait there and I'll get my mobile."

"Trudy, come back here," I yelled, my frazzled state making me narkier than I had intended. "Can't you be serious for just one minute? What are we going to do with him?"

"I've got it," she announced gleefully. "Let's shave his eyebrows."

"Trudy..." I warned.

"Oh, come on. It'd be so funny and just imagine the look on his face. Go on. It would serve him right for coming over here like some psycho and frightening the life out of you like that."

"No!"

"Why not? It would be letting him off easily, I reckon. You should have called the police on him. Then where would he be — in a cell that's where, probably with the same crims he'd be in court with next week."

She had a point. I was tempted.

"No. No one is shaving anyone's eyebrows," I announced firmly, putting an end to her vengeful plans.

Trudy looked at me as though I had just burst her party balloon. "You're no fun."

"One of us has to start behaving like an adult. What are we going to do with him? He's too heavy to move. And even if we did manage to shift him, where would we put him? I don't think your neighbors would appreciate us dumping him out on the landing now."

"We'll just leave him where he is," Trudy said, with a dismissive wave of her hand.

"We can't do that."

"Sure we can. I don't think he's going anywhere in a hurry. And just think, tomorrow when he comes to feeling like forty buckets of shit, you can let him have it. Blast the crap out of him. Won't that be fun? It's my bet going by the state of him that he won't even remember coming over here. How confused will he be?"

I looked across at his lumpen form with concern.

"Look," Trudy added. "If you're really that worried about him coming to during the night, you can always come in and sleep in my room. We'll even lock the door if it makes you feel better. But I'm telling you now, he's out for the count. Nothing short of an earthquake is going to wake him before tomorrow morning." Trudy chuckled. "I wouldn't like to be living in his head when he does wake up. It's going to be real ugly. He's going to wish he was dead."

I was still shaken up from his earlier outburst. Even with him out cold, I found the sight a little intimidating. What if he woke up in the middle of the night and started yelling and screaming all over again? Could the three of us handle him on our own? Then it dawned on me that they shouldn't *have* to deal with him at all. He wasn't their problem. He was mine, *was* being the operative word here, and tomorrow morning I was going to tell him once and for all to get the hell out of my life. How could I have ever thought he was the one? Lying there with a trail of drool slowly pooling on the carpet, he looked like a poor excuse of a man and I had to ask myself what I'd ever seen in him.

Trudy, who I might add was not one to let the presence of an unconscious intruder spoil *her* evening, made a big show of stepping over him, *accidentally* tripping over his ear in the process, and made her way over to the telly, picking up the remote control with an air of defiance.

I couldn't stop thinking about what he'd said. Could it be true? Had I just been part of his grand plan to get a leg-up in the legal profession? Could I have been that gullible? A trophy wife? Me? It would have been funny, if it hadn't been so pathetic.

"Trudy, can I ask you something?"

"Sure. Ask away, hon."

"Why do you hate Brad so much?"

"I would have thought *that* was obvious. Take a look at him there. Why do *you* reckon? I hate him because he is a complete prick, that's why."

"But when I first started going with him, you guys seemed to get along all right and all of a sudden, this cold war sprang up between you two."

Trudy put the remote down and turned to face me, tucking her legs under her. "You really want to know?"

I nodded. I needed to know. Brad's final words were doing the rounds of my head. Was it true? Had I really been that blind? Could anyone be that much of an arsehole and I was the only one who didn't see it?

Trudy appeared reluctant to continue, giving me the impression that whatever had gone down between her and Brad, it wasn't something she felt comfortable talking about.

"He didn't make a pass at you, did he?" I asked.

Trudy's eyes almost popped out of her head. "What!" she shrieked. "No, God, no! Oh, Jesus, what makes you think that?"

I shrugged. "Well, whatever it was, you don't seem all that keen to tell me about it. So what else am I supposed to think?" I wasn't angry with her, just confused. Trudy usually took great delight in telling me everything, even things I didn't want to hear, like the size and shape of her latest beau's donger. It wasn't like her to be coy.

"No, believe me, it's nothing like that," she sighed. "Look, do you remember that time we all went out to that nightclub down by the waterfront? It was just before you and Brad moved in together. You remember, we met up with Becky and the usual crowd from the salon."

Slowly, it came back to me. It was Trudy's birthday and we'd arranged to meet for a big night out. Normally, when I went out with the girls, Brad gave it a miss, preferring to swing by the Leagues Cub where his mates hung out. I was desperate to show him off, though, and after a week of pleading, he agreed to come out with us. After that, things got a little hazy. I vaguely remembered Brad being annoyed with me for having a few too many drinks that night and taking me home early, but very little apart from that.

"I remember I got plastered. Why, what happened? I didn't make a complete fool of myself, did I?"

"No." Trudy laughed. "Well, no more than usual, but you remember my friend Izzie's boss, Darrell?"

"Yeah, of course. Izzie used to go out with him, didn't she?" I recalled.

Trudy laughed. "God, yeah. What a shock for her when he came out. Still, gay or not, he is a top bloke, even if it did break her heart at the time."

"Yeah, of course. Hard to forget something like that. Should have been obvious, mind you. I seem to remember he was really into George Michael at the time."

"Yeah, well, he kept giving Brad the glad eye."

I was confused. "What do you mean?"

"You know, the *look!*"

All of a sudden, the penny dropped. Darrell had been flirting, and with Brad of all people. If it had been anyone else but Brad, I would have thought it was hilarious. Darrell usually kept his gayness on a leash, especially in mixed company.

"Let's just say your *boyfriend* didn't take it very well."

"Jeez, what happened and where the hell was *I* at the time?"

This was dreadful. I can imagine the scene. Brad was the most homophobic man I knew. I couldn't believe he never told me about it.

"You were off throwing yourself around the dance floor with Izzie's sister, Andrea, at the time, I think, or maybe you were in the toilets throwing up. I don't know. But anyway, Brad got real nasty. Threatened to beat Darrell to a pulp. Poor Darrell was mortified. Said his gaydar must have been completely screwed and began apologizing profusely. But typically Brad refused to see the funny side, and when I jokingly suggested that maybe he was protesting a mite *too* much, well, he went mental. I'll admit I'd had a few drinks too by that stage and probably should have kept my mouth shut, but he called me and Darrell every disgusting name you can think of. Then threatened poor Darrell that if he ever so much as looked at him again, he'd get a bunch of his footy mates and do him over."

I could only stand there, stunned. Darrell was the sweetest man anyone could ever want to meet. Just the thought of Brad threatening him like that was horrifying.

"After that, Brad and I had this huge row and I think I might have suggested that maybe he was repressing his true feelings. I know it was nasty, but I couldn't help myself. Pompous idiots like him bring out the worst in me."

I could do nothing but stare at Trudy, slack-jawed. "How come no one ever said anything to me?"

Trudy looked a little embarrassed. "I know we probably should have mentioned it, but we all knew you were totally stuck on him at the time and the last thing we wanted was to spoil things for you. Then, soon after, you moved in with him and you seemed so happy." Trudy shrugged. "Being homophobic isn't a crime. I just thought he was an arsehole, that's all, and I suppose he never forgave me for hinting he was gay."

I couldn't stop thinking about what he'd said earlier. Could it be true that he never really loved me? That he was only marrying me to acquire the partnership at work? It was all too much to take in at once. Only one thing was certain. I wasn't wasting one more tear over him.

* * * *

The next morning, I was relieved in a way to discover that Brad had exited the flat sometime during the wee small hours. I hadn't heard a thing and wondered how someone in his condition could have left without waking the entire unit. The lounge room looked unaccountably spacious without his bulky besuited body taking up precious room. Had it not been for the damp drool patch on the carpet and the slight odor of vomit emanating from the bathroom, I might have believed I'd imagined the ugly episode the night before. But no, it had been real all right.

Still, something inside me told me I hadn't seen the last of him.

Chapter Twenty-Seven

"Where the bloody hell is Sienna?" Prue bellowed, slamming the phone down. "Brooke, have you heard anything from her?"

Shaking my head, I tried desperately to melt into the background.

Although the girls had dropped quite a few hints concerning Prue's reputation for inciting terror in the most battle-hardened hooker, I'd been reluctant to believe them — until tonight. She was a wolf in Country Road clothing and I was Little Red Riding Hood about to be eaten alive. It wasn't that she was openly spiteful, like Dr. Chisholm. She didn't make fun of me or put me down. It was more the underlying threat of what she was truly capable of. Prue had an aura of menace about her.

She glowered at the clock. "Bloody girl should have been back from the Plaza twenty-five minutes ago. Brooke, give her a ring and see what's holding her up now. Tell her I have three more bookings for her and to get her arse back here pronto."

As Prue took off out the back to sort out who to send out to a couples booking, I grabbed the phone and quickly punched in Sienna's mobile number. She took what felt like ages to answer and I prayed she wasn't in the middle of something — something kinky, that was. Just I was about to give up, she finally picked up the call.

"Sienna, it's Brooke," I whispered urgently. "Prue's going mental here and wants to know where on earth you are."

I wasn't exaggerating. Prue *was* mental. More than mental. I was terrified of her.

"Fuck!" I heard her mutter under her breath above the sound of running water in the background. "Tell her to keep her bloody hair on. And while you're at it, you can also tell her that I'll be back just as soon as I wash *the fucking vomit out of my fucking hair*," she suddenly bellowed down the phone.

"Oh, my God, is everything all right?" I asked lamely, wondering if she was ill.

"No, it fucking well isn't!" she continued to yell. "That arsehole currently lying puking his guts out in the next room was blind drunk by the time I arrived, thanks very much! Instead of a bloody tip, I copped a head full of fucking fish of the day."

And with that she hung up on me. Puking clients, another work-related hazard. Who would have guessed? It certainly wasn't *Pretty Woman*, that was for sure. I only hoped she was getting paid extra for it.

"Well, did you get hold of her?" asked Prue, emerging from out the back.

"Yes," I replied trying to keep the tremble from my voice.

"*And*? Where the hell is she?"

"Um...she said to tell you that she's very sorry but she's been held up a little. Apparently her last booking was really drunk by the time she arrived and threw up all over her."

Prue swore under her breath. "Jesus, who the hell booked him in? Christ, haven't I warned you girls before about that."

"Um, I think it might have been you actually," I responded quietly, glancing over to the booking sheet.

Prue glowered. She didn't look at all impressed with my perceptiveness. What was I supposed to do? Take the blame? Going by the filthy look I received, it seemed so.

As she tore off out the back again, I closed my eyes and rested my head in my hands. I was exhausted and as a result of Brad's abusive house call the other night I hadn't slept well these past couple of nights.

"Hey, don't let her get to you, petal," whispered Leanne, who along with everyone else in the place had heard Prue's rantings. "Honestly, you're going great."

I looked up at her and stared in disbelief.

"No, seriously. I think she likes you."

Yeah, sure, maybe in the same way a Russian circus owner likes his dancing bear.

This was the first time I'd had the pleasure, if that was what I could call it, of working with Prue and I fully expected to be sacked before the night was over. It was bedlam. Roslyn, the receptionist who usually worked weekends was off looking after her sick kids at home, so as a result I'd been called in to help out along with Leanne. And thank God for that. Without Leanne to

318

back me up, I swear I would have been a gibbering mess by now.

It was Saturday night and we were flat out. It was a long weekend and in anticipation Prue had called every girl in the book into work. Keeping track of five or six girls a night could be hectic, so not surprisingly ten were proving more than a little challenging. The phones hadn't stopped ringing and since eight o'clock there had been a constant stream of taxis coming and going. And if that wasn't bad enough, it felt as though we'd had every bloke within a ten-kilometer radius through the doors tonight, from pimply teenagers sent in by their mates for a dare and promptly kicked out again by Prue — we're not running a fucking crèche, she yelled out after them — to a rowdy group of blokes in their thirties staying in town over the weekend for a conference. Then there were the usual unlucky-in-love pub and club dwellers, who, sick of going home horny and humpless, dropped by for a quickie before stumbling off home to boast to their mates about the hot bird they picked up. And that didn't even count the regulars.

It wasn't even midnight and I was exhausted already.

The only upside to all this madness was I hadn't had time to dwell on Brad, and in particular what had become of our once-happy relationship. Or, more to the point, the happy relationship I'd *thought* we had. Even now, I cringed just thinking how I used to bore the tits off everyone raving about how in love we were and how wonderful he was and how lucky I was to have him.

For the millionth time I asked myself how I could have been so stupid. But I suppose if nothing else, at least something positive had come of it. I had finally decided to take Leanne up on her offer and was moving into her spare room next week. It wasn't a difficult decision. After taking a look at the place I had instantly fallen in love with it and, as an added bonus, Leanne's flat looked out over the water. It was fantastic. I could finally get my life back together away from Brad's stifling presence and maybe even consider taking up some kind of study like Leanne. One thing was for sure. I knew I'd have to move out of Trudy's as there was no way I was putting Trudy and Becky through a repeat performance of My Ex-Fiancé, the Drunken Arsehole.

At Leanne's urgings, I was also contemplating changing my mobile number just to be on the safe side. Not only would it ensure my privacy from Brad but, as an added bonus, I could also sever my ties to my mother until such time as she stopped harassing me. I figured I'd have at least a few days' grace before my picture starting appearing on the sides of milk cartons.

To my relief I hadn't heard any more out of Brad since his pre-dawn retreat, but that wasn't too surprising considering the state of him at the time. I only hoped he gave himself alcohol poisoning.

"Brooke, honey, can you go out the back and ask Scarlett if she's up for an hour booking? New guy. In the lounge. Wants a tiny twenty-year-old brunette."

I looked at Leanne in utter disbelief. She had to be joking! By this time of the night Scarlett was looking very much on the wrong side of haggard. Let's just say she'd had a rough night.

Leanne noticed my concern but merely shrugged. "Hey, the bloke's no oil painting himself. Just tell her to slap on some more makeup and dim the lights. He'll never know!"

Here we go, I thought, making my way out to where Scarlett was showering in the staff changing rooms.

"You *must* be fucking joking?" she exploded after I relayed Leanne's message. "Christ all-fucking-mighty, my pussy is practically raw. Jesus, I thought that last bloke was never going to blow. Talk about getting his full thirty minutes' worth!"

"Um, do you want me to tell Leanne to get Olivia or Candy?" I asked, not knowing what else to say. Well, what does one say to that? Sounded horribly painful. Every hooker's nightmare.

Unfortunately Prue chose that exact moment to walk out the back. With bat-like hearing, she'd heard every word of our exchange.

"Scarlett," she barked, "it's not even midnight yet and the phones are still running hot. I couldn't care less if your damn pussy is ready to burst into fucking flames. Try using more lube, but get your lazy arse out there. That bloke's paying cash, he wants a twenty-year-old brunette and seeing as Sienna's not back yet, it's your booking! Understood?"

Scarlett muttered something in the affirmative and reached down for her bag.

I gave her a sympathetic look and tried not to wince.

Clearly too tired to argue back, Scarlett threw on a tiny black shift dress and buckled a wide belt around her waist before pushing past me to where her next client was waiting out in the lounge.

Unfortunately, Prue wasn't finished with me just yet and began firing off orders like a drill sergeant. "Brooke, go and get Scarlett's room ready for her. Make it the Red Suite. With any luck, her bloke won't notice she's not exactly a cheerleader. And remember to check the lube."

"Okay," I mumbled, trying to psych myself up for yet another jaunt into the seedy end of the business.

Ever since the fateful Marmalade Man episode, I had employed every available means to avoid what had since become my very own Room 101. *The room of horrors. The room where no one can hear you scream.* Mostly the girls were sympathetic. Unfortunately for me, Prue wasn't one of the girls and my fear of her far outweighed that of the red room. Still, I had to admit she had a point. The lighting wasn't the best in there and red was mercifully Scarlett's color. Regardless of Scarlett's urgent need for camouflage, revisiting it made me feel decidedly edgy and I couldn't help but feel Robert Fletcher's spirit remained together with the slight odor of his preserves fetish.

I grabbed a handful of condoms from the cupboard, scooped up an armful of towels and made my way out the back. The Red Suite was the nearest one to the lounge area and I could hear the sounds of muffled conversation together with what I recognized to be *Bambi's Bouncing Bimbos* playing on the telly. After placing the towels neatly at the end of the bed together and arranging the condoms in a little fan shape on top, I quickly checked the lube as I'd been instructed by Prue. A brief scan of the room later, I deduced that it was all systems go for Scarlett's hopefully myopic client.

I was almost ready to walk out when I spotted Scarlett's bag of goodies in the corner next to the bathroom where she'd obviously dumped it on the way out to her meet and greet. The girls were always making oblique references to Scarlett's legendary bag of dirty tricks, so naturally it got me wondering what she was packing in her arsenal tonight. I stuck my head out of the door to check for any sound of Scarlett. The coast was clear. Not that I expected she'd be pissed off at my intrepid curiosity. Quite the contrary, it was more for the very real fear that she might insist on talking me through a guided tour of her kinky implements of pleasure.

Carefully easing the zipper open, I peeked inside.

Jesus Christ. It looked as though she was firing on all cylinders tonight. Not only were there at least half a dozen dildos of every size imaginable, from minute to *ouch*, but she was also sporting what looked like real police issue handcuffs, a gag, numerous bindings in a variety of colors and textures and, lastly, what appeared to be a strand of beads?

One thing was for sure, Scarlett might be sporting a raw pussy, but that poor bloke out there was about to experience an hour of *lurving* he was unlikely to forget in a hurry.

Suddenly from beyond the Red Suite came the unmistakable sound of raised angry voices, one of which appeared to be masculine. I dropped Scarlett's bag, my earlier curiosity now replaced by a growing sense of unease. This couldn't be good. By now there was little doubt in my mind the commotion was coming by way of the reception and cold alarm slithered deep inside my belly.

"Where the hell is she?" boomed a man's voice throughout the brothel.

It was a voice I vaguely recognized. A very pissed voice. Above the din I heard Prue yell out furiously, "Who the fuck let this dickhead in?"

Being the coward I am, I decided to stay out the back for the time being, tossing up whether to stay put in the kitchen or risk becoming a part of what was rapidly developing into a really ugly situation out the front. My heart was thumping painfully. I hated confrontation. I dreaded scenes full-stop. What help would I possibly be? No one ever listened to me.

It sounded as though furniture was being upended out the front. I felt sick with dread. Behind me, the back door beckoned. My escape route to freedom. I could slip out and no one would be any the wiser. I could pretend I'd nicked out for a can of cola or packet of chips. I eyed the open door. Three feet and I'd be away.

Alas, I couldn't actually bring myself to go through with my cowardly plan. Not only would that be the most gutless thing I'd ever done—and *that* list is shamefully long and illustrious—but if I left Leanne to cope with all this on her own, I'd never be able to look her in the eye again, which might prove to be a bit awkward seeing as I was hoping to move into her spare room next week.

"Brooooooke. I want Brooke. Where is she?" came a disembodied voice from beyond the kitchen.

I prayed that I was experiencing some kind of stress-induced auditory hallucination.

"I'm not going anywhere until I see her! Brooooooooke!"

Surely, it couldn't be. Unfortunately, I knew full well it could. It wasn't merely a bad dream. It was worse than that. It was Brad, my own personal nightmare. Why tonight of all nights? Prue was going to kill me. Oh, God, I was going to be sacked for this.

I ran through my options. Apart from fleeing from the scene like a criminal, I had no other choice but to go out there and pray that I still had a job after the smoke settled. What did he possibly think to achieve by coming in here, apart from ruining what remained of my life and causing me untold embarrassment? *What a mess.* When I'd walked out on him, I *never* imagined that he would sink to this level of spite just to get back at me.

Slowly, feeling like I was about to face my own execution, I made my way out toward the reception area.

The first person I saw was Leanne, looking on with undisguised horror, both at Prue who was seething and practically incandescent with rage and Brad who was nothing if not on the ugly side of drunk. Going by Leanne's pallor, it was my guess that she was the unlucky culprit who had unwittingly let him into the brothel. I felt awful. It was all my fault. After all she had no way of knowing who he was.

"Brooke," slurred Brad, finally spotting me standing beside Leanne. "There you are. I've come to see you...I want to buy you for...um...how much is it for an hour?" he asked Leanne who was by now mute with shock, "Fifty? A hundred? I want the works!" he announced to everyone present.

I wanted to die.

"Brad, for God's sake go home. *Now!*" I hissed as my face drained of blood. For perhaps the first time in my life, I was way past blushing. I felt ill.

But how on earth had he found out I was working tonight? Either he was stalking me or...oh, God, earlier in the evening I'd had a string of phone calls where the caller had hung up on me without saying a word. At the time I hadn't thought anything of it. In a place like this, it was hardly an uncommon occurrence. Unfortunately, tonight, it was my guess it was Brad.

By now, practically everyone in the brothel had got the gist of my current domestic drama and apart from the tape playing in the lounge, there was not a sound to be heard.

"What's the bloody world coming to if a man can't come into a brothel and get some sex?" Brad roared, throwing his arms about like he was addressing the High Court.

At that, Prue finally snapped. "Righto, buddy, that's it. Are you going to piss off and sober up or am I going to call the cops?" she yelled, not in the least bit intimidated by his size or his inebriated condition.

For some reason, Brad thought this quite funny and stumbled over toward the desk. "You can't kick me out. This…" he said, pointing to me, "this is my fiancée."

Prue shot me a filthy look. Clearly she was not impressed with employees dragging their domestic disputes into the brothel.

"I'm not leaving till I get some of what she's been throwing out to every bloke around here," he yelled, dragging his wallet out of his pocket and grabbing a handful of cash from it. "Come on, Brooke. Take it and I'll show you how a real man deals with a slut like you."

I stood there stunned as a shower of five- and ten-dollar notes rained down on me. Leanne stepped forward to intervene but I knew then that this was one thing I had to deal with myself and put my arm out to stop her. Suddenly all the rage I had been suppressing since the other night erupted.

"Get out!" I screamed, desperate to put an end to this hideous scene. "Right now! What do you think you're doing here?"

"Hey, what's the big deal?" He smirked, clearly enjoying my growing mortification. "I'd have thought you'd be pleased and anyway, I'm not asking you to do it for free. Isn't that what you wanted? A big man to take care of you?" He sneered. "Well, here I am. If it's kinky sex you're after then, hey, I reckon I'm up for it."

I stared back aghast. "You're drunk and you're making a complete fool of yourself, Brad. Now leave me alone. And don't you *ever* come near me again!"

Brad laughed. "Ah, you don't mean that."

"Wanna bet?" I growled.

"And what are you going to do then, work in a place like this for the rest of your life? Christ, I would have thought you'd know a good thing when you saw it. No man is going to want you after this. You should be grateful that I'm willing to take a whore like you back after all you've done to me."

Prue meanwhile had slipped out the back by way of the client lounge. I wondered whether she was going to grab a weapon of sorts. Maybe a gun? Up until then it hadn't occurred to me how vulnerable we were in here. Leanne was standing close by ready to intervene and to my horror one by one the girls were emerging behind me to see what the commotion was all about.

"Who the fuck is this wanker?" I heard one of them ask.

"Jesus, it's the arse-wipe lawyer I ditched," replied Scarlett, her disgust evident. "Brooke's ex, by the sound of it."

I prayed for the ground to open up and swallow me. The girls were looking at me as though I was mad and no doubt asking themselves what I was thinking, getting caught up with a psycho like him.

Brad swayed, dangerously close to falling into the client lounge. "Hey, what's the matter? Playing the whore didn't bother you too much that last time. So what's your problem? I'm just giving you what you've been gagging for and paying you for it as well. You can go and buy yourself something nice. Just like being married."

I stared back in horror.

"Well, that's why you were marrying me, wasn't it? Like I was marrying you for the family image I needed for the partnership?"

I burned up with shame. Thankfully I was saved a response by Prue bursting through to the reception area with two of the burly conference men in tow. Somewhere away in the distance I heard the sounds of sirens. Clearly Prue wasn't taking any chances.

Before he had time to hurl any more nasty taunts my way, Prue's two conscripts grabbed Brad and wrestled him to the ground, just as Sienna burst through the back door closely followed by two police officers who had seemingly heard the call over the radio and run over from the station across the road.

It happened so quickly that it wasn't until Brad was bundled unceremoniously into the back of the waiting police van that the whole ugly scene hit me. Turning to Leanne, I burst into tears.

Oh, God, I'd turned Brad into a ranting madman!

"Oh, honey, are you all right?" Trudy asked, sitting beside me in the kitchenette as Scarlett placed a steaming cup of tea in front of me. Leanne thought it best to ring Trudy to take me home after the police finally left with Brad screaming and yelling from the barred windows of the police truck. Exhausted and totally humiliated, I was in no condition to argue.

I sniffed. "Trudy, what have I done?"

"You haven't done anything," Scarlett interrupted. "Jesus, Brooke, I would have thought you of all people, with your fancy clothes and posh manners, would have had better taste in men than that." Shaking her head, she wandered back out the front muttering, "Fancy anyone putting up with that pompous arsehole. You'd have to be mad."

Trudy looked up at Leanne. "I'd better get her home."

"Yeah, I think that's a good idea. But before you go, Brooke, I really think you should get a restraining order out against Brad."

"I don't know. I don't really think he's violent, just drunk and not thinking straight."

"You say that now, but if tonight's anything to go by, I reckon it's only luck that he hasn't got physical. Brooke, think about it, do you really want to take that chance? Jesus, look at him tonight. If Prue hadn't dragged those two blokes out to help out I hate to think what might have gone down. You really have to do something, or next time could be a whole lot worse."

"I'll see how I feel tomorrow."

Leanne was right. He had really scared the life out of me tonight. And it seemed I wasn't the only one. Prue was insisting on pressing charges against him for the damage he'd inflicted on the place. It was nothing short of a miracle she hadn't sacked me.

Instead of giving me my marching orders, Prue came up to me after the police left and put her arms around me.

"Don't let that bastard ruin your life, Brooke," she said. "You seem like a really nice girl. You've got everything going for you and you deserve to be treated better than that. Listen to me. Get rid of him, like out of your life for good, and forget about him."

Words to live by. *And* from a lesbian ex-hooker.

Chapter Twenty-Eight

"Oh, God, I'm sorry it took me so long to get here. I was stuck in Sydney last night and only just got your message. What on *earth* is going on?"

It was Sunday afternoon and I felt dreadful muscling in on poor Simon's weekend, but I didn't know who else to turn to for advice. Leanne had rung the police station an hour ago and apparently Brad had been released earlier in the morning once he'd sobered up and now both she and Trudy were on my case to get a restraining order taken out against him.

Trudy, having let Simon into the flat, was all smiles.

"Brooke, you never told me it was *Simon* who was representing Scarlett."

"What?"

"Simon is Darrell's partner. I can't believe you've never met him before. What a coincidence," she gushed, ushering him into the living room where he spotted me sitting dejectedly, my eyes raw and swollen from crying.

Simon sat down beside me and gave me a brotherly hug. "Jeez, Brooke, what's all this about Brad getting *arrested*? My God, are you all right? I'm sorry, but your message was a little confusing."

After I filled him in on the past few days' dramas, he leaned back on Trudy's lounger and shook his head in disbelief. "Bloody hell, I had no idea he'd take it this hard."

"You're telling me. Oh, God, Simon, I feel terrible. If I hadn't interfered in Scarlett's court case, none of this would have happened, I'm sure."

Simon looked a little confused. "What on earth has *that* got to do with *this*?"

I told him about Brad going on about me ruining his career.

"Look, I'm not quite sure what he was going on about there, but it was no one's fault but his own that he lost the partnership."

"*What?*" I shrieked. "Are you telling me he didn't get it?"

Simon shifted, looking a little uneasy. "I feel terrible. I should have called you last week and filled you in on what's been going on at work, but honestly, I had no idea he'd go off the rails like this."

"Filled me in on what exactly?" I pressed, searching his face for some answers, something to explain Brad's sudden decline.

Simon ran his hands through his hair and sighed. "It's a really nasty business."

He certainly had a point there.

"It seemed one of the partners, Tom, discovered last week that Brad had been interfering with witnesses and leaking key evidence to the opposition in some of my cases. Clearly an attempt to make me look bad in the eyes of the partners. By the looks of it, he was so desperate to gain the partnership that he wasn't willing to leave anything to chance. Not only was he trying to discredit me as a lawyer, but he spread rumors about my private life as well. It was only last week when one of our rival's legal teams came to Tom and revealed what they'd discovered that the true extent of what he's been doing came to light. Not only was he sacked from the firm, but as a result he could well be disbarred over this."

"So it wasn't my fault?"

"How on earth could it be your fault? It was hardly a secret that he's been obsessed with the whole partnership issue for months, well before that dinner party."

"So it had nothing to do with Scarlett's case being taken away from him?"

Simon looked at me in disbelief. "Of course not. Is that what you've been thinking now?"

I nodded miserably.

Briefly I considered confiding to him the business about Robert Fletcher but in the end thought better of it. Brad was entirely responsible for his own downfall. A weight of guilt lifted from my shoulders.

"Well, don't. He can blame whoever he wants, but the fact remains that this was all his own doing."

"I know Brad doesn't deserve anyone's sympathy, least of all yours, or mine for that matter after what's he's done, but I'd really hate to see his life and career go down the toilet over this. Is there any way you think you might be able to persuade Prue to drop the charges?"

Trudy, who up until now had sat quietly, suddenly exploded. "You can't be serious. After everything he's done to you, that bastard deserves all that's coming to him."

Simon shook his head. "I don't know. Even if I can convince this Prue to drop the charges, he might have already ruined his own career, at least as a criminal lawyer."

Just then the door buzzer went off and I instantly tensed, thinking back to the other night. Trudy looked across at me, knowing exactly what was going through my mind.

"Don't worry. You stay there and I'll go and see who it is," she said, jumping up from the lounger and disappearing around the corner to the front door.

I watched anxiously. I couldn't cope with yet another ugly scene from Brad. Not today. My nerves were stretched to breaking point as it was. From around the corner came muffled voices and my heart leapt to my throat.

Simon leaned over and put his hand over mine. "He wouldn't be that stupid."

I didn't know about that. *Coming into the brothel last night wasn't exactly the action of a man thinking rationally, was it?*

It was then I heard my mother's voice, and I groaned. Bloody hell. Could my life possibly get any worse?

Bursting into the room, Mum rushed over quickly, followed by Dad, and practically threw herself at me as if I'd just come back from the dead.

"Oh, darling," she cried, "are you all right? Tina called me this morning and told me *everything*. You poor, poor thing. Are you all right? He hasn't hurt you, has he?"

I glared at Trudy, who at least had the decency to look guilty. She shrugged helplessly.

"If that bastard has laid so much as a finger on you, I swear I'll tear him in two," growled Dad.

God knew what Trudy's mother had told my parents. Dad wasn't one to threaten violence on anyone.

"I'm fine, honestly."

"Where's the bastard now?" Dad yelled.

"Dad," I cried, "for God's sake, calm down. I'm more shaken up than anything else."

Mum had since forgone her histrionics and straightened up to her full five foot three inches. "Well that's it, young lady. Pack your things, because you are coming home with us today."

My bags were already packed, but in preparation for moving in with Leanne. I tensed, ready for another battle of wills, for there was no way I was skulking off home with my parents. It was time to finally put my childhood behind me and start acting like an adult.

"Mum, stop panicking. I'm not moving back home with you guys and that's final."

"You can't stay here." Mum looked around the flat. "By the looks of it, there's barely enough room for Trudy as it is. Come on, we have plenty of room and I can have a room made up for you in no time."

"Mum, you're not listening to me. I have a job I like and a place to live. I know you're worried and I understand, but I'm moving in with Leanne this afternoon. There's no need to worry about me."

"What about Brad?"

"What about him?"

"I don't think I like the thought of you down here on your own, considering his latest behavior toward you."

"Aunty Jill," Trudy interrupted, "we were just trying to convince Brooke to get a restraining order out against him. At least then he won't be able to contact her or come within something like two hundred meters of her."

Immediately Mum turned to me. "Why haven't you done it yet?"

I sighed. Honestly I felt as though I was ten again. "Because I'm not sure about it, that's why. Simon, what happens if I take out a restraining order on Brad?"

Simon frowned. "Obtaining an Apprehended Violence Order is a serious thing. I'm not saying that you shouldn't look into it, if you truly think you're in a position of danger from Brad, but I should warn you that even if we manage to persuade your boss to drop the charges, an AVO is going to stick and give him a criminal record regardless of the fact that he hasn't been convicted of anything. It could very well destroy his career altogether. But like I said, it's entirely up to you. His behavior these last few days probably warrants it."

I thought about it for a few minutes, while Dad grilled Simon on the possibility of Brad returning to harass me further and Mum joined forces with Trudy and Leanne in completely flaying what was left to flay of Brad's character.

"I should have known he'd end up like this," Mum announced. "It was always his way or no way. But deep down I had my suspicions he was no good for you."

"Mum!" I admonished. "Three days ago you were begging me to go back to him!"

"Oh, I think you're exaggerating a little there, Brooke. And besides, that was when I thought he was a decent young man and you were just suffering from cold feet with the wedding and all."

It was pointless arguing with her about this, especially when we had so much more to argue about.

I turned to Simon. "I'm fairly certain that a night in a police cell would have scared the life out of him without me having to ruin what's left of his career by serving him an AVO."

Behind me came a chorus of complaint. Ignoring it, I continued. "What do you think? Is there any chance of just warning him off?"

Simon thought about it for a moment before choosing his words carefully. "I think we all know I'm not one of his biggest fans, but in all honestly I don't think he is any threat to you or anyone else. Like you said, getting thrown in a police cell is a humbling situation in itself. You're a really nice person, Brooke, and I think in years to come, Brad is going to realize just what a mistake he made by acting the way he did. Rather than you dwell on it, my advice would be to get on with your own life and forget about all of this."

Leaning across, I kissed him on the cheek. "Thank you, Simon. And I almost forgot congratulations."

"Congratulations?" he frowned. "For what?"

"Congratulations on getting the partnership, of course. I'm sure it went to the better person. Who else but a bleeding heart like yourself would have gone out of his way to help a hooker? Scarlett's a lucky girl to have you defending her."

Chapter Twenty-Nine

To anyone passing, we must have looked an eclectic bunch, gathered nervously on the steps outside the large modern court house in town. It had certainly been a tough few days, not only for me but most especially for Scarlett as she waited for her day in court.

As Simon had predicted, Brad hadn't caused any more trouble and by the next day, Prue had calmed down enough for us to persuade her to drop the willful damage charges against him. Not long after I received a call from a very chastened Brad, not only apologizing for his appalling behavior of late, but also humbly thanking me for intervening with Prue. But that wasn't the only reason for his call. It was also to say goodbye. He was letting the lease go on the townhouse and traveling down to Victoria to stay with an old mate from uni for a while, he informed me. I was relieved.

Despite Mum's continuing protests, I had since settled in well at Leanne's and for the first time in years was getting used to standing on my own two feet.

Ironically, it was only the day after I moved I also got a phone call from Sophie to let me know she was heading back to London earlier than expected and inviting me for lunch the following week. Accepting her invitation, I finally decided to come clean and told her about the demise of my relationship with Brad. I had decided to postpone news of my brothel job until after we'd consumed a couple of glasses of wine, but at least I'd finally come to terms with the fact that I was never going to have a glamorous job or a lifestyle to rival Sophie's. Strangely, the more I thought about it, the more I realized I didn't care. I had my independence and one day, who knew, I might even meet a nice man who appreciated me for who I was, regardless of the fact that I worked in a brothel.

Besides, like I told my mother, at least it was an honest living.

There was a definite funeral atmosphere about us as we stood huddled together on the court house steps, soberly commenting on the ugly-as-shit sculptures that appeared to sprout up like noxious weeds all over the place together with the scandalous lack of ashtrays — anything really to distract ourselves from the real purpose of our early morning get-together.

Including Scarlett, there were seven of us altogether, which wasn't a bad turnout considering JoJo and Angel had been working last night. Mind you, from all accounts it had been a quiet evening at Shag Central and by midnight they'd decided to call it a night, which was the equivalent of downing tools at two p.m. for nine-to-fivers. I only hoped Prue never found out or heads would roll.

Center stage and turning quite a few heads, albeit of the male variety, stood Scarlett, decked out in her finest fake-fur-rimmed denim jacket, white lace body-suit and black miniskirt, courageously topped off with a pair of thigh-length black stiletto-heeled boots. Her dress code simply screamed emotional armor. Unfortunately, here in the harsh reality of ten o'clock on a wintry morning, she might as well have hung a big sign around her neck advertising her status as a working girl, and a flash of concern passed over Simon's face.

I suppose when all was said and done, you could take the girl out of the brothel but you couldn't take the brothel out of the girl.

In all fairness, though, her hooker status wasn't the issue here, but still a more sober air might have gone a long way to convincing the judge that she wasn't the violent man-bashing psychopath the prosecution had made her out to be. I, on the other hand, was so nervous about my first-ever excursion to a real-life court house I'd overcompensated in the attire arena, dragging from the grim depths of my suitcase my rarely worn black double-breasted suit and ankle-length black skirt, my funeral attire only saved by the late addition of my much coveted pashmina. Sadly it wasn't until I dashed into the ladies' toilets shortly after arriving at the court house and caught sight of myself in the mirror that I realized I looked like a middle-aged virgin librarian straight out of an Agatha Christie novel.

So with Leanne fronting up in a full-length purple velvet kaftan embroidered with tiny yellow butterflies across the bodice, and Olivia, Angel and Sienna attempting to outdo one another in the world's tightest jeans contest, that left only JoJo looking like she'd just stepped out from a fashion photo shoot. We were attracting more than our quota of attention from those waiting anxiously outside, smoking furiously as they in turn waited for their opportunity to plead their cases.

As I stood reassuring Scarlett, Simon returned after racing off on the pretense of double-checking the order of the morning's hearings.

"Carol..." he began, stopping short, finding himself speared by Scarlett's icy glare. "Sorry, I keep forgetting," he apologized. "Scarlett, I have just found out that Judge Callahan has been appointed to your case this morning."

"Is that bad?" I asked, sensing a sudden tightness in Simon's voice.

"Well, no, not exactly, but he can be a little" — he sighed — "how can I put it, *rigid* in his line of thinking." Throwing a worried look Scarlett's way, Simon cleared his throat nervously. "Scarlett, please don't take this the wrong way, but I don't suppose you have another jacket with you, by any chance? Something a little more demure, perhaps?"

Scarlett looked down at herself and pulled her furry collar closer around her neck defensively. "What wrong with it?" she asked sharply. "It cost me a hundred and twenty bucks."

One hundred and twenty dollars! Good God. I had to stop myself from gasping out loud. It never occurred to me that looking so cheap and nasty was so outrageously pricey.

Simon, being the eternal diplomat, though, employed his prize-winning smile to its best use before continuing to walk the tiniest of tiny tightropes with nothing but a pit of snarling, easily insulted hookers below to break his fall. "Nothing's *wrong* with it exactly, but I just thought perhaps something that didn't draw attention to your, um, present occupation might be a little more appropriate under the circumstances."

Scarlett's face darkened with what could have been insult or perhaps sudden understanding.

Turning to me, Simon gave me the once-over and smiled. I couldn't help but blush. It had been a while since someone had bothered to flirt with me. Given his preferences *and* the fact he was madly in love with Darrell, I couldn't have been more off-track. "Brooke, I don't suppose you might let Scarlett borrow your jacket?"

Scarlett's eyes narrowed as she took in the sight of my Miss Marple-inspired jacket. She didn't have to say anything. Her expression of horror was ample to convey her opinion that she considered it not particularly to her liking.

"Um, well, of course *I* don't mind," I began diplomatically, desperately trying to think of a way of getting Scarlett to see the light without hurting her feelings by suggesting her taste in clothes was sluttish to the extreme. "That is if Scarlett doesn't mind me borrowing her gorgeous new jacket. I've been admiring it all morning," I commented, trying to convince myself more than anyone.

Thankfully, with a little prompting from the girls, Scarlett eventually came around, grudgingly relinquishing her jacket for mine.

The transformation in her was remarkable and, going by the look of approval on Simon's face, just what he'd been hoping for.

Now, I feel obliged to point out that I am not fat. Well, slightly squishy maybe, but definitely not a candidate for Jenny Craig just yet. Scarlett, on the other hand, is tiny, minute, almost microscopic—okay I might be a *little* defensive here—making me feel positively Amazonian in comparison. My point being that my jacket, although designed to be closely fitted with a slightly pinched waist, simply drowned Scarlett's petite form and resembled an overcoat of sorts. However, on the plus side, it did cover most of her exposed cleavage and fell below her knees and more importantly graced her with a little-girl-lost look. In other words, it was perfect. She looked about as much of a threat to the general community as Dorothy from *The Wizard of Oz*—and much the same age after Simon convinced her to scrape off most of her makeup.

Simon was clearly pleased with her transformation.

Scarlett was proving a little harder to convince and kept grumbling about looking like her elderly aunt while pawing at the offending garment in distaste. I tried not to take it personally.

"Brooke, thanks for the jacket, it's great," Simon said, throwing me a look of relief.

"No problem, glad to help." I shrugged, trying not to shiver as the wind picked up, sending the outside temperature plummeting.

It seemed pointless to even attempt to pull Scarlett's size eight jacket onto my lumpen and by now freezing body, so instead I casually draped it across my shoulders, looping the sleeves tightly across my chest in a futile attempt to keep warm.

Ignoring Angel and JoJo, who had since grown bored with being supportive and were now openly giggling at Scarlett's newly acquired Orphan Annie look, Simon glanced down at his watch and turned to Scarlett. "We have half an hour to go before your case comes up. Do you want to go over anything again or are you feeling okay with everything we discussed the other day?"

Scarlett bit her lip, giving away her nervous state. "I'm fine. I just want to get it over and done with. Do you think that bastard who attacked me will be in there?" she asked, anxiously looking past him toward the court house.

"Most likely, but don't worry about him. By the time I'm through with him, he'll feel as though he's done ten rounds with Mike Tyson."

"Promise?"

"Promise." Simon smiled reassuringly. "He'll be squirming in his seat."

Scarlett's face lit up in a smile that bordered on rapturous as she wandered off to talk to Leanne.

"Thanks," I whispered to Simon once Scarlett was out of earshot. It was all I could do not to reach out and hug him.

"For what?" replied Simon, slightly bemused.

"For helping Scarlett. For not judging her. For being a complete sweetie. Do you want me to write a list?"

Simon grinned back. "Only doing my job." He shrugged modestly.

I looked up at him and smiled. We both knew that wasn't strictly true as equally as we both knew that had Brad still been appointed to Scarlett's case, he never would have come out to reassure her like Simon had in full view of everyone. Brad would have kept his strict professional distance. Given the choice, I'm fairly certain he would have preferred to defend her via satellite — from another country.

"Anyway, enough of me, how are you?" he asked. "I know I should have rung and asked before now, but what with work the way it is at the moment, things have been a bit mad. Settled in all right at your new place?"

I gave a half-shrug. "I'd forgotten how much fun it is to share a flat with friends. Thanks again, not only for the advice but for talking Prue around."

"Don't mention it. I was only glad I could help out."

Out of the corner of my eye, I spotted Scarlett making a beeline toward us. Simon glanced down at his watch and made his way over to her, before turning back to us. "We'd better get a move on now or we'll be late."

Suddenly Scarlett looked like a scared child and my heart went out to her.

"Hey, don't worry," Simon reassured her with a pat. "Just remember all the things we went over during the week and you'll be fine."

Scarlett looked up at him beseechingly. "Are you sure?"

"Come on, it's time," he said quietly, guiding her toward the court house before being joined by the others.

* * * *

All thanks to Simon's amazing legal expertise, less than an hour after entering the court house, a very relieved Scarlett was let off with nothing more than a twelve-month good behavior bond for possessing capsicum spray — apparently an offensive weapon according to the law. The suggestion that Scarlett would have taken on someone of his build was plainly ridiculous, with even the judge admitting that there were more than a few conflicting aspects to the prosecution's case. Of course the fact that Simon all but danced rings around her accuser's testimony was the clincher and I had to admit in full flight he was amazing to watch.

Walking out of the court house, everyone was on a high, Scarlett, who found herself in the middle of a hooker-scrum, particularly. I remained chatting to Simon who had another case coming up in half an hour.

It was then I heard someone calling out my name and turned around only to find Paul walking briskly up the stairs toward us. Surprise froze my smile as I tried to figure out what the hell he was doing here.

He laughed, taking in my confused expression. "Hey, no need to look so pleased to see me. I was just passing and thought I'd pop my head in and see how everything went."

"Oh, just passing, were you?" I queried, my raised eyebrows acting like a big exclamation mark. This wasn't a car crash, after all. Rubbernecking was strictly frowned upon.

Paul threw his hands up, signaling his sincerity. "Honestly. Scarlett told me last week that today was the big day and seeing as I had an appointment at the employment agency here in town anyway, I thought I'd stop and say hi," he explained, his blue eyes twinkling playfully in the morning sun.

Looking past me, he smiled. "It looks like I'm a little late. By the look on Scarlett's face, I guess it went well?"

"Very well, thank God. She got off with a good behavior bond."

Paul smiled. "Relieved to hear it. I know she might seem a bit rough on the outside, but inside she's all heart."

I couldn't have agreed more.

Outside of Heavenly Pleasures, it was easy to overlook the fact he slept with prostitutes. Still, I couldn't help but think of him getting it on with the girls and felt decidedly uncomfortable. To my horror, it must have shown on my face. Paul squirmed. I squirmed. God, this was awkward. Then, breaking the awkwardness, Leanne came up behind me.

"Sorry, Paul." Leanne smiled. "But I just need a quick word with Brooke here."

"Hey, no problem. I was just going to congratulate Scarlett."

Leanne dragged me out of earshot of the others.

"Okay, what the hell is wrong with you?" she hissed. "He clearly likes you and you're acting like he's radioactive!"

I stared back, practically bug-eyed with horror. "You must be joking, right?"

"No, I'm serious. He is a sweetie…"

"Um…who sleeps with prostitutes," I reminded her.

Leanne burst out laughing. And not just one little chuckle. She was almost rolling on the floor in the manner of an elephant seal about to give birth. Helpless she was and I in turn didn't get what was so funny.

"Oh, God, I'm sorry, petal," she gulped. "You poor thing. I thought you knew."

"Knew what exactly?" I snapped. "What are you talking about?"

"Why do you think the girls are all so keen to get a booking with Paul? Scarlett especially?" Leanne asked.

I shrugged. If she said he had a huge penis or some kind of exotic genital piercing, I swear I was leaving. Leanne came over all serious.

"Brooke, listen to me. Not all the guys who come into Heavenly Pleasures come for sex, you know."

I frowned. If it wasn't for sex, I *really* didn't want to think what they were up to in there.

"Paul doesn't actually have sex with Scarlett — or any of the other girls for that matter," Leanne plowed on.

"No wonder you're confused. I can't believe no one told you."

"Told me *what*?" I yelped, embarrassed and by now pissed off.

"Apparently, he's an artist."

"What, as opposed to a pervert, you mean?"

"No, I'm serious. He says it's just a hobby of his, a way to relax and chill out, but the girls reckon he's just being modest. I haven't seen any of his sketches, but from what they tell me, he's nothing short of amazing."

"So?"

What this had to do with hookers was lost on me.

"*So,* he's been coming in here to draw the girls — in the nude of course. But they don't mind and to Paul it's a lot easier to book one of the girls to pose for him than try to find a willing model to do it on the outside. He says it costs a bit more but for the convenience it's worth it. And besides, at least in here, he gets some variation."

I was dumbstruck. "So he doesn't have sex with them?" I had to be sure. This was important.

Leanne shook her head. "From what the girls tell me, no. Not that they haven't tried." She winked. "They all think he's gorgeous."

Christ, I must walk around with a bucket on my head. Suddenly something Scarlett said a few weeks ago, about it being the easiest booking she's ever had, came back to me, and it all began to fall into place.

What kind of a fool was I?

I must say the realization that he didn't sleep with hookers came as an immense relief as now at least I could look him in the eye without seeing a man reduced to paying for sex rather than groveling for it like mother nature intended.

Away from the hideous retro carpet and pervasive sounds of porn, I had to admit he was certainly someone Trudy and I might well have snuck a perve at if say we'd been in a nightclub or something. Normal, in other words. More than normal, he was very nice and not at all bad-looking, either. In the time it took Leanne to compose herself once again, it dawned on me that he was actually okay.

Jesus, when did this happen?

The shock almost knocked the breath from my body. It couldn't be true. Surely it was merely a knee-jerk reaction to my recent break-up with Brad. Then, before I could put a stop to it, I recalled every single look he had ever given me along with every conversation we'd enjoyed over the past few months. Could I have secretly fancied him all along? *No! No way!*

I should have been horrified, or at least a little embarrassed, but strangely I wasn't.

Walking toward me, Paul smiled.

"You all right? You seem a little out of sorts."

Out of the corner of my eye, I noticed Leanne retreating at breakneck speed, leaving me alone with Paul.

I smiled weakly, encouraged by his cheeky easy-going manner, and blurted out the first thing that came into my head. "Looking for a job, are you?"

"What?"

"The employment agency? You said you were on your way down there."

Okay, it might have been lame, but it was the most inspiring thing I could come up with under the circumstances and was certainly preferable to some of the other less subtle thoughts whirling around in my head.

Thankfully, he mistook my verbal crash-n-burn for wit and laughed.

Before he had a chance to answer, Simon walked across, effectively putting a halt to our pseudo flirting—well, I wasn't sure he *was* flirting. There was a moment or two of awkwardness as I tossed up whether to be blatantly rude and not introduce them, to protect Paul's brothel-visiting secret, or make up some lie, sparing them both any possible embarrassment. Seeing as my status as World's Worst Liar had been well and truly established, I settled for neutral ground.

"Um, Paul, this is Simon Parsons, Scarlett's lawyer. And, Simon, this is Paul..."

And, of course, I hadn't a clue what his last name was.

"Evertson," Paul added, coming to my rescue.

"Paul's an artist," I interjected.

Paul went to correct me, but before he got the chance, Simon cut in. "Evertson?" he pondered. "Your name sounds familiar. I think we did some work for you a year or two back."

Oh, God, please don't let him be a crim, I prayed.

"Of course. Now I recognize you," Paul answered. "You're from Fletcher and Flyte, aren't you?" He offered his hand for a hearty man-shake.

"That's right and it's Evertson Events, isn't it?"

Paul grinned, while I stood back, confusion robbing me of most of my IQ points and most of my powers of speech.

"Hey, great to see you again, Paul. How's business?" Simon inquired.

"Booming. In fact, that's what brings me into town today. Thought it was about time I began looking for an assistant. God knows I'm dreading it. But unless I want to spend every moment of the day answering phones, I figured it was about time I bit the bullet and hired someone to help me out in the office."

"Sorry," I interrupted, finally finding my voice. "I didn't realize you two knew each other."

Simon smiled at my confused expression. "Sorry, Brooke. We did some legal work for Paul a few years back when he was setting up his company."

"And who would have thought back then I would still be in business?" joked Paul, his eyes twinkling at me.

"And what kind of business *are* you in?" I asked, trying not to sound too nosy. Of course I was dying to know how it all tied in with the brothel-visiting-amateur-artist persona.

"Public relations, actually."

"Oh, *really*?"

It was the last thing I had been expecting. Had he told me he was an undertaker, I couldn't have been more surprised. But on closer inspection, he did possess that shiny, open kind of personality that would be right at home amongst celebrities and crowds of 'In' people. This just kept getting better and better. Not only *didn't* he sleep with hookers, but he was gainfully employed. Now I knew there was a God up there after all.

"Yes, I headed the publicity department of a large Sydney-based TV station for years before deciding to branch out on my own. A huge risk, I admit, but after all the initial work, it's finally beginning to pay off, thank goodness."

"Yeah, and what an amazing coincidence..." Simon began, winking at me.

A spirally feeling of dread warned me what was about to come. I threw a panicked look at Simon, but it was too late. "PR. Brooke, weren't you telling me at that dinner party a few weeks back that you were hoping to get a start in that area one day?"

My face ignited with embarrassment. Of course, how could I forget blabbing on to Simon about my somewhat lofty ambitions to enter the glamorous arena of PR, together with the accompanying lie that landed me in all this trouble to begin with? Talk about a domino effect. *One lie, one pashmina and my entire life crumbles, including my relationship.* Simon's eyes lit up with mischief. I also recalled the amount of wine I'd had to drink that night and my face glowed with embarrassment.

Paul looked somewhat taken aback. "Really? Brooke, I had no idea. Aren't you full of surprises?"

Surprises? If only he knew.

Simon looked down at his watch and cleared his throat. "I hate to rush off like this, but I should be getting back in before my next case. Paul, great running into you again and glad to hear business is booming. Brooke, I'll give you a call in a few days and we'll catch up."

As Simon walked back into the court house, I found myself beset by sudden shyness and lost for words.

"Simon's a great lawyer, really knows his stuff," Paul remarked, filling up the awkward silence that had sprung up between us.

I racked my brains, desperate to think of something, anything to break the wit drought currently playing havoc with my head.

"Paul—"

"Brooke—" we both chorused at once.

"Jinx." Paul laughed. "No, please, you go first."

I wasn't quite sure how to put the question currently doing my head in, so in the end, I thought it best to simply blurt it out. "Paul, why didn't you tell me you didn't pay the girls for sex?"

He looked at me with a glint of amusement in his eyes. "Would you have believed me?"

He had a point there, I suppose. Circumstantial evidence and all. After all, generally men who pay for hookers do so for sex.

"Anyway, what would it have sounded like if I'd walked in there and said 'Hey, could I book a girl for half an hour, but I'm not going to have sex with her?' I would have sounded like a right pervert in denial."

"But surely it would have been easier and probably cheaper to join an art group."

"Well, not really. Most of the groups around here are full of bored retirees, painting pictures of gum trees and boats. Life drawing isn't generally their thing, I'm afraid. When I lived in Sydney, there were a few groups operating, mostly out of the universities, but the times always conflicted with work, so in the end I figured the working girls were my best option. Not only are they comfortable with their bodies, but mostly the girls are more than happy to sit back and be sketched. I get to practice and add to my portfolio and I also get some variety as well."

"But doesn't it bother you that people think you're paying for sex? Not that there is anything wrong with that," I was quick to add.

"Brooke, honestly, it's fine. I've found over the years that girls like Scarlett and Angel are less judgmental than most and it's certainly a refreshing change to the high-strung celebrities I've been used to over the years. Does that answer your question?"

I nodded.

"Well, in that case, Brooke," Paul said carefully, "I hope you don't mind me asking…"

Oh, God, I thought, *this is it. He knows I fancy him and wants to let me down gently.* Suddenly the space between us felt as though it was about to suffocate me. I braced myself for the worst, being too cowardly to simply jump the gun and tell him, yes, whatever it was he wanted to ask, don't bother.

"…but are you happy working at Heavenly Pleasures?"

What did he mean? Happy as in I wanted to stay there for the rest of my life or happy as in it wasn't the crappiest job I'd ever had, that position having already being awarded to the surgery job from hell with Dr. Chisholm?

I shrugged in a lame attempt to appear noncommittal. "It's not the kind of career I dreamed of years ago, but it's okay, I suppose." Then, feeling a little traitorous, I quickly added. "Well, at least it's a job and besides, compared to my last job, the girls are much better company."

"So you have no plans to leave?"

What on earth was he getting at? I felt as if we were playing twenty questions.

"Well, to be honest, at the moment, I'm not really in a position to be too fussy. Why?"

"I understand that this is totally out of the blue and maybe you think I am being a little forward…"

Christ, what was going on with him?

"But I was wondering, in light of what Simon just said, if you would be interested in coming to work for me—as my assistant?"

I opened my mouth to speak but wondered if I was dreaming.

"I realize it's starting out on the bottom rung. PR assistants are generally just glorified secretaries with fewer perks, but it's a start at least. I am not implying that your job at the moment isn't fulfilling or anything, but it would save me the trauma of wading through piles of job applications. Well, if you think you could put up with me on a daily basis, that is?" He stopped for a moment to allow me to decline, no doubt. "Er, you don't have to decide now, of course."

"Are you saying you want *me* to work for *you* — as a PR assistant?"

Paul smiled. "Yes. I know how good you are with the public. If you can manage the kind of people who frequent brothels, surely spoilt celebrities and drunken conference-goers should be a walk in the park? I think you'd be ideal for the job, that is, of course, if it's something you feel you'd like to try."

"*Like to?*" I gasped, the full reality of his offer finally hitting me. "Christ, are you serious? I would *love* to." And the opportunity to spend more time with Paul was certainly a major selling point as well.

His smile lit up his face. "That's terrific. I can't tell you how happy that makes me. I realize you have to give your notice and all…" Paul fished around in his pocket before pulling out a business card and handing it to me. "But here, why don't you give me a call tomorrow sometime and we can meet over lunch, or possibly dinner, in the next few days and sort out the details?"

I took the card from him and stared at it as though it was the key to the city. I longed to pinch myself just to prove that I wasn't dreaming. But no, I was fairly convinced he was serious. He was offering a job, in *PR!*

"I'd better be getting back now. I'll stop off at the employment agency while I'm at it and let them know

I won't be requiring their services, after all. Thanks, Brooke. I'm sure things are going to work out brilliantly. I'll talk to you tomorrow?"

I nodded, grinning like a total loon.

Paul's eyes lingered on mine for a second or two. "I'm looking forward to it," he said meaningfully before turning around and making his way back down the stairs of the court house. He'd gone only a few steps when he spun back again. "Oh, and, Brooke, do you have a passport?"

"Um, yes. Why?"

"I have an assignment in the pipeline involving a soap star turned Hollywood starlet. It may involve a few trips back and forth to L.A. Think you're up to it?" He winked before walking off down the court house stairs and around the corner back toward town.

I couldn't believe it. I was shaking. Looking down at the now crumpled business card in my hand, I experienced a rush of excitement. Me in PR. A real job. And, more than that, a glamorous job and a hunky new boss who was only a hop, skip and a jump away from being my hunky new boyfriend, going by the undeniable strands drawing us together.

Epilogue

Twelve months later

"Now, think, have you got everything?" I mumbled to myself. Looking around the room, I went through the list in my head.

Passports, tick.

American dollars, tick.

My shiny-new, strappy red Jimmy Choo sandals, tick.

Clothes, laptop, charger and, and...

There was something else, I was sure of it.

My heart was hammering. I could hear Paul in the next room, ordering a taxi.

Oh, God, it was time to leave. Our flight was in less than two hours and we still had to get through the city traffic to the airport. I *knew* this would happen. I was starting to panic. Spinning around, I tried to think of what I was missing. It was then I felt two comforting arms slide around my waist, together with the warmth

356

of Paul's lips on my neck, and I instantly started to relax.

"Hey, what's wrong, honey?"

"I just know I've forgotten something," I cried.

"Jeez, going by the size of those three suitcases in the hallway I can't think there's anything you *haven't* packed."

"No, seriously, something is missing."

Kissing my neck, Paul mumbled, "You worry too much. Everything is fine. And besides, if we get to LA and you *have* forgotten something, I'll go out and buy it for you."

Suddenly it came to me! I twisted out from Paul's arms, rushed into the bedroom and through to the bathroom. There is was. *How could I have almost forgotten it? Left it sitting right beside the sink?* I smiled as I picked up my beautiful Tiffany's engagement ring, its rose-gold band shimmering under the glint of a perfectly cut pink diamond. I placed it back on my finger where it belonged. Happiness once again oozed from every pore of my body when I remembered that magical moment everything transformed into a real-life fairy tale – the romantic kind. The *best* kind. As my very own Prince Charming announced the arrival of our taxi, I took a quick look back at what had been an amazing year.

From a burned-orange pashmina, a disastrous phone call to Brazil and a brothel in the seedy end of town to working in PR and traveling the globe with the love of my life. I could hardly believe where events had taken me in this past year. Fate might have – oh, all right, had – handed me a few blows, but it had also bought Paul and me together, and what a story it would be to tell our children one day…or possibly not!

Life was certainly interesting and I, for one, couldn't wait for the next chapter.

Want to see more from this author?
Here's a taster for you to enjoy!

Sex, Spoons and Salsa
Isla Dennes

Excerpt

"I have nothing. No husband. No friends. No life. *Nothing.* I might as well be dead!"

Through a veil of tears, I stared at the wilting rubber plant in the corner and tried to pretend I was anywhere but there. I don't think I could have been any more mortified. I sounded like a hack Shakespearean actor.

Crossing her arms over her matronly bosom, Margarita pushed a fresh box of tissues toward me before settling back in her chair. She didn't appear the least bit put out by my hysterics and I wondered what it would take to get some kind of reaction from her. *Talk about detached.* Fifty minutes into our first session and she hadn't even opened her mouth to impart any words of life-altering wisdom? For all I knew, she could be compiling her week's menus and their subsequent shopping list in her head. Was it possible my father had stumbled across the only deaf-mute therapist in the country?

"Therapy. I still can't believe I'm here," I mumbled tearfully. Had I not been so totally consumed by my own misery, I would have been burning up with shame. "Who goes to therapy, anyway?" I cried, ignoring the frown appearing on Margarita's face. "I'll tell you who—celebrities, bored middle-aged housewives, people who've taken to curling up in corners and sucking their thumbs. Total nutters, that's who! Not me."

This had to be a mistake. I didn't belong there. I didn't *want* to belong there. I wanted to have my life back. But the very act of coming to therapy was in itself an admission I had failed at being a grown-up and was in need of rescuing.

On the drive there, I'd made a promise to myself not to get all caught up in that whole touchy-feely crap. Sure, I might have been led dazed and blinking from the dark recesses of my room—and my mind for that matter—clutching a ratty old stuffed rabbit, my normally well-behaved shoulder-length mousy-brown hair long gone wild and my usually striking blue eyes dulled and barely recognizable. But make no mistake, I was there for one reason and one reason only, and that was to get Dad off my back and, in the process, prove to him what a complete waste of everyone's time and money this was. Alas, once I'd settled into that arse-numbing chair—no sign of a comfy leather couch, much to my disappointment—the silence, combined with the sympathy emanating from every pore of Margarita's round face, had triggered something in my brain—the blabbing switch. Before I could stop it, my runaway mouth had embarked on a journey of its own, climaxing in my recent outburst, still hovering in the air between us like a bad smell no one wants to acknowledge.

God, what have I done? Unfortunately, I couldn't take it all back now. I looked expectantly across to the Beige Linen Oracle—as she was from that moment christened—for any sign she'd come up with the magical solution for my ruined life. I'd done my bit. Surely it was up to her now to sort out this mess? But no, she merely stared back expectantly.

Waiting for exactly what, I wondered? A complete mental breakdown? By this time, I was little alarmed. *Am I a lost cause?* Maybe I really *was* losing my mind. *Great, this is all I need.* If it wasn't bad enough to be a twenty-six-year-old recently discarded wife, on top of that I was doomed to suffer the additional humiliation of losing the plot, going la-la, floundering in the emotional cesspool of life without a float.

Plummeting headlong into Loser Hell without a safety net.

"I wasn't always like this, you know. Once upon a time, I had a future to look forward to." I sniffed, trying to reclaim a little of my lost dignity. "I had a husband, friends and a social life." Yes, all very well and good to point that out now, but the truth remained through no fault of my own, I found myself once again living at home with my parents in the same room I'd occupied throughout my rather tumultuous teenage years, complete with posters of Robbie Williams, Justin Timberlake and Ricky Martin. Ah, the nights I'd spent dreaming of marrying Ricky Martin — who knew?

Resentment had bubbled up inside me, heralding an ill-timed return of teenage angst, directed, not surprisingly, toward those near and dear to me. In all fairness to my long-suffering parents, I have to confess their decision to seek outside help for their loopy firstborn hadn't been something they'd taken lightly. You might even say I'd driven them to it after they'd suffered through six hellish weeks of my rabid mood swings. This, I must point out, had come hard on the heels of the discovery that my moods were not the only things out there swinging.

Why is the wife always the last one to know?

Had it not been for the onset of a particularly nasty little rash on my privates, closely followed by the utterance of three little letters, STD—alas not the telecommunication kind—I might never have found out about my husband's affair. God, the shame of it when my doctor, who, I might add, was old enough to have been practicing medicine before the discovery of penicillin, had turned a deep shade of crimson before quizzing me about my supposedly promiscuous past.

If I have one, it's news to me!

Even while I continued crying buckets of shame in front of Margarita, I still found it difficult to comprehend how I could have been so blind not to see what had apparently been going on underneath my nose. Formerly known as 'Amanda, the five-thirty-step-class-bimbo,' from that day on I could only think of her as 'husband-stealing-silicone-enhanced-Botox-junkie-slut-with-the-clap', *or* 'that fucking bitch' for short.

Not that I'm bitter or anything.

Naturally, I'd done what anyone in my situation would have done and scuttled crying back to Mum and Dad, who, I must say, had been more than a little surprised to have had their dinner interrupted by their wailing daughter. Dad had gone totally mental, even threatening to shoot the Two-timing Lying Bastard dead if he came within sight of the house, therefore saving me the trouble of obtaining a divorce. Don't get me wrong, the thought of playing the part of the grieving widow had lifted my spirits momentarily, but having my shame plastered all over the newspapers— *Venereal Disease Scandal Triggers Family Tragedy*— wasn't something I'd felt I could comfortably have lived with.

Six weeks later and my father had again been mumbling about inflicting grievous bodily harm on 'the bastard'. But this time, I'd suspected that rather than a punishment for breaking my heart, it had been more out of retaliation for having inflicted a psychotic daughter on them in what should have been the peaceful twilight years of their lives.

In the end, out of pure desperation, Dad had decided to call in reinforcements, otherwise known as Rachel, Kim and Janine.

The four of us had been best friends since high school, since the time we'd found ourselves lumped together in the C grade team in the local netball competition. It wasn't as though we'd been fat, unfit or socially awkward, but, looking back on it now, it might have been because I haven't got a competitive bone in my body, Janine simply couldn't give a stuff and Rachel and Kim are incredibly violent and, to this day, consider netball a blood sport.

Back then, I was a shy, awkward thirteen-year-old and they were the cool girls, with the short skirts and permanent sneers on their heavily made-up faces. They had attitude. They had respect. They had class. To say I was impressed would be putting it mildly. Me, well, I was the girl no one saw, or if they did, only to pick on or hurl insults at. They were my saviors — the answer to my prayers. Of course, even then I knew their friendship equaled more a case of pity than any real connection between us — and the fact I was willing to run to the canteen for them every lunchtime and act as lookout while they smoked in the school toilets. Yes, I was their lackey, their stooge, their social groupie, but at least I'd made the In Crowd, and for that reason, I was forever indebted to them for taking me under their wing that fateful day on the netball court.

The savagely bitchy atmosphere that prevailed throughout our formative high school years further strengthened our sisterly bond. By Year Nine, we were indisputably top of the teenage-girl food chain and ruled the Block A girls' toilets with a ruthlessness that would have had seen Saddam Hussein crossing his legs and holding it in rather than risk running the gantlet of the smoky cubicles. Yes, we had finally found our foothold in the vicious world that constituted senior high school.

"It's not my fault, you see," I sobbed, grabbing another handful of tissues. "If I hadn't been bullied into going out with the girls, to that stupid RSL club, I wouldn't even be here. Jeez, it's not like we're still at school. But, no, my Dad had to get me out of the house, even if it meant going straight to Loser Hell, thanks to that bloody retro disco."

Not that I would be gyrating my wobbly bits on the dance floor. My role as passive observer and handbag minder had been firmly established years before with my girlfriends' decree that my 'unique style of dance-floor expression' was scaring off any potential action of the male variety. It wasn't all bad news, though. In recognition of my noble sacrifice I'd be kept supplied in alcohol as payoff to ensure my ongoing cooperation. Thus continued my role as protector of the sacred table.

After all, as Rachel was quick to point out, where you sit in these social occasions is a direct reflection of your status within the hierarchy of the nightclub. Sit too close to the bar, you're labeled an alcoholic. Too close to the toilets, you must be a lesbian. Too close to the door and everyone spills their drinks on you, and the only people who sit right next to the dance floor are, of course, losers.

Our table therefore was strategically the most sought after in the nightclub and jealously guarded. Not only did it give us a clear vantage point from which to spot any hunks as they walked through the door, but it was close enough to the toilets—but not too close to be considered creepy—in the event one of us might have mixed our Kahlua and milks with one too many bourbons, white wines or worse still, Tequila Slammers, and a toilet bowl and a moment of solitude were desperately required.

Walking into the foyer of the RSL that night, I experienced a mixture of disappointment, excitement and apprehension after my six-week self-imposed exile.

Excitement at finally, after three years, being able to fit into my favorite black leather miniskirt again—a broken heart is infinitely more effective than a Jenny Craig diet. Apprehension at the remote possibility of running into the Two-timing Lying Bastard as I made my triumphant return to society. And, to my disappointment, the Club foyer was still hideously furbished in the same bold purple, red and brown décor that once enjoyed a very brief period of being fashionable—May 1977 to January 1978, to be precise—before the rest of the civilized world moved onto the shag-pile and orange Formica era.

I'm not sure what I was expecting. Maybe a brass band to welcome me back into the fold. But realizing that everyone else's lives had carried on in my absence, callously unaware of my recent lifestyle changes, began to put things in perspective for me.

That was until I went to sign in.

Then I experienced a stab of uncertainty. After all, for the first time since the breakup I'd been faced with the question of whether I'd be resorting to my maiden name, or simply tack a Ms. to the prefix of *his* devil-scorned surname. A difficult decision to make, seeing as the Two-timing Lying Bastard's surname was the only decent thing I got out of the marriage.

For two years, five months and four days I had proudly gone by the name of Mrs. Fiona Maxwell, grateful at last to finally leave behind forever Miss Fiona McCrutchen, a name that had caused me endless grief since the moment of my conception, peaking to excruciating torment during my school years.

For months prior to my ill-fated marriage I had proudly practiced writing Mrs. Fiona Maxwell, Mrs. F. Maxwell and even Mr. and Mrs. T. Maxwell over and over for hours on end, until even the girls had begun hinting that maybe I was just marrying him for his nice, normal-sounding surname. In hindsight, they might have been right. After all, using marriage as an excuse to lose a last name that had plagued me since birth might not have been a solid enough reason to vow before God and eighty invited guests, to love, honor and cherish until death do us part — and in the process nearly bankrupt my parents with the cost of the wedding.

Well, decision time. I halted my hand at *M* and considered my options. Reverting back to McCrutchen would surely reopen the trauma of a childhood spent trying to ignore the chants of horrid little boys yelling "McCrusty, McCrusty", but, on the other hand, remaining normal, sane Fiona Maxwell was almost akin to saying I still hungered after his body. *Ummm, somehow, I don't think so!*

And with that last thought, Ms. Fiona McCrutchen was officially welcomed back into the Merryland's Returned Servicemen's League.

Home of Erotic Romance

Sign up for our newsletter and find out about all our
romance book releases, eBook sales and promotions,
sneak peeks and FREE romance books!

About the Author

Married, mother of one son and three daughters, Isla Dennes developed a love of writing while employed in her dream job as the owner of a bookshop in a seaside resort town in NSW, Australia. Not content to simply read every book in the store, she found herself compelled to create novels of her own.

Had she concentrated more on sales and less on writing, she might well have retired a wealthy woman, but writing won out in the end, with the result being a lifelong passion for creative writing across a number of genres, including a brief but regrettable sojourn into horribly sentimental New-Age poetry that's best forgotten...

Isla loves to hear from readers. You can find her contact information, website details and author profile page at https://www.totallybound.com